CHASING EVIL

T0072206

ALSO BY KYLIE BRANT

CHASING EVIL

THE CIRCLE OF EVIL TRILOGY, BOOK 1

KYLIE BRANT

THOMAS & MERCER

This is a work of fiction. Names, characters, organizations, places, events, and incidents are either products of the author's imagination or are used fictitiously.

Text copyright © 2013, 2015, Kimberly Bahnsen
All rights reserved.

No part of this book may be reproduced, or stored in a retrieval system, or transmitted in any form or by any means, electronic, mechanical, photocopying, recording, or otherwise, without express written permission of the publisher.

Published by Thomas & Mercer, Seattle

www.apub.com

Amazon, the Amazon logo, and Thomas & Mercer are trademarks of Amazon.com, Inc., or its affiliates.

ISBN-13: 9781477829844
ISBN-10: 1477829849

Cover design by Marc J. Cohen

Printed in the United States of America

For all my friends and students at Lincoln School

Prologue

E d Loebig whistled sharply. The chocolate-brown Lab, the pup he had high hopes of turning into a hunting dog, paid him absolutely no mind as he continued to race ahead.

"C'mon, Digger—get on back here. Digger!" The mutt responded to neither a cajoling tone nor a commanding one. He gave Ed one goofy look over his shoulder, tongue lolling as though he was having a good laugh at Ed's expense, before continuing to bound from one grassy area to the next, sniffing as if he were in dog heaven.

"I am getting too damn old for this," Ed muttered. But it was his own fault for taking the leash off the animal. He thought the grassy field would be a fine place to practice the lessons he'd been teaching of "come" and "stay." Damn dog was flagging straight Fs in both departments.

Ed gave a quick and futile wish for his hound, Bonnie. Best hunting dog he'd ever had, even up to last year when she'd been ten. But the winter had been hard on the animal, as hard as it'd been on Ed. Arthritis had taken a toll on both of them. And although Ed could still get around well enough to hunt, Bonnie could not. Enter the six-month-old pup, which so far was in the running for dumbest animal on earth.

"Digger. Here, boy. No. Don't even think about . . . Damn!" Ed reversed course and started for the cemetery gate, hoping to head the dog off. But speed was one thing the half-grown mutt had all over Ed's beloved Bonnie.

Outrunning the dog was impossible, so Ed headed back to his pickup. Moments later he was nosing it through the permanently open gates of Oak Hill Cemetery. He saw the dog flopped down under a shade tree and thought his chase was over. After turning off the truck, he approached the animal again, promising himself to confine his lessons to the kitchen from now on until Digger was better trained. If that day ever came.

"Okay. Easy now." He dug in his pocket for a treat, held it out to get the dog's attention. "Here, boy. C'mon over here."

But the pooch saw a squirrel and jumped up to give chase just as Ed made a grab for his collar and missed. The dog lost his quarry at the base of a tree and turned his attention elsewhere. Ed was panting when he caught up and saw Digger engaged in the pastime that had earned him his name.

"Hell, no!"

The neat expanse of dirt leveled over the fresh grave was an open invitation to Digger. Dirt flew beneath his paws as the dog furiously dug for the sheer joy of the act. Ed took a quick look around even as he started for the dog in a dead run. With his luck Molly Summit would be nearby with her blasted camera, and the photo would be splashed all over the front page of the weekly *Slater Chronicle*, headlined "Grave Mistake: Animal Owner Ignores Leash Law."

Ed reached Digger and grabbed his collar, then dragged the animal back to the pickup. The dog twisted and squirmed, but Ed's grip was firm. He opened up the passenger seat and hoisted the animal inside. Then he ran back to the grave to repair the damage before anyone happened by and caught him.

It'd been a couple of weeks since anyone from Slater had died, so this grave had to belong to Ida Sweeney. Ed broke out in a cold sweat at the thought of having to explain to the widower, Mel Sweeney, how his ninety-six-year-old wife's final resting place came to be desecrated this way. He fell down on his hands and knees, a position that would have his arthritic knee howling for a week, and began frantically refilling the disturbed soil back into the hole.

Something glistened in the sunlight, and he stopped for a moment, peered closer. And then he was imitating the dog, cupping his hands to uncover even more, dirt spraying behind him.

Fingers of early-morning sunlight slanted through the overhead branches and across the grave. "Jesus, Mary, and Joseph." He stopped then, scrambled away, tripped, and landed on his ass. His stomach heaved; the breakfast he'd had in the Slater Diner threatened to make a reappearance.

Backdropped against clumps of rich black Iowa topsoil was an unmistakably human hand.

~

"Sheriff Dumont?" Cam Prescott stopped next to the man who'd been identified for him. "Agents Cameron Prescott and Jenna Turner, DCI."

Iowa's Story County sheriff was whipcord lean with deep squint lines radiating from the corners of his eyes. He exchanged handshakes with the agents. "Appreciate you getting your team here so fast. Soon as I got the call from Ed Loebig about what he found, I figured this was one to turn over to the Division of Criminal Investigation. We don't have any open missing persons cases in the county at the moment. I'm guessing this isn't going to be one of ours."

"Maybe not the victim." The two men exchanged a long look. "Could be it's the perpetrator who's local."

They all turned their attention toward the spot where the crime team had used electronic body-sniffing devices to draw parameters around the dig site. It had taken Bob Dumont the better part of six hours to make nice with Mel Sweeney about disturbing his wife's grave. That hadn't been strictly necessary—suspicion of a crime gave the DCI latitude in the case—but Cam was mindful of the politics of the situation. It never paid to try and make enemies out of people encountered in the course of an investigation. That happened often enough on its own.

He caught a glimpse of an elderly gentleman sitting in the open rear door of a sheriff's vehicle. He assumed it was the widower. "This will take several hours, Sheriff." Experience told him that much. "One of the state medical examiners will arrive soon. She'll oversee the actual digging and extraction." The county examiner was on scene, but questionable deaths were autopsied by the state.

"I'll stick around, if you don't mind," Dumont said. He gave a nod in the direction of the car Cam had noticed. "I promised Mel as much." The sheriff hesitated for a moment. "I'll let you be the judge if there's anything to this, but word got around pretty fast about this find. And I've heard from two of the sheriffs in nearby counties. They each took reports in the last several months about someone messing around in some of their county cemeteries at night."

Diplomacy wasn't always a trait that came naturally to Cam, so he took his time framing an answer. "I guess that happens a lot with rural cemeteries everywhere. Kids don't have respect. Go out at night and tear around, try to scare each other."

Dumont rubbed the back of his leathery neck, burned as deep a brown as his face, though it was only mid-June. "True enough. Get our share of thefts here, too. People stealing flowers, grave ornaments, and the like. But Beckett Maxwell—he's the Boone County sheriff—had something you might find interesting. Said he investigated a complaint over in Madrid back at the end of April. Someone thought the recent grave of a family member had been disturbed. Well, Beckett checked it out, but there wasn't much to see. He did say that the grave looked freshly dug, the soil turned over like it'd just been done that week. But the fellow buried there had been in the ground almost a month." The sheriff squinted at him. "Not sure what to make of that, but thought you should know."

Jenna caught his eye. A dull throbbing started in Cam's temples. Rural cemeteries like this frequently relied on volunteers or a part-time caretaker for their upkeep. Other than occasional visits for maintenance or to pay respects, the places were largely deserted. The open gates here were a testament to the lack of security measures taken.

Something told him that his new case was about to take a complicated turn.

Chapter 1

He traced the tip of his index finger down her delicate spine, feeling like a mortar shell had exploded inside him. His senses remained steeped in her—the texture of her skin, the scent of her hair, the glide of her fingers. She had her face turned away so he couldn't read her expression. Probably a good thing. He wasn't sure what would show in his. Stunned pleasure, for sure. The slightly dopey look of a satisfied male. Hopefully none of the uncertainty that was crawling through him. The sensation was as unfamiliar as it was uncomfortable. He bent his head to kiss the curve of her shoulder blade. Watched her slight shiver with fascination.

"This . . . feels like a mistake."

He froze, the words raking over him and drawing blood. Ordinarily he'd agree. She was the last person he would have considered taking to bed, though he'd be lying if he claimed he'd never imagined her there. But she wasn't his type. When it came to relationships, he favored them short and hot. And while their interlude had been spectacularly hot . . . he wasn't inclined to keep it short. That should scare the hell out of him.

He slid his hand down her thigh, then back up, fingers grazing close to her damp heat. "Funny." He brushed a kiss over her shoulder. "That's not what I'm feeling."

"I mean . . ." She gasped a little when his hand inched higher, and his teeth scraped her skin not quite gently. "We should . . . if our work—"

"Work is work. This is something else. Let's let it develop and decide later exactly what it is."

~

"Cam?" Jenna Turner ducked her head inside his office. "Dr. Channing just arrived."

He shoved away from his desk, rose. "About damn time."

Her gaze flickered. "You could try being nice." She stood aside to allow him to exit.

"What fun would that be?"

"I'm serious." Jenna's voice was low as she trailed him toward the front of the Iowa Division of Criminal Investigation building. "Special Agent Gonzalez is really going to bat for us when it comes to resources on this case. I don't remember ever having the long-term expense of two civilian consultants okayed before. First the forensic anthropologist and now Channing. And you've said yourself she's the best. The offender profile she developed for that rest stop rapist last January helped us track him down in less than eight weeks."

"Is that when you became president of her fan club?" Cam turned down a hallway and halted so abruptly that Jenna ran into the back of him. Directly ahead, in a tight knot of DCI admirers, was the noted Dr. Sophia Channing, looking like a regal blonde queen holding court for her minions.

It was hard to say what it was about her that never failed to set him off. Maybe it was her faint air of royalty, that sheen of breeding. Could be the cool way she had of surveying him, as if she were beaming a light into his mind and objectively dissecting it. God knows he'd never been a fan of shrinks. But she brought about a reaction different from most. Probably due to the unflappable poise she exhibited. It always made him want to shock her, to jolt her normally serene expression to something more genuine.

Although Cam suspected she wouldn't shock easily. She'd spent the better part of graduate school interning with Louis Frein, renowned profiler at Quantico's Behavioral Science Unit. In the last decade and a half, she'd interviewed the most notorious serial killers in captivity. There was more, much more to the woman than her appearance. He wished he could forget that.

He waited until his presence had the voices of the other DCI personnel tapering off. There was no way Channing could have been unaware of the reason. But when she didn't turn, he said unapologetically, "Sorry to steal the doctor away, guys, but there's this thing. You know—*work*."

The agency's payroll didn't run to retaining a forensic psychologist full-time, so as with most specialists, Channing's services were contracted on an as-needed basis. She'd worked with the agency often enough to have met some people here, but he was surprised by this slavish display of devotion.

"So good to catch up with you. It'll be wonderful to see you all while I'm here."

Her cultured voice drew smiles all around. Channing didn't seem to affect others the way she did Cam. Which, all in all, was probably a good thing.

With a graceful turn of her heel, she faced him. And he had that same punched-in-the-gut reaction he felt every time he saw her again. "Been waiting for you since last week." They began moving in the direction of his office, Jenna bringing up the rear.

"Since I just finalized things with Special Agent Gonzalez on Monday, I find that highly doubtful."

"Six unidentified bodies with similar injuries, all buried in the same fashion. Didn't take a rocket scientist to figure you'd be brought on board." Cam's long strides were eating up the distance back toward his office, before he consciously slowed to match the woman's gait. He wasn't used to the kind of woman who'd wear heels to work. Not here. "She said you just had to wrap up a few things. Didn't expect that to take three days."

"There was the minor matter of selecting another psychologist to take over the client list for my practice for the duration. By the way, Jenna, I love what you've done to your hair. Is it new?"

"Jesus."

Cam's muttered remark cost him a punch to the shoulder from the red-haired agent. "It is, thanks," Jenna answered. "Wasted on the bunch of cretins I'm surrounded with here—present company included—but I like it for summer." When he turned to look at her pointedly, she began to sidle away. "I believe Agent Prescott wants to catch you up on the case."

Cam caught the doctor's eye. "If it wouldn't be too much trouble," he said with exaggerated politeness. Stepping ahead of her, he opened his office door and waved her inside. He wondered if he was imagining that reluctance slowed her progress as she preceded him into the small area. Probably. He swung the door shut behind them. Who could actually move fast on those four-inch stilts she was wearing?

But when the tiny click of the door's closing had her startling like a deer to a rifle shot, he knew his earlier impression had been correct. His mood darkened accordingly.

He gestured her toward a chair. She set her briefcase down next to it but didn't sit. Instead she clasped her hands before her and walked to the working map spread out across one wall. After staring for several seconds, she broke away to pace the length of his office, careful to give him a wide berth. The show of nerves was unusual. Dr. Sophia Elise Channing was always poised. Always calm. At least in work-related matters.

Cam hitched a hip to a corner of his desk and crossed his arms. Waited. If there was one thing he'd learned about her, it was that you couldn't push the woman into doing anything before she was ready. Even talking.

"Although I'm certain you'll find it unwelcome, I feel the need to clear the air."

"The air feels plenty clear," he drawled.

The quick look she sent him on her return trip across the room held more than a hint of uncertainty. "Our . . . encounter, however brief, can't be allowed to impact our working relationship. In hindsight it's fortuitous that we broke it off when we did since we're going to be working closely on this case."

A slow burn ignited in his chest. In truth it had lodged there more than two weeks ago and been on simmer ever since. "I'd be lying if I said I didn't enjoy encountering with you." He waited, fascinated by the color that washed into her cheeks. He'd never met a woman in his life who still blushed. She had to be a throwback to some genteel ancestor of a sort that was noticeably absent from his own family tree. "But our relationship, short as it was, doesn't impact our working together. I told you before that it wouldn't. And not to be a stickler"—he bared his teeth—"but *we* didn't call it off, and it had nothing to do with work. You kicked me to the curb before I ever caught this case. Since we're clearing the air, we may as well be precise."

He reached out for the baseball that sat on his desk and gave it a toss, retrieving it neatly in mid-descent. It was a prized possession, a foul ball hit over left field at Wrigley five years ago that had cost him only a strained shoulder to snag. Well worth it. "I assume Gonzalez gave you a full copy of the case file?"

The color appeared again, a swift tide that came and went in her cheeks, and he immediately felt like an ass. The wonder wasn't that she'd called a halt to their all-too-short involvement, but that it had ever started in the first place. Outside the occasional case, they had absolutely nothing in common.

Which hadn't mattered a damn for twelve exquisite nights after he'd happened upon her—pensive and not quite sober—on the outdoor patio of Mickey's last month.

He opened his mouth to apologize. He had his share of rough edges. They'd actually helped keep him alive in the long months he'd spent undercover on a federal task force a few years ago. Now that he was back to civilization, however, decades of his mother's tutelage were easier to recall. But the doctor's reaction forestalled an apology before he could formulate one.

"Of course. I've been studying it while arranging things at my practice." Her face smoothed into professional lines, and she moved to the map. With precision she placed one pink-polished nail to the red pin, designating the location of the latest victim. "The cemetery in Milo was your last find?"

Discussion of the current investigation beat a postmortem of their not-quite-a-relationship any day of the week. With a minor sense of relief he said, "Monday, yeah. The discovery finally pushed the assistant director into expending extra resources in this case." One of those resources was Sophie herself. "I've still got agents poring over the obits for every small town in a ninety-mile radius of here. If you want to get town residents riled up, just bring in a team with ground-penetrating radar and gas chromatography devices and tell people we're going to dig up Grandma's grave. It's a real popularity contest."

"You pushed to go ahead and look for other possible victims."

He moved his shoulders. If the Story County sheriff hadn't tipped him off, he wouldn't have known to do so. Would never have continued searching for more than that first one. Dumb luck. Most people didn't realize how often that factored into an investigation.

"Yeah, I've got plenty of victims. What I don't have is ID. And without it I'm getting exactly nowhere on motive. And without that—"

"I know." Sophie tapped an index finger against her lips, something he'd noticed she did when she was thinking. "I started the victimology analysis, but it's impossible to complete without more information about who the victims are and what they represent to this offender. Have you talked to the ME about the newest body yet?"

He shook his head. "The victim didn't look like she'd been dead as long as the other five. Less decomposition. Facial features were largely intact, if unrecognizable. Jenna's working on a forensic drawing." Jenna was a trained forensic artist, and the agency used her talents wherever needed. "She and the consulting forensic anthropologist could also work on facial reconstructions for the rest of them if the ME would agree to it." But since the act would necessitate severing the skull for each set of remains, the always-opinionated pathologist had already vehemently nixed that idea, at least for the foreseeable future.

An expression of delight crossed Sophie's face. "Forensic anthropologist? Gavin's here? It will be lovely to see him again."

"It's been delightful," he agreed dryly. He tried—and failed—to imagine a scenario involving him that would elicit a similar reaction from her, short of falling off a cliff. Since he wasn't the type of man to feel jealousy, he blamed the burn in his chest on the breakfast burrito he'd wolfed down on the way to work.

"How's the victim identification coming so far?"

He set the baseball back down in an ashtray on the corner of his desk. "Nothing but circumstantial ID. We're spinning our wheels going through state, national, and international databases with what we have at this point." Which were hair color, gender, height, and very approximate age and weight. That gave them a long list of possible matches across the country for each victim, but they needed a method of positive verification. "We're also batting zero trying to match victim DNA and fingerprints with CODISmp and AFIS." Which told them only that the victims had no criminal history and that no family member had submitted DNA for a match to any of the missing persons databases. Or if they had, the samples hadn't been entered yet.

"That could mean these are high-risk victims," Sophie pointed out. "The kind no one misses. What about the physical pattern you found with the others? I assume it was present this time, too." She did sit then, crossing her legs in a graceful movement that drew his gaze. The suit she wore was the color of pink cotton candy. It was hard to reconcile the woman wrapped in delicate pastels with the keen, intuitive mind that would construct the offender profile on the deviant they were hunting. Her profiles never made for light reading. They were full of the type of details that a woman who looked like her shouldn't even know about, much less analyze. And realizing exactly how sexist that thought was still didn't make him feel guilty for it.

Layers. That's what was so damn fascinating about the woman. He was getting too damn old to appreciate shallow and transparent, regardless of the packaging. More's the pity.

"This one was tortured, too." His cell vibrated. He took it from his pocket to glance at the screen, rose, and headed toward the door. "You're in luck. Come with me to the morgue and you can see for yourself."

⁓

"You get five minutes. Then you're out of here, unless you have a hankering to watch the next autopsy."

Cam scowled at the petite medical examiner. What Dr. Lucy Benally lacked in stature she made up for in attitude. If he'd ever had a soft spot for raven-haired beauties with an enviable rack, it would have been dashed the first time she spoke. She had a mouth that would shame a sailor, a charm that wore thin quickly. "You called me, remember? At least let us get in the door."

"Us?" Benally looked up from the metal table and turned around swiftly. "There's one too many people in here already. You'd better all be gowned. Oh, Sophia, hi. They drag you in on this one?"

"Obviously," Cam muttered, then waited impatiently as the women exchanged pleasantries. The ME actually seemed half-human when she was conversing with the other woman. Sophie had that effect on people. He'd seen her conduct interviews with incarcerated murderers and coax information from them that law enforcement hadn't. People responded to something in her. It was a trait DCI had cultivated on numerous occasions when they'd enlisted her services.

He nodded at Gavin Connerly, who was propped lazily against a stainless steel counter. Cam didn't envy the forensic anthropologist's working proximity to the ME on this case. Not that the man seemed the worse for it. Nothing much seemed to bother the ponytailed consultant. If anything, he appeared amused.

"I think she's talking about me," Connerly said, grinning. "As the one too many. Somehow my charm and affability always fail to win her over. Sophia, you're beautiful as ever. Come back to California with me. We can live in sin exploring LA's decadence."

"If I said yes, you'd set a sprint record running back to California."

"Then say it." Benally shot the man a look filled with dislike. "He never stops talking. Ever."

Glad the ME's ire was directed at someone else for a change, Cam fingered the mask he'd grabbed. Having had enough stomach-churning experiences in the morgue, he never failed to take one after gowning up. But the usual overpowering smells encountered in here were largely absent. Bodies that had been in the ground with no protection didn't carry the stench of decomposition. They smelled like the soil they'd been buried in. Shoving the mask into the pocket of the protective gown, he went to the stainless steel table nearest him and studied their newest Jane Doe.

"What do you think, Agent?" There was a gibe buried in Benally's voice as she came up behind him.

Cam drew back the sheet and looked the naked corpse over carefully. "She was dead or unconscious when she was buried." He lifted one lifeless hand. "He cut the fingernails on this one like all the rest, but there's no dirt on the tips that would indicate she tried to claw her way out." None of the six victims had been buried in more than eighteen inches of soil. Just deeply enough to be pushed on top of the casket's vault in the grave and then reburied. Had they been conscious, each might have been able to dig her way out.

He peered more closely at the victim's neck. "Most of the skin is intact, which makes me think this one was buried the most recently." The skin had turned a mottled shade of burgundy and brown, making it impossible to determine bruising. "Need an autopsy to see whether she was strangled." Certainly looking for petechial hemorrhage in the eyes wouldn't help. Eyes were the first thing bugs attacked. "The skin shows much less than the expected insect activity. He probably doused this one with insecticide, too." He threw a look at the ME. "The nails don't look loose yet."

"He makes me so proud." Straightening, Cam saw Benally pat her chest, addressing Sophie. "I've taught him all he knows. Of course, that's not much."

Connerly ambled over to join Cam at the gurney. "This one might have only been in the ground a matter of days. And damn all the criminals watching *CSI*." His expression was mournful. "That's probably where he got the idea to spray them. Just to screw up the information we could get from the bug activity."

"Very possibly." Sophie sounded pensive. "Certainly this subject is intelligent enough to kill half a dozen times without being caught. He takes the precaution of cutting the nails, which might harbor his DNA if the victims marked him in any way. He washes down the bodies before burial, again we can presume to rid them of any DNA he might have left behind. No traces of semen"—she raised her brows, throwing a quick look at the ME, who shook her head slightly—"so it would be logical for him to try and slow the entomological evidence. But the spray could also be all about him. To make the postmortem sexual attacks more pleasurable. It would allow him to assault the victims long after their deaths while keeping the insect activity delayed."

Gavin's face looked queasy at that. "Jesus, Doc."

The ME strode over to the gurney and nudged between the two men. "Lean on your lab guys. By now they should have narrowed down the type of insecticide he used, which might be some help."

"It'd be better to prioritize the soil samples," Gavin argued. "Dead bodies release about four hundred different chemicals as they decompose, and an unprotected buried body is going to release them in the soil surrounding it. That's going to give us our best chance of figuring out how long each of them has been in the ground."

Cam made a mental note to check on the soil samples and reprioritize the tests he'd ordered if necessary. They had no way of knowing how long the victims had been dead prior to their burials. And the decomposition of some of the bodies could have been slowed if they'd been buried when the ground was still frozen last year. That would also explain the temptation to use freshly dug graves through Iowa's frigid winter this year. But learning when these victims had started disappearing would be the quickest way to accelerate the missing persons search.

Sophie rounded the gurney to stand over the victim, facing them as Benally spoke.

"I checked first on the trifecta of victim injuries we documented earlier." Lucy ticked off on her fingers. "Evidence of prolonged physical and sexual torture prior to death. Manual strangulation. Autopsy will show whether this victim's hyoid bone was broken in the same manner as the other victims. Significant vaginal and anal tearing. Evidence of postmortem vaginal and anal penetration. The killer hasn't been careless enough to leave semen in her throat or stomach, but maybe we'll get lucky this time around. There's not much doubt this one's connected to the other victims in this case, but I won't say for certain until after the autopsy."

That was hardly surprising. Cam couldn't recall a time that Benally had ever uttered a theory that wasn't supported by ten different sets of facts. "How about the soap used to wash the body?"

"Same ingredients were found on the skin." Benally glanced at the clock on the wall while answering, clearly impatient to have them gone. "I understand the lab already gave you a positive ID on it."

He nodded. Mother's Touch, a popular liquid soap advertised as being gentle enough for babies. The irony was appalling.

"And the burn marks on the victim's back?" Sophie asked.

"Give me a hand," the ME said to Cam. She reached into her lab coat pocket and took out a pair of latex gloves and slapped them

17

to his chest. He raised his brows. They never bothered with gloves when they gowned up to come in here, because they were always under threat of dismemberment if they touched anything.

He rounded the stainless steel table, pulled the gloves on, and reached to help turn the corpse over. "Careful." The pathologist's voice was sharp. "Position your hands like mine. I don't want to lose any skin."

Gingerly he helped her turn the corpse over to expose the back side. His gaze immediately went to the left shoulder blade. There were a dozen marks in all, a random scattering of burns that, at least in the case of the first five victims, had been determined to have been inflicted by a lit cigar.

"The number of burns varies, doesn't it?" observed Sophie. She leaned in to peer closely at the shoulder blade. "At least in comparing the pictures, there didn't appear to be a set pattern to them."

"Maybe there's one for each time he assaults the vic. Or each time she displeases him in some way," Cam suggested. Sophie couldn't have looked more out of place in the macabre setting. As if someone had set a fairy princess down in the steaming outskirts of hell.

"That's a good thought." She moved away, going to stand at the foot end of the gurney. Cocking her head, she studied the corpse silently. "Whatever the reason, we can be certain the motivation for the act is about him, not her. It satisfies something inside him, and he acts for reasons rooted in his psychosis or childhood experiences. It seems to be part of his signature."

Cam shifted position uneasily. This was the part of having Sophie here that made him most uncomfortable. Despite the groundbreaking work done decades ago in the FBI's Behavioral Science Unit, he still had a wait-and-see attitude toward things like offender profiles. It required too much guesswork, to his way of thinking, and he was an evidence kind of guy.

But then he caught sight of something else, and lightbulbs started going off in his head. "Holy shit!"

"Yeah, Super-Agent, I wondered how long it'd take you to catch sight of that." Benally tossed her heavy braid over her shoulder with a practiced shrug and smiled smugly. "I was pretty pumped when I saw it. You just might get a positive ID on this one."

Excitement surging, Cam reached out a latex-tipped finger and traced the tattoo lightly. It seemed to wrap around the back of the left ankle, but the length and width of it were made difficult to determine by the extensive discoloration of the skin. "I'll need exact physical locators and measurements on it. What is this?" He lowered his head to look more closely at it. "Bunch of flowers, right? Be too much to hope that there's a name buried somewhere in the design." An identifying mark gave them far more to go on than gender, height, weight, and approximate age did.

Adrenaline was shooting through his veins. He knew they'd finally gotten their first real break in the case.

"Way ahead of you." The ME reached into her lab coat pocket again and withdrew a slip of paper, handing it to him.

Cam looked from it to her, gaze narrowing. "You could have given me this information over the phone."

"But that would have ruined my fun."

"I wonder if I could ask you to do something for me."

Wincing, he tried to catch Sophie's eye. He'd learned to never phrase a request as a favor with Dr. Lucy Benally. Favors had a way of costing a pair of Cubs tickets or, even worse, his fifty-yard-line seats at Kinnick for the biggest Hawkeye game of the season. Commands worked slightly better with the doctor. The worst thing to happen was for her to get the upper hand.

But it was too late. The pathologist had a familiar glint in her eye as she looked at Sophie. "You want a favor?"

"A bit more of your time, perhaps. I know you're busy. But you have all the photos taken of the victims on PowerPoint, don't you?"

Anyone who'd worked with Benally before knew that she did. The ME was notoriously OCD about things like that. Copies of the photos documenting every step of each body's excavation, coupled with the ones taken in this lab, would be arranged sequentially, along with photo documentation of the autopsy on each. Cam tried to head trouble off at the pass. "None of the other victims had identifying marks, Dr. Channing. As you saw in the file you were given."

"Of course not." She didn't even look at him. Her attention was on the diminutive pathologist. "Lucy would have found them immediately. The file said that not all of the skin on some of the bodies was intact. But it also documented the number of burns found. How can we know every victim had burns on her body or how many?"

Cam winced at the imminent explosion. He'd been on the receiving end of Benally's blistering responses before when he'd questioned one of her findings.

But amazingly, the pathologist beamed. "Good question. I'll show you." Swiftly she walked over to her computer, which stood on a rolling cart in the center of the room. A few minutes passed as she fussed with plug-ins and lowered a white projector screen. She opened the laptop and tapped in a few commands. Moments later the photos in question were displayed before them.

"The victims are numbered in each picture according to the order in which they were found. We can't yet say with complete accuracy the sequence in which they were killed or how long they were buried."

Won't say, Cam mentally corrected. The ME wasn't one to make claims that hadn't been verified and reverified.

Gavin had no such compunction. "Given what we know about Iowa winters and the temperatures in the last several months, we can make an educated guess that all victims were in the ground less than a year. Perhaps for as little as six months. Although bodies will interact more with the surface when buried shallowly, encouraging faster decomposition, the soil temperature would have slowed down the process until the spring thaw."

"Connerly's big on 'educated guesses,'" Lucy said. "But here's something actually backed up by science." She magnified the photos highlighting the burns on each victim. "Where skin was missing, I was still able to ascertain the location and size of burns in remaining tissue and, in the case of victims three and five, in bone. If you look at this"—she flipped through more slides—"you can see where I marked the location of each one found. Even if the skin wasn't intact on the area"—she pointed to a photo—"the burns were deep enough to damage the underlying tissue and bone." Each wound on the bodies shone on the screen like a large white dot. "There's no conceivable pattern, nor is the number of wounds the same."

But Sophie moved closer, a finger to her lips, staring at the slides more closely. "Can you rotate the photos to the right?"

Cam exchanged a look with the forensic anthropologist, but the ME obeyed. Connerly straightened, leaned in for a better look. Then said, "I still don't see a pattern."

"And now rotate them again, please." Sophia's tone was so pleasant, Lucy didn't seem to mind the order present in the words. The photos were turned so they were a full 180 degrees from their original position.

"What do you see now?"

Cam, Gavin, and Lucy looked at one another, then at the photos again. The pathologist spoke first. "Got me. You think they're supposed to be letters? Maybe the killer was spelling something by burning a letter into each victim."

"Yeah, but he wasn't quite done." Cam pointed to each picture in turn. "B-E-N-A-L-L—"

"Smart-ass." He wasn't quick enough to dodge the deadly-sharp elbow she aimed at his ribs. "I think it spells B-I-T-E-M-E."

"No, not letters." Sophie looked at them searchingly. "Nothing?" She opened up her purse, which Cam noted for the first time was the same pink shade as her suit and shoes. Once again he marveled that the two of them had ever gotten together. She was designer clothes, and he was get-me-the-hell-out-of-this-suit as soon as he got home every night. She was soft-spoken, and he was . . . What the hell had she called him once? Charmingly abrasive. They were champagne and beer. Oil and water.

Tinder and spark. Unbelievably combustible. And a smart man didn't play around with fire.

Sophie slipped a three-inch-square mirror out of its case and walked to the screen, holding it over each photo in turn. "How about now?" He, Connerly, and the ME surged closer to stare at the reflections.

"Damn. That looks . . ." Gavin squinted. "Is that . . . ? It looks sort of like a twelve. Doesn't it?" Sophie moved the mirror to the next photo. "And that—is it a fifteen?" He looked at Cam for verification.

"That's what I'm wondering." Sophie's voice was grim. "If I had to guess I'd say he's numbering his victims."

───

He sat on the Centennial Lakes Park bench, his face buried in a newspaper and waited for the approaching jogger. The woman was a creature of habit. Every weekday morning, weather permitting, she headed to an area running path between nine and nine thirty. The trail in this park was only 1.5 miles, according to the map he'd downloaded. This was her third trip past him, and her pace was slowing. She rarely ran more than five miles a day and usually alternated between four parks in the area. Cagey enough not to follow a set routine between them, but that was all right. He'd been following her long enough to familiarize himself with all of them.

As she passed him, he kept the paper shielding his face. He already knew what she looked like. It wasn't the facial features he focused on, anyway. A few days after they were taken even the loveliest weren't so attractive anymore. Personality was meaningless, too. All became obedient when properly instructed, although certainly he'd had his favorites among them.

But the body mattered. Especially the ass.

He lowered the paper, gazed over the top at the woman as she passed by. He liked the way her tits bounced a little, even constrained as they were by the designer spandex. Matching shorts showed a butt that was shapely enough even for his exacting taste. He could feel himself growing hard as he thought of having her to himself.

His meticulous research had garnered no fewer than six possible targets that met every criteria on the list. The hunt was always more gratifying in larger locales. With so many options, he could afford to be choosy, while keeping the others to be considered for a later date. It hadn't taken long for Courtney Van Wheton to rise to the top of his list.

He folded the paper carefully and got up, holding it casually to hide his straining cock. This last surveillance had been a formality. He just had to finalize the details for the snatch.

A smile crossed his lips at the prospect. He was a bit vain about his looks, so he wasn't surprised when a nearby young woman pushing a stroller returned his smile with one of her own. He ignored her. She was too young, and he'd learned long ago the merits of sticking with the mandatory requirements. Van Wheton would be his very soon. He'd come to appreciate the anticipation. Within the first few hours of being taken, she'd be moved out of state. Just vanish, with no trace.

She couldn't know it, but her days of freedom were coming to an end.

Chapter 2

Sophia resisted the slight pressure Cam was bearing on her hip. Facing him was a mistake. Hiding her emotions required an effort that was currently beyond her. She felt shattered. Pleasantly limp and dazed. At least that was the reason she gave herself for the fuzziness of her thoughts.

"I'm not good at this."

His lips curved against her shoulder, and she heard amusement tinge his words. "I beg to differ."

She kicked his ankle, then had her foot captured when he threw a leg over it to pin it carelessly. But she was shocked to hear his voice go sober. "Think I don't know you're the cautious type? We're both a bit out of our element here. But just because something isn't planned doesn't mean it's a bad idea."

Somehow she finally found the strength to face him. When she did she found him too close. Too warm. Too intense. "Usually it does."

He smiled again, and she felt her bones going lax. Up close his eyes were more gold than brown, and humor warred with desire in them. Oddly it was the humor that had her heart rate accelerating.

"Only because you equate planning with control. Admit it." He took her earlobe in his teeth, worried it gently. "Wasn't it just a little bit fun to lose control a while ago?"

To admit the truth would be to lose completely. Because "fun" didn't begin to cover the devastating effect the man had had on her senses. Was still having . . .

—

The ring of his cell phone was a welcome interruption from the ViCAP reports Cam was poring over. The FBI's Violent Criminal Apprehension Program database was an invaluable way to compare details from violent crimes involving unidentified human remains. His initial queries had yielded little, so he'd inputted more general details of this case. Going over the resulting reams of information threatened to make his eyes bleed. He rubbed them with the heels of his palms before picking up the cell, squinting at the screen before answering it.

"Prescott." Working his shoulders tiredly, he checked his watch. It was after seven. Time to head home, grab a beer, and put his feet up to watch the Cubs game he'd DVR'd last weekend. They'd lost—again—but at least it'd been close. Still worth viewing.

"It's Beckett Maxwell."

"Sheriff." Cam straightened in his chair. Maxwell was the sheriff in Boone County where they'd found the second victim. "Good to hear from you."

"Appreciate the invite to the daily briefings. I plan to start making them, as soon as I'm close to being fully manned again." A tinge of frustration sounded in the man's voice. "Have one deputy out on vacation and another broke his foot falling off a ladder. Not on duty, thank God, but still . . ."

Cam gave a tired laugh. Wondered if he had time to stop by his favorite sandwich shop before it closed. It was a mom-and-pop operation, and their hours were set more by mood than schedule. But their meatloaf sandwiches made up for the erratic hours. "Just tell me you haven't had a report of another disturbed grave, and my day will be complete."

"Not that I've heard. It's something else." Cam heard the rustle of papers. "I've been reading through your briefing reports. Also got the lists you sent."

One of the first tasks Cam had completed was a list of registered sex offenders in the state who had been convicted of violent crimes against women and released in the last three years. The names he'd deemed most promising he'd given to a couple of agents to pursue. The rest he'd turned over to police departments and sheriff offices in counties where the felons resided for the law enforcement officers to coordinate checks with assigned parole officers.

"With two men out on leave, I'm guessing you haven't completed the felon checks I sent."

Maxwell chuckled ruefully. "Getting there. Feel certain I can check off one. No parole officer on the second, so still talking to employers, neighbors, and family members. But something else came up last night. Had a report of a bar fight just outside Madrid's city limits. Guy by the name of Gary Price sent three guys to the hospital in a dispute over a woman. Witnesses all agree the three men moved on Price first, but I ran everyone's name as a matter of course. Price just moved to the area eighteen months ago. Did sixteen years in Missouri for an attempted carjacking. The woman driving resisted, so he beat her badly enough to put her in a coma before taking off with her car. When she came out of it, she ID'd him. Had seen him at the garage she had her car serviced at."

"Sounds like a scumbag all right." Cam checked the time again, hopes of grabbing that sandwich growing dimmer. "But not the kind of scumbag we're looking for."

"Maybe not. Probably not," Maxwell corrected himself. "But one of my deputies took the statement of the woman at the bar last night, the one at the center of things. Price had attached himself to her, and she couldn't shake him. She finally told him in pretty plain language to leave her the hell alone. He grabbed the back of her neck and pulled her close, holding his lit cigarette an inch from her forehead, and told her she'd look real good wearing his brand. That's when the other three guys moved in, and Price put them all down before leaving."

Cam straightened in his chair, interest caught. "But Price has no history of sexual assault?"

"Nothing shows up on his sheet."

"How long has he been out of prison?"

There was a sound of rustling papers again as Maxwell located the information he was looking for. "Four years. He moved outside of Madrid as soon as his parole was up."

"What brought him there?"

"Couldn't say. Maybe the property. He got a pretty good deal on the acreage he bought at auction."

Cam mulled the information over. Price was clearly violent, but a sexual sadist developed over a long period of years. It was unlikely that he'd suddenly evolved into one after a stint in prison.

Unless he'd never been caught for past sexual crimes. It was entirely possible that there were other graves, scattered over the state—or farther—that had gone undiscovered.

"Price likely has nothing to do with these crimes."

"You're probably right about that."

"You going out to see him, anyway?"

"I figured I'd swing by and have a look at him myself this evening."

Mind made up, Cam had a mental picture of that meatloaf sandwich sprouting wings and flying away. "I think I'll keep you company on that trip."

The sun was doing a slow bleed across the rose-and-black horizon by the time Maxwell's county-issued Jeep made its way down the rutted lane leading to Price's house. A large dog of indeterminate breed raced down the gravel drive toward the vehicle, barking a warning. Beckett pulled to a stop in front of a two-story clapboard farmhouse, next to a newer-model black Dodge Ram pickup.

Cam scanned the area. Across a graveled expanse, a large machine shed situated at the back corner of the property nestled close to a hulking rustic barn. A small metal corn bin that looked as if it hadn't seen use for decades sat like a sentinel next to the barn. Part of the sheet metal on the bin had come loose and gaped open on one side. There were two other smaller framed wooden buildings on the opposite side of the property. Both were gray and weathered, each leaning crazily, as if goading the next straight-line wind to flatten them.

"Pretty isolated out here," Cam observed. The dog had stopped a dozen yards away from their vehicle, still heralding their arrival. "The last farmhouse we passed was five miles back."

"Price bought just the building site and five acres. The farmland surrounding the property was sold separately," the sheriff answered, putting the Jeep in park.

Cam squinted into the distance. A fully grown windbreak of fir trees provided privacy on three sides. An open field of six-inch corn faced the property across the gravel road to the front. Then he looked at the Ram. "That Price's truck?"

"Fits the description I got from the Department of Motor Vehicles." Turning off the ignition, Beckett peered out the window toward the dog that gave no signs of tiring. "Let's hope that animal is all bark, no bite."

"I'll do better than hope," Cam gibed, opening his car door. "I'll let you lead the way."

He rounded the car and joined the sheriff to walk through the open wire gate and up to the house. Keeping a wary eye on the dog, he noticed the kitchen door was open. Light spilled through the screen door onto the paint-worn wooden porch. "Looks like someone's home."

"Did I mention this guy's former parole officer in Missouri said he was given to fits of rage and had anger management issues?"

"Sort of picked up on that." The dog behind them drowned out the sound of their ascent up the four porch steps.

"Boone County sheriff, Mr. Price," Beckett called out as he pounded on the screen. There was no sign of a doorbell. "I'd like to talk to you."

Cam peered through the half-open door. It led into a kitchen caught in a 1960s time warp of avocado green. A light from the adjoining dining room lit that area, showing an overturned chair and a bottle on its side. Beer ran across the scarred table and trickled in a steady stream to the threadbare green carpet below.

"DCI, Mr. Price." Cam tried again, pounding hard enough to have the screen door rattling on its hinges. "Come on out here so we can talk."

Silence greeted his words.

Cam nodded toward the lightweight navy jacket hanging on a doorknob inside the kitchen. An unmistakable shape protruded from the pocket of the garment. "That looks like an illegal firearm."

"It's a felony in a con's possession," Beckett agreed, his hand on the baton at his waistband. "Our duty to check it out."

"My thoughts exactly." Cam reached out, opened the screen door, and stepped inside the kitchen. Beckett was right in back of him. Once inside he stopped, his gaze going to the bottle on the dining room table. Liquid still leaked steadily from it. Whoever had spilled it hadn't done so long ago.

"Mr. Price?" Beckett called out.

Cam did a semicircle around the adjoining doorway to check for anyone hiding just inside it before stepping into the dining room. A quick scan showed it empty. He could see now that next to the bottle was a paper plate with a mound of bones and half-eaten chicken wings on it. A white Styrofoam take-out container next to the plate was empty, save for grease stains and crumbs. Wide-slatted blinds covered the double front windows in the room. An ancient box fan sat on one windowsill, drawing in the cooler evening air. Its motor labored like the grinding gears on Cam's first Honda.

A flat-screen television hung on the wall of the darkened room next door, looking out of place among the dated furnishings. The shelves below it were stacked with electronics. The TV was on and tuned to ESPN. One analyst droned on to another about an upcoming baseball game.

"Someone was in a hurry," murmured Maxwell from behind him.

"His hurry probably started as soon as we headed up the lane." Cam sidled along the wall, skirting the heavy furniture lining it. Mentally sketching the house's dimensions, he figured the darkened adjoining room led to the front door and to a stairway to the upstairs. The only question was which the man had used.

Or whether he was in the shadowy next room, waiting for them. Perhaps with another weapon.

He stopped to listen. There was nothing to hear over the fan. Something about the stillness was disquieting.

Half turning his head, he gestured to Beckett, and the sheriff backtracked across the dining room to flank the other side of the double-size entry into the living room. "Gary Price!" he called out, his hand on his weapon. "Boone County sheriff. Show yourself."

Cam's hand crossed to his shoulder harness, his fingers hovering. His skin prickled the way it had when he'd been deep undercover, and a scene was about to go wrong. The image on the television switched to the opening pitch. He waited, barely breathing. Thirty seconds. Sixty.

A door banged open. The two men moved as one, swinging into the room, weapons in their hands. A man stood framed in a doorway leading to the upstairs.

"Get your hands up where we can see them. Up! Up!" Cam shouted.

"Jesus Christ. What . . ." The man's hands raised slowly as Beckett went to frisk him professionally.

"He's clean."

Cam holstered his weapon as the other man yelled, "What the fuck are you doing in my house? You got a warrant? Huh? You damn well better have a warrant!"

"Are you Gary Walter Price?" Beckett asked, reholstering his weapon.

The man lowered his hands. "Who the hell wants to know?"

"Boone County Sheriff Beckett Maxwell. This is DCI agent Prescott. Answer the question."

Sending a look in Cam's direction, the man smirked. "DCI. What's that stand for? Dicks of Iowa?"

"Funny guy," Beckett observed. "We haul in all the jokesters and give them all the time they need to work on their stand-up routine. Something about a cell seems to dampen the sense of humor, though."

"Yeah, yeah, okay. I'm Gary Price. Now tell me what the hell you're doing in my house."

Cam eyed him. Price didn't look like the type who could take on three inebriated bar patrons and emerge without a scratch. He was five-ten, 180, with longish dark hair, and sported a day's growth of beard. His sleeveless undershirt bore evidence of the meal they'd interrupted. His jeans and tennis shoes had seen better days. Cam's gaze lingered on the prison tats on the man's throat and knuckles. He'd done hard time. Which meant he was a whole lot more threatening than he appeared.

"Why didn't you answer when you heard us calling?"

"Didn't hear you. I went upstairs to put my damn pants on." The man's voice was a snarl. "I was sitting at the table trying to catch a breeze when I heard the dog raising hell. There's no law saying a man's got to answer the door in his boxers, is there?" He stopped, his gaze going between Beckett and Cam. "This about the fight last night? 'Cuz a deputy already took my statement. Got a bar full of witnesses who'll tell you I didn't throw the first punch."

"I've read the statements." Beckett's voice was hard. "I was more interested in the part where you threatened the woman who was trying to brush you off."

"Bullshit." The word was released on a breath of disgust. "Bitch was probably exaggerating."

"The bartender backed her up. You like to burn women, Price—is that your thing? Light up a cigar and hold it to their skin? You like to put your brand on them?"

Some of the man's truculence seeped away. Now he just looked wary. "I don't know what the hell you're talking about. I smoke cigarettes, not cigars, and I didn't do nuthin' to that bitch. She says different, she's fucking lying."

Cam looked at the man's hands again. "You put down three men and don't have a mark on you? That's a trick. You have any ID?"

Price laced his fingers together and flexed them, popping the knuckles. "I got some skills. What's a DCI agent doing here about a bar fight, anyway?" He grinned, showing a chipped front incisor. "One of those pussies I put down work with you? Guess that'd make him a dick of Iowa pussy, wouldn't it?"

"ID, Price."

The man looked at Beckett. "Shit, you found me in my home with my pickup out front. What more do you need?"

"A driver's license for starters." When the man didn't move, the sheriff took a step toward the stairs. "Maybe I'll find it up there."

"It's in my pickup." Price's voice had gone sullen. "Just give me a second to get it."

"Oh, it's a nice night." Cam stepped aside to give the man room to pass. "We'll go with you."

"Suit yourself," the man muttered, brushing by him.

They followed Price through the kitchen and out the front door. The sun had sunk below the horizon, throwing the area into elongated shadows. Cam quickened his stride. His was the first hand to touch the vehicle's door handle. He looked at Beckett over the other man's head. "I'll check it out first."

"What the . . . ?" Cam ignored Price's objection and opened the truck, leaning inside. He wasn't about to stand there passively and give the ex-con a chance to pull a weapon from a hidey-hole inside to use on them. Something about the man was bad, and not just his record. Cam may not know this guy, but he knew men like him. He'd spent his career bringing them to justice.

More, he'd lived in their midst when he'd done undercover narcotics, most recently for nearly two years working to shut down the pipeline of cocaine leading to the Midwest from Mexico. He'd lived like them. Learned to think like them.

The trick was never giving them the advantage.

"Step back," Beckett ordered the other man. "Take it easy."

Cam did a quick but thorough check of the truck's cab and the glove compartment. He didn't find a weapon, but neither did he see signs of a wallet. Backing out of the vehicle, he said, "Don't think your ID's in there."

"I said it was, didn't I?" The man scrambled inside the truck and climbed over the console to bend over the glove compartment. When he popped it open to stick his hand inside, a small light came on. It threw his profile into stark relief. "Right where I left it."

Cam read Price's intent before he moved. "Cover the front!" he shouted to Beckett as he raced to round the back of the truck. Before he'd gotten past the tailgate, Price was springing out of the passenger door and racing across gravel, rocks spewing behind him like tiny projectile missiles.

The dog was back, barking crazily as it chased the fleeing man. He was going in the opposite direction of the machine shed, toward the tumbledown outbuildings. Cam put on a burst of speed, veering to the right. The first structure looked like an old corncrib. Wooden slat boards placed four inches apart comprised the sides. The buildings usually had no doors, open in the front and back. Cam would cover one entrance. With Maxwell on the man's tail, they'd have Price cornered inside.

He turned to see the sheriff disappear around the front. Taking the corner wide, Cam slid on the loose gravel, went down to one knee. Muttering an obscenity, he righted himself and drew his weapon, sidling along the back of the leaning structure.

As he'd guessed, there was no door, just a yawning expanse of darkness that had swallowed Price. The wood slats that framed the entrance were rotted and broken, poking out at jagged angles like broken teeth. Cam could see nothing in the interior shadows. "You've got no way out of this, Price," he called, his eyes straining to make out a shape inside the darkness. "Don't make it harder on yourself."

"Going in," he heard Beckett say.

It was on the tip of Cam's tongue to shout a warning. Right now they had the man contained, but once the sheriff entered there would be virtually no way for Cam to distinguish between two struggling shapes in the shadows.

But before he could say a word, he saw a figure move in the darkness. There was a sickening crack of wood splintering against something solid. He swung around the corner, weapon trained, eyes straining in the darkness. "Maxwell?"

A shadowy figure leaped over a crumpled heap at the other end of the structure and streaked outside.

"Fuck." The sheriff's voice was slurred as he got to his feet. Swayed. "He's loose."

Cam spun on his heel and raced out of the building, around the corner. He saw Price run past the next decrepit building, get lost behind it. Putting on a burst of speed, he sped by it, too. Caught sight of the man disappearing into the thick line of firs marking the perimeter of the property.

Gray shadows melded with black. In the twilight before full night, the moon wasn't yet out. There was just a sprinkling of stars to light the area. Cam tried to recall what was beyond the tree line. More fields, probably. Which would be a wide-open space, a blessing for a foot pursuit.

His breathing settled into the practiced rhythm used when he jogged most nights. The dog's barks were growing more infrequent, and they were now behind him. Maybe the animal was giving up the chase. Cam raised his hands to protect his face as he burst into the grove. Needled branches clawed at his arms, his head. Ahead he could hear someone panting and knew it was Price. The man was tiring.

He burst from the trees and could make out the fleeing man fifteen yards ahead of him. Ten. Filled with a renewed spurt of adrenaline, Cam picked up speed.

The figure ahead of him leaped through the air. It took a moment for comprehension to filter through. When it did, Cam tried to halt his forward impetus, slowing but not managing to completely stop before slamming into the barbed wire fencing delineating the property from the adjoining field.

Brilliant explosions of pain radiated from a dozen different spots. Cursing vividly, he heard the wild cackle of laughter ahead of him as he paused to extricate himself from the wire. The sound torched something inside him. Solidified purpose. Gritting his teeth, he backed up several feet, then ran forward, placing his bloody palm on a metal fence post to stabilize him as he vaulted over it.

Had Price chosen to lie motionless in the field, he would have been nearly impossible to see in the darkness, at least from a distance. But the sound of his progress across the planted field was as good as a spotlight.

Cam had never been a sprinter. He ran for fitness only, and he'd never developed a runner's love for the act. But right now his routine served him well as muscles pumped in familiar response, despite the stinging pain and the blood he could feel trickling down his skin.

Headlights speared the darkness to the left, a vehicle moving fast down the gravel road. It swung around the corner, the slash of light spotlighting the area and the man Cam was pursuing. He was closer than Cam had thought. About thirty yards separated them. Price was half stumbling with exhaustion, but he was still moving quickly, his legs eating up distance across the ground.

The vehicle was racing along the road in front of them, headlights perpendicular to the field but still giving enough light for Cam to see Price ahead. The man tripped, nearly went down. He righted himself, but the action cost him, allowing Cam to narrow the gap between them. Ten yards away now. Five.

When Price stumbled again, Cam dove forward, hitting the man in the back with the weight of his body. They fell hard and rolled, each grappling for the upper hand. Price swung a clenched fist, and Cam threw up an arm, absorbing the blow with his biceps while he drew his weapon and pointed it at the man's temple.

The fight drained out of Price like steam escaping a boiling pot. Cam could make out the figure of someone jogging in the field toward them. Realized it was the sheriff. The vehicle he'd driven, headlights still cutting through the darkness, was parked along the road beyond the field.

"You're making a mistake here," Price wheezed from beneath him.

Cam eased his weight off the man and yanked him to his feet, weapon still trained on him. "The mistake isn't mine. Gary Walter Price, you're under arrest for assault on a law enforcement officer and a host of other shit I'll think of on the way back to the vehicle."

Beckett stepped forward and grabbed the man's arms, cuffing them in back of him.

"Okay, just wait a minute, will you? Wait . . . Jesus, not so tight."

"I'm sorry—you find these cuffs uncomfortable?" The sheriff turned him around and gave him a push to start him toward the Jeep. "Compared to, say, a board to the head, I don't think you have much to complain about."

"The thing is"—Price looked over his shoulder from one of them to the other—"I was lying back there. I'm not Gary Price. I'm his brother, Jerry."

"So where were you when this was all going down earlier?"

The real Gary Price stood just outside the screen door on the front porch of the farmhouse, backlit by the light in the kitchen. He bore an unmistakable likeness to his brother. Unlike Jerry, though, he bore evidence of the fight the night before. The knuckles on his big hands were battered, and one eye was nearly swollen shut, ringed with shades of purple and blue. The two were the same general height, but he had a weightlifter's build, thick through the shoulders and chest.

"Been here all night. Must've been out in the shed. I do auto repair. Got a car out there I'm working on." Despite the mild temperatures the man wore jeans, a torn T-shirt that strained across his torso, and a watch cap. Price craned his neck to look at the sheriff's darkened Jeep. Beckett was leaning against the vehicle, talking on a cell. "You got Jerry out there?"

"I do." Cam gave a slow nod. "Made some calls once he stopped claiming to be you. Your brother's in violation of his parole by being out of Nebraska."

A roll of the man's shoulders passed for a shrug. "Not my problem. Can't help what he does. And you had no call to be on my property in the first place. Got half a dozen witnesses last night who'll swear I didn't start that fight."

"Got a couple witnesses who will swear you threatened to brand a woman with your cigarette," Cam countered. Now that adrenaline had faded, dozens of spots that had encountered the barbed wire were sending up a chorus of pain. "That something you make a habit of? You like to burn women?"

The man's mouth quirked for a moment in fleeting humor. "Bitch needed an attitude adjustment. Might've wanted to give her one, but I didn't. So again, you got no call to be on my property."

"Oh, we weren't just on the property," Cam responded, testing him. "We were inside your house." He watched the stillness come over the man's features and knew he'd scored a hit. "That jacket hanging in the kitchen? The gun in its pocket gave us cause to enter. Your possession of a firearm is a felony. You'll get another ten years for that charge."

Price jerked around to stare hard inside the open doorway. The jacket was still hanging on the knob where it'd been earlier. Cam could see the glint of the firearm in the pocket. "Dumbass," the man muttered. Then he turned to face Cam again. "It's not my coat. Or gun." He shrugged again. "You're welcome to take it. You'll see the jacket isn't my size. Won't find my prints on the weapon, either. Doubt you'll get a warrant once the judge knows that, but even if you do, you won't find nothing in my house. I've stayed out of trouble for four years. I'm not going back inside."

"Maybe not," Cam responded, watching the man closely. "But your brother is."

There wasn't a hint of emotion in the other man's expression. "That's his problem."

———

Cam looked up from the laptop he was manning at Beckett's desk as the sheriff reentered the office. "Got the younger Price brother booked?"

"He's not going anywhere for a while." He held up an evidence bag with the weapon they'd taken out of the pocket of the jacket found in the Price home. "Figured I'd send this with you to drop off at the lab."

Cam nodded. The jacket had turned out to be at least a size smaller than Gary Price could comfortably wear. Which didn't mean the gun didn't belong to him, but Cam knew what a judge would say. Unless they found the man's prints on the weapon, they were out of luck. "We don't have a prayer at this point of getting a warrant, which is too damn bad because I'd like to get a look inside that machine shed." He picked up the thick packet of paper he'd printed off and offered it to the sheriff. "Here's some light reading on your newest guest. Unlike his brother, Jerry Price does have a record of sexual assault. A lengthy one. He's currently on parole after serving ten years of a sixteen-year stretch for rape. His dirtbag lawyer got him off on the kidnapping charge, even though he held the woman for three days in the basement of his house. Choked her unconscious several times, just to revive her and rape her again. A mailman heard her screams for help on his delivery and called nine-one-one. She was rescued before Price could kill her."

Beckett stared at him, the sheaf of papers in his hand forgotten for the moment. "So we've got one brother beating women half to death in order to steal their cars and another who's a sexual deviant."

"Throw in a property isolated from prying eyes, and Gary Price interests me enough to keep him under surveillance for a while."

"So happens that I've got a deputy with a broken foot who isn't up for much else." The sheriff grinned. "Teach him to stay off ladders, anyway."

Relief flickered. Cam knew he couldn't spare anyone from the task force to watch the Price place long term. Not without something solid linking the brothers to his case. "Glad to hear it. You might want the name of your deputy's doctor, though. That lump on your head probably needs to be looked at."

The other man touched his head gingerly. Managed not to wince. "I'm fine. Probably lucky the damn board was half-rotted. And that my head's as hard as it is. Maybe you should follow your own advice." He raked Cam with a look. Smirked. "I'm guessing that suit's a goner. Too bad. You can never go wrong with pinstripes."

For the first time Cam looked himself over to assess the damage. "Shit," he muttered, taking in the multitude of small tears in the gray fabric. Even his white shirt bore a couple of holes. And both sleeves of his suit coat looked as though he'd been on the wrong end of a tug-of-war with a roving band of Chihuahuas. "This means I have to shop. You know how much I hate shopping? I should have taken that snake down harder."

Beckett grinned. "Don't forget about a tetanus shot. No telling how old that barbed wire was. In the meantime, I'm going home to get some ice for my head and a cold beer. I know you've got to drive back, but you're welcome to join me for one before you go."

Tempted, Cam considered for a moment. It was late, and he hadn't eaten since lunch. Still, nothing about his apartment was the least bit tempting. Since Sophie had put a stop to things—just as they'd gotten interesting—his apartment seemed emptier than usual. Which was troubling for a man who'd always valued his privacy. His only pressing tasks of the evening included giving this suit a decent burial and tending the cuts he'd sustained from his first close encounter with barbed wire. Neither was particularly appealing.

"Throw in a side trip to grab a sandwich and you're on." He rose, having made up his mind. The suit and the cuts would wait for a little bit.

And the tetanus shot could wait even longer.

Chapter 3

'm . . . stunned." Sophie looked from the full plate before her to Cam and then back again before giving her head a little shake.

"That I know how to cook? Don't be. I like to eat. Makes sense to learn to prepare my favorite foods. Especially when they aren't easy to come by around here."

He picked up half of the shrimp po'boy sandwich he'd made from scratch and lifted it to his lips, enjoying her visible caution as she did the same. He wouldn't be offended if she wasn't a fan of the dinner. Not everyone liked Creole dishes as much as he did. But her look of surprise, followed quickly by pleasure after that first bite filled him with satisfaction.

"Oh, it's wonderful!" She took another bite. Chewed reflectively. "What's that sauce?"

"Homemade rémoulade." He set down the sandwich to scoop up some dirty rice and washed it down with a sip of the wine she'd brought. He wasn't much of a wine drinker, but the dry white went pretty well with the meal. "I found a little market in the East Village that flies in fresh seafood daily. You have to get there early, but they'll take orders, too. Didn't get as lucky with the produce. I've never stepped foot in Louisiana, but I was introduced to Creole food at this little out-of-the way restaurant in Pomona. The owner was from New Orleans, and I went back often enough to get to know him." He gave her a wink. "Taught me some of his secrets."

He mentally damned his expansiveness when her attention switched from the meal to his words. "Pomona. When you were in Southern California on that multiagency task force? You spent over a year out there, didn't you?"

"Closer to two." He avoided her eyes, concentrated on the food. It wasn't fair to equate her questions with the ones from the agency-ordered shrink. Sophie's interest would be real. Casual. And his future with the agency didn't weigh on the answers he gave her.

But fair or not, something inside him shut down at her quizzical gaze. Food he could discuss. It was the only part of the experience out there that was untainted by memory.

"I don't mind cooking when I have the time," she said easily, reaching for her wineglass. "Although it seems sort of a waste for one person."

"I agree. It's quicker and easier to do takeout, especially during the week." He recognized the out she'd given him. Knew his sudden reticence was the reason for it. And it occurred to him that if they had a future—big if—he was going to have to learn to talk about his time undercover. Sophie Channing wasn't the type of woman to tolerate half-truths and evasion.

He just wasn't certain he was capable of giving her more.

___

"Kendra Blanchette Williams." Sophia sat in the first row of chairs in the DCI conference room four days after joining the investigation, her gaze, like the other occupants in the room, on the PowerPoint Cam was running. "Divorced, two children. She's the first victim we were able to put a name to, thanks to the tattoo on her ankle. Six months ago her vehicle was caught on video surveillance entering a parking garage in Davenport on her way to a doctor's appointment. She was last seen four hours later when she entered the First National Bank's main office and withdrew twenty-five thousand dollars in cash. She was never seen alive again.

"When we added the details surrounding her disappearance to ViCAP, we were able to dramatically narrow the list of possible victims to those who disappeared under similar circumstances. The investigating detectives in each of the missing persons cases on this list are contacting the families of victims to ask for DNA samples to provide positive matches and IDs. We have a tentative match on dental records for one other victim so far, Cassie Wright Urban, who disappeared three months ago from Kansas City, Missouri." The next photo flashed up on the wall, showing an African American woman in her midforties beaming for the camera. "I'm going to let Dr. Channing speak about the victimology analysis and offender profile she's been working on."

Sophia rose un-self-consciously and turned toward the audience that included, she now saw, the very senior brass—DCI director Unger and Department of Public Safety Commissioner Edding. After years spent on faculty at the University of Iowa and as a sought-after keynote guest at national forensics conferences, she was no stranger to public speaking. "There are strong similarities between the two identified victims on that list. I'm guessing after we have positive IDs on all of them we'll be looking at a victimology pattern of single wealthy females, late thirties to early fifties, attractive and in good shape. They're low-risk victims but move about their respective communities freely, increasing their exposure. Both ID'd victims lived in gated neighborhoods, but they were taken outside their homes. The offender reduces his risk by approaching them as they go about their daily lives. He likely stalks them, following them for an extended period of time, learning their routines. There doesn't appear to be any particular physical type he's targeting. The fact that the victims are single allows them to make bank withdrawals without a cosigner. He appears to select them primarily for their wealth."

"And he just happens to also be a sexual sadist in addition to a thief." There was a quick murmur of agreement from the others in the room at Agent Tommy Franks's remark.

Sophia nodded. "We can switch to the offender profile if you like." She turned and took copies of the report she'd developed and handed it to Franks to take one and pass the rest down the row. "This is an evolving document, but it gives us a starting point. Our offender is likely male, early to late thirties. He probably suffered some sort of abuse as a child, as the majority of sexual sadists have. He's threatened by women. He feels the need to subjugate them, sexually and physically. And he's been at this awhile."

"Because of the victim numbering?" This from Jenna.

"That, and because he's likely been developing over time." It always helped to discuss a deviant like this in objective terms, to keep her mind from lingering too much on the incredible suffering of the victims involved. She had to detach to be able to do the work. It was a skill she was constantly perfecting. "Right now the offender is equally motivated by profit and by the ability to act out sadistic sexual fantasies. I think we'll find when he began he was motivated primarily by anger, retaliating for acts perpetuated on him as a child by an adult who had control over him. Or he may have begun striking out because of the failure of a trusted adult to protect him."

"So what you're saying is that he got smarter over time."

She threw a quick look at Cam.

"He evolved," she affirmed. Since Sophia had never been one to stand behind a lectern, she began to pace. "He probably began with violent fantasies as an adolescent and enacted them on high-risk victims as he grew bolder." She turned slightly and nodded toward Urban's photo still showing on the screen. "Pairing the profit motivation with the deep-rooted sexual deviation could have taken years to develop." She caught the warning in Cam's eye and paused, annoyance trickling in. Although their ill-fated time together hadn't seemed to factor into their working relationship as she'd feared, they still had professional differences, and this was one of them.

"It's also possible that the victim selection isn't suggestive of an evolving signature at all, but an indicator that we're working with a team of offenders who have dueling motives."

The room erupted in a flurry of questions and comments. Sophia raised a palm, waited for silence. "It's a possibility," she stressed. "Although no offender DNA has been recovered on the bodies of the victims, we do have two very different styles of sexual assaults before and after death. While the victims are alive, they are savagely and repeatedly tortured in addition to, or more probably in conjunction with, the rapes. But during the postmortem sexual assaults, there are no corresponding injuries beyond some abrasions and lacerations that could have occurred during the body disposal. This may indicate one offender who is gratified by the sight and sound of his victim's terror. Or"—she lifted a shoulder lightly—"it could mean a team. One assaulting the victims while they're alive, and the other after. When you consider the difficulty involved in controlling the victim as she's released to go into the bank, and then having her come back to the vehicle with the money, a team sounds plausible. One to drive, one to secure the victim."

"Statistically, how probable is it that we're talking about a team of killers, Dr. Channing?"

Cam's question was no less irritating for being expected. "It's thought that as many as twenty to thirty percent of serial killers work in teams."

"So we can be eighty percent certain our guy is working alone."

Honesty forced her to admit, "Statistically that's probable. But we should remain aware of the possibilities. This offender has defied statistics in other ways, by targeting victims interstate and straying outside one race in his selection of them. In some ways that makes him—or them—outside the norm for this type of offender."

"Next steps?"

Sophia's gaze went to the woman in the front row who had listened in silence up to now. Maria Gonzalez had risen through the male-dominated ranks of DCI to the position of special agent in charge for zone one in the Major Crime Unit a year and a half ago. Sophia had worked with her on cases in the past, but she was difficult to read. Gonzalez wasn't given to casual conversation. Sophia couldn't recall one fact about her personal life. She was slight, with intense dark eyes and silver threading through the black hair she kept pulled back in a no-nonsense style.

Cam answered. "I've received status updates from the lists we sent out to law enforcement around the state regarding violent sexual offenders released in the last few years. There are a few names we'll be following up on. We're also working on a location profile. Until we get approximate time of death on the victims, we can't be sure how long the the unknown subject kept them. But Dr. Channing thinks it's likely the women were held for weeks at a time. We'll also continue trying to match vics to those on the ViCAP list and follow up with DNA matching when samples are submitted to the missing persons databases. There are still calls coming in from sheriff offices in state wanting us to check suspicious sites in county cemeteries."

"You haven't checked them all?" Gonzalez's question was sharp.

"We prioritized them according to proximity." He glanced at Sophia, and she addressed the question.

"I've included a geographic profile with my report. It's likely this offender is in Iowa operating around Des Moines because he has some sort of anchor to the area. Home, job, family, or another loved one. I suggested limiting the scope of the search. It's unlikely that the offender would bury six bodies in this radius, only to bury another two hundred miles away in the southeast corner of Lee County."

Cam took over again. "Right now there are fifteen ViCAP cases nationwide where the victims were last seen withdrawing large sums of cash. I've spoken to every detective of those cases. As we identify the six bodies we have so far, we might find something else linking the women. In the meantime, we're holding off investigating reports from cemeteries farther from the anchor area until we have more information."

He stepped forward, picking up a stack of paper from the table in front of them and handing it to Jenna to pass out. "We've sent this bulletin to every state law enforcement agency in a two-state radius for dissemination to their local police. It explains the nature of the crime and urges them to alert banks."

"There's nothing in any of this information guaranteed to pacify a jittery public."

There wasn't a change in his stance, in his tone. But Sophia was coming to know Cam well enough to sense his irritation at Gonzalez's remark. "It isn't intended for the public. Pacifying them isn't my number one concern, anyway. Catching this guy is. We're not exactly standing still on this. As we ID each victim and get a better idea of her last hours, we'll have even more to go on. We've submitted Jenna's forensic sketches of the victims to the databases and are going through those hits. This case is breaking open with the first two victim IDs. We're following all leads."

The SAC gave a tight smile. "I have complete faith in your investigative talents, Agent Prescott. But the bodies were found here. The media frenzy is here. And we need something to calm the public and to assuage the reporters immediately, not weeks from now."

Suddenly wary, Sophia clasped her hands. There was tension in the room, its source unidentifiable to her. This wasn't her world, and she was unfamiliar with the agendas and politics that governed it. But it didn't take a doctorate in psychology to realize that every group functioned within a set of unique parameters. And she was the only one in the room to not understand which one had been breached.

"I'll leave the politics to you," Cam said shortly. "Along with the jurisdictional complications." With at least one of the victims being from out of state, there would be questions regarding which law enforcement entity had priority.

As if by unspoken decree, chairs scraped, and people began to rise. Sophia watched as Gonzalez approached Cam for a private word. Moments later they walked out together, Cam with a carefully neutral expression on his face.

"What just happened?" she murmured to Jenna as the woman drew near her.

Jenna grimaced. "Grass meets brass. Typical."

Sophia must have looked as bewildered as she felt because the other agent explained. "Grass." She thumped herself on the chest. "Meaning those of us with feet on the ground running the case often are brought up short by the demands of the brass—our superiors." She shrugged. "Obviously the agency is feeling some pressure from the public over this investigation. It was to be expected. Juicy case like this? I stay away from newspapers out of self-defense, but it's hard to ignore the headlines. Anyway, it's not our problem. That's why Gonzalez gets paid the big bucks, right?"

Pensive, Sophia turned to follow Jenna out of the room. She might be the outsider here, but her time on faculty at the U of I had taught her all she needed to know about interdepartmental politics. She couldn't help but wonder about the conversation going on between Cam and his superior.

"It's not your call."

Gonzalez's level tones didn't fool Cam. She was holding her temper in check. After years of working closely with her prior to her promotion, he knew the signs. But he didn't back off. This was too important.

"Too much information released to the press is always a bigger problem than not enough. The media can screw up a case more often than help it. You know that. At least you used to."

The woman came half out of her chair, slapping her hand violently on the top of her desk. "You don't have to lecture me, Prescott. I've spent considerably more years in the field than you have. But despite what you think about my current position, it comes with certain responsibilities. And handling the media is a headache that isn't going to go away. A case this big has every newspaper in the state calling for updates. PR needs to feed the jackals regularly so they don't start feeding on us. They need a new morsel to chew on and digest every couple days."

"We release ID on two of the victims as soon as their families have been notified." Cam reached for calm. The media was the bottom rung of his worries. Lower. He resented even the need for this conversation. "That should satiate their feeding frenzy for a while."

"What about the Price brothers?"

He fixed Gonzalez with a look. "What about them?"

The woman never flinched. He'd appreciated her tenacity when they'd worked cases together. Found the quality a helluva lot less endearing now that she was his superior.

"You didn't mention them in the briefing today. Are they considered people of interest in this case or not?"

"If they were, I would have included that, wouldn't I? Jesus, Maria." Suddenly spent, Cam rubbed the back of his neck. "I've got law enforcement in the county keeping an eye on one brother, and the other is still locked up for the parole violation. Are they capable of running something like this? Possibly. But without anything solid to connect either of them to the case, we're effectively logjammed there." Once again he gave silent thanks that Maxwell was handling the surveillance of Gary Price's place. The weapon had come back bearing only Jerry Price's prints. A search warrant for the farm was out of the question.

"At this point there are four or five violent offenders in the state we're looking at. But I wouldn't label any of them persons of interest. That's all we need, having some enterprising reporter follow up on such a comment by nosing around and tipping the offender off before we get to them."

A glance at her face showed she was unimpressed. "I'm well aware of your disdain for dealing with the media."

"As I recall, you used to share it."

Maria gave him a tight smile and leaned back in her chair. Her hair was grayer than it had been when they'd partnered together. There were a few more lines on her face. He wondered if they came from the job or from worry about her son. She'd raised the boy on her own, and he'd been in and out of trouble for as long as Cam could recall. With a jolt he realized the "boy" had to be in his early twenties now. It always surprised him anew that time had passed while he'd worked the task force. As if those events had transpired in a freeze-frame, and when he'd finished, time should pick up again from when he'd left.

As if reading his thoughts, Maria said, "While you were gone, I worked that child prostitution case operating in the Quad Cities. Remember hearing about it?"

By necessity, Cam's undercover identity had been cloaked in isolation. There had been no contact with family. Friends. Coworkers. He'd reported to one person, an FBI handler, who'd also relayed messages between Cam and his mother. At least that had been the original promise, and one he'd trusted. It hadn't been until much later that Cam learned just how badly the fed had violated that agreement.

The memory soured his mood further. "I recall," he said shortly. "I had plenty of time to catch up on my reading while I was on administrative leave." First there had been the debriefing. Then the medical leave for the superficial gunshot wound. It had taken far longer than it should have to be deemed fit to return to duty. And that experience still rankled.

"It was good investigative work." His compliment was sincere. Gonzalez had been one of the best investigators he'd ever worked with. And the details about the harrowing life the children had been leading would tug at the most hardened heart. Maria's file was no doubt filled with commendations and superior evaluations. But he'd be willing to bet it was that final case that sealed her promotion.

"And Phil Brown was a good MCU assistant director." Her voice had gone as tired as her expression. "But he was crucified throughout the case. Local kids were being snatched and forced into child prostitution. All of a sudden our long-held custom of protecting the integrity of our cases by releasing as few details as possible wasn't enough. The successful resolution of the investigation didn't pacify parents who blamed the agency for not releasing more information that might have allowed them to protect their children from being kidnapped. You think Brown had planned to take early retirement?" She shook her head. "Don't kid yourself. The agency went into full cover-your-ass mode, and he was the sacrificial lamb."

"And Assistant Director Miller learned a lesson from his fate." A sense of foreboding filled Cam. Sure, he'd read the case files, caught up on agency gossip, but the upper-level politics didn't always trickle down to the agents. He hadn't known of Brown's forced retirement from the helm of the Major Crime Unit. But hearing the story behind it now didn't surprise him.

"Damn straight." Gonzalez nodded. "I was promoted with a new set of expectations, and I'm judged harshly on how I handle the media. I'm not complaining. That's the reality of my job, at least for the foreseeable future. The victim ID will keep them happy for a while. But I have to consider my next move before I need it. I agree that it would be detrimental to the investigation to release the information about how the killer is selecting his victims. That should be for LEO eyes only, at least for now. But we live in a *CSI*-savvy society, and criminal profiles are sexy." To Gonzalez's credit, she grimaced as she said the words. "Releasing a portion of the behavioral profile Dr. Channing put together would go a long way toward putting a cutting-edge forensic face on this investigation. One the public will understand and approve of."

"It's pandering, pure and simple," Cam argued, losing the tenuous grip on his temper. "And it serves nothing in the long run. You heard Sophie." He saw the look in the director's eyes when he used the name. Realized his mistake immediately. But it was too late to rectify it. "The profile is an evolving document. Release one thing now and another later, and the media could spin it that we've been chasing our tails. Not to mention that it unnecessarily frightens the segment of the public that doesn't find criminal profiles sexy."

He could see Gonzalez was unmoved, and he mentally cursed. Long nights and a weekend spent working the case had left him even less diplomatic than normal. The rest of his team was working nearly as long hours as he was. And he was forced to argue about what to release to the press?

"Look." It was a stretch, but he reached for calm. "I appreciate the resources you've attained for this investigation. And I happen to think it's paid off. We dug up the last of the bodies a week ago and have ID'd two victims already. We've nailed down a pretty solid MO for the killer. The lab's promised to rush the results on the soil samples, which will help Connerly determine how long the victims have been in the ground and in what order they died. That's lightning speed on a case like this, and you know it."

The director pressed the flat of her palm to her forehead, a sign Cam remembered. She suffered from migraines. It wasn't the first time he'd given her one. "This isn't going to be your decision. Keep me apprised. I want to see the lab results as soon as they come in. And go over the case files on the missing persons short list you compiled with a fine-tooth comb. One of them might have a key detail integral to this case."

He tucked away the rest of his protests and his temper. Was mostly successful. "I know how to do my job." He got up, intending to head for the door.

She fixed him with a long look. "If I didn't believe that, you wouldn't have been named lead agent on this case."

On the surface the words were innocuous. Complimentary even. But something in her tone alerted him. He stopped to turn to more fully face her. "You had someone else in mind?"

Maria didn't look away. Her dark eyes turned shrewd. Assessing. "You've only been back on the job from your undercover assignment for a year. Some might say you need more time to reacclimate yourself to agency work."

A humorless smile pulled at his lips. "Because I spent nearly two years on a multiagency task force investigation that my superiors urged me to join? No good deed goes unpunished, apparently." But it was more than that, he knew. His struggles with post-traumatic stress after returning from undercover had been a factor in delaying his return to his job. Had obviously been weighed in determining his placement on this case.

"You're lead." She rose, indicating the meeting was at end. "But both of us have something to prove here. And a lot to lose. It'd be best to support each other in our respective positions."

Sophia was on her way out of the building, her mind already full with plans for the evening. She needed to send a long chatty email to her parents. Usually Sunday evenings were reserved for contact with them, but they were traveling in Europe. And last night she'd spent most of her time immersed in the profile she was developing. Then there had been calls to return to Dr. Redlow, who was overseeing Sophia's private practice client list. By the time she'd finished catching up on correspondence, it had been well past eleven.

A frown marred her brow as she considered the fact that she hadn't heard from her parents lately, either. Both academics by profession and inclination, Helen and Martin Channing had been dismayed by her gravitation toward forensic psychology. With the benefit of hindsight, Sophia could freely admit that her plan to split her time between teaching at the university level and forensic consulting had been doomed for failure. It had been an effort to pacify her parents, and her then fiancé, who'd been equally disturbed by her "dark work," as Douglas had dubbed it. They'd disapproved of her decision to leave the University of Iowa and her marriage. Their disagreement was civil, barely mentioned anymore. But sometimes silence could be more stressful than the most violent argument.

She hurried her step, heels clicking on the tiled floor. Their reaction was predictable but difficult, in the way that parental disapproval was always difficult for an only child. She'd been a dutiful daughter, always doing the expected. Boring, Cam would call it, and she knew there was truth to that. But it was doing the unexpected that always landed her in emotional quagmires. First by taking up Louis Frein on his tantalizing offer to study at Quantico.

More recently by her short-lived affair with Cam Prescott.

The memory brought a surge of heat to her cheeks. Maybe she was programmed to act totally out of character once a decade. She hadn't yet come up with any other explanation of why, after knowing Cam professionally for years, she'd decided to take him home one night last month and try him on for a couple of weeks.

The "fit" had been devastating. Addictive. And for the always-in-control Sophia Elise Channing, absolutely terrifying.

"Hold up for a minute, would you?"

She jolted at the feel of Cam's hand on her arm. She'd been so immersed in thought, she hadn't even noticed him. But there he was, as if conjured by her memories.

Ridiculous to feel this zing of electricity at his touch, at his simple request. *Juvenile*, she mentally corrected. Sophia had never been the type for crushes and overactive hormones, not even as a high schooler. And she was far from a teenager now.

"Of course," she answered casually. And just as casually stepped out of reach. It was useless to wish she'd done the same weeks ago when she'd looked up from her drink to see him standing there. Until then she'd had a solid guard against the man. How he'd managed to fragment her defenses in a matter of a few days remained a mystery.

He looked at her quizzically. "The way you were tearing by my office I thought maybe there was a fire and I just didn't hear the alarm." His gaze swept to her feet. Lingered. "Impressive. Never would have thought you could move that fast on those stilts you wear. There should be an Olympic event for that."

Though he wasn't quite smiling, the masculine creases beside his mouth had deepened in amusement. It was surely a measure of her weakness that she found the expression so attractive.

"Care to strap on a pair and race?"

Cam cocked his head, as if considering. "Think those pink things you wore the other day come in twelve wide?"

The mental picture conjured of him tripping along in canoe-size open-toed pink pumps was ridiculous enough to draw a laugh. "You'd be surprised. But I'd be happy to check it out for you."

He folded his arms, the stance pulling his suit coat across his shoulders. His suit today was a deep brown, several shades darker than his hair. "On second thought I think I'll stick to my Nikes. Running will still be torture, but at least I can walk afterward. I got your email." The segue was so abrupt it took her a moment to follow. "I think we can probably arrange it."

She must have looked as blank as she felt, because he added helpfully, "The email you sent today? About travel for the victimology analysis."

Feeling foolish, Sophia hitched the strap of her bag higher on her shoulder. "It's not imperative, of course. I could conduct the interviews with the identified victims' families by phone. I just thought the proximity of their hometowns would provide a rare opportunity to see where and how the victims lived. To talk to friends and neighbors . . ."

"Yes, you said in your email." This time an actual smile pulled at one corner of his mouth. "Go ahead. I'll be anxious to hear what you come up with. How long do you plan to take?"

Sophia did a mental calculation. Both Davenport and Kansas City were within three hours of Des Moines, but the distance from one to the other would be closer to five. "Three days."

"All right. I'll contact you if a need arises before you get back." Someone called his name, and Cam turned to see Special Agent Franks gesturing to him.

"I'll keep you updated," she promised. And watched him move away with a purposeful stride, his mind obviously already on the upcoming conversation with the older agent.

It occurred to her for the first time to wonder if there were any ill feelings about Cam being named lead investigator on this case. With Gonzalez promoted to SAC, Franks was the most senior agent in the MCU. She could think of a couple of others who had been there longer than Cam, as well. Before transferring to MCU, he'd started out with DNE, the agency's narcotics enforcement division.

Turning toward the door again, Sophia pushed out into the still-bright sunshine and headed to her car. She'd worked with many agents in all four zones of DCI's Major Crime Unit in one capacity or the other over the years and knew Cam had always been highly regarded. But the recent multiagency task force assignment he'd worked had probably added luster to his reputation.

Unlocking her car and slipping inside, she wondered if anyone else suspected how much the undercover experience had cost him.

———

The doorbell rang even as she was mentally congratulating herself for her rapid packing. She'd decided to leave tonight and set up the interviews in Davenport by cell on the way. The bell rang again, signaling a lack of patience or maturity. Sophie was betting on the latter. Livvie Hammel, her neighbor next door, had a seven-year-old who was as charming as he was precocious. Last week he'd come over to proudly show her his frog collection. She could only hope that he hadn't developed a newfound fondness for snakes.

While she could see the cuteness in the miniature tree frogs, Sophia didn't do reptiles.

A check of the Judas hole showed a grim-faced Cam on the other side. Her stomach sank as she fumbled with the lock and pulled the door open. "What's wrong?"

He was already stepping inside, sending a look around. "You packed yet?"

"I . . . Actually yes." She fell into step behind him as he started for her bedroom. "I had decided to leave this evening. What are you . . . ?" He was already lifting her bag from the bed, and his proximity in the room had her stomach doing a slow roll.

They'd ended up here that first night. Some subsequent ones, too, but the first time . . . She'd stood in this very doorway, logic slicing through the sensual haze like a quick cold blade. *What am I doing?*

The panicked question had dissipated when Cam had pressed her against the doorjamb, his kiss turning the blood in her veins molten.

Exactly what I want to, a dim inner reply had sounded. *For once.*

Belatedly, she realized he was talking. ". . . but you didn't answer. Figured I'd save time and drive over. Wanted to be sure and catch you in case you'd decided to leave tonight." Two quick strides brought him much too close, her suitcase in his hand. "Is this all there is?"

"I'm sorry. What?"

"Move. We're in a hurry." Applying gentle pressure to her shoulder, he nudged her around and through the door.

Her thought processes finally clicked into gear, bringing an accompanying feeling of dread. "I'm assuming there's been a change of plans." Responding to the urgency in his manner, she quickly gathered her cell phone from its charger and slipped it into her bag. Grabbing her purse, she headed to the door, where he was already resetting her alarm. The sight gave her an odd moment of déjà vu. She'd told him the code once when they'd arrived here, their arms full of groceries. It never would have occurred to her that he'd remember it.

"Change of direction." Cam's voice, his expression was grim. "Just got a call from the Edina PD. Three hours ago the Edina USTC bank alerted law enforcement of a large withdrawal requested by Courtney Van Wheton, widow of a successful hedge fund manager in the Twin Cities. The woman was last seen getting into a white panel van, plates unidentified. No sighting since."

His rapid-fire delivery was punctuated by swinging open the door and stepping aside to allow her to precede him. Sophia's earlier trepidation congealed into a nasty knot in the pit of her stomach.

"You think he's found a new victim?"

"The longer we go without anyone seeing her, the likelier that becomes."

Chapter 4

How long have you had this?"

He was sprawled facedown across her bed, taking up more room, to her way of thinking, than was strictly necessary. "You mean my Adonis-like physique? Or my godlike sexual stamina? If it's the latter, modesty forces me to admit that I had a great deal of inspiration toward that end." His voice was muffled against a pillow.

She snickered at that, surprising herself. Sophia Elise Channing was not in the habit of snickering. Of course she wasn't in the habit of lying sweaty and tangled with a hard-bodied sexually ravenous and frankly beautiful specimen of man.

Not that she'd tell him that.

"The tattoo," she clarified. She stretched her leg to glide along his, not quite innocently. Enjoyed the play of muscles in his back as they jumped in response.

"Which one? The one on my arm or my ass?"

"You don't . . ." She stopped midsentence to double-check.

"Aha." He flipped over, his lazy grin quirking the corner of his mouth. "Made you look."

"Your arm." But couldn't prevent a small answering smile. Honestly, the man was incorrigible. Which wasn't surprising, given what she'd already known about him. But the hidden depths she caught glimpses of intrigued her. Before he closed up, shut down, or turned her curiosity away with a well-aimed quip. She expected him to do the same now and couldn't prevent a faint tinge of disappointment.

But he surprised her by answering. "Fifteen years ago or so. Army intel."

His response was no less surprising than was the fact that he'd answered at all. He had a number of ways of evading questions that skirted too close to the personal. "A compass?" She traced the black arrows on his biceps lightly with one finger. "What does it signify?"

His gaze was sober. Pensive. And uncharacteristically honest. "Undercover work has lots of gray areas. Easy to lose your way if you don't remember which direction you're heading."

"And did you? Lose your way?" she dared to ask.

Bleakness settled into his eyes. His voice. "I'm still trying to figure that out."

~

It was a three-and-a-half-hour drive on I-35 from Des Moines to Edina, Minnesota. Cam passed the time acquiring more background and periodic updates from Paul Boelin, the Edina chief of police. Upon arrival at the wealthy Minneapolis suburb, they followed Boelin's directions to the USTC bank building where Van Wheton had last been seen. The branch was closed now, but a few of the employees had remained at Boelin's request.

Cam, Jenna, and Sophie got out of the agency-issued Dodge Charger and approached the officers stationed in front of the darkened bank doors. Immediately the doors opened, and Boelin, a tall, angular-looking man in his early forties, came out to greet them. Jenna had done some research while Cam had driven up here. So he already knew that the man was a twenty-year law enforcement veteran but a relative newcomer to his current position. He'd face some unique challenges in Edina. With almost fifty thousand residents, its upscale shopping area and plentiful parks would attract a constant stream of visitors from neighboring cities. And the three major highways leading out of the city meant that easy access and exit were unlimited.

"Thanks for coming so quickly." The chief acknowledged introductions with a perfunctory nod of his head and led them both inside the bank. "Still no word on Van Wheton. The private school her kids attend has a year-round calendar, and she didn't arrive to pick them up at dismissal time. The oldest, a daughter, missed a dentist appointment this afternoon. No one has heard from the mom. Not the kids, dentist's office, or school. She's been widowed for nearly five years—car accident. Husband left her very well-fixed."

"How much did she withdraw?" Cam wanted to know.

"Fifty thousand cash." Boelin lowered his voice and said, "More than some clients would be allowed, at least without prior notice, but sounds like Van Wheton is one of the bank's premier customers. The branch manager had shared your alert with his employees, but the personal banker helping Van Wheton was also concerned about accommodating a valued client." He broke off as a middle-aged woman in a discreetly pin-striped suit strode up to them briskly, the authority in her bearing heralding her identity.

"Are these the Iowa law enforcement people we've been waiting for?"

Boelin made the introduction. "Charlotte Dillon, bank president."

Cam stuck out his hand. "Special Agent Cameron Prescott, DCI. My colleagues, Agent Jenna Turner and Dr. Sophia Channing." He noted the speculative flicker in her eyes when the older

64

woman turned to Sophie, but he didn't explain further. "Is the personal banker who helped Van Wheton still here?"

"Yes, of course. Angie Gassaway. She's in her office." The woman hesitated. "I've spoken to the branch manager. He assured me that Angie followed all banking regulations during her interaction with Ms. Van Wheton." Dillon was clearly in damage-control mode. "She quite properly filled out a CTR during the interaction documenting the client's stated use for the cash, as required by federal law."

"We're not here about the paperwork, Ms. Dillon. But we'd appreciate a word with Ms. Gassaway." Cam gave a slight nod to Jenna and Sophie to follow the woman before turning to Boelin. "I'd like to see the security footage, if it's still on-site."

The chief nodded. "I can show you a copy. Got the original at headquarters, seeing if we can get more from it with enhancements."

"Enhancements." Cam fell into step behind the man. "Like a license plate number? Or a shot of the driver?"

The man shot him a quick hard grin. "You don't ask for much, do you?"

———

Two things upon meeting Angie Gassaway struck Sophia. One was her youth. The pretty brunette couldn't be thirty yet. And the other was the lingering fear in her eyes. Sophia was content to observe silently as Jenna led the bank employee through the events of the day.

"Yes, large cash withdrawals are somewhat unusual requests, but not as much as you might think," the woman said somewhat shakily in response to the agent's question. "Ours is a wealthy community. I guess I can tell you we keep enough cash on hand to handle several large monetary withdrawals daily. Not all the size of Ms. Van Wheton's, of course. She seemed to know that her request would trigger a CTR. That's a form we have to fill out for every cash transaction over ten thousand dollars."

"And what reason did the client give for needing the cash?"

Handing Jenna a copy of the form she was discussing, Gassaway responded, "She said it was for a horse she was purchasing for her daughter, Tiffany. She mentioned that the girl's birthday was coming up and what a good rider she was getting to be. The girl's riding coach had a line on a thoroughbred with an excellent bloodline." The banker shrugged helplessly. "I mean, I don't know anything about horses, but it sounded plausible. You'd be surprised by the number of people who deal only in cash."

"Had you ever waited on Ms. Van Wheton before?" Jenna asked.

"Not me personally, but I've seen her in here." The woman lifted a shaky hand to smooth back her hair. "She usually heads right for the manager's office. I was shocked and a bit nervous when she came to me."

"Was there anything unusual her manner? Did she seem relaxed, anxious, afraid?"

"Oh, not afraid, I don't think. A bit fidgety with the time it was taking to fill out the paperwork, but it would have been as long even if she'd seen the manager. She was more chatty than I thought she'd be. Not exactly friendly, but she mentioned her daughter several times. How happy Tiffany was going to be with the horse, that sort of thing. I think I was much more nervous than she was. Honestly, I never even thought about that bank alert until about a half hour after she'd left."

"And who did you talk to once you remembered the alert?"

Gassaway looked uncomfortable at Jenna's question. "Well . . . to be truthful . . . it wasn't until an hour or so later that I said something.

I kept telling myself it couldn't possibly be relevant in this case. I mean, the Van Whetons have done business with this bank as long as I've been here. Longer. And then I got busy. But before I went to lunch I told the manager, Vaughn Sinclair, about it, and he called Mrs. Dillon, who tried to contact the client. When she was unable to reach the customer's cell, she contacted the police." She clasped her hands tightly on the desk before her, fingers clenched. "You don't know how much I wish I'd mentioned it to someone right away. But it just seemed so far-fetched. I mean, the Van Whetons? Who would dare?"

‎ ⁓

Sophia watched the security images twice through without comment. Each time she was attuned to the victim's body language as she approached the white panel van. Despite Gassaway's assertion, Sophia saw anxiety and nerves in the woman's rigid posture, her jerky movements. Van Wheton was dressed casually in knee-length spandex tights and athletic bra covered by a loose-fitting sleeveless cotton top. She carried a designer purse in one hand and a worn leather slouch bag in the other. Presumably the money was in the bag, although Sophia wasn't quite certain how much space was required to carry fifty thousand dollars.

There was no hesitation in Van Wheton's actions when she reached the van, which was running. She opened the side sliding door and let herself into the shadowy interior, although the angle of the images showed clearly that the passenger front seat of the vehicle was empty. Sophia reached forward to stop the tape in its final seconds, for the last clear shot of the victim before the door closed. It wasn't merely nerves she saw in the woman's eyes at that precise moment.

It was the bleakest fear.

—

"Why isn't anyone out finding my mom? What are you all doing here?" Seventeen-year-old Chelsea Van Wheton's demand might have sounded imperious were it not accompanied by the tears streaming down her face. "There have been cops here all day, and now you guys, so who the hell is out looking for her?"

"Entire teams of other officers, all of whom are reporting directly to your chief of police." Sophia watched the long-legged teen swing out of her chair to pace around her well-appointed bedroom. Cam had asked Sophia to take lead on the interviews with the girls, assuming, rightly so, that the two would be fearful and traumatized by the day's events. Boelin had already interviewed both, with the girls' grandparents present, and neither had shed any light on the day's activities.

But Sophia thought they might be able to offer insight on their mother's personality, on her routine, and that could prove helpful. "I know every hour must seem like an eternity, but you have very well-trained investigators on this case. In the meantime, any little thing you can share could aid in the investigation." She turned toward the silent daughter, Tiffany. At fifteen she looked much more like her mother than did her sister, with the same pointed chin and hair color. Clutching a large ragged stuffed bear, she seemed younger than her years. "You said you don't ride anymore?"

The girl shook her head. "I haven't ridden horses since I was a kid. Maybe ten or so. I don't get why everyone keeps talking about horses. My dad wouldn't buy me one then because he said I'd outgrow my obsession with them." She hunched her shoulders. "I did."

"I don't understand how this could happen to my mom," Chelsea put in insistently. "She's hyperaware of security for all of us. After my dad died, she upgraded the security system on the house. She wouldn't even let me drive myself to school, still insisted on picking us both up and dropping us off herself, or sending a driver. It's embarrassing. And now she's the one who vanishes? Just like that?"

"Can you think of anything she might have wanted to buy with the cash?" Sophia offered a gentle smile. "Maybe she just didn't think it was the bank's business so she told them a story about a horse. Does she collect paintings? Sculptures? Do charity work?"

"She buys stuff, sure. But why couldn't she just write a check for anything she wanted?"

Tiffany's lips trembled. "After my dad died . . . mom promised us over and over that she'd take care of us. That she'd never let anything happen to us. And yeah, she was way overprotective and everything. But now to have her gone . . . There's no way she'd leave us like this. Not if she had a choice."

Sophia recounted the conversation to Cam and Jenna on their way to the motel an hour later.

"Boelin mentioned they didn't really have much to offer, other than the locations where Van Wheton liked to run."

"From her dress, it looks like she was picked up wherever she was jogging. If we can figure out where she ran yesterday, we might find someone who saw something."

"We got more than that from the girls' interviews, at least I did." Sophia rolled her shoulders tiredly. She was much more of an early bird than a night owl. Her brain grew positively fuzzy after 10:00 p.m. Which, in retrospect, might have been the cause for her lapse in judgment a few weeks ago when she and Cam had ended up sharing a drink together. And much, much more.

She gave herself a mental shake and continued. "We talked before about how the offender might be controlling his victim. Van Wheton was inside the bank for nearly twenty-five minutes. Why does the UNSUB believe so absolutely that she's coming back to the van with the money? How does the offender know she isn't alerting the police from inside?"

"Maybe he wires them prior to sending them in," Cam remarked. His features were hidden in the dark interior of the vehicle until a passing pair of headlights speared through the shadows, throwing his profile into sharp relief. "Or he might have figured some way to get video, too, to make sure she wasn't handing off notes or triggering some sort of silent alarm."

Sophia was silent for a moment, digesting that. "Yes, of course he would want some assurance, wouldn't he? And remote surveillance would be much less threatening to him than following her inside, lingering in the vicinity to make certain of her obedience."

"Boelin's department is poring over the interior bank cameras for the time Van Wheton was inside, in case he did just that," Jenna put in.

"So you've given up on the idea of two offenders working together to keep control over the victim?"

Although she didn't detect any sarcasm in Cam's remark, Sophia couldn't be certain. "It's too soon to say. But I think we're overlooking the easiest way of all to control someone from afar. Their fear for a loved one. From what her daughters said, Courtney Van Wheton was very security conscious. She was also hypervigilant about her daughters' safety. What if the UNSUB used a parent's natural fear for her children to control her? Maybe he convinced her somehow he had access to one of them. That they were in danger if Van Wheton didn't do exactly as he said." It didn't escape her notice that they were all talking as if it were certain the woman had fallen victim to the same sadist who had buried six women in Iowa. Nothing had been proven yet.

But Sophia didn't kid herself. The details of the day were eerily similar to the last time anyone had seen Urban and Williams.

This time she could hear the frown in Cam's voice. "Van Wheton has daughters, and Williams had kids, but Urban didn't. Not unless you count ex-stepchildren as old or older than she was, who were spread out across the country."

Leaning forward, Sophia argued, "But Urban did have a disabled mother in an assisted-living facility only thirty minutes from her home."

"That's right," Jenna muttered around a yawn. "I remember that from the file. Fear—it's the ultimate leverage, isn't it? Wiring the victim prior to sending them into the bank makes good sense but doesn't guarantee obedience. Some gutsy victim could have tried passing a note or yanking off the wire and getting help. There was nothing in the ViCAP files about failed attempts of similar crimes. But if the victims are made to believe the life of a loved one is in danger, their cooperation is almost guaranteed."

"If she's connected to Urban and Williams, these three women were wealthy and privileged. They lived in gated communities. Van Wheton's daughters mentioned several times how security conscious their mother was. The offender could find easier prey to kidnap, torture, and murder, but these wealthy victims were riskier. Which may motivate the UNSUB as much as the money," Sophia mused aloud, struck by the sudden thought. Serial offenders often started with low-risk victims, but as their needs evolved, so did their motivations. Some required a greater escalation of danger to heighten their own enjoyment in their crime. She'd once consulted on a case where a serial rapist attacked females in their own homes while family members were sleeping down the hall.

71

"It's a good thought." Cam was silent for a moment. "The Van Wheton girls didn't report being approached by any suspicious strangers in the last few months, but all the offender needs is the ruse. He just has to convince the victim he has access to the loved one. It'd take even more planning, though. Not only would he have to stalk the victim; he'd have to acquire in-depth knowledge about their family members."

He shook his head. "Hell, it's all supposition at this point. Right now we can't even be sure that Van Wheton was taken by the same twisted bastard burying bodies around Des Moines."

No one said anything in response to that. But Sophia knew that the more time that passed without a word from Van Wheton, the likelier it was that the offender they were trailing had found another victim. She was as certain of it as she was that she'd found another commonality in the victimology analysis.

She sat back, pulling out her phone and bringing up the copy of the notes she kept on it. *Women with dependents*, she typed slowly, squinting in the darkness. It was reasonable to conclude the offender managed to convince his victims that he had the ability to hurt their loved ones if he wasn't obeyed unquestioningly. Instilling that sort of fear would be exhilarating to the type of sadist they were seeking. Wielding absolute control over his victims added to his godlike mentality. And what could be more godlike than to hold their lives in his hand? She made a mental note to update her offender profile before turning in that night.

A sneaky sliver of memory supplied her with a visual image of the Van Wheton girls, home with their grandparents. First a tragedy had taken their father, and now their mother was missing. And try as she might, Sophia couldn't imagine this thing ending happily for the two.

There were few other early risers in the motel's complimentary breakfast bar. Sophia used the relative quiet to enjoy her yogurt and juice while she updated the victim analysis and emailed it to members of the investigative team. She was halfway through the *Star Tribune* when Cam walked in, making a beeline for the coffee.

She tilted her head to consider him. His charcoal suit and fresh shave gave him an outwardly civilized appearance, at least to the unwary. The more observant would note the narrowed gaze and straight hard line of his mouth and make sure to remove themselves from his path. At least until he'd had his first dose of caffeine.

Sophia watched in mild amusement as he filled a cup halfway with coffee and then paused to drink before pouring more. He turned away from the machine as he sipped, his eyes meeting hers from across the room. But she wasn't prepared for what she saw in them when he caught sight of her.

Heat. It flared in his gaze, frankly carnal. It stole her breath, had her stomach tightening in a hard fist. She'd seen that look often in the short time they were together, but not at all since she'd delivered her carefully constructed speech ending it between them. She'd almost convinced herself that his feelings had changed.

It had certainly been more comfortable to believe that. Shaken, she glanced away, her gaze darting back to him when he slipped into a chair at her table.

"Sophie," was all he said by way of greeting. His voice was gravelly in the morning, sandpaper dragged over silk. To her regret, his eyes had taken on a familiar guarded expression. "Not surprising to find you up at the crack of dawn. But at least you're not singing today. It's a scientific fact that everyone hates a morning person, but singing at dawn is cause for justifiable homicide."

She picked up her juice, something inside her easing at the banter. He'd caught her in a duet with Taylor Swift while she made the morning coffee one day and hadn't let her live it down. "Justifiable?

Odd thing to hear from someone in law enforcement. And studies actually show that morning people overall are happier than night owls." She brought the juice to her lips, eyed him over the rim of the glass. "Something for you to consider when you awake snarling and lethal."

"Well, of course they're happier," he countered, reaching over to help himself to the sports section. "They've got the world arranged to their timeline, don't they? The rest of us dance to their schedule. How would you morning larks like it if the workday started at a decent hour—say, noon—and lasted until nine o'clock?"

Tipping her glass in a slight salute at his point, she conceded, "I wouldn't fare so well. My mind is usually mush by eight."

"That explains a lot, since when we met up at Mickey's it was after ten."

Her hand froze in the act of returning her glass to the table. He didn't appear to notice. His gaze was lowered to a baseball headline. But she knew intuitively that the verbal grenade hadn't been lobbed casually.

Choosing her words with care, she said, "I guess you could say I was having a bit of a pity party for myself that night. I was grateful you interrupted it. I detest people who insist on feeling sorry for themselves, even if it's me. Especially if it's me."

He gave up the pretense of reading. "You don't strike me as the wallowing type."

"Ah, but I was." Sophia thought back to that night a few short weeks ago. Somehow the wound that had been so fresh and raw on the evening in question had dissipated to an irritating occasional sting. She knew that could be attributed to the man seated across from her. But although Cam Prescott summoned a tangled host of unidentified emotions, gratitude wasn't among them. "I'd just heard from my ex-husband." Idly, she played with the strap of her iPad cover. "A courtesy call to let me know that he was getting remarried."

Cam raised one dark brow. "And was it a courtesy?" He reached for his coffee again.

"Oh, probably. Douglas and I still maintain a cordial relationship." She gave a wry smile. "Our divorce was boringly amicable. We'd grown apart, with differing ideas about our careers, our futures. I was living in Des Moines by then, and he was still teaching at the University of Iowa. Although my walking into his university office to find him having sex with his teaching assistant on top of his desk hastened the demise of our long-distance marriage, its ending was probably inevitable. He was never happy with my decision to leave teaching to focus on my forensic research and private practice."

He choked a little at that, putting the cup down with a speed that had its contents sloshing dangerously close to the edge. "Let me get this straight. You caught him banging a grad student and your divorce was amicable? Most women I know would have been lunging for the nearest sharp instrument."

She could feel herself coloring. "I'm not very adept in the art of making scenes, but believe me, any number of murderous responses occurred to me. But instead of acting on them, I just stood shellshocked, long enough for him to spring to his feet, pull up his pants, and demand to know why I was there."

His fascination was obvious. "Please tell me you at least punched him then. One good right jab to the gut."

That surprised a laugh from her. Although the thought satisfied in hindsight, she hadn't been capable of it at the time. "Again, out of character for me. I told him very calmly that we would discuss it at home, and then I left. It wasn't until I got back to my car that I remembered we didn't share a home anymore. And really, what was there to discuss, other than the bitter observations about his being the offspring of a promiscuous canine? Instead of going to his house—our house—I drove back to my condo in Des Moines.

After a week of ignoring his calls, I was calm enough to speak to him about a divorce. He concurred."

He stared at her so long she began to fidget. "What?"

"Nothing." He shook his head. "Everything. You're endlessly fascinating. Go on. You said he called to tell you he was getting remarried, sending you into a tailspin."

"No, it was the news that he was about to become a father that proved to be tailspin material," she corrected. And, yes, that memory still had bite. "We had both agreed that we wouldn't have children, that we'd focus on our careers and our research. He'd reminded me often of what happened to academics who took time off for the mommy track. And he'd come from a very dysfunctional home and had little interest in 'propagating a brood,' as he called it. We'd been in agreement." They had been, hadn't they? They'd discussed having a family in the same way they had discussed everything—books, philosophy, and work. With logic and well-formulated pros and cons, the way reasonable people did. She imagined her own parents, both professors at the University of Michigan, had held similar discussions before reaching the decision to have an only child groomed to follow in their footsteps.

But when she'd left teaching, oddly enough the topic of children had never arisen again, even with the change in circumstances.

"So the cheating bastard that you divorced several years ago called to let you know he'd knocked up his latest squeeze and was marrying her. You rightly felt a little betrayed since he'd convinced you not to have kids while you were together, but here he was ready to dive into daddyhood with someone a decade or so younger. At least I assume he hasn't lost his taste for college coeds?"

She shook her head. "But in fairness, we had agreed—"

"Yeah, you said." He reached for his coffee again, drained the cup. "You've got more self-restraint than any ten women I could name, but even the most controlled woman could be forgiven for going out to hang one on when they find out . . . Ah." He set the empty cup down with a carefully controlled movement.

Mystified, she inquired, "Ah what?"

"So you and me, that was rebound sex. Or revenge sex. Maybe both."

Her eyes widened in shock. "It certainly was not. I don't make a habit of getting buzzed and going home with men in a misguided effort to get back at a longtime ex. That behavior would be juvenile and self-destructive."

The man at the next table—who until that point had been happily spreading cream cheese on his three bagels—was staring at them with rapt fascination. Her furious scowl diverted his interest back to his breakfast. Lowering her voice, she leaned toward Cam. "I should have known you'd put the most tawdry slant on our relationship."

"Did I say it was tawdry?" Unperturbed, he returned his focus to the sports section. Turned a page. "There's not a man alive who minds being used for rebound sex. Revenge sex would be a little bitter, but on second thought, you have too much class for that. So it was definitely rebound sex."

It occurred to her that she felt more sheer fury toward this man than she had when she'd walked in on Douglas bent over his teaching assistant. "It. Was. Not. You are, without a doubt, the most illogical, insufferable—"

When he gave her an indulgent smile, she was shocked to feel her fingers curl into a fist. "Of course it was. Douglas—pansy name, by the way—did a number on your confidence. He's bragging about moving on, starting a family with someone else even though he convinced you to set aside any parenting plans."

She gritted out the words from between clenched teeth. "We both agreed—"

He barreled on as if she hadn't responded. "You were at a low point. You felt rejected and unwanted. Rebound sex is the perfect solution. Explains a lot, actually."

Sophia wondered fleetingly if it were possible to strangle a man with a newspaper. To snatch the pages from his hand, roll them up, and wrap them around his throat. "For the last time, whatever there was between us was not rebound sex. That's the most ridiculous thing I've ever heard."

The gold flecks in his eyes were alight with interest as he gazed at her. "What was it then?"

She opened her mouth. Snapped it shut again when she could find no words. *Damn the man.* Wasn't that the exact same question she'd been grappling with for weeks?

"I am not late. It's not late. You guys are just ridiculously early. Why are we up at dawn? Where'd you find the coffee?"

Jenna approached the table, words tumbling from her lips. Sophia shoved her iPad back inside her bag, gathered up her purse, and rose to brush by her. "I'm going up to the room to get my suitcase."

Behind her she heard the female agent say, "What's the matter with Sophia? She didn't look happy."

Her temper spiked to dangerous levels when Cam answered, "Who knows? Maybe she found out she wasn't a morning person after all."

Chapter 5

Y ou don't talk about your training much."

The question was sudden and completely unexpected. Sophia had suspected that Cam had fallen asleep. His face was buried in a pillow, and she was straddling his bare hips, giving him a back rub.

Or at least attempting to. She'd never given one in her life and was doing so now only because she'd lost the bet. First one awake had to give the other a back rub. That's what they'd agreed to last night.

A slight frown furrowed her brow. She'd suspect him of cheating to win this one, except she couldn't imagine how he could feign sleep so convincingly. His eyelids hadn't fluttered once. His heartbeat had remained steady and slow, even when she'd stroked him intimately.

If he had been awake, she'd have been a bit disappointed.

But he was awake now. And curious. She dug her thumbs into the muscles along his shoulder blades, got a grunt of approval in response. "You want to know about my schooling?"

"I want to know what it was like to be trained by Louis Frein before he retired from the BSU."

She resumed her actions, moving to his shoulders. "He was brilliant. Short-tempered but a wonderful teacher. He addressed my graduate-level deviant psychology class one day, and we spoke afterward for quite a long time. He saw something in me I still don't understand. When his offer came to intern at Quantico, I was stunned. He was persistent." And impossible to say no to.

"You did some groundbreaking work with him. Not many get a chance like that so young."

Sophia moved lower and started on the center of his back, alongside his spine. "And you're wondering why I didn't springboard from that to BAU?" she guessed shrewdly. The Behavioral Analysis Unit consisted of FBI agents using the type of research generated by the BSU and utilizing it to solve active crimes. She used the heel of her palm to rub at a knot below his shoulder blade, eliciting a grunt of pleasure from him. "Because I'm not like you. At heart I'm an academic, like my parents. And I don't have a brave bone in my body."

He lifted his head to peer over his shoulder at her. "Don't kid yourself. I've seen you in interviews. Where you go psychologically is every bit as harrowing as where a cop goes physically chasing these guys."

"With the distinct advantage of not getting shot at." Her voice was dry. His unexpected compliment warmed her, but she had no illusions about her capabilities. "My parents were . . . are academics. They expected me to follow their path." That had seemed important at the time.

He dropped his head facedown to the pillow again. It was a wonder he could breathe. "It's a shame to waste talent like yours."

"I'm not wasting it." She paused to admire the play of muscles in his back as they quivered and jumped at her ministrations. Redoubling her efforts, Sophia said, "With private practice I get the best of both worlds. A varied client list and the opportunity to consult with law enforcement on fascinating cases." And wasn't it odd how that circle had been completed, despite her detour to academia? Louis had predicted it would, eventually.

"I meant your massage technique. You're so good at it I don't feel guilty at all for pretending to be asleep when you woke up."

"You . . ." It took a moment for his meaning to register. Indignation quickly followed. "You were not. I checked." She rolled off him, only to have him follow and capture both her legs with one of his.

Laughter lit the gold flecks in his eyes. "You mean when you checked my pulse? Or later when you put your hand between my legs to—"

"You're shameless," she huffed. To punctuate her point, she gave his chest hair a yank. He grimaced but merely shackled her wrists with one of his hands, stretched them over her head. Raked her nude body with a look that sent quick little bursts of fire through her veins.

"Smart," he corrected. "I learned how to control my breathing in the army. Came in handy when I was wounded in Afghanistan and trying to convince a Taliban fighter I was dead. As for the other . . ." She could feel her cheeks heat at the wicked look in his eyes. "I was reciting the Gettysburg Address in my head to distract myself from where your hand was. Although if you'd lingered any longer, I wouldn't have gotten much past 'four score and seven years ago.'"

An unwilling smile pulled at her lips. "Devious and smart. A dangerous combination."

He lowered his mouth to hers. "You forgot charming."

Against his lips she breathed, "No. I didn't."

His head rose. "May I remind you of the vulnerability of your position?" As if to emphasize his words, he shifted his leg to part both of hers. Slid his knee up to where she was damp and aching.

"All right, charmingly abrasive. That's about the best I can do."
A slow smiled curved his lips. "Your best has always been good enough for me."

Walking miles around endless parks to question its patrons went a long way toward helping Sophia regain her composure. Today's plan had been clear before they had retired last night, so she'd dressed in the yoga pants, tee, and sneakers she'd brought for lounging in her motel room. She could hardly traipse around the miles of trails in a suit and heels, her only other wardrobe options.

"I know this isn't your field of expertise," Cam had told her hours earlier, "but you're welcome to pair up with one of us. Jenna will join several of Boelin's men, flashing the victim's picture to park patrons at all the places where Van Wheton liked to run. Or you can come with me. I'll be going over the enhanced security footage Boelin just received."

Although there hadn't been a trace of the maddening man she'd come so close to choking that morning in his terse, matter-of-fact demeanor, the choice had been a no-brainer.

And despite their singular lack of success so far, there were worse ways to spend a sunny June morning than familiarizing herself with Edina's lovely outdoor spaces. A dozen uniformed officers were scattered around the Ashton Creek Park loop. It was the fourth of the area's running trails they'd checked, and although a few people they'd stopped had recognized Van Wheton, none admitted to knowing her or having seen her in the area yesterday.

Jenna walked briskly ahead to stop a young mother strolling with a toddler and infant. Sophia lagged behind, scanning the area. It was a given that the offender had stalked the victim. According to Van Wheton's daughters, their mother had varied her route so the subject would have had to be following the woman to make his move. More likely he'd trailed her for days and chose the area he would snatch her from. *Another big risk*, she thought, bending to retie her shoe, unless his plan to accost Van Wheton depended more on deceit than surprise. None of the places they'd covered so far this morning were especially isolated, although some had trails less traveled than others. Given how security conscious her daughters had said their mother was, it wasn't surprising that the woman's caution extended even to her exercise routine.

Rising, Sophia's gaze traveled past Jenna and the young mother, who was shaking her head and continuing on her way. But even if Sophia was right about how the offender managed to gain his victim's cooperation initially, he'd still want to keep his exposure to a minimum. Maybe he changed his appearance for each kidnapping. She eyed the scantily clad female jogging at a steady pace toward them. Even the vehicle he drove could be different every time. It would explain the lack of similarities that had emerged so far about the disappearance of their other two victims. Although she imagined that Cam's first task once they got back to Des Moines would be to compare the security footage taken at the Edina bank with security images contained in the case files for each of the ID'd victims.

The thought broke off as she sighted a figure in the distance. Frowning slightly, she walked rapidly toward Jenna, her gaze still on the man she'd observed. He was too far away for her to recognize his features, but something nagged her about the way he stood, tall and lanky with hands shoved deep in the pockets of his baggy shorts, shoulders hunched, head ducked.

Except his head wasn't ducked now. His attention was fixed on the barely covered woman jogging toward Sophia. Memory clicked, and she veered off the trail onto the manicured grass, intent on talking to him.

His hair was sandy colored. Shaggy. He fought a losing battle with the slight breeze by repeatedly raking it back from his face with spread fingers, his focus still fixed on the woman sporting only a neon-pink sports bra and spandex tights with running shoes. He maintained a swift gait across the grass in a style that seemed haphazard as he circled around benches and trees. But ultimately he kept a parallel pace to the jogger on the path.

Sophia had closed half the distance between them before he noticed her. Froze.

"Sir, could you help me?" she called, quickening her step.

Abruptly he angled away, heading toward a wooded area closer to the creek.

She walked faster. "Sir? Please stop for a moment."

But the stranger had forgotten his fascination with the jogger on the path. He was now intent on reaching the shelter of the trees.

A sliver of caution filtered through her, although Sophia didn't break stride. After reaching into her bag, she brought out her cell phone. Thumbed in Jenna's number.

"What are you doing?" was the agent's greeting. Sophia tossed a look over her shoulder. Already Jenna was crossing the blanket of grass toward her.

"There's a man here. I'm positive I saw him this morning at Centennial Park." She'd reached the tree line now, and her step faltered. Although the area didn't look particularly threatening, she couldn't be sure what awaited her in there. Most likely the stranger was using the wooded area to slip away from her.

It was the possibility that he remained near, hidden, waiting for her to follow that gave her pause.

"You're sure?" The agent had broken into a run now and gestured to one of the officers across the park to join her.

"I think . . ." Sophia saw a flash through the trees. The man was only yards away. "I'm going in after him. You've got this, right?"

"No, wait for me. Dammit, don't you—"

But Sophia had already lowered the phone and plunged in the grove of trees after the man.

The space was cooler than the open expanse of lawn she'd left. The tree growth wasn't especially dense, but the vegetation was mature. The canopy stretched as far ahead as she could see. Sunlight dappled the ground, filtering through leaves and branches. Under other circumstances Sophia would find it charming.

She scanned the space carefully. As anxious as the man had seemed to avoid talking to her, he was probably long gone. There was a picturesque bridge over an equally scenic creek nearby, according to the park map she'd grabbed on the way from the parking lot. Ordinarily the scene would strike her as peaceful and secluded.

But "secluded" took on an ominous tone if the man was hiding in the area. She continued walking forward, looking around her carefully. Only then did she become aware of the voice, an annoyed edge to it, coming from the cell phone she still held.

She grinned, finally remembering Jenna on the other end. The knowledge that the female agent would reach her in minutes propelled her forward. If the stranger was still in the vicinity, she wanted to talk to him. Sophia pushed through some undergrowth, belatedly hoping it didn't contain any poison ivy. The cell was halfway to her ear when the man stepped out from behind a large oak in front of her. Stood motionless.

She stopped and blinked. A moment stretched by. Two.

"I'm glad you're here," she said in a calm voice. "I wanted to talk to you." The man's loose-fitting shorts were around his ankles. He gave a little hop, as if to draw her attention to the area he'd bared for her attention. She kept her gaze squarely on his face. "I think you want to shock me," Sophia said conversationally, staying put. "What reaction do you like best? When women scream? When they run?" The stranger's manhood, previously fully erect, began a slow descent. "It gives you a sense of control, doesn't it, when you surprise women this way?"

He gathered himself up in one hand, waved his genitalia at her. Again she kept her attention trained firmly on his face. But mentally she urged Jenna to move faster. While it was true that pure exhibitionists were harmless, there were plenty of exhibitionist criminals, as well. Many of the serial offenders she'd interviewed had demonstrated multiple paraphilias, beginning with flashing and window peeking before they had escalated to sadistic sexual assault. If she hadn't been certain backup was arriving momentarily, she would have sprinted away at the first glimpse of him.

"I saw you this morning, didn't I?" Without taking her gaze from him, she cut Jenna's call off. With a single quick glance at her phone's screen, she found the camera application while she continued speaking. "I'll bet you come to the parks a lot, especially when the weather is nice. You like to look at the women, don't you? And you like them to look at you." Slowly, with no sudden movements, she brought the phone up to snap a picture. They might need a reason to arrest him, and he hadn't yet shown a predisposition to answer any questions.

"I've talked to men like you. Treated them." A look of consternation crossed the man's face, and he bent to yank up his shorts. "You use this behavior to seek control in your life. Others have overlooked you. Not taken you seriously. But being seen like this . . . Now people have to pay attention." Fully clothed now, the man looked on the verge of flight.

"You don't know. You don't!"

"I do," she continued calmly, taking a step forward. Where the heck was Jenna? The stranger seemed more sad than dangerous, but the possible danger wasn't far from her mind. The serial killer Westley Allan Dodd had started out with flashing. So had Albert Fish. "But there are other ways to seek attention. More socially appropriate ways that won't get you in trouble. I'm certain you've been in trouble before, haven't you?"

"Sophia? Are you all right?"

The stranger bolted at the sound of Jenna's voice. Like a sprinter off a starting block, Sophia surged after him. She hadn't stayed this long just to lose the man now. "I'm fine," she called as she burst through the trees, dodging the overgrown brush and jumping over the occasional downed branch. "Don't let him get away!"

Jenna was a flash to her left; the agent moved much faster than Sophia did. The stranger stayed well ahead of them, zigzagging from tree to tree as if seeking cover. It wasn't until he bent, then whirled around that Sophia realized his real motive.

"Watch out!"

But Jenna didn't need her warning. She ducked as he brandished a dead tree branch in a wild swing and then rushed the man, leading with her shoulder and dropping both of them to the leaf-cushioned ground. The stranger let out a high-pitched yowl and rolled to his side. Sophia rushed to help the agent, but Jenna was firmly in command. She flipped the man over and wrestled cuffs on him. "Be thankful you didn't actually hit me," the agent muttered, bending to fit a cuff on his wrist. "I wouldn't be so gentle then."

"I didn't do anything!" The stranger had regained his voice as he was brought to his feet. Sophia turned when she heard a crashing approach. Saw the uniformed officer Jenna had summoned coming toward them at a jog. "I have a right to be here. That woman was chasing me. I was afraid."

Jenna yanked him to his feet. "Hear that, Sophia? You scared him." A quick search of his pockets elicited a slim worn wallet, cell phone, and some loose change. After flipping open the wallet, she peered inside. "Well, Carl Frederick Muller, you're going to get the chance to tell us all about how this big, bad blonde made you fear for your life."

Sophia stepped up to the officer when he arrived and showed him the picture she'd taken on her phone. "His name is Carl Muller. He's likely had numerous complaints for similar acts." The uniform gave the picture a hard look before transferring his gaze to the other man.

"Well, that's easy enough to check out." The uniform started forward. His square face was red with exertion beneath his close-cropped salt-and-pepper hair. "I've got this, Turner. We have enough to take him in."

Jenna looked at her, brows raised as the officer took charge of Carl and brought him to his feet, nudging him back toward the park.

"He was at Centennial Lakes Park earlier today. I saw him by the fountain," Sophia explained. "When the officers joined us, he left before we could question him." Now that it was over, the whole ordeal left her with a mortifying weakness in the knees. Jenna, on the other hand, looked as if she'd dearly love to catch up with the handcuffed man and beat an apology from him. The agent's expression surprised a laugh from her.

"Remind me never to get you mad. You look positively fierce."

It took a moment for the agent to tear her gaze away from the officer and the handcuffed stranger. "What?"

Her shakiness had to be a reaction. She forced herself to move after the officer. Sophia was a clinical expert into the most deviant minds known to mankind. But her expertise was with conducting interviews and research. Teaching. While she regularly consulted on high-profile crimes, she'd never been tempted to join the ranks of the law enforcement who chased the men bent on enacting the evil acts she studied. As she'd once told Cam, she'd long attributed her preference to a healthy dose of self-preservation.

The two walked in tandem at a swift pace in an effort to catch up with the officer. "I wish you'd considered my ferocity earlier," Jenna countered, sending her a sidelong glance that reminded

Sophia so much of Cam she almost stopped in her tracks. "Going after him without me was plain stupid."

The female agent even sounded like Cam. "Believe me—I have a cowardly streak a mile wide. Had I not known you were right behind me, I wouldn't have followed him into the trees." She blinked as they stepped back into the bright morning sunlight. Then added sedately, "Actually, you were a bit slower than I would have liked. You need to work on your speed."

When Jenna gaped at her, Sophia allowed herself a small smile. It drew an answering snort. "Let me see that picture." Sophia brought it up on the phone and passed it to the agent, who stopped a moment. Stared at the screen. Then at Sophia. "So that's what I overheard before you cut me off to snap this?" She waved the phone. "Some weenie wagger's doing a shake-the-junk dance, and you just stood there playing Freud?"

"Believe it or not, I was doing a risk assessment," Sophia responded dryly. "Exhibitionists are typically regarded as low-level offenders if no other paraphilias are present. If the behavior Muller exhibited turns out to be infrequent, perhaps brought on by stress or fantasy enactment, he's unlikely to be violent."

"But he was violent. At least he tried to be," Jenna reminded her. They continued walking, closing in on the officer, who was slowed by his reluctant prisoner. "Only superior reflexes prevented my getting brained by that branch."

"But he didn't display sexual violence and aggression." Sophia lifted a shoulder at the agent's sound of disbelief. "I'm willing to bet he has a record of similar acts, but I'm guessing it won't include aggression unless he's cornered. At any rate, my interest in him is focused solely on what he might have seen if he hangs out in the parks as often as I suspect."

They were headed back to the parking lot where they'd left their vehicles. Sophia slowed her step. "Maybe one of us should stay with the others," she suggested. "I'd feel terrible if I interrupted the search for possible witnesses only to discover this guy is harmless."

Jenna eyed her askance. "Harmless? We'll see soon enough downtown. And the officers will continue the canvass. If this lead is a bust"—the agent shrugged—"we can always rejoin them. The fact that Muller was seen at the park this morning and left before he could be questioned is enough to have me wanting to talk to him now."

Sophia hoped she was right. The sense of urgency elicited by the news of Van Wheton's disappearance was growing stronger. She certainly didn't have the expertise to determine which line of pursuit would prove fruitful. But she had a growing certainty that the missing woman could ill afford to have them waste any time.

⁓

Interview rooms differed little, regardless of the location, Sophia decided. Although this one seemed a tad cleaner, for the most part it was identical to others she'd seen.

It wasn't the cleanliness of the room next door that held her attention on the live feed on the TV before her, however. It was the man slumped in one of its chairs. Carl Frederick Muller had indeed turned out to have an arrest record. Lieutenant Bruce Goldman, a plainclothes detective, sat silently across from the man, looking through a file folder spread open before him. His conduction of the interview for the last fifteen minutes had been textbook. He'd started out easy, asking about Muller's interests, sharing his own, an effort designed to put the man at ease. Then he had segued into leading Muller into describing what he'd done for the last two days. Where he'd been. The other man's narrative was disjointed, riddled with contradictions. The detective made a few notes while the man spoke, but he said nothing until Muller's voice tapered off midsentence.

Then the tenor of the interview abruptly changed. "So you like to look in windows while you whack off. Don't you, Carl?" The other man looked away at the lieutenant's conversational tone. "Get a kick out of flashing the goods to attractive women in the parks, too. You've been pretty busy since the weather warmed up. Got no fewer than three arrests since April, which brings you to a total of"—he looked back down at the file contents to do a rapid tally— "almost a dozen complaints. Four plea bargains and two convictions. I figure a slow learner like you, it must be a real sickness, huh?" Goldman raised his gaze to Muller, who remained unresponsive. "Is it the shock value, or do you just never get any other opportunity to show women your junk?"

"They had no right to bring me in," Muller muttered. "Whatever those women said is a lie. I didn't do anything. They chased me."

"Did you forget the picture one of them snapped, genius?" The lieutenant took a copy of the photo Sophia had taken earlier from the file on the table in front of him. Slid it over to the other man. "Not to mention that the one whose head you threatened to bash in is a DCI agent from Iowa. Why didn't you want to answer their questions? It wasn't because you were snapping pictures on your phone again of strange women in the park, was it?"

If anything the man slunk lower in his chair. "No crime in not wanting to talk to people. Just like it's not a crime to take pictures. Of the trees and stuff."

"Except Judge McNeil's orders about that were pretty clear. On account of how many of the women in your pictures ended up being the ones whose windows you peeked in later while playing spank the monkey."

Muller finally looked up then, his voice going higher. "That's not what the judge said!"

"Pretty close," the detective said imperturbably. "Near enough that he'd figure today was a violation of your probation agreement if you were taking more pictures in the parks. You want to make any bets about what we're going to find on your phone when the warrant comes through?" The other man's gaze slid away. "No? Maybe another picture of this woman." Goldman took a photo from the folder and slid it over to the man.

Muller glanced at the photo, then away. "I don't know her."

"Didn't stop you from taking a picture of her a couple months ago, did it?" The detective's tone had hardened, and he leaned forward, all signs of his earlier laid-back demeanor absent. "This picture was among dozens of others they found after you got caught at your last peep job. Problem is . . ." Goldman's voice rose slightly when Muller started to protest. "This woman"—he stabbed the photo with his index finger—"disappeared yesterday, and no one's seen her since. So you'll see why we're asking a guy like you with such interest in this lady here what you did to her."

"He won't respond to that approach," Sophia said, half to herself. "Goldman needs to use finesse."

"Let's give him a chance," Boelin responded behind her, a slight edge to his words. "The lieutenant's got nearly thirty years of experience. He knows what he's doing."

"So does Dr. Channing," Cam surprised her by saying. "She worked closely with Quantico's BSU for five years while she was in graduate school. Didn't join law enforcement, which may account for her stupidity in following this guy into the woods, but she's an expert in her field. Care to wager a bet on the outcome of this?"

Sophia turned more fully to look at the two men. It wasn't quite an accident that the move had her stepping squarely on Cam's toe. The man was the master of the left-handed compliment, but it was his last statement that had her attention.

The two men were eyeing each other with all-too-easy-to-read expressions of male competitiveness. Boelin cast a speculative glance at her. "I'm familiar with Dr. Channing's reputation. But twenty says Muller spills everything he knows in the next ten minutes."

"I've got twenty that says otherwise. And that Channing will get him to talk after your detective fails."

"My money's on Dr. Channing, too." Jenna raised her brows when Sophia narrowed a look at her. "What? The rate you were going, you'd have had him telling you all about his childhood bedwetting problem before I got there."

Shaking her head slightly, Sophia returned her attention to the TV screen, where the live feed showed the interrogation deteriorating.

"I don't know her!" Muller was agitated now, visibly angry.

"You also said you weren't in Centennial Lakes Park this morning, but two people have placed you there. If you lied about that, what else are you lying about? Look at it from our perspective. We've got a missing woman, and her picture was found in the file of photos taken by you a couple months ago. Plus you've got a rap sheet for following some of those women in your pictures home, then going back at night to get a look in their windows while you jack off. So we're out canvassing all the areas the missing woman used to run, and who do we see hanging around? You again." Goldman paused to let his words sink in. "It just doesn't look good is what I'm saying. So you're going to want to tell us everything you know about this lady." The detective stabbed Van Wheton's photo with his index finger again. "And explain why I should believe that you don't know her."

Muller crossed his arms over his dirty T-shirt in a posture that was as telling as his abrupt silence. And despite long minutes of continued questioning, he remained stubbornly quiet.

"Saying nothing is worse than talking to me. Way worse." Goldman softened his approach, far too late, in Sophia's estimation.

"It makes you look guilty. And maybe you have a really good reason for taking her picture before. If you do, now's the time to tell it. You don't want to have to go back in front of the judge if you don't have to, do you?"

"I'll talk to her, not you," Muller said suddenly.

"Her?" The lieutenant looked confused. "Last I checked, Judge McNeil was still a guy."

"No, her. That lady. The one that talked to me before."

"You mean the DCI agent you tried to brain with that branch?" Goldman made a scoffing sound. "You think she's going to be feeling all sympathetic for you?"

Carl sucked in his bottom lip. "Not her. The other one. The blonde. She helps people like me. She said so."

"Dr. Channing? She's a psychologist who works with cops. She helps put guys like you away. You want a sympathetic ear, I'm the one to talk to, not her."

Clearly having made up his mind, Carl shook his head. "I don't believe you. She had kind eyes. She said she understands. I want to talk to her."

"Double or nothing. Another twenty says Channing gets Carl pouring his heart out."

Whirling around in her seat, Sophia frowned at Cam. "Will you stop?"

He cocked a brow at her. "I gave him ten more minutes. The guy shut down in two. You'd better head next door." He nodded toward the exit. "See if Muller has anything important to tell us, or if we're spinning our wheels here."

Nonplussed, Sophia looked at Chief Boelin. There was a reason neither Cam nor Jenna had led the interview instead of Goldman. Interagency cooperation went so far, but the agents were out of their jurisdiction. And that included the civilian consultant connected with their case.

The man fixed her with a look. "I remember reading about you getting Emmett Sanderson to give up the location of his last victim."

Six years ago Emmett Sanderson had been on death row in a federal prison for the kidnap, torture, and homicide of thirty young boys. All but one of the bodies had been recovered when she interviewed him. The man had had nothing to lose and no reason to talk to her. But after days of harrowing interviews, he'd finally given her the details the Detroit police and the victims' parents needed to hear.

She doubted Carl Muller's information, if he even had any to share, was nearly as compelling as Emmett Sanderson's. One of the officers had already verified his story that he'd been at work by 6:00 p.m. yesterday.

He came nowhere close to fitting the profile she'd developed of their serial offender. Although experience had taught her that Peeping Toms could escalate to more violent sexual behavior, this man didn't have the mental ability to craft the extortion part of the offender's MO.

But the photo he'd taken of Courtney Van Wheton a couple of months ago was damning. And if the woman was the latest victim of the offender they were seeking, time for Van Wheton was rapidly running out.

Without another word, Sophia headed to the interview room's door.

———

He yawned mightily, toed open his bedroom door, and shuffled in, naked and dripping. He swiped the towel over his newly shaved head, tried not to miss the recent loss of his normally thick hair. He wasn't balding prematurely like some his age. It seemed a shame to shave it along with the rest of his body hair. But care had to be taken, especially before a night spent breaking in his newest possession. It was hard to say if he enjoyed the fucking or the beatings the most, but if he was unhappy with the take, he usually started out with punishment, to show the bitch what a disappointment she was.

Because in the end, all women disappointed.

But when the money was good, he popped a couple of blue pills and spent the night training his new whore in all the ways she'd need to learn to please him.

Last night the take had been excellent. Fifty thousand. He stood there for a moment and basked in the thoughts of what he would do with that money, one hand going up to rub at his smooth rippled chest. So the sex had been enthusiastic, and the bitch had been used hard and well.

He picked up the remote to turn on the TV. Shit, as much time as she spent jogging, she should've thanked him for the workout he'd given her. Would give her again, after he got some sleep and hit the gym later.

He dropped onto the bed, swallowing a yawn. Watched a clip on ESPN, then flipped to the news, ready to turn the TV off. Until the female news anchor caught his eye.

Propping his head up with a second pillow, he paused to listen, his mind only half on the morning update. He wondered idly how hard it'd be to get at the pretty Hispanic anchor who was trying to look so serious and professional. Her name was public, and once he had a name he could get an address. Wasn't a security system in the world that could keep him out, either. Before he'd hit on the big-time scores, he'd made his living on B and E's. And if he'd happened to case a house with a decent-looking woman living in it . . . Well, the rapes had been a bonus.

He squinted at the news anchor, half considering it. She looked as if she'd love taking it up the ass. His new possession might not have loved it last night, but she'd taken it plenty.

His cock twitched at the memory, so he reached down to stroke it. Only to freeze in the next moment when the TV bitch said, "And now for the latest on the macabre investigation into the bodies found in local small-town cemeteries in the area, we bring a press conference held this afternoon with Special Agent in Charge Maria Gonzalez."

He sat up, scowling at the screen. The familiar rage was there, just bubbling beneath the surface. Those bodies never should have been found. Never! It'd been a fucking mistake, and mistakes weren't to be tolerated. He'd learned that much from his old man, the fucking bastard.

The screen filled with a piñata-faced bitch that blabbed on for a minute without really saying anything. Something in him eased. The state cops didn't have a fucking clue about what was going on. How could they? They had some dead bodies. They couldn't know who the bitches were, or who they'd been before he'd got done with them. The graves being discovered was a royal fuckup, but the bodies could have been buried with a map and a full set of directions and the fucking cops would still be scratching their asses and going on TV to sniff their fingers.

He cackled, a surprisingly high-pitched sound coming from the big-muscled, hairless body. The rage settled back inside his chest, where it simmered until the next provocation.

"The agency is working with noted forensic psychologist Dr. Sophia Channing, who has put together a preliminary profile on the offender in this case." A still photo was splashed across the screen as Piñata-Face started reading. He studied the picture. Good-looking bitch with excellent tits. She'd look even better naked, with his jizz sprayed across her tits and face. And then she'd still be a helluva lot better-looking than that sour old bitch doing the talking.

". . . a violent, sadistic offender, one likely emotionally stunted in his early teens . . ."

What the fuck? He frowned, straightening up in bed, reaching for the volume on the remote.

"The offender was probably the witness to or subject of sexual assault in his childhood . . ."

". . . feelings of helplessness and misplaced aggression . . ."

". . . compensating for his own inadequacies . . ."

". . . may use performance-enhancing drugs to mask a lack of sexual prowess . . ."

"No-o!" he howled, hurling the remote to smash squarely in the middle of the flat screen. But the bitch kept talking.

". . . overdeveloped sense of self evolving into a god complex . . ."

The raging beast had awakened, and it was calling for blood. Channing's blood. "Fucking whore, I'll kill you—I'll kill you," he screamed. Leaping from the bed, he grabbed the table lamp and heaved it to smash the TV. Followed it with the drawer of the bedside table. Then hurtled the table itself at the wall and shattered the screen, bringing blessed silence, finally.

But the words repeated in his head, set fire to the gasoline-soaked rage inside him.

Emotionally stunted . . .

Helpless . . .

Lack of sexual prowess . . .

He continued his destruction of the bedroom, tipping over furniture, smashing everything in his path. And when he finished, chest heaving, a dull dark red washing across his vision, one name was stamped on his mind like a searing brand on cool flesh.

Dr. Sophia Channing.

Chapter 6

You're a diehard liberal. Why am I not surprised? You're lucky your big, bleeding heart doesn't splash on the sidewalk in front of you when you walk."

They'd returned an hour ago from dinner out followed by a movie. It had been amazing enough that they'd settled on one they both wanted to see. Agreement on their opinions of it afterward was probably too much to ask.

"Because I happen to have empathy for a character who made some bad choices?" Sophia drew a card and fit it in her hand. "I'm just saying none of us is perfect. It's human nature to make mistakes. So it behooves us to have some sympathy for those who are trying to rectify their bad choices from the past." She laid her cards down, just a bit smugly. "Gin."

"You must think—what?" He shot her a narrowed gaze and reached over to rifle through the hand she'd laid. "Funny that sympathy you mention has been absent since we've been playing cards. I'm beginning to think I've been sandbagged."

She smiled sedately, scooping up the cards to shuffle them. If *sandbagging* was the appropriate term for letting him believe at the beginning that she'd be an easy mark, he had her dead to rights. But it was Cam who'd altered her suggestion of cards to playing Strip Gin. And if she'd failed to lay down her winning hands at the beginning, and kicked off first one sandal and then the other when she'd allowed him to win at first, well, men were simple creatures at times. And the one sitting across from her had proved amazingly easy to distract.

"You won the first two hands," she reminded him, shuffling expertly. From his sharp look, she immediately realized her mistake. She'd gone to great lengths to be deliberately clumsy in her previous attempts to ready the cards.

"Yeah, and then you won the next six. But to show I'm not a sore loser—even in the face of growing certainty that you're a shark. . ." He stood lazily and unbuckled his jeans. Stripped them down his lean, muscled thighs. Kicked them aside.

Sophia swallowed hard. Perhaps she'd miscalculated. It had been hard enough to keep her mind and her gaze off his bare chest. But now he stood nonchalantly before her wearing nothing but his navy boxer briefs. And what he did for the garment put male underwear models to shame.

It took effort to tear her gaze away from the sight he presented to deal the cards. She lacked the willpower required to ban the X-rated thoughts currently occupying her mind. Frantically, she searched for something, anything, to divert her focus from the hard-bodied male sitting across from her.

"You call me liberal, but I happen to know you're not as hard-hearted as you'd have me believe." With hands that trembled a bit, she set down the pile and picked up her hand, fanning out the cards. "Twice now I've seen you approach a homeless person and hand them something." She moved her cards around to start her runs and sets and reached for a card from the center pile.

Cam looked uncomfortable. "I wasn't giving them money, if that's what you think. Most of these people have addictions of one kind or another. I'm not about to help support that."

She discarded and looked at him curiously, proud that she managed to keep her attention on his face. Mostly. She barely noticed at all the way his biceps rippled in the simple act of reaching for a card. "What was it then?" She'd wondered at the time if it was a business card with the name of a local shelter imprinted on it. Or a bus pass to help them move around the city more easily.

He discarded. "It was just a card directing them to Sanford's. Your turn here. Unless you're ready to forfeit, in which case you've got some clothes to shed."

She rolled her eyes. "In your dreams." Sophia took her turn but didn't let him divert her from her earlier question. "Sanford's. That's a restaurant, isn't it?"

"More like a diner." He reached for his bottled water. Brought it to his lips and drank. She watched, mesmerized as a drop of condensation dripped to his chest. Rolled ever so slowly down the muscled planes. He set the bottle down and reached for a card. "It's no big deal. I have a tab there. Anyone who comes in with a card gets a free meal, and I pay at the end of the month. Doesn't make me a soft touch. It's not like I'm loaning them my car."

His words melted something inside her. No, the man definitely wasn't a soft touch. He couldn't do the job he did, see the things he'd seen, and not attain a certain level of cynicism. But he wasn't jaded. Not even after living nearly two years undercover. And his act of caring warmed her.

There was more, much more to Cam Prescott than she'd suspected, even after working with him peripherally for years. He was irreverent, insightful, smart . . . and too damn sexy for his own good. Or for her peace of mind.

"Take it off."

Her attention bounced back to the game. "I beg your pardon?"

Those devastatingly attractive masculine creases beside his mouth deepened. "Gin. And remember the rules established at the beginning of the game. Jewelry doesn't count."

Rules he'd established, she recalled. But Sophia laid down her cards without comment. Both hands went to the V of her blouse. Slipped the first button through its hole. Then the second. But when her gaze caught his, her fingers faltered.

All traces of humor had vanished from his expression. The heat in his eyes turned them golden. And the look there—the wanting—was heady enough to steady her hands. Her pace remained slow. Teasingly so.

When had a man ever looked at her with that sort of desire? No one had ever made her feel so feminine. So powerfully female. Only Cam. The newness made it frightening. And overwhelmingly seductive.

Another button slipped free. Her fingers toyed with the last one. Drawing the moment out. His gaze was intimately intent. And when the button was loosened at last . . . when the rose-colored top was pushed off her shoulders to fall unnoticed to the ground, she saw his hands flex once. Then he shoved out of his chair and rounded the counter to pull her close.

"I don't want to play anymore," he muttered against her lips. His kiss was hard, ravenous.

When he scooped her up in his arms to stride to the bedroom, she managed to tear her mouth away long enough to murmur, "Thank God."

"Did you mean what you said in the park?" Carl Muller leaned toward her, his pale-blue gaze not quite meeting hers. "That you help guys like me?"

"Yes, I have treated people with similar urges to yours, Mr. Muller. May I call you Carl?" His head jerked in assent. "The next time you go before a judge, you need to insist that your lawyer request a treatment program. One where you'll learn to channel your urges in socially acceptable ways." If this man was a low-threat offender, as Sophia suspected, he'd likely had a hit-and-miss encounter with counselors.

Muller did look up then, a flicker of disappointment in his expression. "You won't help me yourself?"

"I don't live around here, Carl," Sophia said gently. "My practice is three hours away. I do have contacts in the Cities, though. Some of them offer sessions on a sliding-fee scale, or even pro bono. Would you like me to contact someone on your behalf?"

"Someone nice?"

"Definitely someone nice." She leaned forward, lowered her voice confidingly. "I'll do that, because I do want to help you, Carl. Just like I know you want to help me."

He tensed. "I can't help you. I told that detective before. I don't know the woman he was talking about."

Sophia nodded. "I'm still hoping you can help. You see, I don't think you were the one who kidnapped that woman."

His attention bounced to her. "That other guy did. He was rude, too. And mean. Saying those things about me. He doesn't understand. No one does. I have different needs. That doesn't make me a bad person."

She was fairly certain what his needs made him but kept her voice reassuring. "Of course it doesn't. The judge wasn't very understanding, either, was he?"

He plucked at a hangnail. Shook his head.

"The reason you were there today doesn't matter to me. I'll bet you go to a park every day. You have a right to go to public places, right? Your tax dollars pay for them."

He nodded slowly. "They take lots of taxes out of my check. I have a job at a garage on Seventieth Street. Just sweeping up and stocking shelves for now, but I'm hoping to work my way into their detailing department. I'd be good at that."

"I'm sure you would be." She sent him a warm smile. "Everyone needs to set goals. Sometimes we need assistance to achieve them, though. Is anyone in your life helping you with yours?"

"My probation officer helped me get the job. He's not very nice, but he's not as mean as that detective." Carl plucked at his shirt nervously. "And my mom. She thinks I'd be good at detailing, too. I clean her car every Saturday."

"That's good. Everyone needs a little help, don't they? Do you like to help people, Carl?"

Muller's shoulders jerked up and down. "I don't know. I guess."

Hardly a promising response, but he hadn't shut down yet. Sophia opened up the file folder Detective Goldman had left on the table and picked up Van Wheton's picture. "Do you want to know what my goal is?" She set the photo on the table and slid it toward him. "I'd like to find this lady. I want to take her home to her two daughters. They don't have anyone else. Their dad died a few years ago. My goal is to help them see their mom alive again."

His eyes flicked over the picture. Away. Guilt, Sophia interpreted, but for what? Had he attempted to follow Van Wheton home at one point? The gated community she lived in would have stopped him. Or did he know more about the events of the woman's abduction than he was letting on?

"I can't help you."

"Oh." Sophia's voice was crestfallen. "I'm so sorry to hear that. I don't know whom else to ask. You probably know some of those parks as well as anyone does."

"Like the back of my hand," he assured her. "I know where all the trails go and stuff. Some get more crowded than others. I like them best."

"This woman ran in one of the parks nearly every day. Did you see her often?"

"Sometimes." He shook his head a little, and then pushed back the hank of hair the action had dislodged. "I never talked to her or anything."

"Maybe you noticed her talking to someone else."

He thought a minute. "No. No, I don't remember that. I think someone might have wanted to talk to her, but I never saw him do it."

Interest flared. Sophia carefully kept it from her voice. "A man? You saw a man with her in one of the parks?"

"Not with her." Muller bit at the cuticle on his left hand. "He'd just watch her. I saw him a couple times. He'd come to the park she was at, and when she left, he'd leave, too."

"But he didn't talk to her."

Shaking his head vigorously, Carl said, "Not when I was there. But I only saw this woman a few times. And the guy . . . three times, I think. Two other times before Monday."

"You are being very helpful, Carl." Sophia beamed a smile she wasn't feeling in his direction. Her mind was racing. "I think you're very observant."

He looked pleased. "People don't notice me. But I notice them. Like I saw this guy for the first time two weeks ago, and he was always wearing sunglasses. Even if it wasn't very sunny. And he had this newspaper in front of his face, but when that woman went by he always peeked over the top of it to watch her. I thought maybe he'd take her picture, but I never saw him with a phone. He still might have," he hastened to add. "I just didn't see it."

Clearly Muller had noticed the man only because he'd suspected the stranger of having a fetish similar to his own. "Was he wearing sunglasses every time you saw him?"

Carl nodded.

Sophia clasped her hands on top of the photo. Leaned forward. "Even when you saw him Monday?"

"Yes, I said—" He stopped then, as if aware of the trap.

"You said you saw him Monday. He was always watching her, you said. So Monday you were at the same park as this stranger and the woman. This could be very helpful, Carl. Especially if you have a picture of the man."

He shook his head violently. "I don't. I don't take pictures of men, anyway. I'm not like that. Only women. Pretty girls."

"Of course. But he could have been in the background of one of your pictures."

"I told you I didn't take any!"

"All right." He was growing too agitated to be much help, so Sophia went about soothing him. "I believe you." With the warrant coming through soon, the police would discover whether Muller was telling the truth. Any new pictures the man had taken could possibly be enhanced to include others in the background. "Do you remember what the man looked like?"

Muller shook his head violently enough to have his hair tumbling across his forehead again. Sophia pressed on. "Was he blond like you? Or darker?"

"His hair was a lot darker than mine. Sort of curly, too. He always wore a hat, though."

"A hat? Or a cap?"

Looking confused, Muller said, "A hat. Like the one I got at a Twins game once. Only his hat wasn't blue; it was black. I don't know what team has black for its color."

A cap then, Sophia surmised. Although given the popularity of that particular item, it wouldn't necessarily be a ball cap. "Was he as tall as you or shorter?"

Muller squinted his eyes. "Maybe my height. But stronger, maybe."

"You're observant." Sophia's smile was so bright that the man blinked. "I think you're right. Quieter people tend to see more, don't they?"

"I guess." Muller scratched his jaw. "I mean, I do. Sometimes . . . it's like I'm invisible, you know? But I keep my eyes open."

"I'm sure you do. And I think that's how you can help me, Carl." Sophia deliberately kept the conversation personal. Muller wasn't predisposed to do anything to help the police, who he feared. But she thought maybe she could convince him to assist her. "Have you ever seen TV where an artist does a drawing of a person described by a witness?"

"No-o. But once when I was a kid my mom took me to the Minnesota State Fair. And a guy drew a cartoon of me and let me keep it."

"That's sort of what I'm talking about," she said encouragingly. "The other woman in the woods today. Do you remember the lady with red hair?"

Muller visibly sank in his chair, and his voice went flat. "She's a cop, too."

"She's an agent with DCI in Iowa." The differentiation was deliberate. In order to get him to cooperate with Jenna, Sophia had to make him regard the other woman as he did her, rather than as he viewed law enforcement in general. "She's my friend. We're working together to help that woman in the picture. Agent Turner is a good artist, too. If you describe the man you saw a few times in the park, she could draw a picture of him."

His expression turned sly. "If I help her, will the police let me go?"

"I can't answer that question, Carl. I'm not the police. But even if they don't, I'm sure your lawyer could tell the judge that you assisted us. That and the promise of treatment you'll have when I give you names of some of my colleagues who will help you . . . both will go a long way in your next defense."

Seeming to mull over her words, the man took his time answering. But in the end he just lifted his shoulders. "I guess. I mean, what do I have to lose?"

⁓

Jenna's initial entry had agitated Muller so much that Sophia had offered to stay in the room. Although she was aware that the agent usually worked alone with witnesses in a nonthreatening environment, she feared the man would shut down completely if she left.

And after she'd subtly positioned her chair around to be closer to Muller, the man had seemed to calm. Even more so when Jenna made a point of shutting off the camera in the room.

The agent's tone was easy as she snapped open the briefcase she'd retrieved from the trunk of Cam's vehicle and withdrew her sketch pad and pencils. "Do you do any sketching, Mr. Muller?"

The man shook his head. "Not since I was a kid. I was never much good at it."

"I've been drawing since I was young. With your observation skills, I know you can help me make a reasonable sketch of the man you saw watching the lady in the park." The agent's manner couldn't have been more different from when she'd encountered Muller earlier in the day. But Sophia knew the man would remember that first meeting. She just hoped her continued presence here would ensure his cooperation.

Jenna was experienced at putting people at ease. Rather than getting started right away, she spent several minutes establishing rapport, going so far as to send out for the can of Sprite Muller requested.

"The way this is going to work is I'm going to listen to your description of the man you saw in the park and ask you some questions about him. I might show you some pictures I have in a notebook in this case, too." Jenna thumped the briefcase on the floor with her toe. "That sound okay?"

The man's gaze slid to Sophia, who smiled encouragingly. "I guess," he muttered.

"You said you saw the stranger watching the lady in the park several times. How close did you get to him?"

"I dunno. The closest was about, like, from here to the door, I guess."

Sophia measured the distance with her gaze. Eight feet. It was plenty near enough to elicit a good description, if the angle had been right.

"Tell me what you remember about him."

Muller launched into a verbal description that differed little from the one he'd given to Sophia earlier. Jenna listened, her head cocked slightly, her gaze never leaving him.

"That's pretty good. What can you tell me about his hair?"

"It was brown. Medium, I guess. Not that short because I could see it curl below his cap in the back."

"How about around the ears?"

Carl had to stop and think at that question. "No-o. It didn't hang over his ears."

"What can you tell me about his eyes?"

"They were always covered by the sunglasses. And the newspaper. I never saw them."

"The same sunglasses? Or different ones each time?"

Slowly, painstakingly, Jenna drew Muller out on each tiny detail the man could recall about the stranger in the park. Then she started to sketch. Sophia was fascinated by the way the agent could draw and talk to Muller at the same time, seemingly never getting distracted from either task. She'd draw, push the pad toward Muller, and ask for further details. At other times she'd reach for the big book of facial images she'd brought in her briefcase. The notebook was tabbed in an endless array of sections. Some focused on chins, others on noses or eyes. And then she'd ask, "Which of these is most like the man you saw?" Sophia was amazed to see that there was even a section in that notebook for images of caps.

Under Jenna's expert questioning, even Muller's most vague answers became more exact. He examined the pictures she showed him closely, and the agent would change the composite to more exactly match his clarifications.

Even so, it was a tedious process. While Sophia found it intriguing, she was also aware of the passing time. Each minute that ticked by meant Courtney Van Wheton was farther away. Or perhaps by now she was at her final destination. Maybe her torment had already begun.

Because there was no point in the thoughts, Sophia tried to push them away.

Jenna had been at it for more than two hours when she finally said, "Are you sure? Take a good look now. Is this the man you saw in the parks watching the lady in the picture?"

"That looks like him."

"Anything else you want to change?"

"Nope." Muller slurped loudly from his can of Sprite. "That's the guy I saw before. That's the one who was watching her on Monday."

Sophia leaned in to peer more closely when Jenna ripped the sketch off the pad and nudged it toward the man.

The man in the drawing had pleasant features. Attractive even. Thick, wavy dark hair could be seen beneath the black-billed cap he wore. The nose was straight. The mouth—in her estimation—a little sensitive. It wasn't a face to stir caution if he stopped and asked for directions. This wasn't a man to incite fear.

Staring hard at the sketch, Sophia wondered if the man depicted in it was the one who had raped and tortured six other women before dumping their bodies in open graves in Iowa.

And if he were the same man who had kidnapped Courtney van Wheton.

He roamed freely through her condo, picking up her things, looking at them, setting them down again. It hadn't been difficult at all to find where Dr. Sophia Channing lived. Not for him. Her security alarm was better than most, but there was always a way around them.

And she didn't have a dog. He fucking hated homes with dogs.

Midafternoon sunlight slanted through the blinds. In broad daylight he chanced being seen by nosy neighbors, but all they could report was a van with the glass company's logo across the street, and a man wearing the company's uniform working on the broken glass in one of Channing's small garage door windows. It was the same van that had been used to snatch his newest possession. Now a different color with a magnetic logo on both sides to match the glass company's, it wouldn't stand out even if the cops had gotten a description of it in Minneapolis. Sleight of hand. It was human nature to see normal in daylight and threats at night. People saw what they expected to see.

Most people were idiots.

Carrying a case of tools, he'd walked nonchalantly up to the garage door. It'd taken less than three minutes armed with a wedge of wood and length of wire to open the door. Anyone watching would believe he was repairing the window and that he had an opener. He was that smooth.

It was important to get an idea of the home's layout to plan his approach. Look for weapons first. He hadn't found any guns, but there were still the bedrooms to search. Casing the place in advance gave him an idea of where she'd run, where he'd trap her, and a chance to plan an escape route.

A check of the spare bedroom showed no weapons and no men's clothes. He paused in the closet, eyeing an empty place on the floor next to a large suitcase. Wheel prints left an indentation in the carpet. Maybe the doctor wasn't home. Maybe she'd taken a trip and wouldn't be back for days.

The thought of having to wait made his gut and his chest tighten. He slammed shut the double closet doors, and the noise calmed him. Boredom hadn't set in with his new possession. She'd entertain him until he found Channing.

But the bitch would pay for making him wait. They always had to pay.

More quickly now, he moved to the master bedroom. No sign of men's clothes here, either, and something inside him eased a bit. A husband or roommate meant it'd be easier to grab Channing away from her home, but it was looking more and more as if he could just slip in here anytime he wanted and surprise her. Maybe take her while she was having breakfast, or just climb into bed with her while she slept.

He dropped down on the lace coverlet, imagined holding her trapped and helpless beneath him. Some duct tape over her mouth, and no one would suspect what he was doing to the stupid bitch. He could slit her throat when he was done, cut off her tits and stuff them up her cunt. Show everyone that she was worthless. And what she'd written about him meant nothing.

After bounding off the bed, he crossed to the dresser. Opened the drawers and ran his gloved fingers through her things. He could do this. Touch what he wanted. Take what appealed to him. Just the way he'd do whatever he wanted with her.

One drawer held panties, and he pawed through them, brought out a scrap of lace and ribbon to his face, inhaled deeply. He imagined it smelled like her. Tasted like her. Delicately, he licked the crotch.

Through the blinds he caught sight of a neighbor checking the mailbox and frowned. He'd have only a few hours with Channing, and that wasn't long enough. No, not long enough to show her that she was stupid and useless and a fucking disappointment. He wouldn't be able to take his time and punish her the way she deserved. Unless . . .

He shoved the panties in his jeans pocket, deep in thought. There was no reason to hurry this when there was already a perfect spot to keep her. A spot where he could take his time. Make her pay for writing those things about him.

A slow grin crossed his face at the thought. It'd be a change from his usual strategy, but they were his rules to break.

And if ever a bitch needed to be shown her place, it was this one.

Chapter 7

W ell." Sophie drew the word out teasingly. "I learn something new about you every day."

"I'm an open book," Cam murmured. His eyes were still closed. His breathing ragged. How was it possible to get more intense every time he touched her? Moved inside her? God help him. If it got any better, he'd need a wheelchair to get out of bed. And still count himself lucky.

"Hardly," she said dryly. "You're about as forthcoming as a vault. But who would have thought the steely-eyed DCI agent was ticklish?"

He popped open an eyelid to consider her. "Steely-eyed? Please, this endless flattery is getting annoying. And my feet are sensitive, not ticklish." He winced slightly when he got a pinch in response.

"Ticklish," she said firmly. "In another minute I would have had you begging for mercy."

Both eyes open now, he rolled to an elbow to consider her. "Honey, I was already at your mercy. And I seem to recall doing a bit of begging a few minutes ago, too." Delighted with the immediate flush in her cheeks, he leaned down to nuzzle his nose against the soft skin there. "You're amazingly easy to embarrass."

"I'm . . . not used to this sort of thing."

Something inside him stilled at the admission. "Apparently talent like yours doesn't require practice."

Surprisingly she smiled, a lazy feline curl of her lips that had his gut tightening in response. God, he was pathetic. But her answer distracted his reawakened desire. "No, I mean . . . this." She gave a vague gesture between them. "Easy banter and post-coitus repartee. Is this normal for men, or is it more customary to fall asleep?"

He felt a quick flash of amusement at the slightly academic tone. There was a scholarly aspect to the woman that was all the more fascinating in light of her naked and mussed appearance. "Since the only man I've been to bed with is me, I'm going to have to plead ignorance on that." He slid his hand over the lovely curve from hip to waist. Back again. "But in your case, I tend to think any man who's so easily sated lacks both imagination and stamina." Her quick laugh turned to a gasp when he lowered his head and replaced his hand with his tongue.

Her skin was satiny. Her body endlessly fascinating. Cam tested the curve of her hip lightly with his teeth. He couldn't get enough of her. The shape of her, the feel, the smell. He wasn't some damn teenage kid who'd just bedded his first girlfriend. The female anatomy held no surprises for him.

The thought was made a mockery when his mouth moved to explore the expanse of her stomach. There was a whisper of muscle below the silky skin. Strength below softness. That contrast was present in her personality, too. Polish glossed over competence. Beauty paired with finely honed steel. Intelligence coupled with the most gut-wrenching glimmers of vulnerability.

He paused to dip the tip of his tongue in the swirl of her naval. He needed to get a grip before this fascination turned into something more. Something deeper.

The thought should have sent a cold arrow of reason through his brain. But his mind remained pleasantly fuzzy. She drew a leg up then, and he took the opportunity to stroke the sleek skin of her thigh. To follow the path of his hand with his lips. In his experience the hotter the start of a relationship, the faster it burned itself out. Endings were inevitable.

But damn, he was not ready for this to end . . .

~

"Dammit, Sophie, pick up." Cam left another terse message while pounding at the door of her condo again. Which was probably a wasted effort, since she'd already failed to answer the doorbell.

She was probably on her way in to headquarters. He glanced at his watch. It was still early, though. Barely seven. He normally didn't see her around the DCI building for at least another hour.

Still in bed then. He slipped his cell back in his pocket and propped his hands on his hips. That scenario was definitely one that didn't bear considering.

They'd gotten back late from Edina last night. They'd stayed another day after Jenna had done that sketch using Muller's description of the man he'd seen watching Courtney Van Wheton. They'd canvassed the area's parks again yesterday, this time armed with photos of Van Wheton and the sketch. In addition to a few who'd recognized the woman were a couple of people who recalled seeing the man in the drawing, which at least made Cam certain Muller hadn't been blowing smoke about the guy.

But no one had seen the man approach Van Wheton. No one remembered noticing him in the park on the day the woman disappeared. Nor had the woman's traumatized daughters recognized the man.

The abductor had done some planning, he thought with disgust. The enhanced image from the security image at the bank showed plates on the van that had proved to be stolen. And as the vehicle had driven by the camera, the driver giving a friendly wave had been immediately recognizable.

Either Fred Flintstone had turned to a life of crime, or the offender had taken the precaution of wearing a mask.

But they still had a sketch of a man that might be the UNSUB. Cam had ended up leaving a copy of it with Boelin for distribution to the news organizations up there before heading back to Iowa. It'd been almost midnight when he'd dropped Sophie off at home. He wouldn't blame her if she was catching a few extra hours of sleep.

He considered the rest of the neighborhood. People were starting to move around. Collect their papers. Walk their pets. Leave for work. It wouldn't be long before one of them wondered what the hell he was doing on Sophie's front porch.

Cam actually started to turn away. He could keep trying to call her on his commute. She'd answer the phone eventually, right?

But maybe not before she'd watched the local morning news.

A scowl settled on his face. Damn Maria, and damn "the reality of her job." Despite the conversation they'd had before he'd left, the SAC had gone ahead with a press conference in which she'd released Sophie's criminal profile. Not only that, but some enterprising reporter had found a picture to pair with her name. Despite a few professional differences he and Sophie might have, he knew they'd share similar opinions on actions such as the one Maria had taken. They muddied an investigation with no real hope of furthering it.

And he didn't want Sophie to be caught unaware, the way he'd been this morning when he'd opened the *Des Moines Register*. With a little online digging, he'd discovered that the local TV station had run breaking bulletins with the news for a couple of days.

He headed back toward his car parked in the drive. Hesitated and eyed her garage door with its narrow tinted windows. So sue him; he recalled her security codes. It wasn't as if he hadn't tried to void that and all other memories of the time they'd spent together. Unfortunately, his memory of all things Sophie related remained stubbornly entrenched.

Hell with it.

Wheeling around, Cam marched to the garage door. Punched in the code. It wouldn't hurt to see if her car was there. At least then he'd know whether . . . Ducking his head under the rising door, he saw that her sleek black Prius was parked neatly on one side of the garage.

Without giving it another thought, he headed through the space to the door that led into the condo. It was locked, as he'd figured, and protected by her condo unit's security system. He entered that code, too. He'd just have to take his chances that her outrage at his actions was tempered by concern for those taken by Gonzalez.

"Sophie?" He poked his head inside the condo. Noted that the purse she'd had with her on their trip sat on the table just inside the door. Which didn't mean much. The woman literally changed purses to match shoes. A feminine accessorizing he normally found baffling, except that it was all wrapped up in the fascination she still held for him.

But he was working on that. Cam walked farther into the condo, closing the door behind him. He wasn't mooning over the woman like some seventeen-year-old pining for the head cheerleader. There were hours every day when he never gave her a thought.

It was the nights that were still giving him problems.

"Sophie!" Even as he tried again, he noted her car keys sitting next to the purse. He did a quick walk through the space. It was all one story. He checked out the kitchen. Empty. The automatic coffeemaker had a full carafe. No mug was in evidence on the counter or—with a few extra steps he verified—the sink. A quick look out the back window showed no one in the miniscule yard or on the patio. The small sunroom, guest bathroom, office, and second bedroom were also empty. Music was coming from the direction of her bedroom. She had one of those iPod alarms. It had been a source of conversation between them once. He preferred to waken to silence and she . . . Well, Sophie had the unfortunate taste to prefer waking to a barely-out-of-her-teens singer wailing about bad breakups.

The recollection almost brought a smile to his lips.

He halted his progression through the condo just outside her open bedroom door. He was close enough to hear the shower running. A peek inside showed the bed only slightly mussed, with pillows askew. It was minus the lacy feminine comforter that had been on it the last time he'd been there. The door to the adjoining bathroom was also partially open. He jerked his head back to avoid seeing farther into that room.

Deliberately pitching his voice louder, he said, "Don't get mad, but I figured once you heard what I'm here to say you might forgive my coming in like this." With effort, he kept his gaze from straying toward the bathroom. He'd expected some sort of outraged protest, at least. He knew for a fact that one could shower in there and carry on a conversation with someone in the bedroom. They'd once had a spirited discussion in just that way over the merits of waffles over pancakes. Waffles had won, of course. That hadn't even been a contest.

"I tried calling, but you didn't pick up. So anyway, here's the thing." Propping his shoulder against the wall outside the bathroom, gaze determinedly turned toward the bedroom window, he gave her a brief rundown of what Gonzalez had done and why. "Believe me—I tried to talk her out of releasing that profile before we left.

Thought I'd succeeded, to tell you the truth. I didn't want you to get ambushed by the news looking at the paper today because—big surprise—it's splashed all over the headlines."

When she still didn't respond, a trickle of unease slid down his spine. Sophie wasn't one of those women who believed in the silent treatment. If he'd offended her by coming in like this—and that was a given—she'd let him know in a civil tone that flayed despite its evenness. Then she'd deal with the news he'd come to share.

But she wasn't saying anything. And the queen of green, as he'd once dubbed her, was environmentally sophisticated. She even shut off the water while brushing her teeth in order to conserve.

She definitely didn't take long showers.

The trickle of unease became full-fledged trepidation. "Sophie?" He nudged the door farther open with his foot. "Soph?" He took a couple of steps inside her room and paused, catching sight of something on the floor. Rounding the bed he saw it was the beige suitcase she'd carried with her on their trip. It was on its side, contents spilling carelessly from it.

The blood in his veins iced. Six quick steps took him to the half-open bathroom door. He pushed it open with his elbow. The walk-in shower was clearly empty, although the water was still running. The door to the shower stood open. Water pooled in small puddles on the floor. One towel bar had been partially pulled from the wall and hung from the remaining screw. The flowering plant usually kept on the counter was on the floor, its container smashed. The rugs were in disarray, and pinpoints of bright-red spots dotted the tiled floor.

A fist tightened in his stomach. Cam tamped down fear, let instinct take over. He backed slowly out of the bathroom. Reached down to slip off his shoes and set them on the edge of the dresser. Swiftly he backtracked out of the room, crossing to where she'd left her purse. He knew she didn't retain a landline.

Checking the cell phone he found in the front outer pocket, Cam discovered her last call out had been three days earlier. Which meant she hadn't contacted an ambulance or a neighbor about an emergency. But the call log showed one missed call last night at 12:32 a.m. The name *Livvie* appeared next to the number. He pressed the call button, waited impatiently until a woman picked up.

"Hey, sorry about calling so late last night. Minor crisis averted here, at least for the short term, but still need your help with something."

The voice was naggingly familiar. A moment later he placed it. "You're the neighbor." Livvie Hammel had the condo on the left. She and Sophie had seemed friendly the one time Sophie had been unable to avoid making stilted introductions when she and Cam had encountered the woman in the driveway. Already he was going to the front door, opening it, and stepping out on the porch.

There was a pause. Then a guarded, "Who is this?"

"Cam Prescott. I'll be at your front door in ten seconds." He disconnected the call and strode to Hammel's porch.

He had the distinct sensation of being studied for several seconds through the peephole before the door finally opened. The woman's freckled face looked worried. "Why do you have Sophia's phone? Where is she?"

"I was hoping you could tell me. You haven't seen her this morning?"

Hammel shook her head. "I haven't seen her for a few days. I assumed she was on a job somewhere."

"She was." Deliberately he refrained from giving her any details about the scene he'd found inside Sophie's apartment. "I dropped her off a couple minutes to twelve. She didn't answer your call at twelve thirty-two. How did you know she was home last night?"

"My condo's the opposite floor plan as hers. Standing in my bathroom, I could see that the light in hers was on. I took the chance that she was still up and called."

"If she needed help for an emergency of some sort, who would she contact?" His questions were coming rapid-fire, barely waiting for her response.

The woman's expression had switched from wariness to concern. "Me first, I think. We're friends. Carrie Solberg lives down the street. We all hang out sometimes, but Carrie's on a cruise. So definitely me. What kind of emergency? What are you doing at her place, anyway?"

He ignored the question, thinking rapidly. If there was one thing that he'd learned about Sophie in their time together, it was that she thrived on orderliness and precision. Cam had often teased her about her adherence to routine. He couldn't imagine her going to bed without unpacking her suitcase and putting it away.

And before turning in every night, her cell was placed on the nightstand. Without exception. In case one of her clients needed to contact her during the night, she'd once explained. It had made perfect sense to him. He always kept his cell close, too.

But her phone hadn't made it out of her purse. Her clothes hadn't been put away. Which meant that whatever had happened to Sophie had likely occurred last night sometime between twelve and twelve thirty.

"Okay, thanks."

He turned to leave, already planning his next action.

"Don't even think about leaving without telling me what's happened to Sophia!" Hammel stepped barefoot onto the porch, her eyes fierce. "What's going on? How'd you get in her condo, anyway?"

"Hey, it's the dude with the 'tude. Cool. Can I see your badge?"

The boy who now stood in the open doorway was a miniature of his mother in every way except for gender. About seven or eight, Cam calculated, although he didn't know much about kids. His red hair was a shade brighter than his mom's and hadn't been combed that morning. His left foot was encased in plaster from the base of his bare toes to his knee. He was supporting himself on crutches.

Livvie Hammel flushed. "Not now, Carter. Go to the kitchen and start thinking about what you want for breakfast."

But the boy didn't move. He was studying Cam's pants interestedly. "His lap doesn't look greasy. I still don't get it."

Involuntarily, Cam glanced down at his trousers. "What?"

"Carter." An edge of embarrassment firmed Livvie's tone. "Kitchen. Now."

The kid didn't move. His brow wrinkled, he said, "Dr. C said that, though, remember? You said, 'Hey, what's going on with you and hunkalicious,' and she said it was over because he was a greasy laps judgment. And then you said, 'But he was tasty, right?' And Dr. C said he was absolutely delicious. But you never did explain what greasy laps judgment was, and I just looked and his lap isn't greasy."

Whatever else the kid had been about to say was muffled by the hand the woman clapped over his mouth. Twin flags of color rode high in her cheeks. "I swear the child can't hear me tell him to stop using his crutch as a bat in the house, but he can hear a whispered conversation thirty yards away."

Despite the urgency surrounding the matter, Cam couldn't help asking, "Greasy laps judgment?"

She grimaced as she loosened the hand she had over the boy's lips. "Egregious lapse in judgment. A trait shared by Carter on occasions too numerous to mention."

"Ah." The phrase sounded so like Sophie that it brought a quick hard smile to his lips. One that faded in the next instant. Urgency was pulsing through him, getting more and more difficult to contain. "Did you see anyone around her place yesterday, before she got home?"

"No, sorry. Carter broke a growth plate in his foot a few days ago, and it's all I can do to keep him entertained. I've been home trying to keep him off it this week. That's kept me too exhausted to focus on much else."

The kid was giving Cam a look that was probably supposed to be angelic. It failed miserably. He looked like a pint-size evil genius. "What was the crisis you called Sophie about last night?"

She jerked her thumb at Carter. "Slugger here woke up wanting a drink of water. While I was fetching it he decided to use his crutch to play Sammy Sosa. Sent a tennis ball through his bedroom window."

Cam looked at the boy. "Sosa, huh?"

"He's the all-time home run hitter on the Cubs," the kid informed him. "Soriano only hit thirty-two last year. He's never going to come close to Sosa's record."

Sad but true. "Good point." Cam switched his attention back to Livvie. "How was Sophie going to help with a broken window?"

"Not help, exactly, but I just wanted the name of the outfit that repaired hers this week. I figured since they already knew the area, maybe I could drop her name and get them out here without being put on a waiting list."

Everything inside him stilled. "She had a broken window this week?"

"Yes. Well, I don't know exactly what was broken." She glanced at the boy. "My son saw a van from a glass shop out front. When was that, Carter?"

"Day before yesterday," he replied without hesitation. "I had to stay in the living room while you were hiding clues for the scavenger hunt. It was boring, so I was looking out to see if maybe Ryder or Zach were outside on their bikes."

"What kind of van?"

"Dark blue. It had a sign on it that said Dr. Pane. I thought that was funny and told Mom the doctor was visiting the doctor." Carter looked at Cam for his appreciation of the humor.

Ice slicking down his spine, Cam had heard enough. "Stay available. Someone will be back to talk to you." This time when he walked away, Hammel didn't try to stop him. Heading back to Sophie's, he pulled his cell from his pocket, his fingers oddly uncoordinated as he hit speed dial for a familiar number. He could hear the kid's voice behind him.

"Hey, Mom, how come he gets to wear his socks outside?"

He stopped at his vehicle and opened the trunk with his free hand. Reached in and started digging around in his crime scene bag to make sure he had shoe covers as well as gloves. When Jenna finally answered, he didn't bother with a greeting. Politeness was beyond him at this point. "Get a crime team to Sophie's condo. Here's the address." He recited it without having to think. "I don't know what happened. She's not here." In short, succinct sentences he explained what he'd found without going into his reason for being there.

"Tell them to hurry." The words settled in a hard ball in his throat. It took effort to force them out. "I think someone got to her."

—————

"Be sure to have them run my latents for comparison prints along with Sophie's." Cam was crouched next to Aubrey Hartley, one of the criminalists. She was in front of the kitchen door, rolling the electrostatic dust print lifter mat across the tile floor in front of the door. Her blonde hair was pulled back in a stubby ponytail.

The white Tyvek coveralls she wore couldn't quite hide the girth of her pregnancy.

She arched a brow, but her movements never slowed. "You mean you were as careless with your prints as you were with your shoe impressions?"

"I didn't expect to find a crime scene here."

Something in his bleak tone must have alerted her, because she paused to look at him. "I'm just giving you a hard time. Don't worry about it. I've already taken an impression of your shoe for elimination purposes, too. Where'd you touch when you were looking around?"

"Today? The security panel outside and inside the garage." Her brows lifted higher at the admission. "The knob from the garage door into the house." He stopped then, tried to think. "The door-jamb to the left of the master bedroom door. But I've been here before when Sophie was home."

Aubrey's expression went impassive at she interpreted his words. He'd been a guest here. Moved freely around the space. They'd find his prints on cupboards. Doors. In the bathroom. A shudder wanted to work through him at the thought of the bathroom. He and Sophie had once made love in that shower. The very one she'd likely been abducted from.

"Don't worry about it, Cam. We're going to pull out all the stops on this one."

He caught sight of Maria entering through the front door, shoe covers and gloves donned. Nodding to Aubrey, he rose and crossed the room to meet her. She was scanning the activity in the condo, wearing a slight frown. Jenna was huddled in a corner of the dining area, a cell pressed to her ear. A second criminalist was dusting the doorknob of the entry from the garage. Yet a third was selecting light sources with which to examine the blood samples in the bathroom.

"I hope you're not jumping the gun here." Gonzalez held up a hand to halt any protest he might have made. "You explained the details when you called me, but, like I said then, there are any number of explanations for Sophia's absence. I would have preferred you look into all of them before ordering these resources."

"Dollars and cents? Is that what we're quibbling about here, Maria?"

Her look was dark. "Don't take that tone, Prescott. Not when the details of what happened here are still in question. She could have hurt herself in a fall and called an ambulance."

"Except there hasn't been a call out on her phone for three days."

She went on as if he hadn't interrupted. "Or she might have walked over to the neighbors and gotten a ride to the ER."

"Her friend lives right next door and never heard from her. We've called the area hospitals. She hasn't been admitted. Jenna's checking with the urgent care clinics, even though most don't open until eight and I was here at seven. Tommy's doing a canvass, but so far no one around here has reported anything amiss."

Maria's gaze narrowed. "You brought Franks in on this, too?"

"I was trying to keep it quiet," Cam snapped. He paused, struggling to tuck temper away before going on. "I didn't want to unnecessarily alarm anyone. Kitchen door was unsecured. All the doors operate on the same security system, but they can be opened from the inside without having to disarm it."

"It's like she walked out of her own accord."

He continued as if she hadn't spoken. "Kid next door saw a truck bearing a glass repair shop logo here a couple days ago. I've been running down the names of those businesses in the area."

His cell rang. Cam took it from his pocket and checked the screen. It was Connerly, the forensic anthropologist working with the ME. "Take a look in the bedroom and the bathroom, and let me know if you think the scene looks like Sophie left here on her own," he said shortly. Turning away before Gonzalez could answer, he spoke into the phone. "Prescott."

"Hey, Cam, we got a breakthrough here."

"Not a breakthrough—it's a possible scenario." He could hear Benally's correction in the background.

"It's more than a possibility. Probability factors in the ninety percent range. That's good enough for this California boy."

"Maybe you and Lucy can argue the point on your own time." Given the circumstances, Cam's patience was nil. "What do you have?"

"The lab got back to us earlier this week with the chemical breakdown in the soil surrounding each of the victims. I can tell you with a high degree of certainty which of them has been in the ground the longest. Even better, I can give you a good approximation about the order in which the vics were buried. We had it pretty close timing it by the dates of the original burials, but we were off some."

He released a breath. Yesterday he would have been ecstatic at the news. Right now it bottomed out on a list of his priorities. "That is a breakthrough. Nice work."

"Not the overwhelming enthusiasm I was hoping for, but a bump up from Negative Nancy here."

He heard Benally's response. "I told you to quit calling me that."

Cam saw María exit the bedroom. He knew from personal experience the woman was a helluva poker player. He also knew her tells. The flare of her nostrils gave lie to her carefully blank expression.

Nerves jittered in his gut. In that instant he realized he would rather have had her continued disagreement about what had gone down here. Even a thread of hope would have been better than the utter blackness that descended upon him the moment he recognized that the SAC was finally convinced.

The voice in his ear reminded him that he was still on his cell. "Gavin, have either you or Lucy spoken to Dr. Channing recently?"

The man was silent for a moment. "Sophia? I haven't talked to her since you guys came to the morgue. Can't speak for Lucy." Cam heard the man pose the question to the ME and her negative response.

Gonzalez jerked her head in a signal for him to join her. "Okay, I'll catch up with her later. Listen, great work on the burial sequence. I'm in the middle of something here, but I'll be in touch." Disconnecting, he swiftly strode across the room toward the SAC. Silently she stepped aside, pointing him toward the bathroom.

Seth Dietz, the tech working in there, had plastic evidence markers scattered around the floor and a few sticky notes on the floor, the sides of the shower, and the walls. Cam knew that meant the areas had already been sprayed with luminol and they'd glowed, indicating a presence of hemoglobin.

"Behind the toilet." Maria's voice was quiet.

Craning his neck, Cam could see the yellow plastic evidence marker she must be referencing but not what it indicated. "What is it?"

Seth looked up. "Just pointed that out to Special Agent Gonzalez. I can show it to you after I finish photographing the room. It's a syringe. Found the plastic top under one of the rugs. Haven't been through the medicine cabinets or the refrigerator yet. Channing might be diagnosed with a condition requiring injections."

"She's not." Cam heard the bleakness in his own voice. Knew Gonzalez had, too. He no longer cared what interpretation she placed on it.

She placed a hand on his arm. "I'll issue a BOLO."

He nodded and she moved away. The be-on-the-lookout bulletin would alert law enforcement in the vicinity to watch for sightings of Sophie. But he knew in his gut it was no use.

She could have been taken by anyone. Cam couldn't lose sight of that fact. In her capacity as forensic profiler, she consulted on any number of cases simultaneously. He had no idea what else she was working on or for whom. She could even have been targeted because of someone she'd interviewed in the past.

But he'd learned to trust his instincts. And they were telling him she'd been taken by the maniac who'd kidnapped, raped, and murdered at least six women. The one who might have abducted yet another from Edina three days earlier.

The deviant who just might be harboring a rage toward the woman who'd written the profile on him that was now splashed all over the media.

Chapter 8

E ddies of pleasure continued to shimmer through Sophia, never-ending ripples in a sensual pond. Her heart rate still bucked and sprinted like a high-spirited filly. Cam's weight, while heavy, was too comforting to want to separate from just yet.

Sophia wasn't inexperienced, but she had been selective over the years. None of the men she'd slept with in the past had managed to elicit an ounce of the explosive response she felt with Cam. The thought had a thread of alarm mingling with recently sated desire. Of course, not one of the men in her past had much of anything in common with Cam Prescott, short of gender. Other than where their careers crossed, the same could be said of Cam and her.

Before grad school her life had followed a predictable, if dull, pattern. Her childhood had consisted of arranged playdates with children of other professors at the university. Lessons for flute, piano, and French, all of which she'd excelled at. And because a well-rounded child required physical activity, there had been golf, soccer, and tennis. None of which she'd excelled at.

When Cam took a long ragged breath, she delicately traced his spine with the tips of her fingers, pleased when his damp flesh quivered beneath her touch. Her teen years at the all-girls school had been filled with science club, chorus, band, and dates with carefully selected suitable young men, some the same playmates from her childhood.

And all of it so controlled and planned it was as though she'd been raised inside a glass bottle. If she'd chafed at the firmly set parameters of her life, there had at least been no outright rebellion. Sophia had been raised much too well mannered for that.

Until Louis Frein had smashed that glass chamber, introducing her to a world her parents would never have chosen for her. For the first time in her life, she'd deviated from the path her mother and father had selected. More, she'd found a career at once challenging and fulfilling. It was the only choice she'd ever made that was totally her own.

She'd been paying for that deviation ever since. First with the never-quite-dissipated disapproval of her parents and then the disintegration of her marriage. Hefty prices for her decision. Perhaps well worth it, but she'd certainly learned that choices came with a cost. Which was why it was easier . . . wiser . . . to remain in control. Impetuous decisions invited far-reaching consequences. She preferred a guarantee that throwing caution to the winds wouldn't come back to bite her in the end.

Which made inviting Cam Prescott into her life even more inexplicable.

With an effort she could tell cost him, Cam rolled heavily off her. "Sorry." He positioned them both so they were on their sides, facing each other. Looping an arm possessively around her waist, he buried his face in her hair. "You should have gotten a crane. Are you still breathing?"

"I'm not quite sure how to summon a crane. If the situation had gotten dire, I am armed with the secret knowledge of your ticklish spots."

She could hear the smile in his voice. "A wise woman doesn't give away all the weapons in her arsenal."

"A wise woman doesn't get herself in situations where she requires an arsenal." So why was she even now scrambling for her scattered defenses? She felt totally, achingly vulnerable with him. What she knew about the man, other than the obvious, would barely fill a thimble.

He was sexy but opaque. Hard with glimmers of compassion. Reticent yet intuitive. And despite her respect for No Trespassing signs, both figurative and literal, suddenly that reticence disturbed her.

"Are your parents alive?" she asked suddenly.

"Why?"

"I'm assuming you do have parents."

"I came about in the usual way." His hand began to slide lazily up and down the curves and hollows of her waist. "I have a mom. There must have been a dad at some point, but he was gone before I knew him. And then there were men." His voice went flat. "Some better than others, but most whose charm disappeared about the time they convinced my mom to move in with them. My mother sees the best in absolutely everybody, but I learned at a young age that some people have no best. Just traits that make them a little less than a total son of a bitch."

Her heart lurched a little at the thought of him as a young boy, a revolving door of strange men in and out of his life. She had clients with similar backgrounds. Knew well the dangers of exposing a child to that lifestyle. "Did she marry any of them?"

"She's married now. Not then." One of his feet began to stroke hers. "When I was ten, I got a paper route. Then another. A guy gave me a job delivering small orders from his grocery store on my bike. When I'd saved two hundred dollars, I thought it was a fortune. I took it to my mom, who still had a black eye from her latest 'fall.' Dumped it in her lap and told her she didn't need men to take care of her anymore. I was old enough to be the man."

"Oh, Cam." Her heart quite simply melted. She could imagine him as he must have looked then. Too determined and serious for his age. With those golden-brown eyes that even then saw too much. And she knew, without being told, how much of the boy still existed in the man.

"My mom's a crier." There was an indulgent note in his voice. "Happy, sad, tired, proud . . . She's an equal opportunity weeper. So, she cried, of course. Then she hugged me. Then she packed. It was just the two of us after that. She worked a series of low-paying jobs, and I pitched in. We scraped by. She married Larry about six years ago, after dating him at least that long. Good guy. Not a son of a bitch."

And that easily, that simply, her alarm quieted again. It was such a small thing, this freely revealing a snippet of his past. But for this man every nugget shared was like gold.

Sophia sighed a little, slipped an arm around his neck. "Cam. What am I going to do with you?"

He cupped her jaw, leaning in to whisper a kiss against her mouth. His voice took on a hint of wicked. "I have a few suggestions."

It took effort to open her eyes. Sophia struggled to surface from an ocean of unconsciousness. Her limbs were weighted. Her mouth felt as though it were filled with sand. There was a jackhammer at the base of her skull, drilling reverberations that were echoed by the drumroll in her temples. Her thoughts were muzzy. She must have the mother of all hangovers. But she hadn't drunk any wine last night, had she?

Lying there another few minutes, she became aware of a dark foreboding simmering inside her. The mattress she was lying on was soft. Too soft. It wasn't the firm mattress she'd selected when she'd moved into the condo. She must be in Cam's bed.

The thought had her trepidation easing. Pleasure filtered through the confusion. She'd never woken with a headache in Cam's bed. A night spent tangled up with him always left her limbs weak and her mind dazed. The man had the most amazing hands. And mouth. Her palms itched to explore his hard body again. To map every intriguing place where sinew and muscle met bone.

Something furry skittered across her foot, jolting her fully awake. Biting back a scream, she sat straight up on the mattress, kicking awkwardly at whatever had disturbed her.

Her actions intensified the pounding in her head. Sophia placed one hand on the mattress next to her, waiting for a wave of dizziness to pass.

"Bitching about your quarters already? Typical woman. Never happy."

Something wasn't right. Cam's voice sounded unlike him. Its pitch was higher, with an edge she'd never heard there before. The foreboding returned twofold, morphing into panic. Sophia forced her eyelids open. Threw up a hand as a shield when a bright spotlight drilled into her eyes. The shadowy man next to it seemed to split into two, the images wavering before they melded again.

It wasn't Cam, but a stranger. The realization washed over like a douse of ice water. And she wasn't in a bedroom at all. She swung her head wildly to take in the confines of her prison; the action sent waves of nausea through her.

"Where am I? And who are you?"

"Who am I?" The stranger was huge. At least he seemed that way, shrouded in shadows. Five-ten maybe, but with the build of a dedicated weight lifter. Muscles bulged unnaturally in his chest, arms, and legs. Even his neck was thick, causing his bald head to appear to sit directly upon those massive shoulders.

Comprehension was dulled. It took moments to observe that the stranger was completely naked.

And so was she.

The realization had Sophia drawing up her knees, wrapping her arms around them as if donning armor. She was seated on a blow-up mattress placed on cracked and crumbling pavement. One wall of her cell was stone, the sides wooden. And the front where the stranger had stationed himself to peer in at her was fashioned of metal bars too wide to completely wrap her hands around. What was this place?

Memory quickly followed on the heels of that question. The man wasn't a stranger at all. He'd come into her bathroom last night while she'd showered.

That recollection seemed to open the floodgates, and memories rushed in on a torrent. She'd seen an intruder in the bathroom only seconds before he'd opened the shower door to drag her, kicking and swinging, from the tiled stall. With one of those muscle-bound arms holding her pinned against his chest and his free hand clapped over her mouth, their reflection from the vanity mirror had been something from a horror show. The helpless victim struggling with the masked intruder.

But sometime in their struggles his mask had worked up. She'd gotten a quick look at the features of the man now glaring at her with naked venom in his eyes.

It'd been like glimpsing hell.

"Not so high-and-mighty now, are you?" The smile that split his face made her shudder. "Most cunts aren't once someone shows them their place in this world. I'm gonna be the one to put you in your place, all right. You and me got a score to settle."

"How can that be? I don't even know you." Sophia was shocked by the reasonable tone she managed, even while everything inside her shrank in fear. "Maybe there's been a mistake."

"Oh, there has been. A big mistake. And you made it, bitch. Or should I call you Dr. Bitch?" The stranger seemed to be enjoying himself now, one foot raised to rest on the lowest metal bar, his hands wrapped around another. "Looked you up on the Internet after I saw your lies all over the news a couple days ago. Just because you got a bunch of letters after your name doesn't make you an expert on people you don't even know."

"You're angry with me," she said evenly, trying to make frantic sense of what he was saying. "Why don't you tell me what I did to disappoint you?"

"That!" The rage that bubbled out of him appeared so suddenly, so violently that she reared back, even with the closed gate and space between them. He stabbed a finger at her. "You called it right there. All women are disappointments sooner or later. Goes without saying. But you . . . Who the fuck are you to say those things about me? Inadequate? Displaced aggression? You're going to pay for lying 'bout me getting fucked up the ass when I was a kid. You'll be begging me to end you." He pressed his face close to the bars, his face red, chest heaving.

Every organ inside her body froze. This had to be a nightmare. Sophia squeezed her eyes tightly closed, willing the scene away. But he was still there when she reopened them.

He'd quoted snippets from her profile of the offender in Cam's case. But how could that have been on the news? When? She still couldn't make sense of it.

"And you'll die, all right. But on my say, not yours. First I'm gonna hurt you." He said the words as if savoring them, and they seemed to calm him. "You can't even imagine how much I'll hurt you. And then I'll do it all over again. Those letters after your name don't mean shit to me. You're just tits and ass and cunt, no better than the rest of your kind. I'll use you like a filthy whore, and when I get tired of you, you'll be dead. Then the world will know you're nothing. Less than nothing."

"Did a woman make you feel that way once?" she hazarded a guess. "Is that why they have to pay?"

"You want to know what makes a man like me tick?" The temper had vanished as quickly as it had appeared. He seemed almost amused. "Well, I'm going to educate you about that. I'll educate you real good until the only question you'll have left is when are you going to die."

He pushed away from the gate, rattling it on its hinges. "You think about that until I come back for you."

He strode out of her line of vision. She couldn't seem to move, and she couldn't blame her immobility on whatever drug he'd injected her with. Fear kept her limbs leaden. Her mind frozen. But a couple of thoughts were clear enough. The man they'd been seeking so diligently had found her.

And he didn't look at all like the stranger depicted in the forensic sketch Jenna had drawn.

⁓

The usual conversational buzz greeted Cam when he hit the briefing room. At his entry, however, the noise shut off as abruptly as if someone had flipped a switch.

He caught the eye of Tommy Franks and gestured for him to join him up front. The older agent had been running the briefings in Cam's absence, and Cam wasn't the type to elbow the agent aside upon his return. There was no place in their line of work for glory hounds.

With Franks at his side, Cam began without preamble. "As you all know, there have been major developments in the case in the last few days. We'll address the most pressing first." He gave a nod in Jenna's direction, and she started the PowerPoint. A professional shot of Sophie appeared on the screen at the front of the room.

If the room was silent before, now it was tomblike. "Sometime between eleven fifty-eight last night and twelve thirty-two this morning, we believe Dr. Sophia Channing was forcibly abducted from her home. The intruder somehow entered her locked garage and accessed the house through the attic crawl space. A BOLO alert was issued at nine thirty. The Des Moines police department is manning a hotline and dealing with the tips coming in from the alert. So far none of them has elicited any leads on her whereabouts."

He scanned the room's somber-faced occupants. "You've heard about another possible victim in Edina. When we were up there coordinating with the chief of police on the case, Dr. Channing pointed us toward a potential witness. With his help, Agent Turner drew a forensic sketch of a person of interest in this case. We're using the FaceVACS system to compare the sketch to mugshot databases."

It helped to try to discuss the events dispassionately. To reach for some distance so logic would be unclouded by emotion. But Cam knew the effort would be beyond him. Judging from the expressions of his colleagues, he wasn't alone in that.

"We've got a seven-year-old boy living in the condo unit east of Channing's who saw this vehicle in front of her home two days ago midafternoon." At this cue, Jenna switched to the next photo, which depicted the first in a series of sketches she'd done with Carter. "It's a midsize cargo panel van. Probably fewer than ten years old since he noted no rust. Other than the color, it's a match for the one on the security footage of the Edina bank when Van Wheton was snatched. This van had signage on the side, either painted or a magnet."

139

The next slide showed the logo and words that had so delighted Carter:

Dr. Pane
For all your glass needs
Painless repair for home, auto, buildings, equipment

Next to the words was a cartoon-faced four-paned window with stick arms and legs, a stethoscope hanging from its neck. Cam wasn't surprised they hadn't gotten more description of the vehicle from the boy. He was a kid after all. But he'd provided a detailed recollection of the logo and sign, and that might be prove to be enough.

"A neighbor across the street also remembers a dark-colored van parked in the spot, although she could provide no further details about it or its driver. Dr. Channing has the second from the end unit on the street, with a small backyard that's bordered on all sides by adjacent yards."

Jenna flipped to a diagram of the back of Sophie's condo. "We found the back door on her unit unsecured by the alarm system while the other exits remained connected. He probably took her out the back way. There's no fence between her yard and the neighbor to the east, a six-foot wooden fence around the yard to the west." He pointed to each in turn. "And a black chain link surrounding the yard directly behind her. That leaves these two paths for his escape." He used a laser pointer to indicate each way around the link fence.

"We think she may have been injected with something prior to her abduction. If the intent of the injection was to immobilize her, he carried her out. Possibly wrapped in the comforter taken off her bed. So his shortest route would be this way." He traced a trail to the west from the end of her backyard.

"Beyond the house on that corner and across the street is a cul-de-sac with guest parking. We haven't found any residents there who noticed a dark-colored van in the area last night. We still have a contingent of DMPD officers canvassing the area, showing the sketches of the Minnesotan man and the van. Maybe we'll get lucky. A crime team has finished with Dr. Channing's condo and is now focused on the most likely path taken once the abductor left the house."

Cam turned to Tommy. "Agent Franks has been chasing down the glass company lead." Stepping aside, he let the other man take over at the mike.

"Dr. Pane is a real company, with its main office in Des Moines with branches in Waukee, Ankeny, and Urbandale," Franks began. Jenna flashed a PowerPoint slide with the logo sketch and the company's logo side by side. "The description given by the boy is a good match for the actual logo. But the company uses yellow vans, not blue, and the owner can find no record of a service call to Dr. Channing's home. Nor do they have a record of doing business with her in the past. We're currently going through their employee list, past and present, and cross-checking the names for criminal histories. We're also looking into properties owned by them in all four locales."

Cam had scrutinized the company himself. They'd been in business fifteen years, and he'd found no serious public complaints lodged against them. But that didn't mean there wasn't a rogue employee in their midst. Or someone outside the company with access to their properties.

He tamped down the fear and impatience that throttled through him. Emotion could dull instinct, blind him to facts. He was going to need every ounce of logic he could summon to catch this bastard before Sophie was . . .

. . . raped . . .

. . . murdered . . .

By sheer force of reason he shoved aside the inner voice that could drag him into a useless raging abyss. The best way to help Sophie now was to remain as objective as possible.

It was the least of the insurmountable tasks he was faced with.

"How can you be certain Dr. Channing's abduction is tied to the case you're working?" The question came from Story County's Sheriff Dumont. He sat near the back of the crowded room, flanked by Beckett Maxwell and Pat Grogan, the sheriff from Warren County.

Cam stepped forward to take the question. "We can't," he said flatly. "But it's a reasonable assumption. We think ours is the only forensic case she is currently working on." He nodded toward a DCI agent sitting in the front row. "After the warrants came through, Agent Loring spent the better part of the afternoon going through her computer and files in her home office. We're still waiting on a warrant to examine those in her downtown office, as well. Loring will continue to focus on past cases Dr. Channing consulted on, and check on offenders she helped put away."

"That's a lot of scumbags to look at," Beckett Maxwell put in. There was a murmur of agreement in the room.

"It is. We'll cross-reference them to the same type of offender we're searching for in the investigation of the bodies. The sketch of the man in the Edina park will be submitted into databases. At the same time, we're also concentrating on the Dr. Pane lead. If Channing's disappearance is flagged as priority . . ." He met Gonzalez's gaze from her seat near the back, and she inclined her head slightly. "Correction, since it has been flagged a priority, I expect feedback from the lab on the trace evidence within days."

He refused to contemplate what days might mean to Sophia's well-being.

"Beckett, any report on the surveillance on Gary Price's place?"

Maxwell stood, shaking his head morosely. "Wish I had something to share. There have been a few vehicles in and out, which might account for the repair business he claims to have going. No cargo vans. We've only got someone on the place part-time, though. Got a deputy out there eight hours at a stretch, alternating days and nights, and a sheriff who takes a few hours after duty." There was an answering chuckle from Dumont. "I did finish the cross-check on the offender list for my county, and that should be on your desk. Nothing popped on that, either, but elimination is part of the process. Had a couple judicial emergencies in the county that's slowed getting Jerry Price before a judge on the weapons charge." He sat down, and Cam gave him a nod of thanks.

"In the meantime, we have a tentative identification of one more victim as Alyssa Wentworth, from Sioux Falls." A picture of the victim taken in happier times was flashed on the screen behind him. "When the news of Van Wheton's disappearance went national, her case detective contacted us. He recognized the sketch Jenna had done of Wentworth." Cam had juggled the call that afternoon while still at Sophie's condo. "He'd been on vacation while we were following up with similar cases on ViCAP, but he'll make sure we have DNA samples inside a week."

He waited for Jenna to flip to a slide showing a map with each of the cemetery locations bearing a red flag with a number. "We've been able to firm up the sequence of when the bodies were buried. That narrows the time between the legitimate burials and the body dumps. In your briefing report, you'll find a copy of the suspect sketch Agent Turner composed with the help of a witness in Edina and an image of the van used to abduct Courtney Van Wheton." Similar copies would be sent to law enforcement agencies throughout the state and the bordering regions.

"We have no positive proof that Van Wheton is linked to our ongoing investigation, but the details surrounding her disappearance suggest that she is. Agents Beachum and Robbins will head up the comparison of surveillance footage available for each of the identified victims and Van Wheton. Samuels and Patrick have been canvassing the areas surrounding each of the rural cemeteries for neighbors who might have seen something suspicious."

He glanced in Jenna's direction. "Agent Turner has been putting together a comprehensive list of the caretakers and volunteers in each of the rural cemeteries and cross-referencing them for criminal history and links to any of the ID'd victims. I'm pulling traffic camera images on southbound highways from the Minnesota border to see if we can get a glimpse of the van that abducted Van Wheton."

"What's our timeline here, Cam?"

He sent a quizzical glance at Brody Robbins, the youngest agent on the case. He was one of the additional agents added to the case by Gonzalez while Cam was in Minneapolis. The man was already looking as if he regretted his question. But since he had the case leader's attention, he barreled on. "I mean, I've read the case file, but I don't have it memorized. Dr. Channing—if she was taken by this UNSUB—how much time . . . ?"

His question trailed off, but the agent's meaning was clear enough.

"Now that we have ID on a few of the victims, as well as their approximate time of deaths, we can be certain that the offender keeps each of them for weeks at a time. Based on what we know at this point, the window ranges from three to five weeks."

Cam tried to make the words sound encouraging. But there was nothing encouraging about the mental picture that emerged of Sophie at the hands of a sexual sadist for weeks. "Obviously, in the case of Van Wheton and Channing alike, time is of the essence."

Gonzalez rose and headed toward the exit. After opening the door, she met his gaze, made a slight motion with her head, and left.

Cam shoved the assignment papers to Franks. "Agent Franks will finish passing out your assignments. Until the briefing same time tomorrow, I want to be updated by each team of agents every two hours. Just a brief report of progress sent by email. If it's pressing, call me."

He strode out of the room and down the hall, already dreading the upcoming meeting with Maria. Unless she had news for him, a one-on-one with the woman would serve no purpose. And it just might torch the powder keg of resentment that had been building inside him ever since he'd learned she'd released that profile to the public, practically on the heels of their last meeting.

Because he didn't trust his simmering temper, Cam took the length of the journey to try to tamp it down and tuck it away. Only when he felt he had himself firmly in check did he give a cursory knock on Maria's office door. Pushed it open.

"Judge Cooper contacted me with some concerns about the scope of the warrant on Channing's downtown office," she began without preamble. She looked up at him from her seat behind her desk and made an impatient gesture for him to sit. "Because of patient confidentiality, the judge is reluctant to open her client files unless we can show reason to believe one of them may be behind her disappearance."

"Damn Judge Brennan's retirement." Cam bit off the words in frustration. "Cooper can be a pain in the ass to deal with, but I knew Butler was on vacation. Since Channing's life is endangered, I'd think the exigent circumstances would be convincing enough."

"Cooper is new. He's still overly cautious."

Which had Cam mentally relegating the judge to the bottom of the list the next time a warrant was needed. He took a moment to think. "What's the name of that psychologist who took over Sophie's practice?" Memory supplied it a moment later. "Redlow.

We found the information in Sophie's files today. Tell the judge we have no objection to Redlow being present at the search. When it comes to patient files, the psychologist can do the reading and just give us the information that might pertain to the questions we pose regarding patient likelihood for violence."

"You're okay with that?"

"No, it's ridiculous. But I want to get in her office tomorrow at the latest." The search wasn't all that pressing. He doubted Sophie had kept duplicate copies of her private forensic consultation business at her office downtown, but he wanted to be thorough. Ex-offenders she'd profiled likely posed a much higher risk to her than anyone she'd counseled, and they'd found those files on her home computer.

"All right. Rewrite the request with the new scope and parameters." She eyed him shrewdly.

He hadn't sat down. He was much too wired for that. But giving way to the energy coursing through him by pacing her office would be too telling. So he leaned against one of the uncomfortable wooden chairs she kept for visitors, clenching his fingers on the top of it.

"How you doing?"

He thought he detected the barest tinge of sympathy in her tone. It raised his hackles like nails on a chalkboard. "Just fine, Maria. How you doing?"

Her dark eyes narrowed. Cam noticed for the first time the circles beneath them. He couldn't summon a shred of concern for that.

"Don't try that tone with me, Cam. I know you. We've worked together for years. And I heard you gave your prints for elimination purposes at Channing's apartment today."

"I was first on the scene."

"The criminalist said you told her you'd been there socially." Her gaze skewered him, as if trying to read his mind. "Since when did you get social with Sophia Channing?"

Something inside him froze. He hadn't even considered that his former relationship with Sophie would automatically exclude him from tracking her abductor. And if the abductor happened to be the same man who'd raped and murdered six women already, that exclusion would mean Cam was off the case altogether.

Feeling as though he were stepping around land mines, he let impatience sound in his voice. "I socialize with lots of people I work with. Tommy. Jenna. Castle. Boggs. You. At least I used to." He shoved away from the chair, as if anxious to go. Which didn't take any acting skill at all. "About the only people I do socialize with are people that are connected to my job. What's the big deal?"

"And there's nothing else? No other relationship between you and Dr. Channing?" She was watching him closely, but he was no longer worried. She was fishing. She didn't know anything about his past relationship with Sophie, although she might suspect.

Cam was a helluva poker player, too. And he didn't have any tells. His survival undercover had depended on that. "We're not involved, if that's what you mean."

She leaned back in her chair, fiddled with some papers on her desk. She wasn't fooling him. Maria Gonzalez made no casual movements. She could sit still as a snake on a stakeout for hours at a time. "How'd you get into her apartment this morning?"

"The back door was open, remember? And before you ask, I'd gone to warn her that you'd made the profile public. It's still splashed all over the *Register* today. I heard it was in the news for days. I didn't want her to be ambushed by it or by any reporters that might come nosing around." He tried to keep his seething resentment at her actions from his voice. Was only marginally successful.

There was a flicker in her gaze. There and gone too quickly to identify. "I don't think releasing the profile had anything to do with her disappearance."

Her words raked over him with jagged fangs, leaving blood in their wake. They almost caused him to unleash all his pent-up bitterness over her act. Almost. Until he saw her duck her head a little. Not in shame, but to prevent him from reading her expression.

She was playing him. Trying to goad him into a reaction that would prove, once and for all, if there was anything personal between Sophie and him. The realization acted like a dash of cold water on the coals of his temper. "We'll have to agree to disagree on that."

Her head came up sharply at his wry tone. "I still maintain it was the right decision."

Cam had had enough. He needed to think that Maria's defense of her actions was simply to get a reaction from him. Much more of this, and he wouldn't be able to make himself believe it.

He turned to go. "I'll be sure and ask Dr. Channing her thoughts on that when I find her."

Chapter 9

Cam awakened to the sound of his own ragged breathing. He lay there, his eyes adjusting to the darkness in the room, waiting for his heartbeat to slow and the tenseness in his muscles to ease.

This particular rendition of the nightmare was new, but his reaction to it was familiar. His spine prickled with fear-induced adrenaline. His pulse still surged through his veins. Taking a deep breath, he forced himself to do the deep-breathing exercises that would calm his runaway physical reactions.

Only then did he become aware of the steady breathing beside him.

Sophie.

Cam's eyelids opened, and he stared fixedly at the ceiling. It'd been a while since he'd been bothered by the recurring dream. He'd had his share of flashback-induced panic attacks in the weeks following his return from deep cover. They'd eventually receded, but the nightmares were the last remnants of the PTSD that had dogged him since that time. At least they were manageable now. The cure was several minutes of deep breathing, or, barring that, a punishing sprint on the treadmill.

But deep breathing wasn't helping, and the treadmill was in the corner of the bedroom. Not an option.

Carefully, he eased out of bed and padded to the adjoining bath, swinging the door shut behind him. Cam propped his hands on the counter and leaned against them, for the first time aware of the perspiration that drenched his body.

He'd spent long months railing at the occurrences and at his own weakness. Because no amount of sheer determination was enough to push aside the episodes. As much as he'd despised the time he'd spent with the agency-ordered therapist, he'd grudgingly come to accept that willpower alone meant shit when battling inner demons.

The door opened then. A soft voice sounded. "Cam?"

His eyes slid shut. "I'm fine. I'll be out in a minute."

But a moment later, he felt her arms slide around his waist. Her cheek pressed against his back. "You're not fine," she murmured. Her hair brushed lightly against his skin. "You're clammy. Bad dream?"

"I'm all right," he repeated. And realized in that instant that the words weren't a lie. His pulse had calmed. His heart rate was slowing. "As long as you're awake, I think I'll take a quick shower, though."

"Good idea." When she released him, he wasn't so certain he agreed. But she was back a moment later, pressing a towel into his hand and then moving to the shower, turning it on. The light remained off, a fact he was grateful for, but weak slants of moonlight filtered through the window blind.

He followed her, hanging the towel on a hook, and stepped inside the walk-in shower. She surprised him yet again by getting in after him.

"Sophie . . ." As a protest, it was pretty halfhearted. He could think of one way to banish the lingering darkness from the dream, but he had no intention of using her that way. It was weak, and he was a man who avoided weakness at all costs.

The woman standing before him slicking back her wet hair presented a vulnerability of another sort entirely. One that might prove to be his undoing. "No one has ever called me that before." Her hands slid around his waist. Lowered. Squeezed his ass.

His thoughts jumbled. "Sophie? You're kidding."

"I've always been Sophia, even as a child." Her hands were busy. Clever. "Sophie sounds like somebody else. Someone less serious. More adventurous. Sometimes when you say it, it feels like you're talking about another woman." She took him in her hand then, and when her fingers closed tightly around him, his breath escaped in a sharp hiss.

"I don't want another woman." The admission would have scared the hell of him if he were capable of rational thought. He picked her up and she wrapped her legs around his hips, reaching down to guide him. "Only you."

And as he slipped inside her, he had the dim fleeting thought that this might be what healing felt like.

Cam's office was silent but for the whisper of shuffling papers and the tapping on keyboards. Jenna had been the first to join him there, resisting all his efforts to send her home. Shortly after, Franks had shown up, taken one look inside the office, and silently fetched chairs from the staff room. Cam hadn't even attempted to convince the man to leave. Cam figured that the two agents, like him, weren't going to get any sleep while Sophie was missing.

So they'd all settled in for the evening. Cam had borrowed the coffeemaker from the staff room, and empty cups littered the office. He was seated at his desk, but he had stripped off the suit coat and tie and loosened the neck of his shirt. Franks had done the same. He and Jenna had their feet propped up on another chair in front of them, laptops balanced on their thighs. Other than slipping out of her shoes, Jenna still looked as fresh as she had when she'd come to work that morning, a fact that would have baffled Cam had he taken the time to consider it.

But his focus was on the data they'd split between them. Somewhere in the vast wealth of information the agents' assignments had yielded might be buried the one lead they needed to locate Sophie's whereabouts.

Franks had hit a brick wall early in the evening. He'd been checking each individual on Dr. Pane's past and present employee list for criminal histories. When he'd found nothing of note, he made a copy of the cemetery caretakers Jenna had put together and began looking for a name that might appear in both groups.

Cam had finished running criminal checks on the cemetery caretakers. He'd found a few misdemeanor charges among the individuals on the list, but no one had struck him as dangerous. Now, with a second copy of the Pane employees, he was combing through the DMV database for vehicles owned by each, looking for titles to cargo vans.

"Are my eyes bleeding? They should be bleeding." An hour later Jenna scrubbed the heels of her palms over her eyes. "Just reading the interviews and profiles Sophia did on these deviants over the years . . . It's not a question of whether any of them would be capable of reaching out to her. Sick bastards." She'd been given the task of taking Loring's earlier assignment one step further and looking at offenders Sophie had once consulted on. Cam knew the files wouldn't make for easy reading.

"How many are actually out of prison?"

She glanced at her notes. "Of the ones she conducted interviews on when they were already imprisoned, three are dead. Good riddance. And another is in hospice, dying of emphysema. Albert Lancer was released last year, but he's eighty-seven. I sent his parole officer an email, but hard to see an octogenarian as the offender we're seeking." She peeled down a wrapper of something and brought it to her lips.

Cam stared at her fixedly. The dry cheese and crackers he'd scored a couple of hours earlier from the vending machine were a distant memory. "What's that?"

Franks looked over.

Taking a big bite, Jenna chewed with obvious enjoyment. "A granola bar from my purse. Useful things, purses. You can carry all sorts of necessities in them."

"You have any more?"

His wheedling tone didn't seem to faze her. "Maybe you should check your wallet. That's where guys carry everything they need, right?"

"You owe me, Jenna," Tommy pointed out. "Remember that time I changed your flat?"

"That was five years ago." She took another large bite. "Statute of limitations on payback is three years. Everyone knows that."

"Don't be mean." Cam's stomach rumbled. "I made coffee for you tonight. Poured it for you, too."

"And I carried in the chairs you're using from the staff room," Tommy said. His lean face looked feral. "I can carry them back. Now. I'm sure you'll be plenty comfortable sitting on the floor."

"Whining and threats. Hunger really doesn't bring out the best qualities in you two." Reaching down, she withdrew two more bars from her purse and threw one to each of them. "Remember my generosity the next time you're tempted to tell a joke about gingers."

She settled back as Cam and Tommy made short work of the snacks. "As I was saying before I got interrupted for feeding time, so far there are few conceivable leads looking at the already incarcerated perps Sophia interviewed. Given the nature of their crimes, none of them are getting out of prison for a couple more decades." She paused to polish off the rest of her bar, rolled up the wrapper, and shot it neatly into Cam's wastebasket. "And not one of the dirtbags on cases she's consulted on in the last dozen years are released yet. Of course, I'm not done going through all of them. And that's not to say that one of their embittered family members wasn't behind Sophia's kidnapping. Or that some twisted serial killer groupie isn't doing the bidding of one of the sickos. But . . ."

Her voice trailed off, but Cam could easily fill in the rest of her statement. That line would be futile to follow, the possibilities infinite. They could work only the most promising leads. He couldn't allow himself to consider the less plausible ones, no matter that they remained distant possibilities.

It was more probable that this case had led to Sophie's abduction. And that meant she was at the mercy of the sadistic sexual offender they were seeking. He elbowed aside the bleakness that settled inside him at the thought.

"If she'd been threatened in some way, if one of the guys she helped put away had reached out, she would have told someone about that, right?"

"Absolutely." Cam didn't even have to think overmuch about Franks's question. *I don't have a brave bone in my body.* The words she'd once spoken sounded in his memory. Although he didn't agree with them, he also knew Sophie was too by-the-book to not notify the authorities in that eventuality.

"Haven't run across any reference to a threat from one of them." Jenna made herself more comfortable on the chairs she was using to stretch out. "I'll go back to looking. But reading this stuff about these sickos is like diving into a cesspool. It's hard to imagine Sophia immersed in this all the time."

Cam remained silent. He'd often had similar thoughts, but Sophie was remarkably well balanced for someone who dealt with the darkness she encountered on a daily basis. There was more to the woman than met the eye. He'd learned that for himself.

And if he wanted to trail her to wherever she was being kept, he couldn't—wouldn't—consider what sort of darkness she was encountering right now.

⸻

Sophia huddled on the blow-up mattress, desolation sweeping over her. She'd found the comforter from her bed wadded up and tossed carelessly to the side in one corner of the cell. Although the temperature was mild, she'd wrapped up in it as if donning armor. Even that small bit of familiarity had provided comfort. There was little else to calm her. She'd lost her voice hours earlier yelling for help in vain.

Which told her the place had to be remote. The stranger hadn't bothered to gag her, so he must be certain there would be no one in the vicinity to offer assistance.

She was alone here. The place was large. Dark. Cavernous. Tiny tentacles of light pierced the walls in random pinpoints of sunlight. The sparse light hadn't helped her decide what this place was. The gate on her cell was about six feet tall, with wide round bars three inches apart. It was held in place with a small rectangular box lock of some sort secured to the exterior. By placing her feet on the bars of the gate, she could climb it like a ladder, but for only a few feet before her progress was halted by woven wire fencing that penned her in at the top. The edges of the wire were pulled over the wooden walls and secured in place.

The confines of her cell made it impossible to see to the right or left. All she could see ahead of her was emptiness. Was hers the only cell in the building? She couldn't be sure.

The place smelled old, with faint indistinguishable odors mingling. There was a ceiling far above her. But if there was a floor

above that, no sound emanated from it. Her prison could be a basement of some sort. Or a barn. Her cell could easily have once been
a stall. Or it may even have been a modified parcel holding pen in
an ancient warehouse.

Which didn't narrow down the location at all.

Think! Sophia ordered herself as she paced the confines of her
cell. The area was approximately ten by twelve. It was empty, save
for the blow-up mattress. The floor was more gravel and dust than
concrete. Which told her only that the structure was old, which
she'd already guessed.

And none of that information helped her plan her escape.

She'd done one thorough search of the space. Going to her
knees, she started another. Running her fingers over the limestone
wall at the back, Sophia jiggled each stone, testing it for looseness.
All held fast. No matter how hard she tried to twist and push, she
could find no leverage to move any of them.

Limestone quarries were plentiful in Iowa, and many founda-
tions a century ago were built of the material. The first apartment
she and Douglas had rented in Iowa City had been housed in a wonderful old Queen Anne, which had a dirt-floor cellar with walls just
like the one behind her. Given the number of creepie-crawlies she'd
encountered whenever venturing to that basement, she'd always suspected the stone walls of harboring numerous fissures and cracks.

But that certainly didn't seem true of the one in her cell.

After an hour of fruitless effort, she gave up and moved to the
walls. Her right shoulder still throbbed from where she'd earlier tried
throwing herself against the wooden panels, in the hope of breaking a board. This time she exercised more caution, investigating the
length and width of the wooden strips that comprised the sides.
Sophia could stick her fingers under the bottom slats with an extra
inch of clearance and run them about four feet before encountering
a wooden board placed vertically. Her heart sank at the realization

that the sides were likely two-by-fours nailed together, with braces placed halfway. And unless she found a board rotted with age, she didn't stand a chance of prying one off.

She set about exploring them, pulling on the bottom ones with all her might. There was give in a couple, but try as she might, she lacked the strength to free any of them. The higher boards were placed one on top of the other. Much too close to get her fingers in the gap between, or even to look between the boards at what might be next to her.

The wood was undoubtedly old. She studied one wall for a moment. The weakest area on each should be midway between the vertical posts bracing them from the other side. Sophia let the comforter drop to the mattress, drew back her leg, and, using the ball of her heel, aimed a solid kick in the center of one of the slats.

Pain sang up her leg, but the board remained intact. Eyeing it balefully, she grabbed the comforter and used it to cushion her foot before trying again on another. Her foot was protected this time, but her efforts were met with a similar lack of success.

Ruthlessly tamping down the despair that threatened, she tried over and over, kicking repeatedly at every board she could reach. Although some shook under her attack, they all held firm.

Frustrated, she studied the cell with new eyes. Only then did she realize the occasional threads of light showing through cracks in the structure were getting dimmer.

It had been after midnight when she'd been abducted from her shower. It had been full dark when she'd come to last night. Or maybe it had been early this morning. How long since the UNSUB had left her?

An even more terrifying question was how much time did she have until he came back?

Her knees went to water then, and she stumbled back to the mattress, sinking upon it in an ignominious heap. There wasn't a doubt in her mind that her kidnapper was the man responsible for the six sets of human remains dug up in the cemeteries. The same stranger responsible for the abduction of Courtney Van Wheton. But she'd called out to Courtney by name earlier. There had been no answer.

Sophia had spent more than a decade analyzing crimes every bit as horrific as those this offender was responsible for. She'd worked nearly as long developing victim profiles for the unfortunates who had been targeted by men like him. In order to accomplish her job, an emotional distance was necessary.

But that distance was impossible now. She was immersed in the nightmare. Tiny tendrils of fear curled throughout her system. It was getting harder and harder to keep them at bay. Objectivity was difficult to summon when an inner clock ticked away the passing minutes and hours. But she realized she'd be capable of the clearest thinking before she was victimized herself.

The thought had Sophia surging from the mattress. She turned her attention to the woven wire effectively penning in the top of her cell. It couldn't be reached by standing in place, or by stepping atop the mattress.

Striding to the gate again, she tried not to focus on the fading splinters of light. But a renewed sense of urgency fueled her actions. Grasping one bar in her hands, she climbed up as far as she was able. It moved a little on its hinges when she climbed it, each small shift of position separating it a fraction from the ceiling of wire above. The top rung of the metal gate met the wire when it was closed and would have to swing outward in order to clear it.

She reached out to press against the wire fencing at the right front corner. It was secured tightly for as far as she could stretch. But the pressure she put on it bent the wire slightly. Tilting her head up, she considered it.

The openings between the wires were two inches by three, she estimated. The wires were crimped hard every two inches to hold them together. Not as thick as a chain-link fence people would put around their yards. Not as flimsy and malleable as chicken wire. She'd never been allowed to have pets as a child, but a friend of hers had had two rabbits kept in a cage fashioned with similar wire but slightly thicker.

Shifting position, she started at the opposite end. She reached out to pry at one of the coiled wires securing one section to the next. Quickly sliced her finger.

She popped it in her mouth, reconsidered. Next she reached up above the gate and pressed as hard as she could on the wire. It held firm. Climbing as high as she was able, she ducked her head and pushed on the wire with all her might. A small gap appeared between it and the top of the gate.

Hope slivered through her. It was only two inches or so, but Sophia was filled with new purpose. She just needed something to wedge up there, to separate the wire from the top of the gate enough for her to climb through the resulting space.

Quickly she descended to retrieve the comforter. Fabric wasn't going to be the most effective material, but it was all she had available. She spread it out, then rolled it as tightly as possible.

The ecru and ribbon lace couldn't have looked more out of place in her prison. Before she could slam that mental door shut, she had an image of Cam sprawled out atop it, his arms wrapping her tightly to his chest. The feminine backdrop couldn't have contrasted more sharply with his tough masculinity.

Pain from the memory shimmied through her, and she quickly forced it aside before it could weaken her resolve. She couldn't afford to be distracted or weakened thinking about the past. Couldn't afford to rely on others . . . Cam . . . to rescue her.

Time was running out.

Filled with a renewed sense of urgency, she ran back to the gate and climbed two rungs, struggling to maintain her balance while she reached up to wedge the roll she'd made from the comforter into the space between the gate and the wire. Triumph spiked through her as the wire bent a fraction. Redoubling her efforts, she twisted the roll of fabric, forcing it harder. The wire caught at all the little holes in the lace, slowing the progress, but patiently she freed each snagged area to push it through farther. When she had the folded comforter wedged halfway, she tested the gap it created in the wire.

Her heart plummeted. The gap of two inches was actually narrowing before her eyes as the wire pressed down on the forgivable fabric. It had the bulk, but it lacked the firmness necessary to act as the wedge she needed.

Tears of frustration welled. Sophia forced herself to think. Maybe she could use the fabric to protect her fingers as she tried to unwrap the wire where it was crimped together. But even as the idea occurred, she knew it was doomed to fail. She needed a tool of some sort, and nothing in her search had—

The thought fragmented when a noise split the cavernous confines of her prison. Ancient hinges gave a protesting creak. Her system quite simply froze.

And then a voice pierced the darkness, shooting her spine with panic.

"I came back for you, Dr. Bitch. Just like I promised."

"I might have something. Where's that file folder of violent sexual felons released in the state recently?"

Both Jenna and Tommy straightened in the chairs. Franks picked up the folder in question and slid it across Cam's desk.

Without shifting his propped feet, Cam leaned forward to grab it. He flipped through until he found the name he was looking for. "Stacy Marchand."

"Stacy? That name would get a guy some special attention in prison." Jenna muffled her yawn as she spoke.

"Not a guy," he said absently, still trying to find the page in question. "A sister of one of the cons . . . Ah." He pulled out the sheet he was looking for and held it up. "Sister to Gilbert Humphrey. He was released eighteen months ago after serving twelve years for attempted murder." Cam had checked on the man himself when he'd gone over the list previously. He stopped to refamiliarize himself with the details. "Abducted a woman from her car in a department store parking lot at gunpoint. Drove her to a wooded area and raped her repeatedly. Later tried to cover up the crime by setting her on fire."

"Twelve years?" Franks uttered the words like an oath.

"He agreed to serve as an FBI informant in another investigation and had his sentence reduced. When he got out, he lived with his sister for a time. Stacy Marchand." Adrenaline was rapidly firing along his nerve endings. "I came across her name a couple hours ago. She's worked for Dr. Pane for the last eight years, according to their employee records. The Des Moines branch. And the DMV has her listed as owning a 2005 white cargo van. Bought it in 2010."

Franks stared at him. "So he uses his sister's van to abduct Van Wheton from Edina. If we're talking the same guy, maybe he paints it before abducting Sophia. Problem is DMPD has already searched all the Dr. Pane properties with the owner's permission. Found nothing."

"But we didn't search the Zip's Auto and Salvage properties." Cam passed the page he was looking at over to Tommy. "That's Humphrey's current employer, according to the information on his parole sheet." He reduced one screen on his computer, opened another, and searched for the company. Before he could finish his search, Jenna was speaking.

"They've got a scrap yard on East Elm. Proprietor is one Ernest Zipsy. I'll run a property search under his name. See what else he owns."

Cam turned his attention to running Zipsy for priors. Minutes later, Jenna announced, "Two other business properties are listed with Ernest Zipsy as the owner. One is on Raccoon. That street would be adjacent to Elm. Might be the headquarters for the scrap yard. The other is south of the Martin Luther King Parkway. From the assessed taxation rate, it's not much of a building."

"Meaning it's not one of the structures currently targeted by the urban development going on in the area." Cam knew many of the historic buildings in that neighborhood were being refurbished as trendy lofts and boutique office spaces. But other streets were still lined with abandoned buildings and warehouses.

He paused, did a quick scan of what his search had brought up on the man. "Twenty years ago Zipsy went away for running a chop shop. Five-year stretch. Looks like he's been clean ever since. Or at least he's avoided getting caught."

Mind made up, Cam looked at Franks. "Call Treelord." Steve Treelord was the DMPD lieutenant heading up the city's law enforcement assistance on Sophia's abduction. "Have him get someone to sit on Humphrey's apartment for the duration." At least keeping the man under surveillance would ensure that he wasn't free to terrorize a victim, if indeed he was the offender they were seeking. He switched his attention to Jenna. "Check whether Humphrey has a license. And whether he has any moving violations. Maybe we'll catch a break and one will have been recorded by a red-light camera in the vicinity we're looking at."

He picked up his own cell and dialed a familiar number. "I'm going to call Fenton." He saw her expression and accurately interpreted it. Hounding Al Fenton, the lab manager at the DCI criminal laboratory, was a waste of time and energy. It was doubtful much had been done yet with the evidence collected at Sophie's.

But nagging never hurt.

Cam was about to leave the first in what he figured would be a long string of voice messages. But to his surprise, Fenton answered on the first ring.

"Actually I was just about to call you." Cam could visualize the manager running his fingers through his thinning hair. The man was midfifties, with a perpetually harried expression. It came, Cam imagined, from constant calls like this one asking for updates.

"You have something from today's scene already?" The remark was intended to provoke. Then they'd start the inevitable two-step about a timeline for results. He knew the lab was open only until five, and some of the tests took days to administer. It was all part of the dance.

"We're running a DNA comparison test on the blood samples we found on Dr. Channing's bathroom floor with samples taken from her toothbrush." Cam must have made a sound of amazement because Jenna and Tommy glanced up at him. "If we rush it, we can have results ready sometime tomorrow. Latents will take longer. We've got elimination comparisons to do, and then you can submit the unknown prints to AFIS."

It took a moment for Cam to find his voice. "That's fast work, Al."

"There's more." A note of satisfaction threaded through the man's voice. "We've got a couple sole prints from the garage doorway into the condo, one in Dr. Channing's bedroom, and another in the kitchen. Sneakers, size eleven and a half. I've got an analyst running the tread pattern against known brands. Might get lucky there. And dirt was collected from where it was ground into the carpet in a couple places. Aubrey is doing an analysis right now."

Hope bloomed. Cam remembered a criminalist tagging the spots. If the dirt had come from a shoe tread, it could give them a hint about where the offender had been. Possibly even point to an occupation.

Then shock hit him. "Aubrey?" He checked his watch. "What's she still doing there?" He wasn't terribly surprised that the lab manager was still there at this time. The man was a well-known workaholic. But the lab's budget rarely ran to overtime.

Fenton's tone went defensive. "I'm still here because I had paperwork to catch up on. And if a few of the analysts insist on staying to finish the tests they were running on their own time, I'm going to turn a blind eye. A lot of us have attended forensic conferences with Dr. Channing. She helped write a grant last year to secure a freestanding fuming chamber for the lab. People here . . ." He paused for a moment, and when he continued his voice sounded gruff. "Well, let's just say a lot of us think highly of her."

Cam was surprised, but he shouldn't have been. Sophie had that way with people. An innate ability to connect. He could only be grateful that she generated the same depth of loyalty from the lab personnel as she did from the agents at DCI. "She'll be touched, Al."

"Yeah." Fenton cleared his throat. "You just make sure she gets home to hear about our efforts as soon as possible, okay? Tyler Skarlis will be doing the toxicology analysis on the syringe found in her bathroom first thing in the morning. No telling how long that will take. Depends on whether the contents are substances we commonly test for."

From working around crime lab criminalists for years, Cam knew Skarlis was considered by his peers to be nothing short of brilliant. Given the lab's chronic backlog, coupled with the test requests for priority-flagged evidence from this case so far, the efforts Fenton and his crew were putting forth on Sophie's behalf were staggering.

"Sounds like you've got things well in hand." Cam was still a little stunned, but he couldn't have asked for a better update. "I'll let you get back to work."

"I'll keep you posted," Fenton promised.

When he hung up, Jenna was eyeing him impatiently. "That's the longest conversation you've had with Fenton without uttering a veiled threat or bribe."

"I never threaten." He felt obliged to set the record straight. Intimidation was in the eye of the beholder. And the lab manager didn't respond to it, in any case. "Benally is the one who requires bribes to get a tenth of the cooperation Fenton is showing us tonight." He told the other two agents the gist of what he'd just learned from the man.

Franks whistled softly. "I have to say in my thirty years with the agency, that's a first."

"It's Sophia." For a moment Cam thought Jenna's eyes were shiny. An instant later he decided he'd been seeing things. "That's the effect she has on people. The toxicology results might give us a valuable lead, too."

"Maybe." Cam's response was noncommittal. The more common the substance, the faster the results, he knew. But that also meant they'd be harder to trace.

He turned his attention back to Gil Humphrey. Although the lab was moving at unprecedented speed, they were still talking a fifteen- to twenty-hour window to hear anything. Those were hours in which Sophia was still in danger. Vulnerable.

A sense of bleak desolation settled over him. It was a struggle to battle through it. Maybe Gonzalez was right. Maybe he shouldn't be anywhere near this investigation. Because God help him, it was getting harder and harder to concentrate on getting the job done when images of what might be happening to Sophie right now were torturing him.

Time crawled to a stop. Frantically, Sophia tugged at the comforter to free it from where she'd wedged it above the gate. Part of it loosened, unfolding as she pulled. Other areas were caught on the wire.

Sophia heard the telltale squeak of unoiled hinges again. The bang of a door closing. Frantic now, her fingers were clumsy as they sought to find all the spots the lace was snagged on the wire.

A drumbeat of fear rolled through her chest. Like counting seconds between a lightning bolt and the inevitable accompanying thunder, she measured his approach. Her ears strained for the sound of footsteps even as everything inside her recoiled from the thought of seeing him again. Another spot of the comforter was freed. Then another. A beam of light shone in front of her cell. There was a scrape of a shoe on concrete, and the light drew closer. Brighter.

She scrambled off the gate, picked up the expanse of comforter, and yanked with all her might. There was a ripping sound. Then the material released with a suddenness that sent her sprawling. She barely had time to backward-crawl to the edge of the mattress, pulling the fabric around her as she went, before the spotlight was abruptly blinding her. She threw up a hand to shield her eyes.

"No greeting? That's just rude. Seems I need to teach you some manners, along with a few other lessons."

Sophia battled to draw air into her lungs. It was all she could do to avoid scrambling into the corner, a huddling, shuddering mass of fear. She made herself look at him. Consider what he was. She'd spent her career helping law enforcement bring men like him to justice. The thought shot a little steel to her spine. She might be victimized by him. But she refused to be a victim.

The brave thought dissipated when she noted several threads hanging from the wire above the gate, like billboards proclaiming her recent attempt at escape. She couldn't look away from them. A boulder-size knot of fear formed in her throat. Would he notice?

In the next moment she realized the folly of that particular concern. What he had in store for her involved unimaginable suffering. A failed escape attempt could hardly worsen her fate.

He was dressed for the gym with a sleeveless Dri-FIT shirt that strained across his thick chest, gym shorts, and sneakers. His arms were so corded with muscle he had to hold them a little away from his sides, reminding her of a primate. Sophia recalled again how all the victims had died of manual strangulation. She didn't doubt for a moment that this man could accomplish the feat with one quick flex of his hands around a neck.

"It occurs to me that I've seriously misjudged you." The calm words seemed to emanate from someone else. Someone who wasn't currently cowering in panic. He blinked a moment, and she knew her matter-of-fact statement had taken him aback.

"I said so, didn't I?" He set the light down on the floor next to him. Not a flashlight at all, she realized now, but a portable floodlight of some sort. Powerful enough to bathe the interior of the cell with brightness and bathe the area outside it in a soft glow. "Don't worry. You'll have plenty of chances to apologize."

"Of course. It's what I deserve for disappointing you." He'd used the word *disappointment* when they'd last spoken. The psychologist in her had recognized its significance and filed it away. Curious that the habit of analysis was so automatic even while her physical being was quaking. Her mouth seemed filled with sand. Every word had to be forced out of her closed throat. The unrelenting glare of the light pinned her like a bug to cardboard. A very nearly naked bug. "But I'm a professional. It bothers me that my profile of you was so very wrong, and that I left the public with an erroneous impression of you."

He stepped out of her line of vision for a moment. Came back with a key. The gate rattled as he fitted it to the lock. "You're about to start paying for that, bitch. You'll pay for every word you wrote."

"As I should." Disassociation was critical. Sophia had to find a way to distance herself from the scene emotionally, even as shudders of fear racked her body. She couldn't hope to mount a physical defense against him. Their short-lived struggle in her bathroom had proved that.

But a psychological battle? It was a slim chance. And her only one. "In my profession, mistakes are costly. They shouldn't be tolerated. They especially shouldn't be allowed to stand when there's an opportunity to make them right."

The gate rattled, and then it was swinging open. And then— oh, God, then he was striding inside her cell. Rational thought took flight, and instinct took over. She scrambled across the mattress, one hand thrown up in a futile attempt to ward him off.

Hulking over her, he reached out a hand and grasped her by the throat, hauling her up with one hand and pinning her against the wooden side of the cell. Her ankles dangled helplessly off the floor. "You made a mistake, all right." He shoved her harder against the wall, his face close to hers. Dots swam before her eyes as the breath strangled in her lungs. "Maybe I should film your punishment. Stream it on the computer or something. Show people what happens to fuckups." He shoved away from her then, and she crumpled at his feet, gasping for air.

She lay there for several moments, hauling much-needed oxygen into her tortured lungs. When she spoke, she didn't need to manufacture a weak voice. "You're in charge." Since offenders like this one operated out of a need for power and control, she had to play to that need. Pretend to accede to it. "If you think that will convince everyone of how wrong my profile on you was, of course that's what you should do. My idea is probably not nearly as smart as yours."

Bending down, he wrapped his fist in her hair and yanked her painfully to her feet, grabbing one of her breasts and squeezing it in a viselike grip. "Ideas? See, that's the problem. Every time women go around thinking they have brains, we get mistakes like these. What would happen if dogs started thinking they were smarter than men? Or pigs? Females are on the same level. Lower. Least dogs can be taught to hunt."

Cackling at his own words, he threw her to the side violently so she tumbled to the mattress. He was on her in the next second, his hands running over her body, pinching, probing, squeezing. Panic clawed in her throat. It took more effort than she would have suspected she was capable of to rein in the primitive urge to struggle. Her limbs trembled from the stress of immobility.

"Of course, you're right. And releasing a new profile was probably a stupid idea. You wouldn't want to be interviewed by me so we can get the profile exact. And even if we did, there probably isn't any way to get it picked up by the media."

He stilled. "What the hell are you babbling about?"

It was, she knew, her only opening. "Releasing a new profile on you to the public. Except this would be based on your own words, rather than my inaccurate guesses about you. I've interviewed many famous men who spent their lives outwitting the police while they did exactly as they pleased. But maybe the media wouldn't be interested."

"And you're a doctor? Dumb bitch, the media would eat it up." He rolled off her to sit, glaring down at her. "Most of 'em would chew off their arms for a story like this. But I'm not stupid enough to bring even more attention to myself. Like I want to give the cops more to go on."

It was such a relief to have even that small distance between them that the strength streamed out of Sophia's bones. Tremors of revulsion still shook her. She longed to roll up in the comforter, to shield herself from his eyes. From his touch.

But he was sitting on part of the fabric, making that action impossible. And she knew any attempt she made to cover herself would merely goad him further. Better to focus on a way to keep him from touching her again.

"The police have nothing on this case. Why else would they have brought me in on it? They were desperate. They wanted to convince the public they were making progress, so they released the profile. People don't know how wrong it is, so of course they believe the DCI. They don't realize that you've managed to outsmart them completely."

"I got news for you, bitch. It wasn't that hard. And since I snatched you from right under their noses, everyone already is going to know who has the brains."

"Oh, but . . ." It didn't require acting for her to shrink from the sudden threatening move he made at her protest. "I'm sorry— of course you know this. I consult with law enforcement all over the nation on any number of cases at the same time. I'm certain you've already figured out how to let the media know that my disappearance had nothing to do with any of those other cases I've been working on."

His blow came so quickly Sophia had no chance to dodge it. The backhanded slap was delivered with enough force to snap her face to the side. "You're more trouble than you're worth—know that? I should kill you now and be done with it."

"That's your decision. You're in charge." Sophia blinked back the tears stinging her eyes from the blow. "I only wish I could help undo the idea the public has of you, since it's my fault that the profile is so wrong."

"I'm going to think of a whole new way to make you pay for that, too. Already got some ideas." The smile on his lips made her flesh crawl. But his next words had tiny wings of hope fluttering in her chest. "State cops will probably try to make it look like your kidnapping is related to one of those other cases, just to make themselves look less like a bunch of fucktards."

"They won't want the public to know how badly you're outwitting them."

"I know exactly who would release a new profile." He was sitting close enough that Sophia could see the sheen of perspiration dampening the back of his neck, although the temperature inside the structure was relatively cool. She wondered then if his overdeveloped muscles came from steroid use. "I remember this news gal from a couple days ago. Wouldn't mind paying her a little visit afterward, either, just to thank her." He laughed again, the high-pitched sound like an icy finger stroking down her spine. "Wouldn't that be a kick in the teeth to the cops? Not only did I grab the dumbass consultant they had helping them, I let the public see they don't have shit on me. Everyone would know they're standing around with their thumbs up their asses."

"People would realize who was in control."

He stabbed a finger in her direction. "Exactly. So that's what we'll do. I'll get you some paper, and you can write a new profile. I'll hand deliver it to someone who will get it on the air. And the cops will be the laughingstock of the state."

When he stood suddenly, Sophia felt a sharp blade of relief. He'd leave now. He'd have to fetch a notepad. A pen. She could use the time to work at the fencing again. Or perhaps she should focus on the lock securing the gate to the cell.

He yanked his shirt over his gleaming bald head, and her relief suffered a quick violent death. Her heart stumbled to a stop. Then lurched, pounding in her chest like a runaway locomotive.

"First things first, though. You got a few lessons to learn. And I'm in the mind to start delivering them."

Chapter 10

I t might have been the smell of bacon that woke him. Either that or the coffee.

Cam lifted an eyelid. Definitely the coffee. His brain responded innately to the matter that provided it fuel. But the bacon provided the necessary impetus required to summon the effort to sit up. To eye the tray Sophie was waving temptingly before him.

"What did I do to deserve breakfast in bed?" He reached out to snag a piece of bacon before she could change her mind and make him get up and go in to the table.

"Absolutely nothing." She calmed his fear by sitting on the bed next to him and settling the tray on his lap. "As a matter of fact, you should feel serious guilt for how little you've done to deserve this extraordinary effort."

She filched a half piece of buttered toast and took a bite, eyeing him angelically as he reached for the steaming coffee mug on the tray.

"Now that my suspicions are suitably heightened, I'm sure you'll tell me how I can make it up to you." After a long gulp, he felt human enough to set down the coffee and pick up the fork to attack the eggs. Over hard, just the way he liked them, with ketchup on the side. Apparently she hadn't been able to set aside her culinary objections and douse them with the substance, as was his habit. No matter. Cam scooped up a forkful of eggs and bathed them in the ketchup before lifting them to his lips. Followed up with another slice of bacon.

"Make it up to me?" She fluttered her lashes in mock surprise. "I can't imagine how. Oh, I guess I do have some shopping to do. You could come to the mall with me this afternoon and carry my bags."

He felt a mild pang of panic at the thought. "Or you could just shoot me now." He pointed to the center of his forehead. "Put the bullet here, and get it over with."

She went on without a hitch. "It's promising to be a beautiful day today. They're saying midseventies. Perfect weather to clean the garage."

Cam reached out to grab another pillow to stuff behind him. This playful side of Sophia was still new enough to fascinate. He wouldn't have guessed that it lurked behind the professional demeanor he was used to seeing. There were a lot of things he wouldn't have guessed about her.

"I could eat off the floor of your garage. Garages have grease. They have clutter. It isn't natural to have everything hung up and neatly stored away. I'd lose my man card if I made your garage any cleaner." Enjoying himself hugely, he shook his head, dug into the eggs again. "Sorry. I won't willingly surrender my man card, even for you."

When she reached over as if to take the tray away, he added hastily, "That isn't to say that I'm not willing to do something else to repay you."

Without missing a beat, she reached beneath the tray for the newspaper and held it out to him. The Iowa Life section had been extracted from the bulk of the Sunday *Des Moines Register* and laid neatly on top. "Really? As it happens . . ."

Feeling indulgent, he scanned the headline before him. "Des Moines Arts Festival? I thought that was usually next month."

"It was moved up this year because of the road repair projects slated for downtown this summer."

He made a nonchalant sound and continued eating.

"You've been to it before. You said that's where you got the picture in your family room."

"Lots of walking." He pretended to grouse. Tipping the cup of coffee to his lips, he hid his grin at her crestfallen expression. "Crowds. Strollers everywhere. Plus there's a Cubs game on today. Doubleheader with Cincinnati."

He reached out for the last slice of bacon, but she beat him to it. Brought it slowly to her lips. "Of course I can always DVR the game," he said quickly.

She lowered the bacon back to the plate on the tray. "You could, couldn't you?" Leaning forward, Sophie gave him a much-too-brief kiss before bounding from the bed. "I'm going to take a quick shower before going home to change. You can pick me up at ten."

Cam took the bacon and savored it as he shook out the newspaper for the sports page. He could think of far worse ways to spend a sunny May afternoon than strolling around with Sophie, crowds or no crowds. He knew for a fact that they sold beer at the festival. Probably the only way to get guys to attend, but it worked for him. And ice cream. He was definitely going to get ice cream if they stayed past—

A manila envelope landed on the bedcovers beside him. Frowning, he picked it up. Turned it over. It must have been tucked inside the newspaper folds, but there was no writing on either side. He sent a quick glance toward the closed door to the adjoining bathroom. He could hear the water running. Sophie was already in the shower.

He opened the clasp, half expecting to find some sort of additional inducement to accompany her today. His gut tightened when he saw the images depicted on the pages before him.

There was a picture taken from the street in front of his condo. Another zoomed in on the address plate attached next to his front door. Yet another close-up of the license plate on his car. A shot of the DCI headquarters. And the last was of Cam and another man. One he hadn't seen since that last fateful day in California.

This was the picture he studied the longest. Matthew Baldwin. He remembered when it had been taken. Gabriela, Matt's wife, had snapped it on the afternoon of their baby's christening. Cam had managed to evade accepting the role of godfather for the baby. The hypocrisy of the act had been too much for him to swallow. But he hadn't attempted to stay away from the festivities. Wouldn't have tried.

The danger of any undercover work wasn't just the constant threat of exposure. Or dealing with men to whom human life had less value than a warm pizza. It was getting to know the people he was investigating too well. Getting too close. Seeing them as more than just criminals and recognizing they had good qualities as well as bad.

The scumbags were easy. But not all the people he'd met in the undercover task force investigation had been scumbags.

Despite his best efforts, Matt had become a friend. And that friendship had led to a decision that even now kept Cam awake nights.

Staring at the photo in his hand, he wondered grimly what that decision was going to cost him.

Cam's vision was blurred from reading the ViCAP reports, yet again. There had to be something he'd missed in them. An offender like the one they were seeking didn't spring from nowhere.

He evolved.

That's what Sophie had said, and it was likely true. But there should be similar details from the assaults that would link earlier crimes to the bodies they'd found in the cemeteries. He'd resubmitted a more general search with rape, cigar burns, and the Midwest as the key elements. The result was a ream of data he'd yet to completely get through. Certainly he hadn't hit on an offender matching all three qualities in Iowa.

Yet.

Franks disconnected the call he was on, looked at Cam. "That was Officer Gomez, the uniform Treelord assigned to Humphrey. He's been outside the guy's address for hours, but there's been no sign of him so far."

"One of the terms of Humphrey's release was a six o'clock curfew," Cam said. "I'd like to verify that he's home where he's supposed to be. Call him." Franks was looking the number up in their violent felon file. "And if he doesn't answer, have the uniform go up to his door."

Cam picked up his cell and redialed Mitch Mead. Once again there was no answer. Parole officers were used to being on duty even after hours, so the lack of response bothered Cam a bit. Not that Mead wasn't entitled to a private life. But he'd never had a parole officer fail to answer a call, regardless of the time.

He got up to get the file from Franks. Humphrey's information included not only a listed number for Zipsy's place of business but one for the owner himself. Cam dialed it, shooting a look at Franks as he waited impatiently. The agent shook his head. Humphrey wasn't answering.

After several rings, an irascible greeting sounded in Cam's ear. "Mr. Zipsy, this is Agent Cameron Prescott with the Division of Criminal Investigation. I'm sorry to disturb you this evening. We're trying to locate an employee of yours, Gilbert Humphrey. Could you tell me the last time you saw him?"

"Ex-employee." The words were brimming with frustration. "And if you find the lazy son of a bitch, you can tell him that for me, too. Give a con a break, I thought. Lend a helping hand. Son of a bitch all but spit in my eye."

"Was he at work today?"

"If he'd a shown up for work, I wouldn't be firing him, would I? Two days since I last saw him. And that's what I told that parole officer of his, too, when he called and asked about Humphrey. The guy started out all right, and, hey, hiring an ex-con comes with a pretty good tax break. But the tax break don't mean shit if the guy leaves me shorthanded."

Sifting through the litany of complaints, Cam zeroed in on the one bit of information that interested him. "And when did you last speak to Mr. Mead?"

"Who? Oh, you mean the parole officer. Called him yesterday about noon to let him know that Humphrey hadn't shown up for work. That's our deal. Humphrey is supposed to let the parole officer know if he's sick or something, and then call me. But neither of them called, so I contacted Mead. He said he'd check on Humphrey for me. Never heard from him, either."

It wasn't clear from his voice who Zipsy was more unhappy with, Mead or Humphrey. "Have you ever seen Mr. Humphrey driving a white or navy cargo van?"

The man gave a contemptuous laugh. "Driving? Where would he get the money for wheels? Humphrey took the bus to and from the job."

"What were his duties while he worked for you?"

"Whatever I told him to do. Sweep up the office, or file things sometimes, but mostly I had him showing people cars for parts they were interested in. The guy was strong as an ox. That was one good thing about him. He ran the end loader I have for moving heavier car parts, but I've seen him shoulder a bench car seat and walk it across the yard for a customer like it was nothing. Guy like that came in handy in my line of work."

"So he mainly worked at your salvage yard." Tommy was openly listening, but Jenna was engrossed in something online.

"Where the fuck—" The man apparently remembered at the last moment who he was talking to. He amended his tone. "Where else would he be working?"

"I understand you own another business property." He picked up the slip of paper to read the address Jenna had scribbled on it earlier. But the man was answering before he got the words out.

"Yeah, I own it but there's no business going on there. Just an old warehouse. I use it for storage mostly, but a few months ago I had Humphrey and another guy I employ over there cleaning it up. They're redeveloping some blocks in that neighborhood for lofts and office space. I figure it's only a matter of time before a real estate agent comes knocking on my door with an offer on that space. I don't plan to sell cheap."

Cutting in before the man could expound on his canny business sense, Cam said, "And you have the only key?"

"Got an extra in my office, but, yeah, I'm the only one with access. And I'm careful with my office stuff. I mean, when you hire ex-cons, you have to be, right?"

"I appreciate your time, Mr. Zipsy. If I need more information I'll call you back."

The man's shrug sounded in his words. "Don't know why. Can't tell you anything else. But suit yourself." Without further elaboration he hung up.

"Bingo!" Jenna was doing a self-congratulatory fist pump even as Cam finished his conversation. "Cam, you should go to work for the psychic hotline. Your talents are wasted here. Humphrey has a license but no vehicle. He's been a safe motorist, no moving violations, but there's a traffic camera image of him snapped five days ago, two blocks north of Zipsy's abandoned warehouse. And he's driving a white cargo van." She turned her laptop screen around to show them.

Squinting at the image, Franks observed, "Doesn't leave him much time to paint the van a different color in time to snatch Sophia yesterday."

"He wouldn't necessarily have had to paint the vehicle. He could have foiled it." Cam looked at Jenna, his brows raised. "You've heard of that, right? There's a film you can get to apply over vehicles for temporary color changes. Applies like window tinting. Costs a good amount to have it done professionally, but if a person had some know-how, a cargo van wouldn't be especially difficult compared to a car. Not as many curves and angles to work around."

A slow smile crossed Cam's lips. "Sometimes she surprises you, doesn't she?" he said in an aside to Franks.

The other agent was peering at his cell phone. "Scares me more often than she surprises me." Apparently finding the contact he was looking for, he pressed a button and brought the phone to his ear.

"My uncle's a teacher but paints cars on the side," Jenna said, exuberance from her discovery still sounding in her voice. "I've actually watched him foil a car. Unless you find someone who works cheap, like my uncle, it's not all that much less expensive than a professional paint job. But if you can do it yourself, the cost of the materials wouldn't amount to more than a few hundred dollars."

Cam studied her, half listening to Tommy's conversation. "Where do they buy the materials?"

Jenna was already shaking her head. "I know what you're thinking. Auto stores and department stores with an automotive department would carry them, but my uncle always orders from a discount place on the Internet. A lot of Chinese outfits sell everything you'd need for the job online."

Cam tucked the information away for further reference. First he wanted to be certain that Marchand's vehicle had, indeed, had the color changed. And he needed to talk to Humphrey himself. He would have preferred to have Mead with him when he approached the man, but he wasn't willing to wait around. "Good find, Jenna."

Franks was tucking his phone away. "I just called a friend of mine who's a parole officer. Took a chance, asked if he knew Mead, and he said he did. Not that surprising. The officers in the fifth district are spread pretty thin. He said they'd had a training meeting today in Ankeny and Mead wasn't there." The other agent lifted a shoulder. "Could be on vacation. Or out sick."

Cam shoved away from his desk. "I want answers now. It's only half past eight. Let's drop in on Stacy Marchand this evening and get a look at her van for ourselves. It might be harder to find her at home if we wait until Saturday. I'd like to ask her some questions about her brother."

Jenna and Tommy rose. "And then?" Jenna inquired as she bent to reach for her purse.

Shrugging into his suit coat, Cam said, "And then I want to track down Gilbert Humphrey and have a little chat with him."

Terror had Sophia's brain freezing. She measured the distance to the gate with her gaze. The man hadn't locked it behind him. Then he shifted his bulk, and her heart plummeted. She'd never make it by him. One look at the smirk on his face told her that he was waiting for her to try. That he'd actually enjoy her attempt.

The man's chest was padded to a cartoonish degree. He bore several tattoos, some she recognized as prison tats. She'd seen similar ones adorning criminals she'd interviewed over the years. He had two half sleeves and a large tattoo on his back, as well.

Tendrils of fear curled through her veins as she recalled that this man was every bit as sadistic as some of the most notorious men she'd profiled.

The main difference was the men she'd conducted the interviews on had been safely behind bars. They'd worn shackles and leg irons to the interviews. Here, she was the one kept caged. The one at this sadist's mercy.

His hands went to his waistband. The gym shorts were tented with his erection. Sophia clawed through the fear and panic for reason. "Time is of the essence to release the new profile. But, of course, you know that."

His hands stilled. "Plenty of time for that after some instruction. Crawl over here on all fours and suck me off. Do me real good, and we'll start easy with the fucking before the beating." His wide smile showed a missing bottom left incisor. "High-and-mighty doctor bitch like you has probably never been fucked hard and proper. I'm gonna teach you to take it in ways you never imagined."

The wild flutter of panic had calmed in her chest, replaced with grim resolve. She'd put off the inevitable as long as possible. And then . . .

"I'm eager to learn, but I'm also eager to make amends for the mistakes in the profile that got released."

You have a natural empathy that people respond to. Frein's long-ago words sounded in her mind. *It can be an insightful tool or a weapon to combat the subject's attempts at manipulation. Use it.*

"If you'll agree to be interviewed and I work all night, I can have something ready to be delivered to the media in time for the morning news. You'll want to act fast. We don't want the talking heads discounting the new profile by saying I've fallen victim to Stockholm syndrome."

The man's expression was blank. "What the hell are you talking about?"

Sophia tread carefully. She was completely blowing smoke here, and she hoped the stranger wouldn't realize it. "I'm sure you've seen movies or read articles about it. There's a theory that the longer a victim is kept, the more he or she begins to sympathize with his or her captors. If the so-called experts called on by the media say I've been missing long enough to have fallen victim to Stockholm, the profile won't get the attention it deserves." Although the theory had gained acceptance in the past, it was losing favor with experts in more recent times. Sophia had never ascribed to it herself. The symptoms correlated to the syndrome could more easily be attributed to brainwashing and a natural deterioration of reasoning as a victim adapted to his or her new reality.

But she prayed this man didn't realize that.

"Stockholm syndrome. I think I heard that in a movie once."

A tiny ribbon of hope unfurled as the man didn't move toward her. "You know all this, of course. But a handwritten profile would be best. It would allow a handwriting expert to compare samples of my writing and verify the authorship." She forced a tiny smile. "The most important thing is to correct the inaccurate profile. But the media will be talking about this for days. Everyone will know just how wrong I was about you."

For a bulky man, he moved with lightning speed. The blow snapped her head back. Her ears rang, and tears of pain sprang to her eyes. "And I'm just supposed to believe you're really that eager

183

to get the right information on me out there, huh? You must think I'm fucking stupid!" His voice had risen on each word until he was screaming the last at her.

Eddies of agony shimmied through her right jaw. Even her teeth ached. His anger had risen so suddenly, so violently, that Sophia knew her earlier guess had been accurate. If the man wasn't on steroids, he was on some other substance that increased violence and impulsivity. Which made him even more dangerous.

"I'm not offering to do it for you!" The quaver in her tone owed little to pretense. But her words were pure fabrication. "I don't tolerate mistakes. Not in myself. Not in others. I have to make this right. I owe that to you and to myself. And then I must be punished for my error. My mother taught me that. I expect it."

The way he was studying her made her flesh crawl. It was tortuous to lie there under his gaze, pretending to be docile and subjugated.

Worse still to consider how long it would take for the pretense to become a reality at the hands of this man.

"I had an old man who taught me the same thing. He was tough on me, but it didn't hurt me any. Taught me how to be a man."

Sophia was pretty sure what his father's treatment had taught him. A sadistic predator evolved . . . and often that development began in childhood. She'd have to use what she knew about men like this one, and everything she suspected about this offender in particular for the cat-and-mouse game she was engaged in.

She only hoped she could maintain the farce.

"Okay. We'll get the interview shit out of the way so you can earn your keep correcting the lies you told about me. Wait here." He cackled, bent down to grab his shirt, and pulled it on carelessly. "Guess you don't have a choice about that, though, do you?"

Sophia watched closely as he swung open the gate and pulled it shut after him. He stepped outside her line of vision for an instant, but a moment later he was back, fitting the key in the lock securing the gate. He strode away, taking the spotlight with him. His muffled footsteps grew fainter. Then there was the creak of a door opening.

It hadn't escaped her notice that she hadn't heard him close the door behind him. Which said he wasn't going far. But the relief that swamped her just from being released from his presence for a few moments was almost overpowering. She was only buying herself some time. Time was a valuable commodity in comparison with the other plans the man had for her.

Somehow she had to continue the pretense she'd begun for a few more hours. If she could stall long enough, she might be able to put him off until tomorrow. That would give her another day to find a way out of her prison.

And in that time she'd also have to avoid inciting the offender's temper again. Which would be a trick without knowing his triggers. She touched her throbbing jaw gingerly. She had more than a decade's experience speaking with men like him. Writing detailed analyses about who they were. What had formed them.

But this was the first time her life depended on it.

⁓

"I just told you—I can't show you the van because my husband has it." The truculence in Stacy Marchand's voice was mirrored in her expression. In her body language. Her arms were folded tightly across her chest, a strand of limp blonde hair in her face. Shaking it back, she jutted out her chin. "Why are you interested in it, anyway? It hasn't been in an accident, if that's what you think. We're both of us careful drivers. We get a deal on our insurance, because neither of us has ever gotten so much as a ticket."

"What about your brother, Gilbert Humphrey?" Cam watched her expression closely. "Is he a careful driver?"

There wasn't so much as a flicker of emotion in the woman's expression. "What's my brother got to do with anything?"

"He drives it, too, doesn't he?"

She shook her head vehemently in answer to Cam's question. "No. It's just me and my husband. None of the kids are old enough to drive yet, so we're the only insured drivers . . ." Her voice trailed away as Tommy took the blown-up image taken from the traffic camera two days ago. The license plate and driver were clearly visible.

Her thin shoulders hunched. "Okay, so I let my brother drive it a couple of times. He's got a valid license. It's not a crime. At least . . ." She suddenly looked worried. "That's not insurance fraud, is it? To let someone else use my vehicle? I'm pretty sure it's not, but these policies can be tricky sometimes. I don't want to get jammed up and lose my good driver discount."

"We're not here about the insurance." Cam kept his voice patient. The three agents were standing on the small concrete stoop outside the neat single-story brick home. Marchand was positioned on the other side of the screen door. She'd made no move to open it. He had the distinct impression that she'd like nothing better than to slam the door in their faces.

Though it had grown dark the occasional child went by on a scooter or skateboard. Since Marchand gave none of them a glance, he assumed they didn't belong to her. The dim sound of children's voices came from somewhere in the house. Maybe her kids were all accounted for.

"Look." Now her tone was weary. "I hold down a job. I pay my taxes. I belong to my kids' school parent organization, for god's sake. My brother isn't a great guy, but he's my brother. So he borrowed my van a couple times. If he owes on a ticket, I'm sure I'll hear about it, and then he'll hear about it. He'll make good on it. He's got a job, and he's trying, you know?"

From what they'd learned just an hour earlier, Cam remained unconvinced of that statement. But he had no evidence to disbelieve that Marchand wasn't the hardworking mom that she presented herself as. And he knew just how difficult it would be to have a brother with Humphrey's background.

"Where does your husband have the van?"

"He and his buddies drove it to South Dakota to go prairie dog hunting." She lifted her shoulders. Dropped them again. "They go every year. Just an excuse for a bunch of grown men to get away, drink beer, and act like fools if you ask me, but if it keeps him happy . . . He'll be back in three days."

"And what color was the van when your husband took it?"

Her brows came together. "What do you mean, what color was it? You can see in that picture the agent has. It's white."

"What's the longest time your brother's ever had it in his possession?"

She stared at him with shrewd blue eyes. "I can't figure out whether you're interested in Gil or the van. He's had it overnight a couple times. He needed it to move into his apartment when he got out. He had things in storage to haul. And a couple days ago he used it and didn't bring it back when he said he would. Jim, my husband, was pretty hot about that, because it meant that he had to take me to work and pick me up. But when we went and got it that next night, we didn't say much, you know? Gil isn't a guy that it pays to pick a fight with."

"What do you know about your brother's friends? Where he goes when he isn't at work?"

A door slammed in the recesses of the house, followed by a loud "Mom!" Marchand tossed a look over her shoulder and shouted, "Just a minute." Then she turned to face them again. "I only know a few people he used to be friends with before he went inside. None of them were good people. I have no idea if they're still around. And I make a point of not knowing much of Gil's business, but I know he works at Zip's Auto and Salvage. I've met his parole officer once. Mead, his name is. Gil isn't supposed to go anywhere other than work, church, parole meetings, and maybe the grocery store once in a while. That makes it easy for me to avoid having him here, because to tell you the truth, I don't like having my brother around my kids. Especially my daughters. And that makes me feel like a pretty shitty sister. He's paid his debt to society and all that. But I'm a mom before I'm a sister. So I feel guilty, and I help him out when I can to make up for it. That's about all I can tell you."

A more insistent "Mom!" sounded.

"I'm coming!" Marchand called. She stepped away from the door, obviously intent on ending the conversation.

"I'd like the names of your brother's friends that you remember," Cam said quickly. "Then we'll let you get back to your family."

"Jason Dows, Mike Quinn, and Pat . . . McCormick, I think it was. It was a long time ago. They were all losers. They might even be in prison by now. I don't know and don't care." With that the door closed.

The agents headed back to their vehicles. Jenna had driven with Cam, but Franks had brought a second car in case they needed to split up later. "Seemed sincere enough," Jenna remarked. "It can't be easy for her to have a brother like that in the same town where she's raising her kids."

"We don't know how far she'd be willing to go to help him out," Franks interjected. They proceeded to the curb where they'd parked. "Pretty convenient that the van is gone for the next few days so we can't get a look at it."

"We can always check the I-80 west traffic cameras to verify her story if we need to." But in his gut Cam thought Marchand had been telling the truth about that. "I'm more interested right now in talking to Humphrey myself."

"I'll check out Humphrey's former buddies while you drive to his address." Jenna walked to Cam's car. "Something tells me we're not going to have any better luck at his apartment than Gomez did."

Humphrey lived in a brick apartment building that had given up any semblance of respectability and was firmly entrenched in deterioration. The agents got out of their vehicles and stood on the curb across the street, peering at the structure. Only a few of the streetlamps that dotted the area were on. Cam assumed vandals had targeted the rest. In this neighborhood, repair requests would be slow to be fulfilled. As fast as new bulbs could be put in, others would be broken out.

The door of the black-and-white parked several yards away opened, and a uniformed DMPD officer got out and approached them. Cam made introductions.

"Officer Val Gomez." The officer squinted toward the building. "Place looks a little better in the dark, to tell you the truth. Still no sign of Humphrey. There's an alley with a side entrance to the building, but I've got a clear view of both exits from here. I was just inside forty minutes ago. If Humphrey is in there, he's not answering the door."

"He hasn't been at work for the last two days, so no telling the last time he left the building," Cam told him. Or if he had left, how long ago. "We're going to check it out. Talk to a few of his neighbors. Give Franks a call if you spot him."

"You got it." Gomez returned to his car.

"Any chance one of Humphrey's old pals lives in this building, too?" The three of them waited for a rusted-out black pickup to go by before moving across the street.

"Marchand's a good judge of character. She called it right on a couple of the names she gave us," Jenna reported. The redhead easily kept pace with them. "McCormick is doing a five-year stretch—his second—for receiving stolen goods. Dows got out a couple years ago after doing ten years for manslaughter. His address is in the Pine Hills trailer park. Quinn isn't in the system. It'll take a bit more digging to track him down."

The steps to the building were concrete, flanked with wide brick and cement railings. All were cracked and in need of repair. The front door bore the scars of numerous assaults through the years. The knob turned under Cam's hand, and he pushed the door open.

The foyer was dimly lit by a wire-enclosed bulb. In contrast to the relative quiet of the street out front, Cam could hear a baby wailing, a stereo and TV blaring from somewhere inside, and the sound of raised voices. "Which floor?"

"Third," Jenna answered.

"Of course it is," he muttered. They passed a small elevator with an Out of Order sign on it. He suspected it'd been placed there in the 1980s. They headed for the wide wooden stairway that split the foyer, with hallways flanking it. They climbed the stairs in single file. No one they passed on the stairs looked at them or spoke.

That changed when they got to the second floor. Two dark-haired, unshaven men in white, ribbed, tank undershirts stared at them coolly from their stance leaning on either side of a window. Cam didn't even want to guess why the men had been stationed there. But he recognized lookouts when he saw them. One pulled out a phone as they turned the corner to climb the next flight.

"We just got reported to someone inside," Franks muttered.

Cam figured he was right. Less than an hour ago Gomez's uniformed presence hadn't stopped whatever illicit activity was going on in apartment 209. Cam couldn't even summon the ability to care.

At midnight Sophie would have been gone almost twenty-four hours. An inner clock ticked away every passing minute. It took a massive strength of will to avoid contemplating what she might have suffered in the meantime.

Twelve days. His footsteps down the long narrow hall seemed to echo the words. Too short a time to constitute a relationship. It had begun and ended on Sophie's terms. And really, its ending had come at an opportune time. He was still waiting for the other shoe to drop with Baldwin. The man hadn't reached out again since the delivery of that one envelope. If Cam and Sophie had gotten more deeply involved, there was no way he could have done justice to the investigation of her disappearance. No way he could have shoved aside the tangle of sick fear that surged every time he allowed himself to contemplate her fate.

Nevertheless, his spine was slick with perspiration that had nothing to do with exertion. When they stopped before Humphrey's apartment, his fists were clenched. Someone started out of the apartment next door just as Cam readied to pound on number 318. Seeing the three agents, the woman ducked inside again.

"Mr. Humphrey," Cam called. "DCI. Open the door. We want to talk to you." They waited a minute. Then two. Cam listened closely. There was a jumble of sounds emanating from behind other closed doors in the hallway. But none came from 318. He knocked again. "Mr. Humphrey. Open up." He motioned to Jenna and Tommy, and the pair split, each taking a door on either side of Humphrey's to knock on. Cam pounded again, already resigned to the fact that the apartment was empty.

Jenna was having a similar lack of luck, but the woman they'd seen briefly a few minutes ago had opened the door, keeping the safety chain on. Cam moved to stand behind Tommy.

"Sorry to bother you, ma'am." The agent's voice was smooth. "We're looking for your neighbor. Can you tell me the last time you saw him?"

She gave a quick jerk of her skeletal shoulders, bared by a black, figure-hugging tank. "Don't know. Don't keep track of him. He minds his business; I mind mine. That's the way he likes it, and I don't need trouble. I steer clear—you get my drift?"

Franks persisted. "Have you seen him today?"

She shook her head and sent a furtive glance in the direction of Humphrey's door. "He won't like anyone talking about him. But he hasn't been around lately. Usually we go to work about the same time. But I didn't see him this morning or yesterday, now that I think about it. Someone else was at his door earlier. Maybe the same guy who was there yesterday. I didn't look. He ain't the type you want to rile, you know? Meaner 'n a swamp rat."

"Have you ever gotten a look at anyone who has visited him before that?"

"Saw a blonde woman here with some guy a few days ago, and they had a real loud argument with him about a van." The door was already easing shut. "That's all I can tell you. I don't even know the guy's name. I'm sort of hoping he doesn't come back."

They tried several nearby doors in the hallway, but not one of them opened, even those with sound coming from them. The word of their presence had already spread through the building, Cam realized. And this wasn't the type of place where people were interested in speaking with law enforcement.

"Let's hope we have better luck in the trailer park," he said as they turned to walk away. "Although it'd be nice to know the last time Mead saw Humphrey." He looked at Franks. "Try him again."

The agent pulled out his phone to obey. "When we get outside, I'll look up Marion Thompson's number." Thompson was the director of the judicial district department of correctional services that governed the area. As such, she oversaw the parole and probation officers assigned to offenders in the south central counties of the state. "At least she'd know where Mead is." If the officer was on vacation, Humphrey would have been assigned to another in the interim.

They hadn't gotten more than a few steps before they all stopped. Cam looked at Franks, who still had the cell phone pressed to his ear. Then at Jenna. Without a word they turned in tandem and walked back to Humphrey's door. Listened.

From inside came the unmistakable sound of a cell phone ringing.

Chapter 11

Sophie snuck a look at Cam. He was eating methodically, as if the act gave him no pleasure. She'd think the problem lay in the meal she'd prepared except that he'd once professed to love Italian food. Lasagna was hard to mess up. As such, it was one of her few specialties.

He'd been preoccupied all evening. Before. Even yesterday, when he'd called and begged off going to the art festival. The phone conversation had been stilted and oddly distant. She'd been inordinately disappointed, although of course she understood that professional obligations could crop up suddenly for both of them. In the end she'd gone to the festival with a couple of her neighbors and enjoyed herself. Except for one recurring worry that managed to niggle through every time she began to relax.

The level of disappointment she'd felt at Cam not coming had seemed disproportionate to the newness in their relationship. They'd been occasional colleagues for years, minus the time he'd spent on the task force in California. Their paths had crossed infrequently at social gatherings. Other than that, had he not happened by while she was moping over a margarita at Mickey's, the last several days would never have happened.

She brought the piece of garlic bread to her mouth and bit into it reflectively. It was frightening to think how quickly he'd managed to feel like a part of her life. Which he wasn't, of course. Couldn't be. Sophia was new to casual, but she was fairly certain by definition neither party in such a relationship was to get too serious. So it might be time to start cultivating a little distance of her own.

"I've been terrible company." Her gaze flew to his. His golden-brown eyes were serious.

"Were you preoccupied or ravenous?" she managed lightly.

"I don't know. Both?" He reached over and scooped out some more lasagna. "This is great, by the way. My mom always said the way to a man's heart is through his stomach." His wink was a little wicked and so like him that her worry eased a fraction. "Although I'd be glad to show you a more direct route."

"I don't know." She reached for her wine and pretended to consider. "In the fairy tales shortcuts always seemed to get the characters in trouble. Little Red Riding Hood. Goldilocks."

"But shortcuts can be fun. They're quicker, and you never know what you'll find along the way."

She studied him over the rim of her glass. After taking a sip of wine, she set it down. "I'm someone who prefers signposts, I'm afraid. GPS. Google Earth. I like to know exactly where I'm going."

He forked up a bite of lasagna. "We're going to have to do something about your lack of spontaneity."

It occurred to her that their banter held a deeper meaning, at least for her. She'd veered drastically from her normal path the first night she'd taken Cam home. She'd been in uncharted waters ever since. And, on the one hand, he was right. The experience had been deliciously new. Exciting. Thrilling even.

But she wasn't comfortable without a map, and, at any rate, there couldn't be shortcuts in relationships, could there?

Maybe she could get used to casual. Although Sophia didn't want it, she took another bite of bread. But she wasn't sure she could ever get used to a journey with no particular destination in mind.

The sound of the door closing again had Sophia's eyes sliding shut in a moment of despair. They reopened an instant later, resolve stiffening her spine. She'd been afraid before, especially early in her career. Even sitting across from vile, sadistic men already in prison could be harrowing. To hear the revolting details of their stories. To discern the notes of relish in their voices when they described mind-numbingly brutal atrocities. A few of them had outlined in great detail exactly what they'd like to do with her if given the chance. They'd meant to shock. They'd succeeded. But she'd managed to keep her reaction from them with a display of acting skills she'd never known she possessed. *Act unafraid and you'd be unafraid.* That had been her mantra.

But, oh, it was so much easier to hide fear when she wasn't locked up with a monster.

The man set the spotlight down in front of her cell. Sophia was shocked to see a sack full of food from Bryson's, a popular drive-through restaurant in his other hand. After putting it down, he stepped to the side for a moment and then began unlocking the gate.

Sophia filed the information away. Both times he'd entered he hadn't reached in his pocket for the key. So it was outside the cell nearby, possibly hanging from a nail or hook. Maybe she could reach it now that she knew it was there. The slats of the gate were wide enough for her to reach an arm through. Even if she could knock it to the floor, she might be able to—

"I know what you're thinking." He reached into the full sack and withdrew a sandwich. On cue, her stomach rumbled. She hadn't eaten since they'd hit a fast-food place on the way home from Edina. But thirst was a bigger concern than hunger at this point. Her mouth was so dry, she had difficulty summoning saliva. "You're thinking, can you reach the key? Was he stupid enough to put it where you could get it and escape?"

Taunting her, he held the key up for her to see. Then shifted to replace it before rejoining her. Opening the gate, he bent to grab the sack before entering and closing the gate behind him.

"When my mother would punish me, she'd often make me go in the hallway closet and shut the door." She sent up a silent apology to her mother for the lie. Helen Channing would never dream of behaving so callously to a child. But for all this man's protests, she was more certain than ever that the majority of her profile was all too accurate. By drawing similarities between them, he'd be more forthcoming, whether he meant to be or not. "There was no lock. Once she forgot me, and I was in there all night. But I didn't leave until she came for me."

He threw the bag to her. She fumbled the catch, but made no attempt to open it, despite the pangs of hunger that were gnawing through her. "Because she'd have beat your ass harder."

"No, because my punishment wasn't over." She saw his quick look, kept her expression guileless.

His gaze narrowed. A trickle of fear snaked down her spine. "What are you waiting for? Maybe it was too soon to feed you. Maybe I should have waited until tomorrow."

"I'm waiting for permission to eat."

She felt a flicker of triumph at his look of surprise. He was caught off guard. Sophia didn't know how she could use that to her advantage, but she realized instinctively that her success depended on making him believe the tale she was spinning.

"Go ahead."

There was a covered plastic cup with a straw in the bag. Sophia grabbed that first. Drank. The water was tepid but was an instant balm to her dry mouth and throat. She forced herself to stop after drinking half of it. Only then did she give in to her hunger. It was all she could do to not rip the wrapping from the sandwich and devour it in a few quick bites. But she made herself take a small bite of the hamburger. Chew. It was cold and tasteless. "Thank you."

"Did you think I was going to starve you? I'm not a monster." He made a move toward her. She dragged the edge of the comforter she was wrapped in and got off the mattress to sit on the cement floor, hoping he'd take the gesture as subservient. In reality she wasn't certain she could carry on the farce if he touched her again. "Besides, I got other plans for you. Want to hear a few?" He watched her face avidly as he graphically detailed what he had in store for her.

Sophia held on to the memory of the incarcerated felons she'd interviewed who had tried the same tactic. He was looking for a reaction as much as they had been. But while outward dispassion had been the correct response for those men, this one required different handling. She let none of her revulsion show, but she didn't have to fake the fear in her expression. From the glint of satisfaction in his eyes, she knew it had pleased him.

"Better get this interview over with so we can get to the good part." He reached down to stroke his bulging erection. "My old man always said it was a shame to waste good wood."

His continual state of arousal surely was chemically induced. Sophia wondered if whatever substance he was abusing had left him impotent, or if he took an erectile dysfunction medication as a tool for perpetuating his sexual abuse. Her mouth dried. It was hard to be subjective about the question when faced with the evidence.

"What should I write on?" He hadn't fetched a notepad. She was hoping that meant he'd have to leave. Perhaps for an hour or more. Long enough to try getting away again.

"Book smart, street dumb, aren't you? Typical." He took a pen he'd tucked in his waistband under his shirt and tossed it at her. "Figure it out."

Her heart did a nosedive. He wasn't going anywhere. Wings of despair fluttered in her chest. And this time she couldn't quite banish them by sheer force of will. Sophia felt her final chances to escape this—escape him—dwindling.

But though the interview might only prolong the inevitable, every moment felt like a reprieve. She felt a measure of resolve returning. His earlier words echoed in her mind.

I'm not a monster.

Spoken like a true deviant. She picked up the sack the food had come in. It was slightly damp from the moisture from the cup. Carefully she tore it until it was flat. Then she smoothed the sandwich wrapper, set it aside. The interviews she'd done with incarcerated violent offenders had run to hundreds of pages. The criminal profile she'd developed for this man was nearly twenty.

She'd been given two "pages" to write the correction.

"All right." Drawing upon every hour of experience she'd acquired over the years, she looked up at him expectantly. "My condo doesn't allow animals," she lied. "But I think if it did I'd have a cat. I was never allowed a pet when I was a child. Do you have one?"

"Cats." He made a sound of disgust. "Figures. Worthless animals. Pets are too much damn trouble, but if I had one, I'd have a dog. At least they can learn to obey." The words weren't surprising. Psychopaths and sociopaths normally preferred dogs for that very reason. Cats were willful. And dogs could be counted on for unconditional love.

"And that's important to you. Teaching those around you to obey."

He shot her a quick look. "You'll find out for yourself soon enough."

She went on seamlessly. "Which did you have as a child?"

The man's smile was humorless. Chilling. "We didn't have either. I was the pet. Sounds like you were, too. But I wasn't near as good a student as you. And my mother didn't use closets."

He was referring to the lies she'd told him regarding her childhood. Sophia felt a small glimmer of self-satisfaction. It meant he'd believed them. And it was imperative that she keep spinning the tale to establish a bond between them.

She didn't fool herself that the connection would impact his final plans for her. He'd use what she shared to taunt her. But his expectations of her behavior would be different based on his earliest impressions of her. And that was what Sophia would use to manipulate him, given a chance.

He made a production of stretching out on the mattress. Folding his arms beneath his head. "Is this how your patients do it, Doc?"

"A few do. Many sit in chairs positioned across from mine. The most important thing is for them to feel comfortable."

"I'd feel more comfortable if you came over and gave me a blow job. You do that for your patients?"

Sophia treaded carefully. She needed to project as professional an image as possible to get him to open up to her. But if the proper deference weren't shown, she'd incite another explosive response from him. "I don't, no. But then I don't think I've ever had a client with your intellect. Most can't seem to manage the simplest obstacles life throws their way. You've smashed through all such roadblocks and pulled off the perfect crime." She waggled the pen in her fingers at him. "Quite a difference."

"Most people are idiots. They work at crappy jobs, taking all the shit their bosses shovel their way, and whine about how bad things are. They don't try to make things better."

"How would you advise people to make their lives better?"

He rose to a sitting position in one smooth movement and shot a finger in her direction. "There are two kinds of people in the world. Those that are helpless and those that help themselves. If I want something bad enough, what do you think I would do?"

The answer came without having to think. "You'd find a way to take it."

His smile was crafty. Once again she noted the missing tooth. Made a note of its exact location. Perhaps she could somehow bury a description of the man within the context of the profile.

"Maybe you got half a brain buried in there somewhere after all. Yeah, I would. But I couldn't take anything if people weren't stupid. Like you. Got a fancy security system. Even have the garage entry to the place secured. But you think an automatic garage door protects you. It doesn't." His wink had the hair on her neck rising. "That's what I'm good at. Like you say, I don't see obstacles. I see ways around them."

Sophia was unsurprised. A conscience served as an impediment to criminal behavior. The lack of one put him a step ahead. Because it was difficult to combat an enemy who wasn't bound by a similar moral code.

In the next instant, his demeanor changed. Grew threatening. "You're not writing anything down."

"I have nearly perfect auditory recall." It was the first truth she'd offered him. Gesturing toward the sack and wrapper, she continued. "My profiles run several pages. But I have to make every word count this time. So I'll do without notes and rely on my memory." Not so very hard to do, since she'd be writing a fallacy meant to stroke his ego, rather than a professional judgment.

"Hope for your sake your memory is as good as you claim." He shifted on the mattress to sit, leaning back against one wooden wall. "I'm not known to be a patient teacher."

"Patience is merely permission for people to repeat the same mistakes." The quote could be attributed to one of the offenders she'd interviewed years ago. But this man wouldn't know that.

"Whatever." He lifted a shoulder. His steady stare was unnerving. Sophia found herself wishing that he'd lie down again so she wouldn't have to face him directly. "Mine is running out. So why don't we cut to the chase, and you can ask me about my favorite childhood memory. The day I killed my old man."

***

"I don't know," Isaac Mackey said, stalling in the act of finding the proper key for the lock on Humphrey's door. "Word gets around I'm letting cops into people's apartments, who's gonna rent from me?"

"If you ignore a warrant and end up in jail for obstruction, who's going to rent from you?" Cam's voice was steely. "Open it."

Mackey bore a ratty T-shirt, stringy goatee, and questionable hygiene. He sucked in his bottom lip in what appeared to be a laborious attempt to think. "Maybe I should call a lawyer."

"You understand what a warrant is, right? We're looking for a missing person." It was difficult to temper his frustration. Time had seemed to speed up to sprint pace after Franks had redialed Mead's number a second time, while they'd all stood outside this door earlier. There had been no mistaking the timing of the ringing emanating from inside Humphrey's apartment. "We have reason to believe he was here earlier. His cell phone is still inside. Open the door, or I'll do it myself."

"You better do what he says," Jenna murmured. "No use you getting jammed up in someone else's mess, right?"

Mackey stole a glance at Cam's expression. Whatever he saw there had him hastening to select the right keys from his ring. One for the lock and another for a dead bolt. Once he'd unsecured both, he pushed the door open for them but remained rooted in place in the hallway. "I'm not goin' in. Nuh-uh. Bad enough explaining to this guy what happened. That dude is mean."

Cam brushed by him. "Call the number again." He spoke the words over his shoulder, but Franks was already holding the cell and pressing "Redial." The apartment boasted a kitchen wedged into one corner, opening to a postage-stamp-size living space. Moments later a ringing sounded in the apartment. There were only two other doors, presumably to a bathroom and bedroom.

It was coming from the bathroom. Cam drew his weapon. The other two agents did the same. His gaze met Jenna's, and without a word she moved to the bedroom while they approached the closed door of the bathroom. A few moments later she returned and gave a quick shake of her head. Standing to the side of the bathroom door, he reached out to turn the knob, swinging it open as he and Franks leveled their weapons to cover the space.

But the area was minuscule. Barely big enough for its one occupant.

Who was currently duct-taped to the cast-iron sewer pipe running up the cracked wall behind the toilet.

Cam quickly holstered his weapon to approach the man while Franks left the room. Lifting his head, Cam checked the pulse in his throat. It was weak, but steady.

Jenna picked up the wallet lying at the man's feet. It was empty of money, but both the parole officer's driver's license and employee ID were in it. "It's Mead."

"Humphrey." The word was garbled between split lips, but it had Cam's attention jerking to the bound man. He hadn't realized Mead was conscious. His body was limp. Both eyes were ringed with rainbow colors, and one was completely swollen shut. "Gone."

"Do you know where he went?"

But the effort seemed to have drained the other man. Cam could hear Jenna in the other room on her cell summoning an ambulance before placing a call to Gomez. Franks returned and Cam took one of the knives he'd found by rummaging in the kitchen drawers. The two agents went to work freeing Mead from the tape.

"See this?" Cam called Tommy's attention to a wound at the back of Mead's head that had bled profusely. "He must have been out long enough for Humphrey to drag him in here and tie him up."

"Put up a hell of a fight first, from the look of his fists," Franks observed as he went about slicing through the tape. When the two of them had the man free, it was Cam who caught him and laid him down as gently as possible on the floor. "Call Treelord and get a BOLO out on Humphrey. Give him Quinn's address in Pine Hill. And they'll need to check Marchand's address, too." Even while he'd tended to believe Stacy Marchand, it had been evident the woman was somewhat fearful of her brother. If Humphrey had insisted, he doubted Marchand would have been able to resist a demand to hide at her house.

He went to the bedroom and pulled the sheet off the bed to cover the wounded man with. Then he placed a call himself.

"Mr. Zipsy, this is Agent Prescott again. We're going to need to look at your vacant property tonight. Yes, sir, right now." His glance fell to Mead then, who was moving restlessly. "I realize the hour, but I'm afraid I'm going to have to insist. We'll meet you at the address in thirty minutes."

It was closer to forty minutes before Cam knocked on the window of the car parked in front of the warehouse. The window powered down. "This is a bunch of bullshit." Cam had never met Zipsy, so he couldn't ID the individual behind the wheel, but he recognized the irritable voice. "Drag me out of bed on a fool's errand. There ain't nothing to do tonight that can't be done tomorrow morning. I'm gonna make damn sure your boss hears about this, too."

"How many other entrances to the place?" Cam cut through the man's grousing.

"Got a single door and two double overhead doors, front and back. But I disabled the mechanism to open the front overhead doors. Figure I don't need to be inviting trouble. And the single-door entrance in back is boarded up. Has been ever since some asswipe decided to break in last year."

When the man started out of the car, Cam's voice halted him. "I'll take the keys, Mr. Zipsy. You stay here and wait."

"Hell if I will!" With the aid of the interior light in the man's beat-up car, Cam could easily interpret the jut of his chin. "My property, remember. I'll be the one to go in."

"I'm afraid I can't allow that. And the longer you sit here and argue about it, the more sleep you'll be missing."

The older man argued for a little longer, but in the end, apparently deciding Cam was immovable, he turned off the car and took out his keys. He removed two from the ring with movements jerky with temper. "Top one opens the door lock and the next the dead bolt. You and I are going to have a little chat after you go in there and find the damn place empty." He thrust the keys out the window toward Cam, who took them and started walking away. "You can be thinking about your apology now!"

"Always nice to work with cooperative citizens," Franks gibed as he and Jenna walked rapidly with Cam toward the dark building. The area was totally enshrouded in shadows. Not even an occasional security light relieved the darkness. It was as if the owners of the buildings had given up protecting their investment long ago.

Cam switched on the Maglite he'd extracted from the trunk of his vehicle. Waited for the other two agents to do the same. "According to Zipsy, only the overhead doors are in working order in the back, but be ready in case someone inside heads out that way." He handed his light to Jenna, fitted the top key into the door-knob, and then used the second to unlock the dead bolt. He took a moment to slip both keys into his pocket before taking the Maglite from Jenna, drawing his weapon and easing the door open.

It took his eyes a moment to adjust to the black interior. They swept the place quickly with their flashlights, the beams cutting through the darkness. Then they slowed for a closer look at the area.

The last use of the place had obviously been for receiving. Partitioned holding pens lined two stone walls. At one time Cam imagined the place had been a bustle of activity with semis being packed and unpacked and skid loaders scooting around with heavier goods.

Now the empty quiet was eerie.

The agents spread out, searching the area in a grid pattern. Once Cam thought he heard the scrape of a shoe overhead. He stopped, straining to listen. In the next moment he decided the noise had come from one of the other agents. He continued to the far wall of holding pens, determined to get a look inside each of them. Although the place was empty now, that didn't mean that Humphrey hadn't used it earlier.

Halfway to the stall nearest him he heard another noise, and this time it was unmistakable.

The sound of footsteps upstairs.

Cam whirled, playing his light over Jenna to catch her attention, and then motioning with it toward the upstairs. She and Franks were closer to the door they'd all entered through. By the time Cam had caught up with them, they were shining their flashlights at a battered steel door set in one corner of the interior wall. Its doorknob was missing. Franks reached out and pressed it open with the heel of his palm while Jenna kept her Maglite focused on the stairs inside.

Footprints were visible in the thick dust on each tread. At least two sets.

The agents took the stairs single file, Cam in the lead. He made every effort at silence but couldn't avoid the occasional squeak of old boards. Every time the telltale noise sounded, beneath either his weight or the other agents', he held his breath. Waited to hear footsteps overhead approaching the door.

Or perhaps whoever was up there would find a hiding place to prepare an ambush.

At the top of the narrow stairway was another scarred steel door. It was also missing the doorknob. He took a moment to wonder whether the person upstairs had been the one to remove them.

Weapon ready, he shifted to the opposite side of the steps before slowly pushing the door open. The area was one open space without interior walls. A single portable strobe lit the area. Black paper had been taped over all the windows. Cam realized immediately why the upper story had been chosen. The ceilings were significantly lower here, and crossed with large metal ventilation tubes. Highlighted in the center of the lit space was a nude spread-eagled figure. Ropes secured to wrists and ankles were tossed over the ventilation tubes and retied to hooks that had likely been bolted to the walls for this express purpose.

Blood pooled at the captive's feet. There was a flash of movement from a second person crouched there, and a muffled sound of agony was heard.

"You have two choices." The voice came from the man, who rose to stand before the bound victim. "Do what I say, or die right now like the worthless piece of shit you are. What's your life worth to you?"

Cam had heard enough. He charged through the door, the other two agents right behind him. "Drop your weapon," he barked and sidled along the wall to get an unobstructed shot at the offender. "Now!"

"Clear!"

"Clear!"

Jenna's and Tommy's voices came almost simultaneously. An instant later Gilbert Humphrey lunged toward the victim and Cam fired once, kicking up splinters of wood at his feet. Screaming an expletive, the man jumped back.

"The next bullet goes center mass." Cam's voice was conversational as he drew closer. "Ever had a sucking chest wound? Few recover. But if you're feeling lucky, go ahead. Try to use that knife again."

Slowly, as if the digits were having difficulty taking orders from his brain, Humphrey's fingers opened. The knife clattered to the floor.

"Step back. Further." He waited until the man was out of range of the weapon. "On your belly, hands behind your head. I'm sure you know the position." He waited for the man to obey before moving to handcuff him. Only then did he rise and look toward the victim.

A man. Slight and small of stature but definitely a male. Somehow that awareness had already made its way through Cam's brain, and the disappointment crashing through him was nearly overpowering.

He lowered his weapon. The other agents began working at the ropes keeping the captive upright. His torso and groin was covered with red-stained slices, superficial cuts that would have been agonizing, but none were life threatening. He and the other agents had arrived before Humphrey had gotten what he wanted from the man.

At this point, Cam couldn't even bring himself to care what that might be. With a sense of déjà vu, he took out his cell phone. Called for an ambulance and a police response. He didn't look at the time on his cell's screen. Didn't have to. His mental alarm was shrilling loudly.

Nearly twenty-four hours since Sophie had been abducted. Two victims rescued during that time frame. Neither of them the person they were looking for. At this point they were no closer to finding her than they'd been at seven that morning.

He felt Jenna's hand on his arm then but didn't dare look at her. He was too afraid of what she'd see in his eyes.

Sophie. Her name was a desolate howl through his system, leaving an arctic path in its wake. *Where the hell are you?*

"Do you want to tell me about your father's death?" Sophia kept her tone carefully nonjudgmental.

"Sure." Her captor leaned forward on the mattress, a gleam in his eye that chilled. But the emotion there wasn't directed at her. Not this time. It was turned inward, as if relishing a treasured memory. "I took his hunting knife. Bastard kept it sharpened, to field dress whatever he shot. Never could figure whether he loved hunting or giving beatings best. I hid the knife, and the next time he tried using his belt on me, I cut his fucking throat."

"That must have been satisfying."

He laughed then, that high-pitched cackle that was so at odds with his muscle-bound appearance. "That must have been satisfying," he mimicked. "It would have been a pleasure. I fantasized a dozen different ways to off the asshole. But he died when the oil derrick he was working on exploded. Good riddance. Then there was just me and my mom."

"Tell me about her," Sophia invited. An abusive background didn't cause children to grow up to commit the sort of atrocities this man had. And not all serial killers were the products of dysfunctional homes. But for many of the offenders she'd interviewed, the roots of their violence could be traced to their childhoods.

"Want to know about dear old Ma?" His expression was derisive. "Look in the mirror. She was a worthless cunt just like every other female walking the earth. My father was a bastard, but at least he worked. Stayed away for weeks at a time on the oil rigs, and that was just fine with us. Problem was, I looked just like him. So when he left, everything she woulda liked to do to the old man got done to me."

"She abused you, as well."

He lifted a shoulder, as if unwilling to admit that any woman, at any time of his life, had had power over him. "Best thing about when the old man did come home was watching him whale on her. And once she was on the floor, she was in the right position." Sophia's flesh prickled at the glee in his tone. "He'd mount her right there, on the kitchen floor. Maybe he'd forget I was there. Maybe he didn't care. That's another of my favorite childhood memories. I'd get hard watching and have to run outside to find a knothole or something to whack off in."

And thus violence and sex were forever paired for this man, Sophia thought. Humans were intricate, complex creatures. Others would have survived such horrors at home, becoming manipulative and aggressive without criminal tendencies. Some would have spent the rest of their years building a life that was the exact opposite of what they'd endured. Something inside this man's mind had propelled him to continue the abuse of his youth. To exceed it.

It was as if the memories had opened a floodgate. Sophia listened as much to how he phrased his words as to the content itself, counting the times he referred to himself. Narcissistic personalities used far more *I, me,* and *my* in their verbiage. She drew him out about his school years, unsurprised when he bragged about bullying behavior. Victimized at home, he'd gone on to victimize others at an early age.

When he started to get bored, she'd interject an admiring comment to goad him to continue. If he were dependent on sexual enhancement drugs for performance, time was her friend.

She strove for an expression that was understanding but allowed her fear to show. Her response would stroke his ego and keep him talking. But her attention wandered. Something he'd said earlier niggled at the back of her brain, and she searched in vain for the reference. It had been when he'd spoken of his parents and the violence enacted on the mother by the father. This offender's response to it . . . And have to run outside to find a knothole or something . . .

A knothole . . .

Comprehension clicked into place. Her gaze shifted to the wood wall behind him. The wood was old and dotted with occasional knotholes, which, if she remembered correctly were the weakest area of the wood.

A sliver of hope flickered. Sophia adjusted her gaze to the offender again, her fingers playing idly over the pen she held.

Perhaps he'd leave the pen behind, but she couldn't count on that. Its clip, however . . .

"Or maybe you aren't interested after all. I could probably do a better job showing you than telling, anyway."

She responded to the threat in his words before their meaning. Deliberately, she widened her eyes. "Why would you say I'm not interested?"

Tension had seeped into his muscled body. He looked like a large violent jungle animal readying for an attack. "Don't try to play me. You stopped listening a while back. I'm not stupid."

"No, I'd place you in the gifted range on the IQ scale." Another lie, delivered in an absent yet professional tone. "Difficult to tell, of course, without actually testing you, but based on your achievements, and the ease with which you're duping law enforcement, definitely gifted." In actuality he'd likely score in the average range. The man was organized, a planner, but the dumping of the bodies had been lazy and amateurish. He also had mood swings with bouts of impulsivity that likely would make him react rashly when cornered.

"You were last discussing women's worth, and equating that with the amount each woman you targeted withdrew from her bank account. You said, and I quote, 'Why waste your time on poor bitches when all cats look gray in the dark?'"

He stared for a long moment before laughing, his big body easing a little. "That's exactly what I said. Huh. Doesn't make you smart, though, repeating my words back to me. Parrots can be trained to say the words we teach 'em. Maybe you have a bird brain—ever think of that?"

His sudden bout of truculence was like a minefield that required careful maneuvering. "I certainly realize I'm not in your league. Which makes me all the more anxious to correct the profile and get it out to the public as soon as possible."

"I'm done talking." After swinging his legs over the edge of the mattress, he rose to approach her, his intent clear.

A cold river of dread flooded through her. It was difficult to summon thought when her mind froze. Reason shut down. He reached down to yank her to her feet by her hair. "I'm sorry," she stammered, wildly searching for logic. "I misunderstood. I thought you wanted to get the profile on the early news. Doesn't that air at six a.m.?"

"Plenty of time to give you a taste of what you got coming." He wrapped her hair around his fist painfully, pulling her head back.

"You're right, of course. Maybe they can air it Saturday evening instead."

He stilled. "People need to hear the truth about me as soon as possible. It'll go on at six."

His fingers twisted in her hair had tears of pain springing to her eyes. "I'll need a few hours to write it. And then . . . However you plan to get it to the anchor you have in mind, I'm sure she goes to work a couple hours early to have hair and makeup done." Sophia had no idea of a TV anchor's schedule, but her mind was scrambling. "Will that give you enough time?"

The vicious slap he delivered then would have knocked her to the ground if the hand in her hair hadn't held her painfully upright. "Wouldn't even need that new profile if you hadn't fucked me over in public to begin with." He was screaming at her now, in an abrupt escalation of frustrated fury. "Fucking lying cunt." The man hurled her into the stone wall, and when she fell to the floor, he strode over to kick her repeatedly.

Sophia curled up, trying to make herself as small as possible, every blow sending shock waves of pain flashing through her system. Finally, the edge of his anger spent, he halted.

"You got two hours to get that written. Hear me?"

"Yes," she croaked. She couldn't manage more. Drawing a breath at all was torture through her bruised and battered ribs.

The creak of the gate sounded. Then it slammed shut. She heard the key in the lock. The light receded as he moved away.

Shallow breaths helped. Cautiously, Sophia pushed herself to a sitting position, whimpering when her movements had pain stabbing through her. She'd bought herself some time, but it had come with a cost.

Not as high a price, though, as if he'd stayed.

Two hours. Because standing was beyond her at this point, she adjusted the comforter around her as well as she could manage and scooted toward the pen she'd dropped. She reached for the sack and wrapper, hissing in a breath at the resulting agony. Shifting position an inch at a time, she reached it, and then wondered how she was going to write. The walls were out of the question; a pen wasn't going to function for long on an upright surface. She'd thought to stretch out on her stomach but doubted now she'd be able to manage . . .

His voice sounded from somewhere in the recesses of the structure. The blood in her veins congealed. Turned frigid.

". . . not . . . to see me? You're . . . learner . . . another lesson."

Sophia turned her head wildly, frantically searching for evidence of his return. Why was he back? Two hours he'd said. He hadn't even left the . . .

He hadn't left the building. Comprehension washed through her. There was no approaching beam of light splitting the darkness outside her cell. No sound of footsteps. But still her mind refused to grasp the only possible meaning.

Then an inhuman scream echoed through the building. It was quickly muffled, but the suffering in the sounds bombarding her brought chills to Sophia's skin. Tears of sympathy sprang to her eyes. The noise continued, as did the unmistakable auditory of assault.

"Stop it!" The visceral demand was ripped from somewhere deep inside her. Unplanned and primitive. "Stop it! Leave her alone!"

Because there was someone else held in the building with her. Another woman being attacked at this moment who was on the receiving end of all the frustration and violence the offender had felt toward Sophia.

In all likelihood Courtney Van Wheton was being raped and beaten in Sophia's stead.

Chapter 12

"Tell me why we're here again?"

"I'm doing a favor for my neighbor." Sophia wandered the walkway between the cages, stopping frequently to make cooing sounds of delight. "Livvie wants to surprise Carter with a puppy for his birthday, and he has his heart set on a beagle. She prefers a rescue dog so was going to check out the shelters today while he was at his dad's. But plans changed and she has to pick Carter up . . . Oh, aren't you sweet?"

Doubtfully, Cam looked at the patchy-haired cat she was referring to. It appeared as if it had been on the losing end of a feline brawl. Its tail was half-gone and one ear was so scarred fur no longer grew there. "You must be talking to me."

Ignoring the signs warning her against doing just that, Sophie stuck her fingers in the cage to stroke the tom's side. He responded with a purr that rivaled the sound of a small jet taking off. "In your dreams."

"You'd be surprised. My dreams are extremely vivid, and you're pleasantly attentive in all of them." Enjoying the flush his words brought to her cheeks, he grinned.

At last they moved on to the next cage. Where they stopped again. "An active fantasy life isn't unhealthy," she murmured, making kissy noises to the yawning ball of lint curled up inside the kennel. "Until it borders on psychosis. Then strong medication is recommended."

"Not the recommendation I was looking for." Cam looked around at the size of the shelter and estimated at their current rate of progress they'd cover the place just inside six hours. "I didn't realize you were such an animal lover."

He was bemused by the shock in her expression. "Oh, I'm not. I mean, of course I like them, but I've never had a pet. Frankly, I wouldn't know what to do with one."

"You've never had a pet?" He managed to steer her past three cages before she stopped yet again. "Not even as a kid?" At her head shake, he went on, "Not even a bird or something?" After he and his mom had been on their own, they'd been dirt-poor, but he'd always had a dog. Usually some scruffy stray that would come by and forget to leave. It was hard to imagine a childhood without one.

"My parents didn't consider a pet a necessary part of raising a well-rounded child. And now I don't know what I'd do when I have to leave for days at a time. Maybe I'll get a cat someday. They can be left alone for a while, can't they?"

"So I hear." He tried to keep his personal bias from his tone. He didn't have a dog for much the same reason, but he wouldn't mind having one that required a lot of exercise so he could take it running. But so far he'd put off the responsibility.

They moved on to a cage that held a litter of kittens. One corner of his mouth quirked, both at their antics and at Sophie's response to them.

His cell phone vibrated. Taking it from his pocket, he looked at the caller identification. His earlier good mood evaporated. It was from his former FBI handler, the fed he'd reported to when he'd been undercover. He'd liked the man well enough when he'd been part of the task force. Until later, when he'd realized how badly the agent had betrayed his trust.

This call would be another in response to his forwarding the pictures hidden in his newspaper a few days ago. Apparently the feds were jittery about what the photos meant.

Cam was still wondering the same thing himself.

"I like the idea of rescuing an animal from a shelter like this." Sophie finally moved on, past a few more rows of cages. "Giving them a home and someone to love. It'll be a good lesson for Carter."

"Everyone needs rescuing now and then." He held up his phone. "I have to return a call."

He strode away, feeling her eyes still on him. His words came back to taunt him. People made choices every day. Some good. Some bad.

Cam wasn't at all sure there was any rescue possible from the one he'd made a couple of years ago.

"Humphrey's victim has been identified as Michael Quinn." Cam leaned back in his desk chair and reported the conversation he'd just had with DMPD Lieutenant Treelord. "According to Marchand, he was an old acquaintance of Humphrey's. Doesn't have a sheet, but the narcotics division is familiar with him. Been a bit player in the scene for decades. No arrests." He rubbed the heels of his palms against his eyes. They felt as though they were filled with grit. "That in itself is some sort of miracle."

"Maybe he's just a lucky guy," observed Franks. The older agent was in need of a shave. Cam knew he probably looked as bad. "His luck ran out last night, though."

"According to Quinn, he was snatched a couple days ago, and tortured on and off the entire time. Apparently there was a big score from a drug deal right before Humphrey was sent up and he wanted his share. Quinn didn't have it, didn't have the means to pay it back." He shrugged. The conflicts between known scumbags didn't much interest him. The fact that the agents had wasted their time thinking Humphrey was going to lead them to Sophie did.

"Hopefully Fenton will call soon. Do you want me to start going through traffic camera images again, try to get a glimpse of the van?" Jenna made the offer around a big yawn.

"We've checked out all the ones you found."

"I might have missed—"

Cam shook his head. Wished he could dislodge as easily the bleakness that shrouded him like a blanket. "We've had the owners of the vans checked out. Nothing sprang. Gotta figure the UNSUB was smart enough to look up the location of all the traffic cameras between here and Edina, then drew routes to avoid them."

"Information's on the Web." Franks's voice sounded more gravelly than usual. "That'd explain why Chief Boelin isn't having any luck finding the white van leaving Edina."

"Or seeing it anywhere between there and the Iowa border."

The traffic images would have been their best bet, but the lead hadn't panned out. A lot of manpower hours had been wasted following up on images of white cargo vans and then running the records on each. Doing background checks on the drivers. Nothing had popped at this point.

"We may take another pass at the list of those vans identified from the images." But Cam knew it was a long shot. None of the owners had arrest records, at least for anything violent. And if the owners had lent the vehicles out, the way Marchand had, it would be virtually impossible to trace.

He needed some positive movement. Depression was settling in, partially due, he knew, to lack of sleep. But mostly due to lack of progress. As much as he didn't feel like sleeping, he'd be better for catching a few hours. Sharper. Fresher. And so would the other agents.

"Go home and get a couple hours sleep," he ordered brusquely. "We're spinning our wheels here. I'll call you when I hear from Fenton, and we can start again."

The two agents didn't protest. Cam figured they realized the truth in his words. With no more than a few more words exchanged, they got up and exited his office, leaving the extra chairs behind, apparently believing his space was going to serve as the center of the investigation for the time being.

He regarded the empty chairs broodingly after they left. Investigations were composed of following the best leads. Some panned out. Others led to brick walls. Spending hours on one that hadn't led them to Sophie shouldn't be regarded as a time suck since they'd eliminated Humphrey from the list of suspects.

But anything that didn't result in her rescue at this point was like another tiny dagger under his skin. Time was of the essence. The professional thing—the objective thing—would be to stop focusing on what she might be undergoing right now and focus on getting her home alive.

But knowing that and following his own advice were two different things.

The ring of his cell later had Cam starting in his chair, rapping his knee smartly on his desk. Reaching for the phone, he noted the time. He must have dozed off for a couple of hours.

The second thing he observed was the identification of the caller.

"Tell me you've got something."

"I'll let you be the judge." Fenton's voice was weary but jubilant. "But, hell yeah, I think we found something interesting. We've got the type of shoe narrowed down to three possibilities, and in the morning when we can place a call to the manufacturers, we can give you a definite ID." Cam felt mild interest stirring. The results were of use only when they had a suspect in hand, for comparison purposes to shoes in his possession.

But the information wouldn't lead them to Sophie.

"Anything else?"

"What do you know about ostriches?" came Fenton's reply.

Cam blinked. He actually wondered if the lab manager was trying to get back at him for the times over the years when Cam had hounded him about test results. "Uh . . . I know they're big. They have feathers. I also know it wasn't an ostrich that kidnapped Soph—Dr. Channing."

The man actually chuckled. "Of course not. But the samples of dirt we analyzed didn't come from your soles, or from those of anyone else on the investigative team wearing shoe covers. It's a good bet they came from the kidnapper, and in one of the samples we found a single ostrich hair."

Surprise kept Cam silent for a long moment. "This is Iowa," he said finally. "We've got cows. Pigs. Maybe sheep."

"We've also got ostrich farms scattered around the state. An Internet search shows that."

The information required some processing. "I've heard that hair analysis is under review as a forensic measure." At least one conviction he'd read about had been overturned based on the questioned reliability of that evidence. He didn't want to waste time and effort following another fruitless lead.

Fenton's voice held a note of impatience. "You're talking about a case where they convicted based on a scientist's assertion that a hair at a scene came from a certain subject. We're talking about matching a hair found to a species of animal. The hair isn't human. That was easy enough to ascertain. Human hair has consistent pigmentation and color throughout its length. Animal hairs tend to be banded, with several colors in a short length. The roots and medullas are also different. The FBI has a manual with photomicrographs of common animal hairs."

Cam sat up straighter, tamping down a measure of excitement. "So you were able to match the hair to one of those photographs?"

"Photomicrographs," Fenton corrected him. "And no. Ostriches aren't considered common enough to be found in crime scene evidence. But one of our criminalists, Jack Walsh—I don't know if you know him, great criminalist—did an expansion of the FBI's hair manual as his dissertation. Spent a summer at the San Diego Zoo collecting samples. I'm telling you, Walsh is almost certain this is an ostrich guard hair. Possibly from the head or leg. He can even be certain it didn't come from an emu, although there are similarities between the two birds and they're often raised together. There's no way to match it to a specific ostrich, mind you, but there's no doubting the dirt came from a place where ostriches are or were once kept."

Cam turned to the computer and did a quick search. From past experience dealing with criminalists, he knew that he'd never get 100 percent certainty from any of them. Scrolling through the results on the computer screen, he discovered there were no fewer than ten such farms listed, three of them within half an hour of Des Moines. But two in particular caught his eye.

The locations were in Story and Boone. They'd found bodies in both counties.

A bolt of excitement tightening in him, it took a moment to realize the man was talking.

". . . could also identify traces of manure that might have come from cattle. In this state, that's not much of a lead, but coupled with the hair we found, I'd say you're looking for a suspect who has spent some time on a farm around livestock."

"Thanks, Al." Adrenaline kick-started, Cam was already considering his next move. Some of the ostrich farms nearby were in a neighboring DCI zone. Which meant a different SAC and Major Crime agents. Maria would have to get the territorial issues ironed out.

His mind racing, he began scribbling notes on a piece of paper. "When this is over, I'm going to buy you the biggest steak on the menu. Restaurant of your choice."

"Oh, well." The lab manager sounded pleased. "Actually I'm a vegan, but when we have cause to celebrate, count me in. And, Cam . . . when you find her, will you let us know?"

"Definitely."

After disconnecting the call, he immediately called Jenna. "Call Franks for me. I'm contacting the rest of the agents. Briefing in an hour and a half."

The female agent's voice was groggy. "We've got something?"

"We've got something." He hung up, turned to the computer, and sent out a mass email that would alert the entire team, including Treelord of the DMPD and sheriffs from involved counties. Then he called his SAC and gave her an abbreviated account of the events of the night and the news from the lab. "We've got jurisdictional issues," he ended with. "At least two adjoining districts have farms that will have to be checked out."

"I'll be there in thirty minutes."

"Briefing's not for another hour and a half—"

"I'll be there in thirty minutes." In true Maria fashion, the call was disconnected. Cam couldn't fault her for her lack of conversational skills. Urgency was mounting. He had a feeling that the investigation was finally on the fast track.

He hoped for Sophie's sake that this time he was right.

When his cell rang he frowned, checked the time: 5:30 a.m. And although the number was vaguely familiar, he couldn't immediately identify it. He did, however, recognize the voice on the other end of the call when he answered.

"It's Bob Dumont, Cam."

The sheriff of Story County. Cam's brows raised. "Sheriff. You're up early."

"At my age you don't sleep worth a damn. Checked my email, found your message. Just wanted to say, Joe and Vera Hostetter have been my neighbors for years. The owners of the ostrich farm you mentioned? I can swing by there on my way to the briefing to talk to them. They'll let me go through their buildings, no problem. Been there before, but I hate those damn birds. Sooner bite you as look at you."

A little of Cam's excitement dissipated. "If you can get that done, I'd appreciate it. Might not be the owners we're looking at, anyway, but hired help. Grown children who assist with chores." A thought struck him then, and he added, "Ask whether they've hosted any tours through there recently. Had any visitors. And I'm going to want the names of their relatives. Sons, cousins, nephews, sons-in-law." Stacy Marchand had loaned Humphrey the van he'd used to abduct Michael Quinn. Sophie might not be held on a farm at all. A family member who had visited one could be the UNSUB they were after.

"Will do. I know that they have two girls, Marcia and Chrissy, both living somewhere out west. The Hostetters get help with chores when they travel, of course. Neighbor kids for the most part, but I'll share what I find when I see you."

"Appreciate it."

The call ended, Cam turned his attention to typing up the pertinent points and assignments for the upcoming briefing.

SAC Gonzalez entered his office almost to the minute of her promised arrival. She flicked a dark gaze over the jumble of chairs and empty coffeepot but didn't mention them, getting right to the point. "I'll be putting in calls to the other SACs as soon as they're in. And I'll apprise Assistant Director Miller that the scope of the search is broadening. Am I trying to finagle having you at the searches at the ostrich facilities in other zones?"

Cam shook his head. "I have plenty to keep me busy up here, and I want the searches completed as quickly as possible. They can be done almost simultaneously if I don't insist on being on every scene."

She looked at him through hooded eyes. Not for the first time, he couldn't read her thoughts. "And you're okay with that?"

He knew what she was asking. "I'm okay with anything that brings this stage of the investigation to a successful close."

Gonzalez nodded. It was the politically correct answer, but truthful in this case. He wanted Sophie found, the faster the better. "You think Dr. Channing's going to be found closer by."

She was good at reading him. They'd worked together for years before her promotion, often side by side. "I keep going back to the geographic profile." He nodded at the map taking up a large portion of one wall. Sophie had pinned red strings from each of the body dump sites like wheels of a spoke, all of them coming together in Polk County. Yellow strings signified the cities where the identified victims had been abducted. "Dr. Channing talked about an anchor, some place the scumbag feels safe. Something that ties him to his operational area. It's the same approximate distance from here to each of the dump sites, depending where he's holed up."

"And your gut is saying she's nearby."

He merely looked at her, unwilling to admit how heavily he was relying on instinct to make the decisions of where to focus his attention.

"Go with your gut," she said simply. "It's rarely steered you wrong in the past."

She left his office, her words echoing and reechoing in Cam's head. He stared blindly at the map, considering just how wrong Maria was. He'd made a major breach of professional ethics before the final bust was going down on that recent narcotics task force. And that breach had recently come back to bite him in the ass.

He couldn't afford to make a similar error when it came to saving Sophie.

———

The screams went on and on, spiking through Sophia's ears, blazing across her brain. She could visualize every torturous moment the other woman was experiencing. Could imagine just how easily it could have been her suffering at that instant.

It should have been her.

An unbearable onslaught of guilt arrowed through her. She folded her arms alongside her head, blocking her ears to shut out the sound. But the screams echoed in her mind until she wasn't sure if they were real or whether the earlier ones had lodged there, impossible to shake loose.

She'd thought to buy herself time. Just another day to try to effect an escape. Summon help. It had never occurred to her that there was someone else imprisoned with her. She'd never answered when Sophia had called. Why hadn't she answered?

The next scream shot up her spine. The pain from her ribs was forgotten. How little to endure compared with the suffering being inflicted . . . on Van Wheton? Or another woman?

Sophia had felt helplessness before. She'd assisted in investigations where law enforcement had been too late to save a killer's latest victim. She'd stood by and watched the lifeless body of a five-year-old extracted from the shallow grave a pedophile had dug for him.

But this . . . The feeling carved a jagged hollow through her center. Filled it with despair. And she knew she'd never forgive herself. There was nothing she could do to stop the agony the other woman was enduring.

The knowledge pummeled her with brutal fists. The desolation that followed the thought was debilitating.

Except, there *was* one thing she could do. Determinedly, barely conscious of the tears streaming down her face, she snapped the clip off the pen. Examined it. Once she filed it on the broken concrete floor, she'd have an edge sharp enough to work with.

Crawling across the area, she tucked it beneath the mattress, as close to the wooden wall as possible. Then she returned to the center of the cell and snatched up the torn fast-food bag.

The screams were hideous, one melding into the other, sounding more animal than human. Each pounded a dagger of remorse deeper and deeper into Sophia's brain. Sprawling on her stomach, she ignored the chorus of protest from her ribs. And she began planning a way to write the "profile" while embedding a message the sadist a few yards away wouldn't notice.

But one Cam would hopefully look for.

The monster—it was impossible to think of him any other way—
made a pleased sound. "If you'd a written this to begin with, we
wouldn't be in this mess."

"I'm glad you've given me another chance to get it right."
Sophia's ears strained to hear a sound from his other victim. But
there was nothing. Not even soft sobbing. She wondered if the
woman had lost consciousness. Or worse.

With dull eyes she watched as he read the new profile while
absently scratching his chest. She ought to be concerned that he'd
notice the words she'd hidden in the context of the writing. But
anxiety for herself was difficult to summon. There was only emptiness. A void that echoed the quiet emanating from the other victim.

The gate remained locked and shut. He hadn't bothered to
come in. Hours ago she would have been heady with relief.

That was before he'd brutalized another woman.

"How will you get it to the news anchor?" He'd expect the question, or one like it. But Sophia couldn't find it in herself to care. All
her concern centered on the other female nearby—and the deathly
silence that permeated the structure.

Had he killed her?

Whatever his actions, he appeared sexually sated. His arousal
was no longer evident. The ferocious temper had disappeared,
although she already knew how suddenly it could reappear. The
sadistic monster had been satisfied.

For now.

He looked up. "You did a real good job on this. Of course, I
could have just told you what to write and skipped all the psychological shit. Saved us some time. You're probably feeling neglected by
now. 'Specially since you heard all the fun you were missing out on."

"You were wise to allow me to write it in my usual fashion."
Sophia couldn't—wouldn't—let herself respond to his incendiary
words. But the casual reference to the brutality he'd enacted on the

other woman ignited a torch of temper that burned through her shock and sorrow. "The law enforcement will call upon professionals to verify my handwriting and style of writing. They'll be able to discern that the profile was written in my unique manner."

"That's what I figured." Carefully he laid the sandwich wrapper atop the torn bag and rolled the two pieces around the pen he'd brought her to use. She had a moment to wonder whether he'd notice later that its clip was missing. If he'd realize what that meant, and come back for her sooner rather than later in the day.

Then his gaze rose, his pale-blue eyes impaling her, and something in them made her writhe in revulsion. "But knowing you were listening to us the whole time . . . I think it made me last even longer. I've got plans for you when I get back. You and the other whore. Nothing like the anticipation of a little girl-on-girl action to give me something to look forward to today."

The other victim was alive then, despite his vicious attack. Relief was followed by a flare of hatred, so hot and intense that Sophia almost shook from it. She dropped her gaze in what she hoped he'd take as deference. Or fear. She didn't want him to read the real emotion in her eyes. Her job required objectivity, even in the face of the most horrifying details in a case.

But this was no longer a case. It was her life. Hers and the victim who was likely Courtney Van Wheton. And if they were both to live, Sophia had to be successful in her next escape attempt.

Finally the man turned away. She heard his steps recede as he moved across the building, leaving her in darkness. Something inside her wound more and more tightly with each passing moment, waiting for the telltale sound that would mean she was alone again.

But, no, not alone. Another woman was depending on her success, as well.

The squeak of ancient hinges had her lunging across the cell, as if a giant spring had been released. Ignoring the breath-stealing pain in her ribs, she yanked the mattress away from the wall and scrabbled to find the metal pen clip she'd stored there. It would have been easier to wait for the dim light that would eventually lighten the interior of the structure when dawn broke.

But she couldn't make herself stop. Her fingers groped blindly along the wooden wall in a frantic search until they found the item she was looking for. Sophia clutched the metal piece like a talisman before moving to the edge of the mattress nearest the limestone wall.

It would be useless to search for a board to attack until she had some light to guide her way. She'd use the time to prepare. Holding the tip of the clip in two fingers, she dragged the broken edge across the rough stone to sharpen it. Because failure didn't bear considering, she wouldn't let herself think about what would happen if her idea didn't work.

It had to work. Two lives were depending on it.

***

"Will a member of this team be present at the searches on farms in other zones?"

"No." Cam noted Jenna's faint look of shock at his response to her answer, and he addressed the others in the briefing room. "It would require too much time, and we want this completed as quickly as possible. While it'd be wonderful if we found Dr. Channing on one of the sites, we have to consider it's far likelier that we'll discover it was someone who visited the place who left behind the evidence. A hired hand, possibly. We're also in the process of getting a complete list of employees and volunteers at the Blank Park Zoo." Cattle and ostriches could also be found there.

He glanced down at his notes. "Beachum and Robbins will compare the list of names we get from the zoo with the violent sexual offender list we've been working from. I've already run checks on the owners of each of the ostrich farms in Iowa, with nothing of note appearing in their backgrounds. The MCU agents in the other zones will be gathering information regarding hired men, family members, and lists of visitors. They'll pass along the data as it's compiled."

His gaze cut to where the Story County sheriff was seated. "Bob, you want to tell us what you found on your search of the Hostetter farm?"

The man stood, cleared his throat. If anything his tan had deepened since the first body was discovered. Coupled with his lean build, it gave him the look of well-worn rawhide.

"As I told Cam, I've known the owners for years. Been at their place a hundred times. But I stopped by again, and Joe took me through every outbuilding on the property. He wasn't nearly as understanding about me wanting a look at his basement, but I checked it out." He scratched his chin with a long index finger. "And that's probably gonna cost me a bottle of Kentucky's finest at some point, but I can tell you there's no trace of anyone on the place with the exception of Joe and Vera. I have the names and contact information for the two high school kids who help out with chores when needed. No visitors have been by. They used to host a kinder-garten class every spring, but they had to stop because of liability issues. A daughter and son-in-law just left last week. Their informa-tion's on the list, too, but they live in Cheyenne." He walked to the front of the room to hand a paper to Cam. A quick glance showed a neat listing of names, numbers, and addresses.

"Thanks, Bob." Cam's attention switched to Beckett Maxwell, who was comfortably slouched in his chair next to Dumont. "Anything new on the surveillance of the Price place?"

"Not if you mean new like seeing a herd of ostriches run around the farmyard." A few chuckles sounded in the room. "Had a run-in with Gary Price two days ago." He shrugged. "Pretty hard to do circumspect surveillance when there's nothing around but corn and bean fields. He took offense to having us sit on his place. I listened politely and informed him that we intended to continue. There's some traffic out there. Talked to people in town, and apparently he does do car repair, as he said. We've gotten a glimpse inside the machine shed a time or two, and it's equipped like an auto repair shop." He rubbed his jaw. "What I'd really like is a look in that old barn that butts up against the back of the shop."

"Do you know the property owner farming the land directly behind it?"

A slow smile crossed Beckett's mouth at Cam's question. "I do now. Yesterday I got his permission to walk his fence line. Got within forty foot of the barn, and there is a large double door, but it was closed and secured with a big wooden bar slid across the length of it."

"What about the brother?"

"It's been one delay after the other getting a court date, and Jerry Price remains a drain on the Boone County taxpayers. It'll be a blessing to get rid of him. Whiny little pain in the . . . county budget," he amended. "You'll be happy to know that he's very inter-ested in our investigation. Asks about it all the time. Seems to think he has some information that will help us, while at the same time saving him a trip back to prison."

"Unless that assistance includes some details about his brother and the structures on his property, we're not interested."

Beckett shook his head and slid a little deeper into his chair. It was a wonder, to Cam's mind, that the man didn't end up as a puddle on the floor. "I inquired. Of course he's not talking about a relation. Just some mysterious stranger he met in prison."

The tip line being manned by the DMPD was full of just that sort of vague information. The manpower required to check out the "leads" elicited from it had so far been a drain on resources. "If Price wants to get my attention, he'll need to get specific."

Cam rifled through the sheets on the table in front of him before finding the one he was seeking and holding it up. "Here's something more promising. There's also an ostrich ranch in your county. We need to check with the owners about anyone else they might know of who once kept ostriches and no longer do. Bob?"

"I'll call Joe and ask him."

Nodding, Cam waited for Beckett to come up for the page he was holding out before going on. "We've also got DNA corroboration on another match of one of our victims. Hillary Keogh, age forty-two, from Saint Louis. Jenna and Tommy, I want you to contact the case detective in her missing person's case and familiarize yourself with the details. Talk to the bank personnel who saw her last. Have the detective send the images from the bank security cam for comparison. Loring"—his focus switched to the dark-haired female agent—"there's an ostrich co-op in the state. Check it out. Get a list of past members names and addresses who no longer appear on the site." She nodded, scribbling on a notepad.

"Patrick and Samuels, search for links between the ID'd victims and the person in the grave they were buried with." Cam gave a mental shrug. It was a long shot but needed to be checked out. He surveyed the group somberly. "A lot of you are putting in some long hours on this case. It's appreciated. And it's beginning to show results. We'll run down these leads as quickly and efficiently as possible. Since the sketch we got in Edina hasn't panned out for us, this is the first solid lead we have for the UNSUB.

"Let's use it to nail him."

Chapter 13

Sophia's legs wrapped around Cam's hips, her back bowed. His slow movements inside her were excruciating. Urgency clawed for release. Her heels dug into his back punishingly, but he ignored her silent demand. Instead he paused his movements to untwine her hands from around his neck and raise them above her head. Linking their fingers, he began to withdraw from her, inch by infinitesimal inch.

"Cam!" The word was more plea than demand. He responded with a bruising kiss that belied his teasing movements.

"What do you want?" His words were raspy, spoken against her mouth. "Tell me."

Tossing her head restlessly on the pillow, she arched again, trying to force a closer contact. "I don't . . . I can't . . ."

He dropped a stinging necklace of kisses along her jawline. "I'll give you everything you want. Anything. Tell me."

"You." She freed her hands to fist one in his hair. The other clutched a muscular shoulder. Her legs crawled higher. "All." Urgency was churning inside her, thought impossible. There was only need. Fervent and desperate. Desire, dark and molten, was heating her veins. Every nerve inside her stretched as taut as a bow.

His hips slammed into hers then with a force she welcomed. Returned. Sophia met his punishing tempo and demanded more as she reached for something just out of reach.

She could feel his muscles, tight and straining, beneath her fingers. Heard his ragged breathing. Sensed the exact moment when his control shattered, and his movements went wildly unrestrained.

His loss of control had heat, quick stabbing spears of it, arrowing down her spine. Her world narrowed until there was only Cam and her. Bodies twisting and straining as they sped through the darkness on a race for release.

And when hers ripped through her, shattering sanity, scattering reason, his name was on her lips.

It might have been hours later. Was likely only minutes. Sophia still felt pleasantly weak. Lethargic. And absolutely boneless. It pleased her that Cam's breathing hadn't yet returned to normal. She could feel embarrassed at her total loss of control had she not been certain Cam had been equally desperate. After the explosive climax, she'd be satisfied to never move again.

But a need of another sort was making itself known. And although the last thing she wanted to do was leave Cam's bed, nature would not be ignored.

Sliding from beneath his arm, she reluctantly swung her feet to the floor and stood. He made a sound of protest, but she rounded the bed to head for the bathroom, intent on returning as quickly as possible. Her bare foot stepped on something foreign. Flat and square. "What . . ."

"Hmm? What's wrong?"

"Nothing." Sophia reached down and scooped up what she'd stepped on and hurried into the bathroom. Closed the door and turned on the light. She stared at the object in her hand, gradual comprehension turning to dismay. It was the foil wrapper of a condom.

An *unopened* condom.

She gave a little shake of her head as if to dislodge the sensual cobwebs that persisted. Her reflection stared back at her from the mirror above the sink. Stricken.

Sophia recalled Cam taking it from the drawer of the bedside table. She had a clear memory of taking it from him, intent on sheathing him with it.

And she had an equally vivid memory of him taking one of her nipples in his mouth at that exact moment. Teasing it with tongue and teeth until she'd grasped his head with her hands, whether to stop or prolong the torment, she didn't know.

What she didn't recall was what she'd done with the condom after that. One thing was certain; they hadn't used it. They hadn't used any protection.

The ramifications of that lapse successfully banished the lingering sensual haze.

In all her life, Sophia had never been so careless.

Of course, decades earlier she'd been on the pill. Had remained on it until a couple of years ago when her gynecologist had recommended a break. That hadn't mattered, not then, because she hadn't been sexually active after her divorce.

Until Cam.

A quick mental calculation had some of the tension seeping from her limbs. She should be safe, but the fact remained that safety hadn't even entered her mind.

And that fact terrified her. She was by nature a cautious and meticulous woman. But her normal caution had been spectacularly absent from the moment she and Cam had shared drinks at Mickey's last week.

And Sophia could no longer dismiss the alarms going off inside her over yet another aberration in judgment.

As soon as the dim fractured light began to penetrate the building, Sophia had begun her search. A knothole signified a weakness in the wood. So she identified all the boards along the two wooden sides of the cell that contained one. Limiting herself to those easily within reach, she'd come up with four possibilities. Selecting one, she'd started to work at it.

It was long, tedious labor. The jagged metal end of the clip easily scraped a groove into the aged timber, but it had taken hours just to wear a groove around the knot deep enough to force out the small plug of wood.

Her success had brought a surge of excitement. But that emotion had quickly abated after she'd kicked at the board repeatedly, and it'd held fast in place. So she'd gone back to work, a bit more frantic now, intent on widening the hole.

Pausing to rest her cramped fingers, she took another drink of the tepid water from the now-soggy paper cup. After drinking the last few trickles of liquid, she tossed it in a corner. Only then did she wonder if the monster had fed Courtney Van Wheton.

Just the thought of last night had her breath catching. An auditory repeat of the horrible sounds of the assault would creep unbidden into her mind at random moments, an emotional ambush. And yet it was nothing in comparison to what the woman had endured at the man's hands since her kidnapping. Sophia could hardly bear to contemplate it.

It was that thought, however, that had her redoubling her efforts. She inserted the rough edge of the clip and began scraping at the wood again. The metal often hit a snag in the wood and bent. Each time she'd straighten it, but Sophia worried it would snap in half at some point, making it more unmanageable to wield. Or totally useless.

Better to focus her worry on that than on when the monster would return.

Earlier that morning, she'd again called out to the other woman, but there'd been no answer. Realizing that further effort would be wasted, Sophia had saved her breath. Perhaps Van Wheton was scared. Maybe her injuries prevented her from responding. But thinking of her suffering somewhere nearby kept Sophia working long after the splinters of light allowed in the building grew bright.

Because it kept her stronger to focus on something—any-thing—other than what awaited her if she failed in her attempt, she let her mind touch on the investigation. She knew each of the agents working on it personally. She trusted them.

But most of all, Sophia trusted the man running the case.

Despite the way their relationship had ended, she was certain Cam would stop at nothing to find her. She wouldn't wait for that rescue. Couldn't count on it. But it warmed something inside her to be certain of his efforts on her behalf.

Just thinking of him had a host of unsolicited memories swarm-ing her mind. Mental images of Cam, jaw squared and determined. Or the way his eyes slit when he was vaguely annoyed.

The image of how he looked when he was lazy and sated, a slight curve on his lips. The memory of the long, smooth stroke of his fingers down her spine.

The pang of loss that struck her then was as sharp and searing as any that emanated from her battered ribs. She blinked away the tears that pricked her eyes. This was no time for regrets or for weak-ness. It would take all her strength to outwit her captor.

But, oh, if she let herself, Sophia could long to relive the time she'd once been weak with Cam Prescott.

Her fingers were cramping more and more frequently. She stopped to flex them. Studying the widening hole, she realized it was nearly twice the width of the original knot that had been removed. About an inch and a half across.

Setting down the clip, she moved to the opposite side of the stall. The hole was near the center of the board, nearly three-quarters down its length. Reasoning that the area of the board farthest from the supporting post on the other side would be the weakest, she took aim again. After running across the cell, she kicked at it with all her might. Was gratified to hear a sharp sudden crack when her heel met the wood.

She tried over and over, ignoring the pain in her heel from its continued contact with the unyielding lumber. The pain was meaningless in the face of what the other woman had endured last night.

And it was a reminder of what was in store for her in a few hours if she failed.

The thought fueled her strength, and Sophia gave another hard kick at the hole she'd created.

Then stared, in dumfounded delight, when the board finally split in two.

〜

Because it was just a few miles down the road from headquarters, Cam traveled to the Farm Service Agency himself. And then cooled his heels in the waiting area for several minutes as several jean-clad farmers showed no sign of hurrying through the business they were discussing with the clerk at the counter.

Finally, he skirted the line of customers remaining and rounded the counter to approach an older clerk working at a computer.

"Excuse me."

The look she gave him should have blistered several layers of skin. "You'll have to wait your turn, sir. There are others ahead of you."

He flashed his shield. "I'd like to speak to your manager."

Her lips pressed into a thin disapproving line. "I'll see if he's available."

Rising, she went to a closed door a few feet away and preceded her entrance with a perfunctory knock.

Cam scanned the place. Other than the young woman manning the counter, there was only one other employee in the vicinity, but several empty desks suggested absentee colleagues. A moment later the older woman slipped back out of the manager's door, a disappointed expression on her face. "Mr. Jeffries can see you now."

Starting toward the office, Cam was met by someone who had to be the manager, although he looked for all the world like a fourteen-year-old kid. If fourteen-year-old kids wore Dockers with polo shirts and needed to shave.

"Agent Prescott? Justin Jeffries." The younger man stepped aside and motioned him to his office. And then closed the door upon the avid interest being shown by the woman who'd announced Cam.

Closer examination had him revising his original estimate. The manager actually looked nearer to twenty. Which still had to be years off the mark but made him feel a little better.

"Have to say, getting a visit from DCI is a first." Given his youth, Cam figured the manager had a lot of firsts ahead of him, but he took the chair Jeffries offered and waited for the other man to seat himself behind his desk.

"I'm looking for a crime site that we have reason to believe currently or once held ostriches," he began without preamble. "Chances are it's a rural area, and I thought there might be a federal farm program operators could be signed up for."

The manager shook his head. "If there were, we wouldn't be able to let you look at the records without a subpoena. But we don't have programs for livestock producers, except the dairy program." He gave a sudden flash of perfectly even white teeth. "From what I know about ostriches, I don't think they'd qualify."

"But you do have records of all the farms in Polk County."

Again Jeffries shook his head. "We have records of the commodity producers who are currently or have in the past signed up for a federal farm program." He pointed to a large county map on the wall. "This is our most current map. It probably details most of them, but wouldn't include a lot of the acreages. The producers are highlighted by the yellow dots."

Already feeling as if this had been a wasted trip, Cam rose, his eyes on the map. "Ever heard of anyone who keeps ostriches in the county?"

Jeffries stood, as well. "I know there's an operation in Boone County, because the county director there has mentioned it before. But there hasn't been one that I'm aware of in Polk County since I was a kid."

Attention caught, Cam remained in place. "That long ago, huh?"

Jeffries grinned again. "Born in eighty-five. Know what was significant about the eighties in rural Iowa?"

"Unlike you," Cam said dryly, "I have vivid memories of the eighties. You're talking the farm crisis?"

"Exactly. Farms going under after being overextended by banks, paying outrageous inflationary interest. Livestock and crop prices bottomed out. Lot of farmers were desperate to turn a profit, and that's when some turned to raising ostriches and emus. There's still a market for their feathers, meat, and leather. A neighbor of my grandpa's had a herd. You know what you hear about them eating anything? My brother and I were over at the farm looking at them once. I stuck my comb through the fence, and an ostrich ate it right out of my hand. Could see the comb go all the way down his throat, too." The young man laughed at the memory. "They're actually supposed to be kind of smart, but it was hard to believe it that day."

"Where was this?"

241

Jeffries looked surprised. "The ostriches? Next farm over from my grandpa's, north and east of town. Maybe about eight miles from here."

"Can you draw me a map?"

"Sure." Jefferies got out a pad of paper and started drawing just as Cam's phone began to vibrate. "The house is gone now, and all that's left of the place is this really great old barn. The pasture the birds used to graze on has been plowed under, though. Unlike the eighties, producers these days can't complain about grain prices. A lot of them are farming fencerow to fencerow, conservation be damned."

Only half listening, Cam checked the screen, saw the number for Jenna's cell. "Excuse me," he told Jeffries and turned half away to answer it. "Prescott."

"Cam, you're going to want to head over to KCCT."

"I am?" He took the crudely drawn map the manager handed to him. "Why is that?"

There was a shake to the normally level agent's tone. "A news anchor received a written message that's supposedly from Sophia. There's a note with it that says if it isn't aired today, she'll be killed."

———

Luz Servantez, the pretty Hispanic anchor, looked distraught. The station manager and Drew Harper, the station's attorney, seemed to take turns comforting her. At Cam's questions, the newswoman drew a breath and repeated the story she'd clearly already shared with her coworkers.

"I go on the air at six a.m., and I'm always at work by four thirty to get hair and makeup done. But I was late. We have a new puppy, and it was raising heck in the middle of the night, so we were up for a while trying to settle it down. I went back to sleep and must have slept through the alarm. So"—she drew a deep, shuddering breath and reached for the bottled water in front of her—"I was rushing around and got out to the garage to find someone had smashed the driver's side window on my car. In a locked garage! There was glass all over the seat, and that"—she nodded toward the rolled-up papers—"was on the seat, too. But I really didn't pay attention to the papers. I was too upset about the car, and the thought that someone must have been in our garage. I got my husband up and took his vehicle while he cleaned up the mess and called the police. He unrolled the papers and thought they were trash. But when he saw the writing on them, he figured I'd used them to jot down some notes, so he set them aside. It wasn't until a couple hours ago when he finished dealing with the police and talking to the insurance company that he looked at them again." She paused to take a long gulp from the bottle. Lowering it, she added, "That's when he called me and brought the papers here."

"So he handled them?" Gonzalez asked the woman.

Servantez shot a guilty look at the lawyer. "He didn't know what they were. But he read some of the writing to me on the way over here, so I told Drew and Molly right away. No one has touched them since."

"That's not exactly true." Harper's smile was as smooth as his muted silk tie. "I spread them out to read them after drawing on some driving gloves I had in my car. Clearly we weren't going to make any other move until consulting with your agency."

Obviously the lawyer and station manager had taken the time to have a long discussion about their options before making that call, Cam thought, studying the note grimly. But he'd let Maria take care of that. He was more concerned with the words scrawled on a plain white napkin:

If this isn't aired today, Channing will be dead before dark.

He picked the papers up with gloved fingers and placed them carefully in a clear evidence bag. Sealed it. The lawyer cleared his throat. "Naturally we want to cooperate in any way possible. But we also have a clear interest in the public good, and our viewers deserve to be apprised of this development."

"Will you excuse us for a moment?" The station employees looked at Maria in surprise. "Of course." When neither she nor Cam made a movement toward the door, the manager tugged at the attorney's sleeve and spoke to Luz. "Let's get you somewhere you can relax before you go on again." In a bustle of activity, they all left the room.

Maria walked over to the evidence bag. Looked at the papers inside it for a moment. "Is that Dr. Channing's handwriting?"

"It looks like it. The lab will tell us for sure, but yeah." He stared at the paper, as well, trying to recall the score sheets she'd written when they'd played Gin that time. He'd been intent on keeping score another way, but she'd insisted on keeping track of points, as well. Once she'd trounced him, he'd figured out why. "I've only seen a few handwritten words before. But it does look like it could be hers." He looked up, his gaze catching Maria's. "It just doesn't sound like her writing, if you know what I mean."

"Possibly because the UNSUB was dictating it. She was merely writing down what he told her to."

He nodded slowly. "Maybe. But the professional words used . . . Those are more familiar. The phrases are similar to some she'd use in a profile, but—"

"The rhythm to the words seems off," Gonzalez finished.

"Exactly. It looks like he was intent on having her correct the earlier profile that had been released about him."

"I'm guessing that it wasn't her idea to include the sympathetic portrayal of his intelligence." The SAC read for another minute or so.

"What are you going to do with it?" Cam figured he knew the answer, but the question had to be asked. He'd thought he knew

Maria as well as any colleague he had. She'd proved him wrong by releasing the first profile.

"I'm going to do exactly what the UNSUB wants us to do." Her simple response had something in Cam's chest easing. "I'm going to tell the station to have it read on the air."

～～～

There were eleven Bryson's drive-throughs in Des Moines and its suburbs, and it had taken Cam more than two hours to get the warrants for the security footage at each. There was no telling how long ago the UNSUB had been at the restaurant. Or even if he'd gotten the food himself. But if he had, and if it was recent enough to still appear on the camera, they just might get lucky and get a picture of the offender.

One security company provided the surveillance packages to all franchises of the chain restaurant, Cam had learned, but each owner chose his own level of security. Gonzalez had reassigned extra agents to the case. Cam had promptly given them the task of picking up the copies of images from the cameras and taking them back to headquarters for viewing. If they found any images of drivers in white cargo vans, he'd turn them over to the lab for image enhancement.

During that time he'd also fielded a call from Fenton relaying the news that the blood found in Sophie's bathroom had indeed belonged to her. Turning his attention now to the emailed toxicology report, he scanned it swiftly, then slowed as incredulity surged. He grabbed his cell, punched in a number. Then printed out the report, waiting for Franks to arrive.

When he did, Cam held out the pages for the man. It wasn't long before the other agent looked at him, his expression as grim as Cam's.

"Etorphine? It says that stuff is fatal to humans."

"In veterinary strength," Cam corrected. But the UNSUB would have to know how to lower the dosage to an appropriate amount for humans. A cold river of dread coursed through him. He'd held on to the fact that this offender didn't kill right away. He found himself newly grateful for the appearance of the profile that morning. At least Cam wouldn't have to torture himself with worries that Sophie's abductor might have killed her with that drug.

"It comes with a human antidote," the other agent muttered, still reading.

"Have Jenna help you contact all the veterinary places in the area. Large and small animals. See if they've been targeted for break-ins for pharmaceuticals. Also get the names of their supply reps. If they're anything like pharmaceutical reps who call on doctors, they often have samples of the drugs." He didn't know if they gave samples of the heavy-duty stuff, but he'd once had a doctor give him a new antibiotic to try in sample form.

"Then get a list from the licensing board of vets in the area and run them for arrests in their pasts."

"I'm on it." Tommy's usually taciturn expression held a glint of excitement. "I'll also check with DNE. See if they've got anything on thefts of the drug."

"Good idea." At one time narcotics had operated under the DCI umbrella, but several years ago the Division of Narcotics Enforcement had been formed, and it operated independently of DCI. When Cam had joined as an agent, he'd originally been assigned to the division. Years after he transferred to DCI, a long-ago contact made in those earliest days had gotten him loaned out to DNE again for the federal multiagency task force he'd worked with for a couple of years.

The memory wasn't one he welcomed, so he distracted himself by saying, "Let's hope he didn't buy it off the Web." There were sites on the Internet that claimed to sell pharmaceuticals without prescriptions. If the UNSUB had gotten the narcotic online, their chance of tracing it was minimal.

But with the threat of international narcotics enforcement, he had to hope that stealing the drug would be easier for the offender. He'd already proven amazingly creative at breaking and entering. What additional challenge would a vet clinic hold for him?

"I'll keep you posted."

When the agent left, Cam's gaze fell to the copy of the new profile he'd made before turning the originals over to the questionable documents section of the lab. The analysts there would determine whether the handwriting belonged to Sophie.

He wanted it to be proof she was still alive. Wanted to believe she'd written it. If she had, Cam couldn't imagine her wasting an opportunity to give them some sort of clue about her abductor. Or even where she was being held. He jotted down the first letters of each sentence. The last letters. Every other word in the profile. Every third word.

He came up with nothing.

Rubbing his forehead, he considered the fact that he might be wasting his time. Sophie was under duress. Possibly suffering. That thought twisted and tightened in his gut like a tangle of vicious serpents. Her primary concern would be pacifying her captor. Staying alive. That was a helluva lot more important than risking the man's wrath if he suspected her of embedding a code in the writings.

And yet . . . the paragraphs contained some awkward phrasing the likes of which he'd never heard her speak, much less include in a profile. Like "markings of intellect" and "mood lifter." The choice of words was puzzling. Had she taken them from the UNSUB's speech patterns? If so, they were interspersed with wording more commonly found in Sophie's professional work. It also included more casual language than she would normally use, and one near misspelling. The first time she'd written genius, she'd had an *i* for the *e*, and had to correct by writing over it. And something about the sentence structure bothered him.

It is a sad penchant of society to knock a genius.

Clearly the profile had been written to inflate the offender's ego. The almost misspelled words, *genius* and *intelligence*, each appeared more than a half a dozen times in the missive.

Knock a genius. The slang didn't even sound like Sophie. *Knock a genius. Knock a "ginius."*

Knock. Gin.

Barely breathing, Cam stared harder at the words, afraid to believe it. They'd played Gin only the one time. Strip Gin, as it happened, and she'd sandbagged him. The hell of it was, he hadn't even cared. The game had been win-win, rules be damned.

Rules. It took a moment to refocus. What were the rules of Gin? Sets and runs. Ten cards dealt. Play to one hundred. A bonus of twenty-five points for declaring Gin.

With renewed focus he bent over the profile, scribbling every tenth word from the profile in one column, every twenty-fifth in another.

Going through the writing on both pages, in the first column he quickly realized he had a jumble of meaningless words. But in the second he'd written the words *con, markings, lifter, mouth, missing, bottom, right, bare, headed, color, blew, no, sketch.*

Staring for a moment in amazement, Cam let out an incredulous laugh. "Dammit all, Sophie. You're brilliant."

Because she was alive. She had to be, this missive proved it. And even in the midst of the most dangerous situation of her life, the woman had had the guts to embed a description of her abductor in the profile.

It hadn't taken long for Sophia to work the longer length of board loose from its moorings. Moving it back and forth with all her might, the rusty nails holding it in place gave a screech of protest. A few more tries and it was freed. She'd blinked in astonishment at the board in her hand for a moment, before setting it aside to tear off the other piece.

It proved tougher to release than the first. She kept trying, moving it up and down, then pushing and pulling on it. Sweat slicked down her back, the effort sapping her strength. Finally, it gave with a suddenness that sent her stumbling back across the stall and sprawling on her back.

The aches from her injuries set up a howl of protest. Slowly, determinedly, she rose to her feet and picked up the prizes her hard work had wielded.

Here, at last, were the wedges she needed to pry an opening in the wire above her.

She took one of the boards and climbed the gate as high as the wire would allow. Then stuck it in the narrow opening where the ceiling of wire met the gate and pumped it up and down like a handle in an old-fashioned well.

Her heart lifted when she saw the wire overhead move as it was forced to bend upward and back with the leveraging motion. She labored for more than an hour before she had an opening she thought she could slip through. Then Sophia propped the board atop the gate, holding the wire up and stationary, before moving halfway down the gate to do the same there.

Only then did she allow herself to look at the dim slivers of light allowed into the structure. Her heart sank when she realized that it must be late afternoon. She hadn't realized how long it had taken to get this far in her escape plan.

And she didn't want to consider how many hours she had until the monster returned.

Before she made her attempt, she had the forethought to retrieve the comforter and stuff it through an opening in the gate. Then, focusing on the passageway she'd created in the wire, she decided there was only one way through it. She'd have to snake through the gap headfirst and try to descend the gate on the opposite side, supporting her weight on her hands.

Power walking was the height of her athletic accomplishments. This feat would take far more strength and dexterity.

It would also require an inordinate amount of luck.

Easing her head and shoulders through the space pried between the top of the gate and the wire, she was filled with even more doubts. But freedom was much too close to alter the plan now. A sense of urgency was building, and scenarios where her abductor returned earlier than usual flitted across her mind on an endless reel of nightmarish possibilities. Perhaps the profile hadn't aired, further enraging him.

Or worse, maybe he'd examined her writings more closely and decoded the clues she'd included.

The thought had a cold wash of fear cascading through her. But she couldn't hurry even if she wanted to. Awkwardly reaching for the next lower rung on the bars on the exterior of the gate, she attempted to work her hips through the opening. The wire scraped and abraded skin as she wiggled through, but her progress down the other side was steady.

Until it came time to thread her legs through the portal. While they were still positioned on the bars inside the cell, they were taking the bulk of her weight. Once they left the rung, her wrists had to bear all of it, as if she were doing a headstand. Sophia felt herself slipping and grasped wildly at the next bar. But the momentum of her legs swinging to the other side was too great for her to overcome. She lost her grip and fell the rest of the way to the concrete floor below.

The breath drove out of her chest at the bone-jarring contact. Stars spun before her eyes. Laboring to breathe, she gasped for air. Her lungs were strangled, heaving for oxygen. Long minutes ticked by.

Eventually she attempted a slow, cautious roll to her side. Then got up on all fours. Crawling the short distance to the unforgiving metal gate, she hauled herself to a standing position, taking stock of any injuries sustained in the fall.

Her ribs sang a familiar protest, and there was a teeth-gritting pain in her hip that was new. Her left wrist throbbed even when she kept it cradled close to her chest.

But her legs held her when she let go of the gate. She awkwardly wrapped the comforter around herself and stumbled in the direction from which the offender always came. Toward the door.

Sophia could see now that this side of the structure was lined with cells like she'd been kept in, although none of the others had wire across the top of them. She crept along, progress slower than she'd like because of the shadows. She peered into each cell, but none held a mattress.

And none held the victim she'd heard last night.

Until she came to the cell just inside a huge set of double doors. This cell had wire over the top. And she could make out the figure of another woman curled up on a blow-up mattress in one corner.

"Courtney?"

Her whisper had the female inside the cell trying to turn painstakingly in the direction of her voice.

"Go back." The words were little more than a croak. "He'll come back and punish you. He'll punish both of us."

"We won't be here when he gets back," Sophia promised grimly. She moved to the side of the cell, looking for a key to unlock the woman's cell. But it was too dark inside the building to see it.

Instead, she turned her attention to the big doors five feet ahead of her. If she inched one open, she'd have enough light to be able to search for the key. And once she released the other woman, maybe she could study their surroundings through the narrow opening before attempting to make a run for it.

Did the UNSUB live on the property? Did he reside close by?

The thoughts had her stumbling to a halt, loath at first to even touch the exit that promised freedom. But there was no other way.

Stiffening her spine, Sophia felt along the door for the handle and then pushed with all her might. It barely budged. She pulled inward on it. Nothing. Desperation flickering, she attempted to drag it first one way and then the other. There was no movement.

Panic and frustration warred inside her. Sophia let the impetus of the emotion drive her forward, throwing her weight against the massive exit. Once. Twice. Again.

Battered now in mind and spirit, she finally leaned against it, shoulders slumping in defeat.

Somehow in all the hours she imagined finding a way out of her prison, it had never occurred to her that the doorway leading to freedom would be locked.

Chapter 14

I 've never seen you with your hair grown out before." Entranced, Sophia studied the picture of Cam and another man. It looked fairly recent, but instead of the short-cropped style he and the other agents favored, it was curling over the top of his ears and around his collar in back. It was thicker than she would have imagined. And sun-streaked in a way that gave him a more carefree look. "It's curly."

He never looked up from the kitchen drawers he was rifling through. "I don't have curly hair. Wavy. There might be a slight wave. Not curly. Curly's not masculine."

She looked at the photo again. "Well, in this picture your hair was going all unmasculine on you. I like it. It makes you look less stern."

"You want stern? I can show you stern. Just as soon as you help me find some . . ." His gaze rose then and the rest of his words died. His gaze went still. Shuttered.

Watching the change come over his expression, something knotted in Sophia's chest. Without knowing exactly why, she had the sensation of tiptoeing through a minefield. "Who's this with you?"

"My cousin." He returned his attention to the search again. She didn't know why it seemed as though the hunt for batteries to replace those in his smoke detectors had suddenly become a convenient excuse.

"I thought you told me once that neither you nor your mother had any living relatives."

He shut the drawer he was looking in. "I'll just run to the store and get some. Less aggravation."

But she was dogged. She, the psychologist who respected boundaries in others and only pressed when she felt more transparency was in her client's best interest. Cam's best interests hadn't even crossed her mind. Nor had her usual consideration for others' privacy.

It was getting more and more difficult to quiet the warnings sounding in her own head. She held up the picture. "How can he be your cousin?"

His gaze narrowed, a sure sign of his irritation. "I don't know the actual relationship. We don't have any close relatives. He's my mom's great-uncle's grandson or something. I'm not sure. That makes us—third or fourth cousins? No idea. I never could figure that stuff out."

Slowly, she lowered the picture to the desk drawer she'd opened to help him in his quest for batteries. And when she closed it, she felt as if she were teetering on the brink of a momentous decision.

She was being ridiculous. Repeating the words over and over in her mind like a litany didn't make her feel better, however. Cam certainly had the right to decide which subjects he wanted to discuss with her and which he didn't. He had every reason to declare some topics off-limits.

But he hadn't done that. Instead he'd lied. In her profession one became an excellent judge of honesty. She had no problem being warned off when she was skating too close to the personal. At least usually she didn't.

But she was finding it more and more difficult to balance their intimacy in the bedroom with the lack of it out of bed.

Her own fault. She crossed to the rattan basket he used as a catchall next to the leather couch and flipped through the magazines and flyers in it blindly. She didn't do well with casual. Had difficulty traversing the boundaries and unspoken rules. And it certainly wasn't his problem that she felt as though she were losing a bit of herself in the process.

Unbidden, the unopened foil wrapper from last night flashed across her mind. Sophia didn't even recognize herself in some of the choices she'd made recently. Cam's reticence about something as simple as a photo was a dash of cold water that she desperately needed. He had no trouble whatsoever throwing up walls whenever she veered too close to the personal.

She was the one finding it difficult to maintain defenses. To keep that healthy sense of caution that had served her well all her life. She just didn't know what had her acting so out of character.

"You're not going to find them in there. Forget it. Changing the batteries isn't pressing. I can do it later."

She rose, feeling a little raw from her abrasive thoughts. Not meeting his gaze, she went to where she'd left her purse. "I could use a diet soda, anyway. I'll run to the store for you."

"You don't have to do that. We'll both go. Just let me get my—"

"No." Because the word came out a little more emphatically than she'd meant, she deliberately softened her tone and manufactured a smile. "I have a bit of a headache. This will give me a chance to clear my head." Clear it of this uncustomary dithering and try to figure out once and for all if she was capable of maintaining a no-strings intimate relationship.

Snatching up her keys and hurrying to the doorway, she felt a sense of loss as soon as she stepped through it.

Because in her heart she already knew the answer.

———

"Go back. Before he comes." It seemed to take everything Van Wheton had to force the words out. Given the whispery hoarseness of her voice, Sophia assumed she'd been choked by the offender, and she felt an immediate pang of empathy.

"It's all right. We are getting out of here." She sounded more certain than she felt. There was something about walking about freely outside a cell that solidified her purpose. Once given even a small taste of freedom, there was no way she'd give it up again.

With one hand on the door to guide her, she explored the confines of the building. When she reached the corner, she nearly tripped over a pile of materials in a jumble there. Judging from the cobwebs she encountered, they'd been there for quite a while. Sophia picked up each item, or dragged it closer to the nearest pinprick of light coming in through the cracks. She could see now that the limestone partial wall in the back of her cell continued around the perimeter of the building.

But when she was able to examine each object she'd found in the tiny beam of light, her heart sank. Useless ancient junk, all of it. Pieces of scrap metal that looked like spare parts for some sort of machinery. A roll of rusted wire. A barrel with wooden slats, half-rotted with age. When she heard something skittering inside it, Sophia took a cautious step away.

Even though she couldn't imagine how any of those objects would help her open the door, she continued her search, feeling encouraged. The cell where she'd been kept had been barren. But the building wasn't empty. Not completely. Surely there had been other items left behind.

She continued to search, staying close to the wall, stopping each time she encountered an unfamiliar object. There were lengths of pipe, and she hefted one grimly. If she wasn't able to find a way out, she now had a weapon. Maybe she'd be able to surprise her abductor as he opened the door.

The thought of swinging the pipe through the air and making contact with his head brought twin spears of squeamishness and satisfaction. Sophia had never struck anyone in her life. She had a feeling it would be all too easy with this sadistic UNSUB.

She dragged the pipe along with her, but she had to set it down each time she found something else to identify. Her left hand wasn't capable of holding anything and ached constantly. Under the circumstances, it was the least of her worries.

Her progress was slower than she'd like, and she was acutely aware that the miniscule beams of light were fading. The realization had her hastening her step. That, and the sudden thought that any building, even one as old as this, would likely have a second exit.

She found it on the center of the wall adjacent to her cell. Dropping the pipe, Sophia ran her hands over the rough doorway, slowing when she discovered the seam running the width, splitting the door in half. Comprehension dawned. She had the answer to one question now. They were being held in a barn.

And the thought of just how many of the structures dotted the landscape around the state made her realize just how unlikely their rescue was.

Running her hands over the rough boards, she could find no handle or knob. There was, however, a couple of uniform holes in the wood near the edge that might signify where one had once been.

A new plan took shape in her mind even as she continued along the wall trying to find any other items that had been left behind. One of the pipes on the other side of the barn had been a half-inch in diameter. She might be able to use it as a crowbar to pry the frame off around the doorway she'd just discovered.

But then leaning against the wall twenty feet from the cells, she found the treasure that she knew was going to be her ticket to freedom.

A pitchfork.

Giddy with delight, she clutched it close with newfound possessiveness before doing a tactile examination. The metal handle was loose, and it had only two tines. But each felt solid. And better, they were slimmer than even the smallest pipe she'd found.

Retracing her steps to the split door she'd discovered, Sophia abandoned her original plan. Setting the pitchfork down, she ran her fingers along first one side of the door and then the others, until she found what she was searching for.

The hinges.

⁓

"You sure you want to do this?" The doubt expressed in Beckett's voice echoed that of the Boone County attorney's when Cam had made his pitch earlier. "This morning you didn't give a shit about what Jerry Price claimed to know."

"This morning I didn't have any way of verifying what he said. Now, hopefully, I will. And you don't have to worry." He shifted to get more comfortable. The narrow wooden chair he occupied in front of the scarred wooden table in the sheriff's conference room wasn't exactly cushy. "Your county attorney is no more anxious than you are to offer this scumbag a deal. Most likely Price is blowing smoke to avoid going back inside on the weapon's charge." If every ex-con he'd ever met had the type of information they suddenly claimed to possess when faced with a prison sentence, there'd be no unsolved crimes in the country. "But on the off chance he isn't . . . We're just talking, that's all." Cam shot him a halfhearted grin. "Probably be the shortest conversation you've heard since your last girlfriend dumped you."

Beckett looked amused. "The one where she said, 'You're just too big?'"

"The one where she said, 'I can do better.'"

Unperturbed, the sheriff picked up his radio. "You don't know my last ex. If you did, you'd realize those words were punctuated with a lengthy disparaging commentary about the deficiencies in my parentage." He spoke into the radio. "All right, Owens, bring him in."

Cam waited for Jerry Price to be shown into the room, fairly certain that Beckett was right. Nine times out of ten, these conversations were a waste of time. There was little a convict wouldn't do to avoid paying the consequences of his actions with a stint in prison.

But given the details Sophie had managed to embed in the phony profile that was currently airing as breaking news on KCCT, he'd know whether the ex-con was merely playing him without having to waste more than a few minutes on the conversation.

The door opened and a uniformed deputy held it to allow Price entry. He was doing the jailhouse shuffle, courtesy of the leg chains that matched the set on his wrists. His dark hair was a bit greasier than the night he'd been arrested. His beard was filling in and shot with gray. But jail hadn't dimmed his attitude.

"Well, look who's been shopping." The man grinned at him, edging into the chair the deputy indicated. "That suit's in better shape than the last one I saw you wearing."

"Good times," Cam said mildly. "I like the look you've got going on, too. Not everyone can pull off county orange. But that jumpsuit seems to be made for you."

Price folded his hands and set them on the table; the action sent the links jangling. "Since you're here, I figure the sheriff told you 'bout my offer. The deal is, you make the weapons charge go away, and I give you information that will lead you to the guy kidnapping and burying all those women."

Cam laughed in genuine amusement. "You could draw me a map to his house, and that weapons charge still stands. The best you're going to be able to do with the Boone County attorney is get him to recommend a reduced sentence to the judge, and that's only for information leading to an arrest. Something I highly doubt you have."

"Guess you're not going to find out." Price studied the prison tat on the back of one knuckle in studied boredom. "That's my asking price, and I'm not in the mood to be generous."

"Sorry to waste your time." Cam's chair scraped the floor as he pushed it back and rose. "Thanks, Sheriff."

"No problem." He and Beckett headed for the door.

Price turned to look after them, half rising from his chair. "Hey, now." The deputy put a hand on his shoulder and pushed him firmly back in his seat. Cam turned in the doorway and lifted a brow. "Thought you were done talking."

"You fellas need to learn a little bit about the art of negotiation." The ex-con struck a conciliatory tone. "The deal is, I give a little, you give a little—"

"That's where you're mistaken. There's no negotiation going on here." Cam returned to the table but didn't sit. He set his hands on the table, leaning forward. "I doubt very much whether you have anything worth the price of the gas it took to drive over. But I've made the only offer I'm going to. You talk or I walk. It's as simple as that."

The truculence that came over the man's expression was familiar. "Any lawyer worth his salt could get me a better deal than that."

"Then maybe you'll want to reconsider acting as your own attorney," Beckett put in wryly.

Price didn't respond. His gaze was fixed on Cam. "You staying, or what?"

"You giving me a reason to?"

A jerk of a shoulder served as assent. Slowly, Cam sank into his chair, aware of the minutes ticking by. "Okay, here's the deal. I did time with this guy, my first cellie on my last stretch. He used to say some stuff. Like we'd talk, you know, to pass the time. Perfect crime and all that. Purely theoretical."

"Is that when you practiced your vocabulary, too?"

"I'm no dummy. Neither was this guy." Price's gaze was intent on Cam. "He was only in for five years for his second breaking and entering. Thing is, he told me he committed hundreds of B and E's that they never looked at him for. Did a lot more than that, too, if the bitch of the house was home when he called, if you get my meaning."

"I'm still waiting for you to get to the part where I start to care."

Price flashed a palm. "Wait for it. So we were doing time in Nebraska, but it turned out he'd spent a lot of summers in Iowa growing up. We hit it off. He made a decent haul carrying off electronics and jewelry and what not, but cellie says how he's got bigger plans than that. How he was putting something together when he got out where instead of breaking into houses, he'd be snatching up these rich bitches and making them drain their bank accounts."

"You like TV, Jerry?" Cam made a point of looking at his watch. "Bet you do. Because you got every bit of that story off the news.

There's not an original detail in it, and you are out of time." He made to rise.

"I didn't get this from TV, swear to God." Price thumped his folded hands on the table. "That stuff I said, about him grabbing up wealthy women, that was his deal. So when I heard the news shows, yeah, I thought about him." When Cam continued to look unimpressed, Price said, "I got a name. You check out my cellie, bet you won't find him in Nebraska. Know why? He said he might go to Iowa when he got sprung. Had a grandpa he used to visit by Ankeny. Said the old man used to live on a farm and raise ostriches."

Everything inside Cam stilled. There was no way Price could know the lab results. No way that information had been leaked to the press.

"Yeah, I had a grandpa that raised dodo birds. We used to race them. Tie them up to dog sleds to pull us through the snow."

Beckett's sarcasm broke the silence. Price looked from him to Cam. "Okay that was probably one of the things he was lying about. But you check him out. I'm saying, whoever is snatching those women is pulling exactly the same gig my cellie was planning."

"Name." Cam kept his tone bored although mental gears were spinning. The mention of the ostriches was too unique to ignore.

Price's expression went sly. "I get consideration with the judge, right? The prosecutor agreed?"

"You're getting way ahead of yourself," the sheriff said with a scowl. "What was the cell mate's name?"

"Mase Vance. Mason Vance, but everyone called him Mase."

"I need a description."

Price frowned at Cam's demand. "I don't know. Dirty-blond hair, I guess. Sort of bushy. Blue eyes. Tall as me, but solid. He took some knocks when we were inside. Always thought he was a tough guy, but there's always someone tougher. He bulked up a little while we were in. Said he was going to get serious about it once he was released."

Cam had heard enough. "Why would he come to Iowa?"

"He said his grandpa was going to leave his place to him. Not the farm, some house in a little craphole town around here. I don't remember where. Never heard of it before." He stopped then, leaned back in his chair. "That's solid info right there. You can use it, right? Swing some weight with the judge."

———

"Is there any chance at all that he heard deputies talking about the lab analysis?"

They were back in Beckett's office. Cam was in a chair barely more comfortable than the one in the conference room, his computer balanced on his lap as he combed through databases to verify Price's story.

"It's doubtful but hard to tell. I knew, and so did Owens because he was with me when we checked out the Quade Ostrich Ranch. Pleasant couple," he added sardonically. "Had to get a warrant before they allowed me to step foot on their property. And I can't be certain the dispatcher didn't mention our location to one of the other deputies. So . . ." His shrug was its own answer. There was no way to be sure.

"Okay," Cam said, scanning the computer screen at the information he'd pulled up. "The first part of his tale is true. He bunked with a Mason Vance for Vance's entire five-year stretch."

"The best lies begin with a kernel of truth." The sheriff turned to his own computer. "You got a date and place of birth for him?"

It was contained in the man's arrest record, so Cam read it off. Then he brought up a photo of Vance along with the terms of his release. No parole, as he'd served his entire sentence. Which meant he'd been free to leave Nebraska upon his release and go wherever he wanted, with no one keeping tabs on him.

He studied the man's mug shot intently. It definitely didn't match the sketch Jenna had drawn of the man Muller had seen in the Edina park. But the code in Sophie's last profile had said as much. According to her, they were looking for a bald man, a change easy enough to effect. Similarly the man's missing tooth could have occurred at any time since his release. It wasn't noted in the physical description of the man.

Tattoos were. Half sleeves on each arm and a fire-breathing dragon on his back right shoulder. Give him a couple of years on the outside to bulk up, and this could be the man Sophie had described.

Trouble was, her description would also likely fit dozens of others.

Nevertheless he picked up his cell phone, dialed Jenna's number. When she answered, he gave her an abbreviated account of the conversation he'd had with Price.

"Do you believe him?" She knew as well as he did how little credibility these guys had.

"Verifying the details of this story," Cam said noncommittally. "According to the details Dr. Channing coded in the revised profile, the UNSUB is a weight lifter. Call around to every gym and fitness center in Des Moines and its suburbs. See if they have a Mason or Mase Vance on their membership roster."

After hanging up he did a quick Internet search, but he found no current listings for a Mason Vance in either Iowa or Nebraska. Undeterred, he checked the DMV records. No license had been issued to someone fitting that name and age.

"I don't see an owner of a white cargo van listed under that name," Beckett muttered, scrolling down his screen.

After thinking for a moment, Cam logged on to a genealogy site that offered free one-month subscriptions. He had Vance's name and his place and date of birth. That was enough for a fishing expedition.

After wasting several minutes registering and typing in a search, he muttered, "There he is. Found the son of a bitch."

"Vance?" The sheriff spun around in his chair to stare at him. "How?"

"His name pops up as a descendent when I do a search of his grandpa. The one who was born in Polk County." Real excitement started to hum in his veins. He couldn't forget what Sophie had mentioned in the geographic profile she'd developed. That the offender would be in the area because of something familiar that anchored him here.

If Price was correct about Vance being an heir to his grandfather's estate, that anchor could be the old man's home.

"Ivan Stanford." He read the information off the site. "One daughter, Evelyn Marie Stanford, deceased. She was married to Walt Vance, also deceased. One surviving grandson, Mason Vance. The old man's last listed address was Alleman, Iowa."

"Alleman?" It was clear from the expression on Beckett's face that he was trying to place the town. "Little bitty place. Somewhere around Ankeny, right?"

Cam didn't answer. He was busy typing in another search on the computer. Finding the phone number he was looking for, he stood and powered off the laptop as he made a phone call. "Justin Jeffries," he said as soon as someone came on the line. When the younger man answered, Cam said without preamble, "That place you were telling me about today. The guy who raised ostriches in the eighties. What was his name?"

"Stanford," came the answer. Cam scooped up the laptop and headed for the door at a half run at the response. "Ivan Stanford. Last I heard he was retired and living in some small town nearby. Alleman, maybe."

The flat hinges stretched from door to jamb, and should have taken far less work than the boards in Sophia's cell had. This time, however, she was working one-handed, so her movements were slower than normal. Awkward. When she had removed the hinges, the lower part of the split door still didn't budge. So she used the tines of the pitchfork to pry the old wood away from the jamb. Weathered and rotting, it gave easily. She was able to pull most of the lower door away. A wide shaft of sunlight poured through the opening. The sight of it had her heart kicking a faster beat.

Outside. Freedom.

The sheer joy of being this close made her dizzy for an instant. There were two two-by-fours hammered across the doorway from the outside. She dropped the pitchfork and picked up the solid metal pipe and used it as a hammer to pound the lowest board outward. This timber was fresher and far more solid than the barn door had been. Sophia was sweating and panting by the time she'd knocked it free.

She turned to go back for the other woman, before hesitating. There was no way to know how close her abductor was. He could be living in a house right across the farmyard from where they were being held. He could live across the road. Somewhere close enough to see them immediately when they left the barn.

She scanned the area outside the door she'd broken open. Ahead of her was a scruffy farmyard, rolling to a steep ditch. Across the gravel road was nothing but a sea of green surrounded by barbed wire.

Nearing late June, the corn would only be midthigh. The wide-open expanse of the field offered nothing in the way of cover. If they went that way and the sadist returned, he'd spot them immediately.

She craned her neck to look in either direction. Corn to the left and more farmyard to the right, bordered by another field.

Not wanting to take the time to go back for the comforter, Sophia crawled through the hole she'd created and sidled along the side of the barn to the right to ease a look around the corner. More weeds and brush. A broken-down wooden wagon with rusted steel wheels leaned precariously off to one side. A bean field was ahead of her, the plants only inches high. Scarcely daring to breathe, she made her way quickly along the side of the barn, flattened against it, barely tilting her head to see around the corner.

Nothing. No house. No vehicle. Nothing but more corn.

Relief had the strength streaming out of her, and it took a moment before she could be certain her legs would hold her. Then she made her way back to the door she'd broken open, keeping a careful eye for a plume of dust that would herald an oncoming vehicle.

The horizon was still. The sky was an eye-shattering blue, unmarred by clouds. The sun had faded, signaling late afternoon. Everything around her was peaceful as an Americana painting.

It was such a stark contrast to the evil permeating the barn that she felt a chill work down her nape to snake down her spine. It was all Sophia could do to force herself to go back inside the building. She wouldn't leave without the other woman. She couldn't be certain help would arrive before the monster returned.

But it was hard. So hard to stand inside the relative coolness of the barn and squelch her impulse to bolt for freedom again.

Determinedly, she made her way the length of the building to Van Wheton's cell. This time, with the sun slanting in through the door, she could easily make out the key hanging from a nail two feet from the gate. After retrieving it, Sophia fumbled a little as she fit it into the lock. Turned it. The gate was heavier than she'd expected.

When she pulled it open, the other woman just stared from her seat on the mattress, a mixture of hope and fear on her battered face.

"We're free. But we have to hurry. I don't know how long . . ." How long before he comes back, she almost said but swallowed the words. This woman didn't need a reminder of the precariousness of their situation. "There's no one around. No house that I can see." She tried to force a reassuring smile, but it quickly faded when Van Wheton made several attempts to stand and failed.

"I'm sorry." The words were so raspy they sounded painful to utter. "I can't . . . I don't think I can . . ."

The key still wrapped tightly in her hand, Sophia picked up the comforter and entered the cell, draping their only covering around the woman's shoulders. "Courtney Van Wheton?" she asked gently, wincing a little as her hip protested when she went down on both knees before the woman.

A jerky nod was her only answer. "I'm Sophie." The nickname was uttered without thought. "Put your arm around my shoulder. Let me help you stand." Staggering a little under the woman's weight, she rose. For the first time she wondered if the woman had internal injuries that could be worsened by moving her.

After a moment of indecision, she slid her arm around Courtney's waist and tried to provide as much assistance as possible as they left the cell, using the metal pipe as a crutch for support.

Their progress through the barn was excruciatingly slow. "It's going to be okay. It won't be long now." She kept up a reassuring whisper along the way. But she was already revising her original plan. There was no way the other woman was going to be able to flee to safety once outside. Sophia wasn't even certain how long she could keep Courtney upright. She'd have to find a grove of trees to hide her in. Some brush. Or, barring that, wrap her in the comforter and leave her partially covered by the tall grass in one of the deep ditches edging the gravel road.

Helping the woman through the half door she'd opened sapped an alarming amount of stamina. As much as she mentally railed at herself for being a wimp, the ordeal had weakened Sophia, and her struggle to assist Courtney was tapping the adrenaline-fueled strength she'd drawn on. Her bruised hip hampered her movements, and every time her left wrist was jarred, it sent up a screech of agony.

But then she caught sight of the woman fully in the daylight, and a vise squeezed her heart.

Courtney was barely recognizable. Bruises covered her face and body like an overall tattoo. Her nose was swollen and at an odd angle. Dried blood matted her hair and crusted on cuts and scrapes all over her body. One arm hung limply at her side.

Blinking away tears of sympathy, Sophia murmured, "It's not far now. I just need to get you hidden while I go for help." How the woman had managed to get this far was a miracle. Hope must have provided some much-needed strength, but clearly it was flagging fast.

"I have an idea." Sophia forced encouragement into her voice. "We'll just get you as far as the ditch. Can you make it that far?"

The woman tried to speak. Sophia bent so her ear was close to Courtney's mouth. "Thank . . . you."

Daggers of guilt twisted in her stomach. She was the last person who deserved this woman's thanks. Unknowingly, she'd deflected the offender's sexual assault last night at Courtney's expense. And she knew it would be a long time before she ever learned to forgive herself for that.

"Don't talk. Save your strength." Drawing upon a new well of it, Sophia half carried Van Wheton the thirty yards or so to the nearest ditch. Climbing down the steep side, though, she lost her footing and the two of them tumbled the rest of the way to sprawl at the bottom.

The weeds and grass were long, offering the only form of cover Sophia could see for miles. She spent a couple of minutes searching for the pipe, and then got Courtney settled in the center of the comforter, the pipe at her side. Grabbing the corners on either side of the woman's head with both hands, she tugged. Slowly she pulled the woman along the bottom of the ditch, gritting her teeth against the pain singing up her arm from her injured wrist. There wasn't a soul to be seen. How far before they'd reach a farmhouse? A mile? Maybe two?

The question became moot a couple of minutes later when Sophia spotted a farm drive ahead. Its purpose was to allow the farmer access to the field from the road. Many had drainage pipes under them to keep water from collecting in the ditches.

The sunlight glinting off something metallic beneath the drive was an answered prayer.

"Not much further now," she muttered between gritted teeth, pulling as fast as she was able. "Almost there."

The mouth of the culvert was less than two feet across. Plenty of room for Courtney, but the quarters would be close. Claustrophobic. Sophia used the pipe to clear the culvert of any creatures that might be in residence before helping the woman to a sitting position. "Do you think you could crawl inside?" Courtney's battered face was a mask of weariness. Sophia didn't know how she'd managed to get this far. "You'd be safe there. Out of sight. Then I can run to find the nearest house." A smile pulled at the corner of her mouth. "Maybe run is a little ambitious, but at least I can—" She stopped as the woman recoiled. Panic and hope warred in her expression as she stared at a point beyond Sophia's shoulder.

Turning, she saw what had caught Courtney's attention. Dust plumed on the gravel road a couple of miles down the road.

Caution had her keeping low, but Sophia was already planning how to climb the side of the ditch in time to flag the driver as it went by.

Except the vehicle never got to them. It slowed long before that. A hard knot of fear lodged in her throat, choking her. Eyes wide with alarm, Sophia watched a white cargo van swing into the drive and disappear behind the barn.

Chapter 15

C am waited until the door closed behind Sophie before striding across the room, opening the desk drawer, and withdrawing the picture of him with Matthew Baldwin. He couldn't explain even to himself why he'd printed a colored copy of the photo before handing off the entire envelope to Agent Dietrich. It wasn't only because he was now convinced Dietrich was a lying son of a bitch.

The photo was a reminder.

The longer he stared at it, the more memories swam to the surface. He'd spent the better part of the last couple of years stuffing most of the recollections away. But there had been a few bright moments in those long months undercover. Times that had momentarily lightened the heavy emotional toll that came from living in constant danger and threat of exposure.

This man had been a part of every one of those moments.

It was Matt who had introduced him to the restaurant that had ignited Cam's addiction to Creole food. Matt who'd shared a love of all things baseball, although his team had been the Oakland A's. Matt, whose love for his Mexican American wife had embroiled him in a deadly entanglement with a powerful player in the Sinaloa cartel drug operation.

Matthew Baldwin. The man who'd avoided capture in that last culminating bust, because Cam had made sure he wouldn't be on-site when it went down.

Shoving the photo back in the drawer, Cam turned away, his mind working. The packet of photos could have come from his former friend. Because they had been friends. In another place and time, but there was no other word for it.

Or it could have come from someone within the Sinaloa cartel. After the arrests of many middle-management members of the organization, the first reaction of cartel leaders would be to minimize the damage. Change routes, routines, shipments, so if any of those arrested flipped on the cartel, losses would be minimal.

Their second priority would have been to cast blame and exact revenge on those responsible.

They'd look first for members who should have been at that fated bust but were now conspicuously absent.

Second would be a search to make sure all arrested had ended up in a cell.

Had Cam put a target on Matthew's back by ensuring the man hadn't been at that final strategy meeting? The bust had been a treasure trove for law enforcement. Maps of the routes used, a cache of weapons that would have outfitted a small army, and an armored car filled with product ready to be shipped. The crown jewel of the undercover operation had been the capture of one of the eight highest-ranking members of the cartel.

Baldwin had missed being scooped up.

If anyone bothered to check, Alec Jensen, Cam's undercover identity, wouldn't show up on any prison roster in the country.

Which meant both he and Matthew would have some serious explaining to do if they ever had to answer to the cartel.

Looking again at the photo, he wondered if it was an indication that his explanation was coming due.

—

"We're rollin' silent." Cam communicated the order to the other agents over radio from his position two miles from the barn. Franks was placed a similar distance away on the opposite side of it. Jenna was a half mile in back of Tommy, and Boggs was behind Cam. "If we have the right place and Vance is in there, we don't want this to turn into a hostage situation. Tommy and I will pull within a quarter mile of the site and take a closer look at the area. Maintain your distance at the rear." That proximity would allow them to pick up details of movement around the site with the aid of binoculars.

He put the vehicle into gear and pulled out of the farm lane he'd been parked in. Turned onto the gravel. The hulk of the old Stanford barn could be seen from here. According to Jeffries's information, there was no longer a house on the property, but that didn't mean a trailer or some other temporary living quarters hadn't been pulled onto it. Cam had dispatched Beachum and Robbins to the Alleman address when he'd set off for this site. Their orders were to report any sightings of Vance, and to follow him if necessary. At this point, the agents were reporting no activity around the small bungalow that belonged to the suspect's grandfather. A little circumspect questioning of some locals had revealed that Ivan Stanford was residing in a nearby rest home, suffering from dementia.

—

Cam pulled to a stop closer to the barn and picked up the high-powered binoculars from his gear bag on the passenger seat beside him. Any lingering doubt about his instincts regarding this lead dissipated.

A white cargo van sat outside the barn.

Excitement thrummed through him. If their information was correct, Sophie and Van Wheton would likely be held in that barn or in the Stanford house. The isolated countryside made the barn the logical location to carry out the sadistic brutalities Vance was suspected of. After making calls to Iowa State Patrol and the Polk County sheriff's office for backup, he radioed his agents again.

"Turner and Boggs, tighten up to an eighth mile behind our vehicles. I want a roadblock and tack strips across the road in back of us." He brought up the binoculars to study the structure again. There was a split door on the face of the building visible from the road. Boards had been nailed across it, but the bottom one had been torn off, and the lower door was open.

Cam tried to temper the hope that stirred at the sight. The partially opened door might be for ventilation purposes. It might be there to provide a second exit for Vance, should he need it.

But the way it had been obstructed meant there was another entrance to the place on the other side of the structure. And it would be much harder for Vance to escape if both routes were blocked.

He could feel sweat trickling down his back in spite of the air-conditioning. The heavy armored vest he was wearing was suffocating. "Tommy, we'll use our vehicles to block the exit from the drive and approach on foot. You cover the entrance facing the road."

"I see it," came the laconic reply over the radio.

Scanning the miles of corn and beans surrounding the building, Cam realized there would be nothing to stop Vance from ramming the van through the barbed wire fencing and attempting an escape by driving across a field. He might break a wheel shaft traversing the uneven ground in the process, but they couldn't count on it. "I'll continue around the barn and disable the vehicle. Gear up and let's roll." He edged the vehicle back onto the road.

"Cam, you've got movement in the south ditch a couple hundred yards to your rear."

Boggs's words over the radio had Cam's gaze flying to the rearview mirror as he eased the car to a stop. Something unidentifiable was moving in the tall grass. With one hand on his weapon, the other went in search of the binoculars. Raised them to his eyes. A moment later, stunned recognition slammed into him.

The nude figure of a woman was awkwardly clambering out of the ditch.

Sophie.

A fierce primal spear of joy arrowed through him. She was alive and mobile, if more than a little banged up.

Alive.

"We've got a sighting of Dr. Channing attempting to climb from the south ditch. Boggs, stop to offer assistance. Summon paramedics." The radio burst with excited chatter from the other agents at the news. Cam had to stop for a moment to steady his voice. "If she's capable, put her on the radio, Boggs. She might be able to offer intelligence on what we'll face inside the barn."

It was both heaven and hell to watch the scene unfold from afar. Sophie struggled to ascend the steep side of the ditch. The way she seemed to be favoring her left wrist had a sharp prick of worry grazing him. Cam wouldn't let himself think about the fact that it was likely the least of her injuries. Couldn't dwell on the greasy pool of dread that accompanied the thought.

She'd survived. That was all that mattered right now.

Boggs pulled to a stop beside her and got out of the vehicle. He helped Sophie to the road and slipped off his suit coat to wrap it around her naked form. But when he tried to steer her in the direction of his vehicle, she began talking and gesturing toward the ditch.

Frowning, Cam had to divide his attention between the barn before him and what was transpiring behind him. Franks was at the drive, awaiting further orders. There was no activity around the building. Switching his focus back to Sophie, he saw Boggs accompany her to his vehicle and seat her on the passenger side before he made his way carefully down the side of the ditch again.

"Sophie. Pick up the radio."

There was a long pause, during which time he saw Boggs approach the short farm drive in the ditch, getting down on his knees to peer at something in the culvert beneath it.

"It's Courtney Van Wheton, Cam." The sound of her voice had him sending up a relieved prayer to a frequently absent God. "She's unresponsive. Maybe I shouldn't have moved her. She's badly injured. I was just too afraid to leave her while I—"

"An ambulance is on its way," he broke in soothingly. "Was she the only other victim held in the barn?"

"Yes. He's in there now. The UNSUB. I saw the van pull in there about ten minutes ago, and we hid. I was afraid he'd come looking for us."

"Is he always alone? Armed?"

"He's been alone. I don't know . . . I never saw a weapon, but it was always pretty dark inside." There was a slight tremble to her words. Otherwise her manner was remarkably steady. "He'll be dangerous and if cornered will behave impulsively. Erratically. He has bouts of rage, but he's violent at any time. Oh, and he doesn't match the sketch Jenna drew."

"I figured that from the description you hid in the content of the profile. It's okay. We'll take it from here. You stay put. When the paramedics arrive let them take a look at you."

"Oh, but Courtney . . ."

His gaze returned to the barn. "They'll take care of her, too. And, Soph . . . it's good to hear your voice."

"Yours, too." Her words sounded thick. "Be careful."

He put the car in gear and drove ahead to take position. The entire exchange had taken less than a minute and had served to allay some of his worries for her.

More, she'd given him valuable information that would impact how they'd approach the suspect inside. Cam stopped at the edge of the property and reached over for the whisper mic on top of his gear. Donning it, he zipped up the gear bag and took it out of the car, easing the door shut behind him. As he rounded the vehicle and made his way into the ditch to approach the barn, he saw Tommy exit his car and do the same. Staying as close to the fence line as possible, Cam veered around the scrub brush and a few half-hidden scraps of metal from some ancient farm equipment until he reached the far end of the barn.

He stopped. "We've got a set of sliding double doors, one is standing open." He spoke into the mic in a near whisper. "Looks like a shiny new padlock on the door." The rotted board that had likely once served to slide across the doors to secure them was leaning against the side of the structure.

Cam's gaze turned to the vehicle. It was parked in view of the doors. If Vance was still inside, depending on where he was situated, there was a good chance he'd see any movement around the van.

But if the suspect had gotten there ten minutes earlier, as Sophie had attested, he'd have seen that his captives were gone. So what would keep him inside?

Franks's voice sounded. "There's a big square door near the top of the barn on the east side."

Which meant a hayloft. The original owner would have needed the opening for ventilation, and to load and unload hay for the livestock. "Any method of escape from it?"

"Not unless someone doesn't mind breaking a dozen bones by jumping."

"Stay out of range of it." If Vance had taken position up there, he'd be in perfect sniper position. "Any sign of movement inside?"

"Negative."

Cam crouched low and made a beeline for the van. Crawling under it, he used the tack stick to puncture the sides of each tire before rolling out again. Looked toward the barn. "I'm going in. Cover the back."

Weapon in hand, he ran in a crouch to the yawning expanse revealed by the open door. Set the gear bag down. "Mason Vance," he called in a loud voice. "DCI. Put your hands behind your head and come out." There was no response. All was silent save for the trill of a songbird. The near-complete quiet lent an eerie quality to the scene. He tried again. "Vance! You are surrounded. Come out now. Hands behind your head." As seconds crawled into minutes, he said to Franks, "Let's go."

Weapon drawn, Cam swung around the doorway, scanning the dim interior. There were stalls lining one side. A rickety ladder led from the pulverized and dusty concrete barn floor to an overhead opening near the center of the barn.

He took the left side, Franks the right. Cam looked in each of the stalls. All were gated with the tallest livestock gates he'd ever seen. The gate of the first cell yawned open. Inside it was only a blow-up mattress and a wadded-up Bryson's bag and cup in the corner. His gaze lingered for a moment on the familiar sack. A similar one had served as the paper for Sophie's revised profile. Woven wire effectively penned in the stall from the top, making an escape-proof cell in which Vance could keep his victims.

But not exactly escape proof, apparently. Somehow Sophie and Van Wheton had managed to get out.

A crazy grin threatened at the thought. The suspect was cunning, but he'd underestimated Sophie's training and intellect.

He moved on. The place was massive. There were ten cells in all, but only the first and eighth had been used. Cam stopped a moment at the eighth gate to marvel at Sophie's ingenuity. At least he assumed Sophie had been kept here. A cup was in the corner but no bag. And from the sounds of things, Courtney Van Wheton had been in no shape to escape on her own.

One board was missing from the side of the stall. Parts of it had been used in two spots above to wedge the wire open far enough to allow a slender person to exit. That stall, too, was empty.

Cam took a moment to wonder at Vance's reaction when he'd found his victims gone. The man was prone to fits of rage, Sophie had said. Capable of fits of violence and impulsive, erratic behavior.

He found no one in the cells. Turning to Franks, he pointed upward, and the other agent nodded. Cam retraced his steps to where he'd left his gear. Going to one knee, he unzipped the bag and found a navy cap emblazoned with "DCI." He joined Franks on the other side of the barn and briefly explained his intent. The other agent bent down and retrieved a long length of heavy pipe.

"That'll do. Cover me." He headed back to the ladder, reholstering his weapon. Affixing the hat to the top of the pipe, he grasped a bent wire rung with his free hand and began to climb, the pipe held high above him.

"I'm coming up, Vance!" he shouted. He ascended far enough that the hat atop the pipe would be partially visible to anyone above, half expecting to hear shots fired in its direction.

What he was not expecting was to hear a woman sobbing.

"He's not here! He's not here! Oh, please God, get me out before he comes back."

⁓

Rhonda Ann Klaussen, as the ID from the purse in the van identified her, didn't fit the profile of Vance's usual victims. By her own
admission she had no money. A quick check showed that she'd twice
been arrested a decade ago, once for solicitation and the other time
for assault. What she did have was a long professed association with
Mason Vance, both before and after his time in prison.

"Where is he now?" Cam had been in contact with the agents
he'd sent to Alleman. Vance still hadn't been sighted. While Agent
Loring had found an Ankeny-based health club that admitted to
having a member by that name, the employee Loring had spoken to
claimed that the man had already come and gone that day.

Klaussen was seated in the back of Sheriff Dusten Jackson's
county-issued Ford Explorer, rubbing her wrists. They were red,
with visible indentations from the tight zip cuffs Cam had cut off.
Her feet had been similarly bound. "I don't know. He made me
drive him here, gave me the directions. He never let me out much,
but when he did, he always made me drive."

She was a big-boned woman, but lean, dressed in jean shorts,
a T-shirt, and flip-flops. Below the bleached-blonde hair and heavy
makeup, she looked older than the age on her driver's license. But
her prints had already been taken with a portable fingerprint device,
and the results had come back in minutes. She was exactly who she
said she was.

It just wasn't clear what relationship she had with Vance.

"What did he tell you?"

"Nothing." The sheriff reached into the front seat for something, and Klaussen shrunk away as if expecting a blow. "Mase
is . . . He's a mean guy. And whatever he had in mind wasn't good.
I knew that. Whenever he got that nasty little smile on his face, I
always knew something was coming I wouldn't like. He said he had
a surprise for me. You learn not to ask a lot of questions with Mase.
So I just drove, already shaking. But this place . . ." She gestured to

the barn. "What the hell is it? He said for me to wait in the van and if I moved he'd cut me." She held out an arm, which bore a fresh, barely healed scar. "I know he means it. So I stayed in the van."

"You weren't in the van when we found you." Both ambulances went by just then, and Cam followed their progress with his gaze. Jenna's vehicle followed them. He'd told the agent to remain with the women and report back when doctors had seen the two. Van Wheton still hadn't regained consciousness.

Klaussen began to shake. "Mase wasn't inside for more than a minute or two before he came out, screaming and yelling. He dragged me out of the van and into the barn, raving about all women being worthless cu—" Her gaze dropped. "He uses the c-word a lot. Kept ranting about finding two bitches and bringing them back to burn the place down with all of us in it." Tears welled in her eyes at the memory. "That's when he made me climb the ladder. He tied me up. I was begging and pleading with him." She pointed to her mouth. "So he hit me and told me to shut the fuck up. Then he left. When I heard you calling, at first I thought it was him. He plays games sometimes. Tries to get me to call for help by pretending to be someone else, and then if I do . . . Well, this is what you get if you try to get away from Mason Vance."

She turned a little on the seat, reached in back of her to lift up the hem of her shirt.

In a meandering line over her right shoulder were several round scars that were a match for those found on the six victims they'd unburied. Some looked like fresh wounds inflicted over healed ones.

"He likes to burn people," she said with a catch in her voice. "I always figured someday that wouldn't be enough to satisfy him anymore and he'd just kill me. If you hadn't come along I think today would have been my last."

"Do you believe her?"

"Hard to say." Cam's response to Tommy's question was reflective. The two were in Cam's car parked on the side of a road perpendicular from the Stanford house. "She could be an accessory. Dr. Channing said from the beginning the crimes could actually be the work of a team." But he'd thought if there were two criminals working together, the other might be the man matching the sketch Jenna had done in Edina. Nothing about this case had turned out the way he'd expected.

"Or she could have been Vance's first victim. She says they lived together for a while before he went to prison and practically held her captive. When he went to jail it took her ten days before she summoned the courage to venture out of the apartment they were living in."

"Wouldn't be the first time a victim was forced to be an accessory," Tommy observed.

"It's touchy." Broodingly, Cam watched the elongating shadows from the line of birch trees that edged the property. It was almost dusk, and still no sign of Vance. He found himself wishing he could get Sophie's take on Klaussen. Which was never going to happen, because if he had his way, Sophie would never be reminded of this case again. "If Klaussen's story is true, the grilling she's going to receive will be just one more trauma. She said she was often kept chained in the basement. And we saw the chains when we were inside." After the warrant had been okayed, they'd done a quick walk-through, with the help of a crowbar on the back door. The hasty search had yielded a rifle, a Glock, a list of bank account numbers, and twelve thousand dollars stuffed in a duffel bag in a bedroom closet. Cam had called Maria to give her an update, and she was working on freezing the assets in the accounts.

But the most damning thing they'd found by far was a pair of tennis shoes whose soles looked like a match to the footwear report Fenton had sent him that very morning. The treads still held traces of dirt Cam hoped would be identical to that found in Sophie's apartment.

He had two deputies stationed in bushes closer to the house. Stakeout in a vehicle was a piece of cake in comparison.

"Place isn't as isolated as the barn, but located on the outskirts of town like this, he wouldn't have to worry about nosy neighbors," Tommy noted. The next nearest house was another couple hundred yards away.

"Perfect for a son of a bitch like this one," Cam agreed grimly. "The van is in Klaussen's name. She said she bought it a couple years before Mason showed up in her life again. Claims he took it as his own and doesn't have another vehicle."

"He's got to realize with the two victims missing that someone would be coming for him. We had to have missed the bastard by minutes." Tommy's tone mirrored Cam's frustration. "Dr. Channing said the van had pulled in about ten minutes before she flagged down Boggs. That matches up with the timeline Klaussen gave, too."

Though Cam had headed to Alleman, he was still receiving updates about the search for Vance. And there had been a depressing lack of progress in that area. To have been that close to the man and missed him was the worst kind of timing.

"Probably thought he'd be finding Van Wheton and Sophie fairly quickly, given the location. He couldn't know our arrival would be minutes after his. Instead of killing three more victims, he ended up on the run himself." Cam considered the house across the road. The smartest thing for Vance to do would be to leave the area, but he might also want to get the contents the agents had found in the house. Or maybe he kept souvenirs there. Cam wondered if the sadist was also a collector. A lot of these sick bastards were.

Franks worked his shoulders tiredly. "Missed him by minutes. Thought the search plane might come up with something, but there are usually waterways in fields. I suppose he could have hidden in the grass in one. Made his way along it a couple miles to the next farmhouse."

Or maybe, Cam thought bleakly, the man was long gone. He could have hitched a ride and be on his way out of the state by now. Cam had already checked the stolen vehicle reports in the vicinity, but the closest theft that day had been in Ankeny, during the time a desk clerk at U-Fit said Vance had been working out. She'd identified him from a faxed photo as the suspect they were seeking.

"How long are we going to give it?"

"A few more hours." If Vance hadn't shown up by midnight, Cam would have to review his options. Once it got dark, they'd also be calling off the ground search in the area surrounding the barn. He'd leave in place the deputies the Polk County sheriff had stationed at the nearest farmhouses, though. Vance might be holed up somewhere in the vicinity of the barn, waiting for the cover of darkness before he . . .

The thought trailed off suddenly. A car pulled up in front of the drive across the street and stopped, motor running. "Honey, I'm home," he crooned in a singsong as Franks straightened in the seat next to him. A bulky man in gym shorts and T-shirt got out of the vehicle.

"You getting that license plate?"

"Might be older than you, but there's nothing wrong with my eyes." Franks scribbled it in a notebook he took from his suit jacket.

Vance withdrew his wallet and took out some bills, handing them to the driver. Then he walked up the drive as the car took off, temper evident in every step.

They let him get in the house. Waited for lights to go on while Cam shrugged out of his jacket, took off his tie, and pulled his dress shirt loose from where it'd been tucked in his trousers.

"How do I look?"

Franks spared him a glance. "Like a guy who's been waiting hours to kick some ass."

That was an understatement. "Exactly what I was going for." Cam fastened his holster under his shirt, weapon to the back. Then he reached up to turn off the overhead light. "Showtime."

They opened their doors simultaneously, Cam heading toward the house and Franks making a long circle that would eventually take him to the back of the Stanford property. The other law enforcement personnel would see his approach and be ready.

Cam wanted to give Vance time to get inside, but not long enough to get in the shower, on the phone, or engaged in anything else that might prevent the man from answering the door.

His hammering on the front door wasn't subtle. Neither was the threatening look on Vance's face when he yanked it open, after Cam waged a second assault on it.

"You got a problem, buddy?"

"Actually, yes." It wasn't difficult to summon the frustration rife in his voice. "I'm in town to visit my grandma. You know Hannah Barnett? On Oak and Third?" He turned and pointed behind him. "I tried to leave two hours ago, but the damn car won't start. My phone is dead, my wife took the car charger, Grandma doesn't have long distance on her landline." He bared his teeth, the picture of a man at the end of his rope. "Doesn't seem to be anyone in town under the age of eighty who knows a darn thing about vehicles. I'm hoping maybe you do. Or if that's not your thing, that you'll at least let me use your cell to get a tow truck out here, so I don't have to spend the night sleeping in the damn thing."

Sophie had been right. The guy was big. His arms were roped with muscles and hung a little away from his sides, giving him an apelike appearance. A sly look came over Vance's expression as he peered past Cam. "What kind of car is it?"

"Dodge Charger. I figure I might have blown the ignition relay. But with all the damn electronics in these new cars, hell if I know where to find it."

"New model, huh?" The farce had worked. Vance was shoving his feet into tennis shoes. Probably already salivating at the thought of getting his hands on a new set of wheels. After he'd gotten rid of Cam first, of course. "I'll take a look. I'm pretty good with my hands."

"It's across the street." Cam let the man precede him down the steps, pulling his weapon as soon as Vance's back was to him. "Get down on your belly. Down, down, now!" Agents and deputies burst from their hiding places to swarm the yard.

For all his bulk, there was nothing wrong with Vance's reflexes. He spun around and lunged toward Cam, his meaty fist whistling through the air as it came perilously close to Cam's temple. He dodged, slightly off balance, and aimed a vicious kick at the man's knee, designed to dislocate his kneecap. When it connected, Vance squealed like a girl. Went down hard. He latched on to Cam's ankle, intent on pulling him to the ground. Even with a half-dozen guns trained on him, the man was trying for a weapon.

Cam swung away, one foot purposefully finding Vance's injured knee. The man's scream was hideous. Franks and Sheriff Jackson moved to restrain him as Cam stepped to the side, weapon still trained on the man.

"Mason Vance." A primitive sense of satisfaction filled him as he spoke the words. "You're under arrest for eight counts of kidnapping and six counts of murder." It took four law officers to bring Mason to his feet. It was an oddly surreal moment for Cam to watch the sadistic rapist and murderer who had enacted atrocities on multiple women sniveling about the pain in his leg.

"I'll follow you to the Polk County jail," Cam told Jackson. The sheriff and his deputies led Vance away. The DCI agents headed back toward the house as Cam called for a crime team.

Only Franks stayed by Cam's side, silently watching the sheriff's Explorer turn and head out of town until its taillights were just pin-pricks of red in the distance.

"That some kung fu shit you were doing with Vance?"

"Army Ranger combat training." Cam didn't trust himself to say more. An unfamiliar tide of emotion was still coursing through him. The urge to lay aside his weapon and join the man on the ground, using every ounce of deadly training he'd once received had been so strong, so overpowering that he still shook with the effort it had required to restrain it.

The feeling was unprofessional. Primitive. It had nothing to do with the oath he'd taken when he'd joined the agency and every-thing to do with the six bodies in the morgue, and with the two women currently at the hospital.

It had everything to do with Sophie.

Franks clapped a hand on his shoulder. "All this backup is nice, but sometimes it feels like a shame to have witnesses, doesn't it?"

"You must have a crystal ball in your pocket, Tommy." Cam started for his car. "Because you just read my mind."

Chapter 16

She could have taken the easy way out and done this with a phone call. An email. But that would have felt even more shameful than the knots she had in her stomach just contemplating the upcoming scene.

Sophia had chosen an outside corner table at Legends, hoping the shadows relieved only by the occasional torchlight would give her some much-needed bravery. So far it didn't seem to be working. Her heart was rapping inside her chest, keeping time to her galloping pulse. The margarita in front of her wasn't doing a thing to soothe a throat dry with nerves.

She wasn't good at this. Hardly surprising. In the last several days she'd found any number of things she wasn't adept at. No-strings sexual interludes, for one. Keeping her wits about her as she allowed herself—for the first time ever—to be led by her hormones.

And she wasn't good at scenes. Something told her Cam wouldn't be as civil and accommodating as Douglas had been when they'd discussed the dissolution of their marriage. But nothing about Cam was similar to her ex.

Which was very likely the reason she'd deviated from her usual safe choices in men in the first place.

She'd ordered for them and paid the tab but had barely touched her drink. The beer she'd ordered for him had drops of condensation collecting on it in the warm air. One of them slowly rolled down the side of the bottle. Sophia's gaze tracked its progress with an intensity that would have served better had it been turned inward. She could have benefited from that sort of focus twelve days ago. Or any one of the days since. She could have avoided this upcoming scene.

And missed out on every delicious and delectable moment she'd experienced with Cam Prescott.

Looking up then, she saw him approaching the wrought iron railing that separated the patio from the sidewalk. Her heart turned over in trepidation. He was wearing jeans with a white dress shirt, the sleeves half rolled to his elbows. And Sophia was reminded, quite vividly, of exactly what had made her throw her usual caution to the winds.

Summoning a smile when he stopped near her, she said, "Your beer's getting warm."

"Then I'd better drink it." Rather than going around to the entrance, he stepped over the railing, earning himself a look of disapproval from a harried waitress rushing by. He slipped into the seat opposite Sophia's and picked up the bottle. Took a drink. "Parking is getting ridiculous down here." He propped a forearm on the table and scanned the area. "I like what they've done with this area. Hate the parking. There was no reason to bring two cars. Would have made more sense for me to pick you up."

"I thought it would be easier this way. We need to talk."

His arm stopped midway in the act of lifting the bottle to his lips. Slowly, deliberately, he set it on the table in front of him. Met her eyes. "I can't think of one conversation I've ever enjoyed that started with those words."

It was hard, so hard, to look at him as she stumbled through the speech she'd been practicing all afternoon. "I'm worried that our involvement could negatively impact our work the next time I consult with the agency."

His gaze was watchful. "Nearly three dozen MCU agents in the state. You and I have only worked together a handful of times."

"But still . . . We both work for the agency when I do consult." Her argument sounded inane, even to her own ears. "It wouldn't look good."

"To who?"

He was making this difficult, she thought a bit wildly. Why was he making this difficult? "I've enjoyed the time we've spent together." She was fumbling this. Badly. "I just think it's time we ended it."

Cam said nothing. Just reached for the beer and took a long swallow. He set down the bottle. Remained silent.

"It's not you—it's me."

His mouth quirked in a humorless smile. "You're giving me the 'it's not you—it's me' speech? Honey, I invented that speech. You're doing it all wrong."

She felt her cheeks grow hot. Inexplicably, tears welled in her eyes. "I am. I'm sorry." Rising, she fumbled for her purse. "You must think . . . I'm sorry."

She hurried off, her vision blurred. Behind her she heard him murmur, "Good-bye, Sophie."

And in that moment, she thought she regretted saying good-bye to Sophie almost as much as bidding farewell to her relationship with Cam.

It took a couple of minutes for the door to be opened to Cam. "You changed the security codes. Good." He stepped by Jenna into Sophie's living room. The other agent closed and locked the door behind him. Reset the alarm.

"We also reset the key code on the garage. And Loring nailed shut the attic crawl space from the inside, at least until we can get the security company out here." Jenna was showing the effects of a long day. Cam's gaze went beyond her to the pile of throw pillows on the sofa. It looked as if she'd crashed there for a while.

His gaze cut toward the master bedroom. "How's she doing?" His voice was as hushed as Jenna's. It was after three in the morning. He'd stayed at the jail until it became apparent that they weren't going to get squat from Vance. The only words the man had uttered were to demand a doctor and a lawyer, in that order. His response to all questions had been a variation of one of those requests, made at escalating decibels. So Cam had gone back to Alleman to check on the crime team at Vance's home. They would be working on the search for hours yet.

He hadn't been able to wait hours before seeing Sophie again.

"I wasn't sure the doctor would release her." Because they felt suddenly useless, he jammed his hands into his trouser pockets. "Did he give you a report on her injuries?"

"She wouldn't stay. And I'll let Dr. Channing discuss her injuries with you. But I can tell you that Van Wheton still isn't conscious. The doctors are worried about internal injuries and they're checking for a brain bleed." Jenna looked away, her expression strained. "The way she looks . . . I'm surprised she's still alive."

Cam walked over the couch. Sat heavily. He didn't remember the last time he'd had a full night's sleep. "I can't believe she made it as far as she did once they got out of the barn."

Jenna came to sit beside him. "Somehow Sophia managed to pull her using some sort of blanket carry. I just can't believe it's over."

292

Leaning his head back on the couch, he let his eyes close. For just a minute. "Yeah. It's over." At least the urgent part of the case was finished. There would be no more victims, but now they started the painstaking, methodical piecing together of evidence to build a case for trial that was so airtight, Vance would never wiggle free. "I've got another crime team at the barn," he murmured. "I need to head over there."

But for now he let himself take a moment to enjoy the fact that Sophie was free. Back home, in her own room, in her own bed.

He didn't kid himself that this thing was over for her, though. He still didn't know what Vance had subjected her to. The thought had his stomach tightening. She'd have healing to do. Physical and emotional. He knew from personal experience that sometimes the body healed much more quickly than the mind did.

His cell vibrated in his pocket. Cam's eyes snapped open, and when he recognized the number, he surged to his feet to answer it. "Chief. I assume you got the voice mail I left."

Edina's chief of police, Paul Boelin, sounded jubilant. "I did. Damn good news that Mrs. Van Wheton was found alive, too."

Pacing to the kitchen, Cam kept his voice pitched low. "She's in rough shape, Paul. It'll be touch-and-go."

Some of the elation dissipated from the man's voice. "I'm sorry to hear that. Her daughters are on their way to the hospital to see her now."

"I don't know the details, but she's still alive at this point." That was the fact to hang on to. With both Van Wheton and Sophie. Whatever they'd endured, they'd survived. They were safe.

"Caught a break up here that might help you nail the coffin on that bastard a little tighter." A thread of satisfaction sounded in the chief's words. "I figured since we didn't catch a glimpse of the van used to abduct Van Wheton on any of the traffic cameras heading out of the Cities, he must have planned a route that would take back roads all the way to Des Moines."

"That's what I thought, too." Cam had met with a similar lack of success when he'd checked all traffic cams on southbound roads from the Minnesota border to Des Moines.

"A trip that length, he would have had to gas up along the way. I struck out checking the security videos on the gas stations in town, so I started calling up local police to help me with stations in the towns on southbound blacktops."

Interest flickered. "You got an image of him at a gas station?"

"I did. An image without the damn mask he wore at the bank. The security footage clearly shows Courtney Van Wheton's face at the back window of the vehicle when he was driving away."

"I'll be damned." Puzzle pieces were clicking into place. And when all the pieces were found, the complete picture of Vance's crimes would put him away for life. But Cam's sense of grim satisfaction at the thought slipped away with Boelin's next words.

"That agent of yours did a damn fine job on the sketch."

A nasty pool of dread started to form at the pit of Cam's stomach. "What's that?"

"The sketch Agent Turner did up here with Carl Muller. To tell you the truth, I thought maybe Muller was just yanking our chain, but that drawing matches the image of the driver in the van almost exactly. Eerie, really."

Jenna had come to the edge of the kitchen, frowning at him as she tried to discern the gist of the conversation. When he hung up several minutes later, they looked at each other. Her expression was pale.

"Vance has a partner?"

Cam swallowed around the hard ball of fury that had lodged in his throat. "He has a partner."

Jenna leaned heavily against the counter, absorbing the news. "We shouldn't tell Sophia. She doesn't need to hear this right now."

"I don't need to hear what right now?"

Their heads swiveled at the sound of Sophie's voice. She stepped out of the guest bedroom, tying a robe around her waist. She looked at their faces, and her movements stilled.

"I don't need to hear what right now?"

Cam was the first to recover. He went to her, taking a quick visual inventory. She looked much too pale and much too brittle. As if she'd shatter at a single indiscreet word.

"You need some sleep."

She stared at him with sober eyes. She could have been looking at a stranger. "I don't want to sleep."

Cam looked a little helplessly at Jenna. "Did the doctor write a prescription for a sedative?"

"I don't want to sleep," Sophie repeated plainly. "What I want is for you to tell me who you were talking to just then."

"It was Chief Boelin." When she waited, saying nothing, he added, "The Van Wheton girls are on their way to the hospital to be with their mom."

A flicker of emotion chased over her face. "That's good. Having them there . . . It might help." She looked at the couch then and said, "Jenna, you don't have to stay. I'll be fine."

"I'm too tired to drive now," the agent said easily. "You don't mind if I hang out for another few hours, do you?"

"Of course not. I'll get you some sheets."

"I'm fine. Really." To accentuate her words, Jenna went back to the sofa and dropped down on it, stretching out. "But I can't sleep if I know you're still awake."

"Maybe I am a little sleepy." Sophie looked at Cam. Her blue eyes, usually so full of life, were opaque. "Would you mind coming with me for a few minutes?"

He followed her into the guest bedroom. Swung the door shut behind them. Although he'd poked his head in there a couple of times, he'd never spent time in it before. Realizing why she had chosen the room to sleep in had his chest going tight.

There would be too many memories in her bedroom. In her bath. Nightmarish reminders of when she'd last been there. "Maybe you should have gone to a hotel tonight."

She turned to face him, sitting on the edge of the bed, hands folded in her lap, back straight. He was reminded for an instant of the evening she'd ever so delicately extricated herself from his life.

"I wasn't raped."

The pronouncement was uttered baldly. Unsure of how to respond, he said, "I'm grateful for your sake. But you were brutalized. Emotionally. Physically." One of her wrists was encased in a soft splint. A bruise bloomed a brilliant shade of purple on her jaw, and her bottom lip was split. Cam didn't want to think about what other injuries the robe was hiding.

He was far more concerned about the ones on the inside.

She went on as if she hadn't heard him. "I told you that so you'd know. I didn't suffer. Not the way Courtney did. It was traumatic, yes. I was frightened—more than I've ever been in my life. But I'm not going to shatter with the delivery of bad news. I won't fall apart at hearing a gruesome detail. Please tell me what Chief Boelin had to say that had you and Jenna so freaked out."

He tried for a smile. "It's been a freaked-out sort of day, but I think we've got things under control for the—"

"I can tell when you're lying." The words, delivered in that too-dispassionate tone, stopped the rest of his statement. Her intense gaze was difficult to meet. "I wish I couldn't. But I know you're lying now, and it's more upsetting to me than any truth you could tell me. And after you go, I'll sit and worry about what you're keeping from me. That won't be good for my emotional health. So I think you need to tell me straight-out."

She sounded so like herself, so much the practical, professional Dr. Channing, that he almost smiled. But there was nothing amusing about this moment.

He went to sit beside her on the bed. Stared straight ahead. "You could have died." A hot ball of emotion surged to his throat. "That's difficult to forget."

"I know." Her fingers reached for his hand. Squeezed. "Thank you for bringing the cavalry today."

A breath forced out of him at that. "You didn't seem to need any help. You were halfway to Ankeny by the time we figured out where to find you."

"Not quite." She looked down, her hair hiding her profile. If his hand weren't still in hers, he would have lifted it to brush the hair from her face. "I've heard bits and pieces, but can you tell me the rest? Everything that happened after I spoke to you on the radio."

Because it seemed important to her, he gave her an abbreviated account of the events of the day. But it was the news of Rhonda Klaussen that seemed to shock her the most.

"Where is she now?"

"The Polk County jail." At Sophie's swift look, he raised a brow. "She can be kept for up to forty-eight hours without being charged. We need time to check out her story. She can't be allowed to go free before we're sure she wasn't an accessory."

"What have you found out so far?" The concern in her voice would be better utilized if it were aimed at her own well-being. But at least she'd lost that expressionless mask she'd worn minutes earlier.

"She has a long history with him. There are cigar burns all over her back. Some old and others more recent. She said she'd been kept chained in the basement much of the time, and we found the shackles down there. That's about all."

"The burns . . . Was there a number?"

Cam tried to recall, annoyed with himself that it hadn't occurred to him before. "Not that I could make out. They were all in a row."

They looked at each other, saying simultaneously, "One."

"She was the first," Sophia breathed. "The one he began to hone his skills on. Did she have a high-risk lifestyle?"

He nodded slowly. "Most likely. She's got a couple pops, one for solicitation."

"I'd like to interview her."

"No." His tone was emphatic, and his fingers tightened on hers. "No," he said again, when she looked at him askance. "You're done with this thing. I'll make sure Gonzalez backs me up, too."

"I think she'd find the information I can get from Klaussen to be valuable in painting a clearer picture of Vance. But if you insist, I won't ask to speak with her." She paused a beat. "If you tell me what you were talking to Boelin about."

He narrowed a look at her. "Shit. I've just been sandbagged again. You've had practice at that, and the hell of it is, no one expects it coming from you because you've got that whole golden angel look going on."

Turning away, she said flatly, "I'm no angel. I'll call Gonzalez myself. I think I can convince her."

"Okay." He took a breath. Hoped he wasn't going to regret this. "Boelin tracked down an image of the van that was used to abduct Van Wheton. It was caught on a security camera at a gas station heading for Iowa. Got a clear look at the driver and a glimpse of Van Wheton in the back window."

Something inside her seemed to ease. He wished he could brace her for the rest. "So that's good news," she said. "One more piece of evidence against Vance."

"The driver matched the sketch Jenna did. Of the man Carl Muller saw in the Edina park."

For a moment it was as though her body melted. As if all the strength streamed out of it. Releasing her hand, he placed his arm around her waist, obscenities on his lips.

"No, it's all right." But her protest was far too faint for his liking.

"It's not, but you will be. Do you understand me?" He placed a crooked knuckle under her chin to turn her face to his. "I will never let anyone hurt you again. No one will get near you again."

Her smile was tremulous. "A team of offenders. It explains so much. The pre- and postmortem assaults seemed so different. The care he took with the bodies prior to burial. Partially to cover up the evidence, yes. But I think there's more to it."

And this was exactly what he didn't want her thinking about. "You'll be in protective custody. You can go wherever you're most comfortable, and one of us will be with you at all times. Whoever you choose. Wherever you want. A hotel or one of our homes. There will be someone at your side until we catch Vance's partner."

"A hotel would be inconvenient for everyone. But so would having an unwanted houseguest indefinitely." Her words would have sounded reasonable if he hadn't felt her slight shudder. She wasn't unaffected by this news. Hell, neither was he.

"You'll come to my place." Belatedly he realized he should have made the statement sound a little less like an order. "It's familiar. There's a second bedroom. Plus, I'll let you take over my home office and organize it. You know you were wanting to."

She actually smiled at that. The sight lifted something inside him. "Ah, the infamous Prescott win-win. How can I resist?"

"You can't." He brushed his lips over her hair in a gesture too light for her to feel but one he suddenly needed. She'd found him all too resistible not so long ago, but that was different. That had been . . . Well, he didn't know what the hell that had been. But this wasn't personal. It was his job. And Cam didn't trust anyone to do that job as well as he could.

Because the next person who tried to get at Sophie Channing was going to have to walk through him to do it.

Acknowledgments

If I wrote novels based on my own expertise, the books would be short indeed. As usual I owe a shout-out to several people who put up with my endless questions in an attempt to lend credibility to the plot.

A big thank-you goes out to Division of Narcotics Enforcement SAC John Graham for his prompt responses to my endless nagging. I appreciated all the insights and can heartily agree that the coolest guy in any novel is always going to be the narc.

Thanks are also owed to FBI forensic artist Lisa Bailey for her time, talent, and knowledge, and for being the inspiration for one of my characters! To John and Justin, the FSA men in my life, for answering all things agriculture related. Bruce Reeve, laboratory administrator, generously provided answers about the workings of the DCI Criminalistics Laboratory. And Ryan Boder at suretyCAM Security helped me figure out how to get my villain into the places he shouldn't be. I appreciate everyone's help!

As always, any errors were mine alone.

TOUCHING EVIL

TURN THE PAGE FOR A PREVIEW OF
BOOK 2 IN KYLIE'S EXCITING CIRCLE OF EVIL TRILOGY.

Chapter 1

"C'mon, Jonah. Don't be such a wimp."

"You try carrying a pony keg on your shoulder. Through the woods. At night." Jonah Davis puffed as he stumbled on the winding path. Branches of scrub bushes scratched at his arms and snagged on his jeans. How the hell had he gotten stuck doing all the work while Spencer Pals got to help Trina Adams over every fallen branch and around each tangle of brambles?

'Cuz Jonah had been a dumbass. He'd figured to impress Trina by being all macho and shit. Yeah, she was going to be real impressed about the time he fell over of a heart attack and the keg knocked her on her fine little ass.

She turned, flashlight in her hand, to give him a melting look. "Are you sure you're okay, Jonah? You should make Spencer take a turn. That's so heavy."

His chest swelled. "I've got it. You just watch out for Spence. He thinks these woods are haunted. He's liable to piss himself if he hears a noise."

"Fuck you," Spence said.

She gave a tinkling laugh, and the sound of it went straight to Jonah's groin. Before today Trina Adams had never so much as glanced his way in the hallways of East High, but there was nothing like the promise of a kegger to help people make friends. He'd looked at her, though. He'd looked plenty. She was Jennifer Lawrence cute with a smokin'-hot body that would look even hotter under his.

Before the night was over, he was going to know that from personal experience. Sometime after this keg was gone and she was feeling awfully friendly toward the guy who'd carried the damn thing the whole way.

"Shh." Spence threw out an arm to stop Trina from going any farther. Probably copped a feel while he was at it, too. Spencer was that type of guy. "I think I heard something."

"Here we go." But Jonah was none too sorry to put the pony keg down. Even if they hadn't yet reached their usual party spot. "Is it a ghost, Spence? Or maybe a zombie." In an aside to Trina, he said, "You should see Spence in the morning. He looks like an extra from the cast of *The Walking Dead*."

She laughed again, and his dick took a bow. Thank God she couldn't see how damn happy she made his pants.

"Listen, Hulk, there's someone up ahead."

Jonah shot Spence a glare. He hated that nickname. But then he heard the noise, too. Voices too distant to really make out.

"You think the others beat us here?" he asked doubtfully. The spot next to the Raccoon River had always been his favorite spot for keggers. But not everyone coming tonight knew where it was. He'd had to pass out maps.

"I don't see how."

Trina handed the flashlight to Spence. "Whoever it is, let's sneak up and scare them."

"Okay. Be vewy, vewy quiet."

She muffled a laugh at Spence's stupid cartoon character imitation, and the two of them went off. Neither waited for Jonah to wrestle the keg to his shoulder again and nearly have cardiac arrest doing it.

Somehow this wasn't going at all like he'd planned.

By the time he caught up with them, the sweat was snaking down his back. Even the back of his shorts was wet beneath the jeans. He made a grimace of distaste. Butt sweat was really the worst.

Twin shushing sounds came from Spence and Trina. Since they were crouched down behind a rock, he set the damn keg down. Again.

But his flare of annoyance vanished when Trina reached up to grab his hand and yank him down beside her behind the huge boulder. "You won't believe this. There's a couple down there making out. And the guy's like . . . old."

"Not old-old," Spencer corrected in a whisper. "But like Halston's age."

Trina smothered a giggle with one hand clapped over her mouth. "What if it is Mr. Halston?" She and Spence snorted with laughter.

Jonah craned his neck to see. Halston was one of the gym teachers and an okay guy. And he wasn't old. Not really. Maybe Jonah's mom's age. Forty or so. But Halston was married. And Jonah just couldn't see any married guy boning on the banks of the Raccoon River. What would be the point when a couple had a house and a bedroom where they could get their ugly on?

The place Trina and Spence had chosen wasn't the greatest vantage point. They were well hidden behind the jutting rock from the people yards below them. But they also couldn't see shit. Jonah moved farther away from Trina so that he could peer around the edge of the rock.

They could hear just fine, though. Not so much from the woman, but the guy. He seemed to be doing most of the talking.

"This will have to be the last time we're together like this. I know, I know. I feel it, too. Shush. Darling, are you crying? Don't cry." The guy touched the woman's face, but Jonah couldn't really see it at all in the darkness. It didn't really matter, though. The stars were bright enough that he could occasionally get a glimpse of bare skin.

His stiffie stood at attention at the thought.

"Don't cry. We still have tonight. One more time. Our favorite way."

Jonah's eyes about bugged out of his head. The guy was doing her up the ass! Oh, man, this was better than a porno flick. Far better than *Cracked Rear Entry*, the DVD Spence had filched from his dad's collection.

"Get ready."

Jonah pulled his head back to protest. "No, man. Let them finish. I hate to interrupt a guy in the middle of getting some." That should be written in the man rules or something. It just seemed wrong. Unless it was that creepy Roland Ott, who'd been trying to get in Jonah's mom's pants for weeks. Jonah would interrupt that as much as possible.

But there was no talking to Spence and Trina. "On three, okay? One, two . . ." The two stood up, shining the flashlight down on the couple, screeching, "Get a room, already! Zip it back up, Daddy Long Leg!"

That last was from Spence, because, well, he was an idiot. But not to miss out, Jonah rose too, hoping for a better glimpse of the naked woman.

The man jumped, yanking his pants up, grabbing at something on the ground. "Fucking little monsters! I'll kill you!" He started for the rocky incline toward them, and Spence screeched like a girl.

"Gun!"

Trina caught the woman in the flashlight beam then and shrieked as if she'd seen an ax murderer. Jonah grabbed the light to steady it, because the woman was just lying there. Maybe the guy had drugged her or something.

But then he screamed, too, every bit as high and girlishly as Spence had.

Because the woman below them was more zombie than woman. Some of her skin was gone, and there were places where her bones showed through.

The woman was dead.

"Run!" Dropping the flashlight, he grabbed Trina by the arm and yanked her along. Back into the woods. Crashing through the brush. Leaping over downed limbs. Pushing aside branches. They ran until they got to the road. Where Spence already had the car running and ready.

Jonah pulled open the back door and shoved Trina inside. There was the sound of a gunshot. Then another. The guy was screaming something, but Jonah wasn't waiting around to hear what. He leaped into the car, sprawling on top of Trina. "Go!" Spence took off, leaving the zombie lover behind.

And leaving the zombie woman lying on the banks of the Raccoon River.

———

Division of Criminal Investigation agent Cam Prescott stood silently watching Lucy Benally work. He'd known better than to request her when he called. Cases were assigned at the ME's office on a rotating basis.

But Lucy had autopsied the six female bodies they'd discovered buried in rural cemeteries around Des Moines three weeks ago.

Cam knew she monitored every call that came into the ME's office and would insist on being at the scene. She wasn't the most senior pathologist on staff. Just the best at throwing her diminutive weight around. That suited him fine. He may often have quibbles with her personality, but she was the best.

This case called for the best.

Polk County sheriff Dusten Jackson ambled over to him. "I might have broken protocol by calling you personally, but with the Vance arrest still fresh in my mind, I thought you'd want a look at this scene."

Mason Vance was a sadistic sexual deviant Cam had arrested just days earlier on eight counts of kidnapping, seven counts of rape, and six counts of murder. Dr. Sophia Channing, the forensic psychologist consulting on the case had been Vance's latest kidnap victim. And as Cam watched Benally zipping up the body bag, he couldn't shake the thought that Sophie had escaped a similar fate only through sheer guts and cunning.

Jackson slipped his hands in his uniform pants pockets. "This one wasn't found in rural cemetery buried on top of a burial vault, but do you think . . . Is it possible she was one of Vance's victims?"

"I'll let you know after I talk to the ME." He looked around. "Where are the kids who reported this?"

"Back at the road. I didn't see any need for them to watch what was going on. The parents are anxious to get them home, so once you've spoken to them, go ahead and release them. The biggest one—Jonah—seemed to get the best look at the guy. Also seemed to have the best head on his shoulders, but hey, it was a pretty gruesome scene. And they're kids."

"I'll talk to them in a few minutes," Cam promised. First, though, he needed to speak to Benally before she left the scene.

"Prescott," she greeted him without preamble as he approached her. "Somehow it's not surprising to find you where it's damp and dark."

"Ah, the famed Benally wit," he shot back mildly. "Immature…and yet not funny."

"I'm hilarious." She stood then, nodded at her assistants, who lifted the body bag onto a stretcher and began the careful transfer through the woods to the waiting ME vehicle. "I do stand-up in my free time." She watched the progress of the stretcher as it entered the woods and then switched her focus to Cam. "You want to know if there's a chance this one is related to the first six bodies."

"There are no more missing persons reports matching Vance's MO from the other crimes." The offender had targeted wealthy single women primarily for their looks and bank accounts, and he'd cast a wide net, hunting both in and out of state. Each victim had last been seen withdrawing a large amount of cash from her bank.

The next time they'd been seen was when Benally had extracted them from shallow graves.

"Then this body can't possibly be related to the others." Lucy tossed her long dark braid over her shoulder and peeled off her gloves.

Cam gave a mental sigh. "Quit toying with me, Benally. I'm asking."

She looked up at him. Way up. What the woman lacked in stature she made up for in attitude. Way overcompensated in that area, to Cam's way of thinking, but she was usually worth the aggravation she caused him.

"I'm going to have to get her in the lab and take a better look," she began.

Cam was used to the hedging. To the ME, perfectionism was an art.

"The skin wasn't totally intact on her back. But there are wounds that look an awfully lot like cigar burns."

He reached up to rub the back of his neck. "Shit."

"Yeah, shit." Lucy's face was grim. "No way could I make out a number, but maybe when I get her back to the autopsy suite."

Vance had numbered his victims, branding them with lit cigars. Cam had recently discovered the first victim, a woman named Rhonda Klaussen, who was still alive and had been kept chained in the offender's basement. Sophie thought Vance had practiced his atrocities on Klaussen as he evolved. The six bodies in the cemeteries had been numbered up to fifteen.

But that left a lot of numbers unaccounted for.

"Sophia was the one who figured out Vance's system. Maybe she'd like to come to the lab when I'm ready with this one."

"No." He ignored the warning signs in Lucy's darkening expression. The woman didn't take kindly to the word. Cam didn't particularly care at the moment. "Dr. Channing is no longer a consultant on this case."

"Well, shit, Cam, she wrote the damn victimology report. I think if this victim turns out to be related to the others, she's the best equipped to bring in on this."

"We'll see." His answer was noncommittal. But his objection wasn't. Sophie was still healing from the trauma she'd been through. He wasn't going to compound that trauma by yanking her back into the center of this case again. "Keep me posted."

With the aid of his Maglite, he walked across the clearing and made his way up a steep embankment. When he exited the woods, he played the light over the people and cars still gathered there. Picked out the big kid Jackson had mentioned right away.

Jonah Davis was sitting facing the road in the open back passenger door of a car. After a few words to the kid's father, Cam approached the kid and led him through the story he'd already told a half-dozen times tonight.

Listening without interruption, Cam waited until Jonah had run down. "See that red-haired agent over there?" Cam pointed to where Jenna Turner was questioning another teenage boy, who looked considerably more shaken up.

"Yeah, I've seen her." Jonah gave Cam a wink, man-to-man. "Walking hard-on material—am I right?"

Cam just looked at him. Waited for the kid to visibly quail before continuing. "She's a forensic artist. If you got a good look at the guy, she'll be able to use your descriptions to draw a sketch." He took a folded-up piece of paper from the inside breast pocket of his suit coat.

Shaking it open, he passed it to Jonah. "Agent Turner did this sketch a couple weeks ago with a witness we interviewed up in Edina."

The kid stared at the composite drawing, mouth hanging open. "But . . . but . . . that's him! The zombie lover guy!" Mr. Davis swiveled in the front seat, a concerned look on his face.

"Settle down, Jonah. It's okay."

"No, Dad, this is the guy we saw." Jonah stabbed at the sketch with his index finger. "I got a really good look at him. Not so much the woman, at least not until the end. But this is the guy. I swear it."

With a sense of bleak resolve, Cam tucked away the sketch. Gave the kid's father the okay to take Jonah home.

Then he walked a few feet away and called Loring, the agent he had stationed with Sophie in his absence. "We've got reason to believe that the man identified by the Edina chief of police as Vance's accessory was seen revisiting one of the victims tonight," he told her tersely. "How is Dr. Channing?" A little of the tension seeped from his body at Loring's response. "Good. She doesn't have to know about this." Maybe Loring would stand up better to Sophie's gentle probing than he did. He could hope.

Not for the first time he wondered if he should have arranged Sophie's protective custody to be overseen by another agent.

But Cam knew he'd never entrust her safety to anyone else. Not when they'd discovered Vance hadn't been working alone.

Not while Vance's partner was still free. When the man had every reason to go after the only surviving victim who could provide the testimony that would send Vance away forever.

About the Author

Photo © Lee Isbel of Studio 16

Kylie Brant is the author of thirty-five romantic suspense novels. A three-time RITA Award nominee, a four-time Romantic Times award finalist, a two-time Daphne du Maurier Award winner, and a 2008 Romantic Times Career Achievement Award winner (as well as a two-time nominee), Brant has written books that have been published in twenty-nine countries and eighteen languages. Her novel *Undercover Bride* is listed by *Romantic Times* magazine as one of the best romances in the last twenty-five years. She is a member of Romance Writers of America, its Kiss of Death Mystery and Suspense chapter; Novelists, Inc.; and International Thriller Writers. When asked how an elementary special education teacher and mother of five comes up with such twisted plots, her answer is always the same: "I have a dark side." Visit her online at kyliebrant.com.